Opening a Window

The Streets of Cardiff Series

Book 4

Anne Main

Opening a Window

Book 4

Streets of Cardiff Series

Chapter 1

1954

It was bitterly cold; the promise of spring might be just around the corner, but winter hadn't yet loosened its icy grasp on the freezing streets of Cardiff, a late cold snap had gripped the city. Unexpected snow was starting to fall outside in the darkness; fat white flakes drifted down softly like feathers, settling on window ledges, coating the roofs of Wilson Road with frosted sparkles, silently gathering against the chimney stacks, and lining the gutters with glitter. Heavy grey clouds hinted at more snow to come, if this kept up then by tomorrow morning there might even be enough snow for snowballs.

Ivy hugged herself and wriggled deeper under the cosy blankets of her rumpled bed. She was still basking in the delicious warm glow of their lovemaking and her heart was so happy she felt sure it might burst with joy. It was the first time Billy had made love to her and she wanted the evening to last forever.

"Please stay Billy… just a bit longer." She pleaded clinging to his taut muscled body, nuzzling his neck. The luminous hands of the alarm clock said it was already past ten o'clock.

"No, I must go," he kissed her again, reluctant to leave the arms of the woman he loved. "Look at the time Ivy. I've got to walk back…. I'll have missed the last bus to Caroline Street already and the snow is coming on." He unentangled himself from her embrace.

Billy kissed her once more, softly on the lips and got out of bed. He would not stay the night at Wilson Road even though June was staying overnight with Nanna Betty and Bampa Gag. It was not the worry of impending snow driving Billy out of Ivy's warm bed, he'd decided that until they were married he wouldn't cause tongues to wag or rumours to start about Ivy by staying the night at her house. Ivy had had enough nasty rumours, sneers, and bitchy remarks to last a lifetime. It was only a matter of weeks to wait until their wedding; Billy could be patient.

"Goodnight my beautiful girl, I'll see you tomorrow," Billy whispered. He slipped on his clothes and with one last tender kiss he left to walk back to the flat he shared with his brother George and George's wife Alice.

The tiny two-bedroomed flat was nestled above The Tasty Plaice fish bar, the family's prosperous chip shop business on Caroline Street. Billy knew George and Alice were looking forward to the day he would move in with Ivy too. With a baby due soon the young couple didn't have room for Billy to stay with them for much longer and he certainly wouldn't find a welcome at his parent's house now that he was engaged to Ivy Benson.

It had been two nights since Billy turned up on Ivy's doorstep after his release from prison, and as soon as she saw his smiling face and was wrapped in his warm embrace, it was as if the whole weight of the world was suddenly lifted off her shoulders. She felt as if she could breathe again.

Whilst Billy was in custody, falsely accused of the murder of Ajo Abbas, her heart was broken like a mirror shattered into a thousand pieces. Ivy had been so utterly miserable and despairing that she couldn't eat or sleep; her life was a black void without him. Now Billy was back, and she was like a bird released, content and free to dream of a happier life with the man she loved. She couldn't wait to marry him.

"I love you so much Billy," she whispered as he kissed her goodbye.

When Billy made love to her for the first time that night, it was like a whole new world was revealed to her and she gasped with delight. Ivy had only ever known her fumbling, grunting, insensitive husband Jimmy Benson, a man who took what he wanted from her body and treated her like dirt.

Jimmy robbed her of her virginity when she was just a lass of sixteen, she'd never known the gentle touch of a man who loved and respected her. Making love with Billy was a revelation; a joy to be savoured.

For Jimmy, coupling was brutal, animalistic sex, devoid of love and affection; she hated it, and she hated him. Foul-mouthed Jimmy Benson, a man so drunk and needy that when he lay in her bed, he would pin her down without so much as a caress and claim her; and afterwards he would fall asleep snoring, leaving Ivy to cry in the darkness with despair. Ivy had heaved a sigh of relief when her advancing pregnancy revolted him so much that he took to sleeping in the spare room and now that Jimmy was dead, she rejoiced at having a second chance of knowing true love and happiness with Billy.

At first she'd been shy with Billy, ashamed of her battered body, to be naked and exposed with all her stretch marks and flaws, but Billy was tender, loving, kind.

It touched Ivy's heart when Billy even caressed and kissed her scarred stomach, with its legacy of pregnancy and the hysterectomy. He looked her in the eyes and told her she was beautiful, and she knew that he meant it; in Billy's eyes she was perfect.

Billy took time to make her feel desire and when she hovered on the edge of release, he slowed his rhythm until they came together with a rush of ecstasy Ivy never knew existed before; afterwards, Ivy cried.

"What's up my love… have I hurt you," he'd whispered anxiously when she came.

"No, Billy, you've made me feel whole again," she sobbed cocooned in his strong arms.

Later when Ivy was drifting off to sleep watching the silent snowflakes gather on the windowsill outside her bedroom window, she wondered how she could have gone through life without knowing such love and pleasure between a man and a woman was possible. Ivy vowed to herself she would do everything she could to build a happy life for her daughter June and the man she loved; she would make sure Billy never regretted choosing her as his wife.

Billy was prepared to give up so much to be with her, he was even willing to break from his parents if it meant defying their wishes and marrying Ivy with all the baggage she brought with her; Ivy knew Jimmy's reputation had stained her in the eyes of so many people. Ivy couldn't blame Les Thomas for hating her; for wanting better for his son.

Jimmy Benson might have ruined her happiness in life, but she was not going to let him ruin her happiness in death. Her miserable life with Jimmy was a time she needed to forget, to shut away forever; she mustn't dwell on the past, she told herself; only look ahead to her new future. This life with Billy was her chance of happiness and she would grab it with both hands. The thought of spending the rest of her life with Billy and June was beyond perfect.

For the first time in a long time, Ivy slept peacefully through the night. She slumbered on blissfully unaware that in a small, cramped bedroom on snowy Caroline Street, her best friend Alice Thomas was struggling to bring a new life into the world.

Chapter 2

Deirdre was carefully polishing the crystal sherry glasses before returning them to the glazed cabinet in the corner of the sitting room. Across the walnut table, which sat proudly in the bay window, small piles of freshly washed ornaments and keepsakes were waiting to be put back in their rightful places.

The glass shelves and display fronts of the cabinet had been polished to Deirdre's satisfaction, now all that remained was for the treasured objects and knick-knacks to be arranged to best advantage.

Deirdre had spent all morning emptying the cabinet and washing her precious possessions in hot soapy water until they gleamed, before returning things to a pleasing order on the display shelves. Outside, the sky might look like a leaden sheet crowding the bay but for Deirdre, the start of March meant spring cleaning and the sitting room display cabinet was one of the more satisfying jobs on her list of things to do.

"That looks much better Bobby," Deirdre addressed the tatty ginger and white cat lounging on the windowsill. The aloof old moggy was overseeing proceedings with a lazy stare.

"Your fur doesn't help things Bobby, getting fluff and dust everywhere, and if you knock my best vase over again I'll have your guts for garters." Deirdre wagged her finger theatrically and the cat ignored her.

Yesterday Bobby had capriciously decided to wander dangerously close to a small cut glass vase containing some sprigs of fragrant wintersweet placed on the window ledge. The vase had wobbled and toppled and was on the brink of falling off the ledge when Deirdre rescued it from impending disaster.

Bobby regarded her with a bilious stare as if to say *the vase was in my way,* and then the cat settled down to groom its mothy fur coat on the very spot vacated by the offending object. Recognising the house was more Bobby's than hers by rights, Deirdre sensibly relocated the vase to the mantlepiece; Bobby had won again.

"My friend James is joining me for a cup of tea this afternoon, so you'd better behave yourself Bobby or you'll find yourself put out in the garden for a few hours, like it or not." Deirdre popped the last few items on the cabinet shelves and gave the walnut table a final rub to remove Bobby's paw prints.

Deirdre had to admit, she was unexpectedly nervous about James Pugh coming into her home. Of course, she'd taken the step of inviting him to pop round for afternoon tea and a chat, but now that he *was* coming, she felt a flutter of anxiety deep in her stomach. For a woman who had just turned sixty, she'd never invited a man into her home before or spent time alone with any man apart from the vicar and her solicitor Mr William Williams.

Don't be ridiculous, pull yourself together, it's just a cup of tea, nothing to worry about, she chided herself.

Deirdre had distracted herself all morning with the soothing tasks of polishing, cleaning, and baking. A fresh batch of butterfly cakes topped off with sherry icing sat on her pretty cake stand in the kitchen, all ready for afternoon tea, and the sitting room smelt nicely of lavender beeswax.

Deirdre appreciated James Pugh had developed a heightened sense of smell since he'd lost most of his sight in the Great War and it bothered her that old Bobby might have a lingering odour to offend her neighbour's sensitive nose. The smell of fresh baking and polish would certainly distract from any trace of Bobby.

Deirdre knew it was just silly mithering on her part and James wouldn't judge her, or her home, but she so wanted the afternoon to go well; they were beginning to become close friends and it was important to her to make a good impression.

James Pugh was just the sort of sensitive, noble, man Deirdre would have admired when she was a young girl, but somehow despite living on the same street, she never noticed James Pugh until he returned home a broken man shambling around the streets of Roath with his white stick to guide him. Then she pitied him and all the other broken men she saw and passed by.

James Pugh was a few of years older than she was, which might help explain why she only vaguely remembered him from that time when he lived on Alma Road. At the time her own thoughts were too fixated elsewhere to be noticing the men and lads who lived in the same long street as herself. Her heart had been captured by Richard Owen, a well-mannered, twenty-five-year-old solicitor's clerk who was sweet on her; all the other men who might have flitted through her daily existence merged into a blur, Deirdre only had eyes for Richard.

Richard hadn't ever told Deirdre that he loved her, but she knew they were starting to grow close and in her heart she hoped that fondness would turn into love.

Deirdre knew that she wasn't a conventionally pretty girl when she was younger, but she had been described as handsome and she accepted the compliment with pride. She had fine, regular features with a delicate complexion and honest blue eyes and Richard Owen acknowledging her finer points had started to court her in earnest.

The romance was just beginning to flourish when Richard felt compelled to join up with so many of his friends and fight for his country. There had been no promises between them to keep, and the budding romance was still in its infancy, but Deirdre had all the bright hope and optimism of youth that she might indeed have found a man who loved her.

The day the whistle of the recruiting Sargent swept up the boys and men of Alma Road, including her own brother Edmund, and led them off to battle, she didn't notice the young James Pugh amongst the chattering throng, her eyes only searched for her beau Richard Owen to wave him off

.

I'll wait for you she'd called as she waved and smiled brightly, little knowing that she would spend the rest of her life waiting.

To begin with Deirdre, like so many others, believed the great lie that the War was to be a brief and glorious escapade over by Christmas, and she waited for Richard to return home to her within a few months.

But the War was far from brief and glorious. As the months passed it turned out to be more chaotic and bloodier than anyone could ever have imagined. None of the men who left Cardiff would ever return home undamaged to their loved ones; all would bear scars.

The fairy tale promises of an early Christmas victory rang hollow and when the dreadful news came that many fine men had lost their lives in April 1915 fighting at Gallipoli, including her darling Richard Owen, Deirdre knew then that her one chance of finding love and marriage had died with him.

Like countless others Richard *never* returned home; in battle his broken body was scattered to the winds and buried in the mud…and there he stayed.

As the years passed Deirdre joined the swelling ranks of other women still young, but not young enough or pretty enough, who were overlooked and left to live out their lives as spinsters without hope of ever finding someone else to love them.

Deirdre, unable to fly the family nest, turned her attention to being the best and most useful daughter her aging parents could ever have hoped for. Maybe love, a home and a family of her own was not a life meant for her, but like thousands of other women left behind by circumstance and the lack of young men, she would settle for what she had and make the best of it.

To her eternal shame and regret, Deirdre never enquired after the young, blind man she sometimes saw shuffling past her on Wellfield Road, like her, he too had become invisible, lost amongst so many other damaged men who stood on street corners, hands out asking for change.

Deirdre vowed to make up for her past insensitivities and decided that she would treat James with all the respect he richly deserved. She was older and wiser now and if her brother Edmund had taught her anything it was that happiness was fleeting; she needed to be bolder, take chances and enjoy life more.

"Out you go, you grumpy old baggage," Deirdre scooped up the cat and tickled it under the chin. Bobby started to purr until he saw Deirdre was heading for the back door and he scrambled to be put down.

"Oh no, you don't Bobby, its time you went outside for a wee and if you behave yourself you can come back in later. And remember, you'd better be on your best behaviour or else you'll find yourself locked out all afternoon."

Deirdre knew her threats were baseless and so did Bobby. The cat stuck its nose in the air, raised his plumed tail and sauntered up the garden path without a care in the world.

Chapter 3

When Billy returned to Caroline Street it was nearly midnight; he was surprised to see so many lights blazing in the flat above the chip shop as he walked up the road. *That's odd; Alice and George must still be up.* Billy's feet and toes were numb with cold, and his face stung from an hour's walk in the driving sleet and drizzle. His walk back from Ely had been bitterly cold and slippery; treacherous sheets of black ice were forming on the pavements and threatened to whip his legs from under him. Only the thought of Ivy's love kept him warm.

His evening spent with Ivy had been beyond his wildest dreams, he still glowed with the joy of loving her. There was no fear of discovery or risk of pregnancy to worry them, just the two of them free to enjoy each other without the need to hold back.

With Ivy he didn't feel ashamed of revealing his body which still bore the marks of his teenage acne, with Ivy he could just be himself; she'd always loved him just the way he was. He understood what it was like to feel damaged, shy, and fearful of judgement uncertain of an imperfect body. Billy felt that in many ways he and Ivy were kindred spirits; survivors of adversity and in his eyes, she was perfect too. He loved her so much it almost hurt.

Arghhh!

Through a crack of an upstairs window, Billy heard the most piercing, blood-curdling scream shattering the night. Fumbling with his key in the door lock Billy raced up the stairs to the flat above taking two steps at a time.

His brother George was pacing the floor, his head in his hands.

Arghhh….oh, oh, arghh!

The screams and shouts emanating from within the bedroom were tortured; loud guttural moans and groans punctuated the high-pitched screams.

Billy knew then it was Alice he could hear yelling as if she was being murdered.

"Shouldn't you be with her?" Billy asked anxiously.

"For Christ's sake Billy what do you take me for?" George said snappishly. "I can't go in there even if I wanted to. The midwife told me to wait out here… I feel bloody useless!"

George sat down in the chair for a moment then instantly leap up again as another high-pitched scream pierced the night.

Arghhh

"Bloody hell is it always like this?" Billy could see George was worried; agitated his brother was pacing up and down raking his fingers through his hair.

"I don't know," George moaned. "It's been hours since she started. I called the midwife like Alice asked me to, but now nothing seems to be happening; it's been ages… she's been screaming blue murder for hours on end and it sounds like she's in agony…. and there's nothing I can do to help." George mopped his forehead. A thin sheen of sweat glistened on his brow.

Billy slipped his arm around his brother's shoulders; he could feel his brother's chest heaving as he struggled to keep himself together for Alice's sake.

Thinking of Ivy's ordeal, Billy feared for Alice and the baby. *Poor George.*

"Shall I go for a doctor?" Billy offered, desperate to help.

George shrugged his shoulders and raised the palms of his hands. Midwife Marion Spears had told Billy to keep out of the way unless she called for him, but that seemed like ages ago. "I don't know what to do Billy, surely the midwife will come and get me if that's what she wants... I've never known anything like this before and no-one tells you what to expect." George felt frightened and exasperated in equal measure.

Arghhhh....huh, huh,huh, Arghhh

George raised his eyes to the heavens, the high-pitched yelling was like torture to him, as piercing as the scrape of nails on a blackboard and as heart-rending as the howling of an animal with its leg caught in a trap. *"Dear God!"* George muttered superstitiously. The Thomas family were not church-going, but George respected Alice's deep Catholic faith, he wished he knew what words to utter at a time like this.... *Where was God when you needed him!*

Huh,huh,huh,huh.....arghhhh

With one last stupendous push and a bit of help from Marion Spears a greasy, streaked baby boy slid into the world.

After a moment of blissful quiet, the sound of lusty wailing was music to George's ears.... Alice's screaming had stopped, only to be replaced by the high-pitched mewling of a new-born announcing its arrival into the world.

George and Billy looked at each other; relief flooded George's face; Billy felt sure he could see tears in his brother's eyes. "Congratulations George, it sounds as if you have a son or a daughter," Billy slapped his brother on the back and hugged him.

Within moments Marion Spears popped her head around the bedroom door. "Congratulations Mr Thomas, you have a son. Your wife has given birth to a healthy baby boy, with a grand set of lungs on him." Marion was busy wiping her bloodied hands on a large towel.

"Now put the kettle on, I'll need plenty of hot water to clear up with in here and I'm sure Mrs Thomas could do with a nice cup of tea." Marion Spears said crisply. After a particularly traumatic delivery she was used to dealing with shell-shocked husbands who stood about looking like spare parts; men who turned into blubbering wrecks feeling that someone should be looking after them after the ordeal. Marion's no-nonsense air usually set matters right.

"Your wife has had a bit of a tough time Mr Thomas, and she will take a while to heal and recover, but in a few weeks she'll be fine. What Mrs Thomas needs now is lots of peace and quiet and plenty of rest."

"Thank you, Mrs Spears," George muttered sheepishly uncertain of what to say next, for a moment he looked like a chastised schoolboy.

"I'll put the kettle on," Billy offered.

"When can I see her… I mean them?" George asked.

"Just give me a few minutes to make your wife presentable and to tidy things up a bit and then I'll call you through…. Birth is a messy business Mr Thomas, that's why we midwives like to keep you men out of the way; it never helps to have a mother worrying about her husband when she's got a job of work to do."

Ten minutes later George crept into the bedroom. Marion was busy tidying away her forceps and suturing equipment, a greasy placenta was wrapped in newspaper for George to dispose of; Alice lay in bed looking exhausted but happy.

The baby, tightly swaddled in a clean towel lay quietly in Alice's arms, "just look George…. isn't our son beautiful?" Alice whispered.

Every bone and muscle in her body ached and she felt utterly exhausted by her ordeal, but above all she felt deliriously happy; her baby was safely delivered, and it was a beautiful, healthy boy, perfect in every way.

"You are wonderful," George kissed her gently on the forehead and peeped in at the sleeping baby. "He is beautiful Alice, even if he did cause you a lot of trouble… I do love you." He stroked her brow and pushed back her greasy lank hair from her damp forehead.

Alice sank deeply in the pillows and sighed contentedly. "Can we call him Rhys…I think it would suit him." She murmured.

"Rhys? Yes, if that's what you would like… Rhys Thomas it is then," George laughed looking at the tiny crunched-up face tucked under the warm towel, "and to make the old man happy shall we call him Lesley for a second name?"

At that moment Alice was none too enamoured with her Father-in-law Les after he'd picked a fight with Billy over marrying Ivy. But she'd got her way on the Christian name, so it seemed churlish to veto the middle name of George's choosing. "Rhys Lesley Thomas, that's nice," she said sleepily, her eyelids were fluttering closed.

"Off you go Mr Thomas, I've given your wife a shot of morphine to help with the pain and to help her sleep a little, your place will be on the sofa tonight and *every* night until Mrs Thomas feels well enough." Marion Spears said crisply as she ushered George out of the tiny double bedroom.

"I'd best be off now and leave you all in peace, at least the snow has stopped," Marion observed through the window as she wrapped her thick, blue woollen cape around her shoulders.

Marion Spears collected her things in her black Gladstone bag; she promised Alice and George that she would return first thing in the morning to check on how things were. The feisty, capable midwife mounted her bike and cycled cautiously into the frosty night.

"Bloody hell Billy, she's a piece of work, I certainly wouldn't want to get on the wrong side of her. The way she's spoken to me all evening you'd think all this was my fault." George muttered as he poured himself a bottle of beer to wet the baby's bottom.

"Of course, it's all your fault you daft 'apeth… it's always a man's fault when a woman is having a baby, and from what we heard tonight it's a wonder they ever let us men get anywhere near them." Billy joked. "Pass us a bottle 'an all…. Here's to little Rhys… and to women for putting up with us," Billy raised his glass.

George downed his beer in one.

"You can have my bed tonight George and I'll take the sofa, from the look of you, I think you need a good night's kip." Billy grinned.

It was already 2am and the night was fast disappearing, tomorrow the chip shop would be busy and there would be plenty to do with a new baby about the place. "Thanks…Goodnight Billy," George ambled off to snatch a few hours' sleep in the spare room.

He had a son.

Chapter 4

"Alice has had a little baby boy Mam, and they've named him Rhys," Ivy traded gossip with her mother over a cup of tea.

Billy had called by briefly early in the morning with news about Alice and the baby, but he couldn't stop long, he was needed to do the lion's share of the work in the Tasty Plaice today. His brother George was trying his best to help Alice and run a few errands under the strict instructions of midwife Marion Spears. Billy was needed to step up and run the shop.

"That's wonderful news Ivy, I'm so pleased for them both, did Billy say how heavy the baby was?" Betty had brought June back home from her overnight stay in Inkerman Street and was eager to hear all the latest news. Betty was very fond of Alice, as a young girl Alice Tranter had been Ivy's best friend and she'd stuck with Ivy through thick and thin.

"He's a whopper Mam, 7lbs 10oz so Billy said, with a fine pair of lungs on him…. And I gather it was quite an ordeal for the poor girl. The midwife says Alice's going to be all right in a few weeks' time, but she's feeling a bit battered and bruised and is being told to stay in bed and rest. George is absolutely made up about it being a boy."

"Father's usually want sons and mothers want daughters…. My Mam always had this rhyme *a son's a son 'til he takes a wife, a daughter's a daughter for the rest of my life.* It didn't stop her letting my Da throw me out though." Betty said ruefully, "still that's all water under the bridge now, although Gerald told me a while back that my Mam is still alive and living in Canton."

"Alice told me she hoped it would be a girl a few weeks ago," Ivy said swiftly, she could see her mother was starting to get maudlin. Betty had mentioned her own mother a few times of late, Ivy half expected her Mam to try and track down her elderly mother and repair the rift. *Families could be strange things.*

"Alice said she wished for a girl, but George wanted a son to continue the family name, I expect she'll try for a girl next time" Ivy chattered on. It went without saying that Ivy would never give Billy a son to carry on the Thomas family name, and that for Ivy there would never be a next time, but Ivy didn't have an envious bone in her body, and she was genuinely thrilled for her friend's good fortune.

June ambled into the room cradling her favourite dolly *Margaret* in her arms, rocking it like a baby.

"June knows the stork brought Aunty Alice a baby boy in the night, don't you June?" Ivy winked at her Mam.

June nodded solemnly and continued to rock *Margaret*. "Will the stork leave us a baby too Nanna?" June looked up at Nanna Betty with her trusting almond eyes.

"I don't think so my lovely," Betty scooped the child up on her knee and gave her a big hug. "You see Aunty Alice didn't have a little baby to love so the stork brought her one, but your Mam's got you and you're just perfect…. the only little girl your Mam ever wants."

Ivy struggled to choke back a tear and mouthed *thank you* to her Mam over June's head.

"I'd best get back home and sort Bampa Gag's dinner out or else Nanna will be in trouble, and we can't have that can we June?" Betty glanced out of the window, "at least the snow didn't hang around for long, apart from some under the hedges it's all fizzled away thank heavens."

"I know Mam, but June was so disappointed not to have a chance to make snowballs this morning, it was all gone here by nine o'clock." Ivy chuckled remembering June rushing up the garden path with Nanna Betty in tow on the hunt for traces of any remaining snow.

Betty rose to leave." Oh, by, the way, I'm popping in to see Aunty Phoebe this afternoon Ivy, so I'll tell her the good news about Alice and the baby. I saw Phoebe on Wellfield Road yesterday when I was doing my shopping and she said she wanted to tell me about something that was puzzling her, she was quite mysterious about it…. I wonder what it can be?"

*

Phoebe had hunted high and low but there was no doubt about it, her silver and onyx rosary, a treasured first Holy communion present from her late Godmother Alys, was nowhere to be found.

She could have sworn she left it in the back parlour hanging on the armchair or on the little side table next to her armchair. After attending Sunday mass and using her rosary for prayers, Phoebe would invariably leave the chain on, or beside her favourite armchair in the sitting room for use throughout the week. But this week it was nowhere to be seen.

Despite hunting under chairs and searching down crevices the finely worked chain with black beads had vanished. In vain Phoebe turned the room upside down in her search for it, even searching impossible places like down the back of the old writing bureau Deirdre had left behind. There was nothing for it but to admit the rosary was lost. *It was a mystery*.

Phoebe tried to wrack her brain and recall if she really did place the delicate silver chain with the tiny onyx beads and silver figure of Christ in its usual position *or* could she possibly have lost it on her way home from church.

The chain was so light and delicate, it was possible she'd dropped it in her rush to return home from mass and not noticed the loss. The rosary wouldn't have made a noise *if* it had fallen out of her coat pocket on the way home or even in the church.

Phoebe widened her search.

Phoebe had already retraced her steps on her usual route to St Paul's, her eyes scanning gutters and crevices, and she enquired in the church office to see if a cleaner had discovered it. She'd searched behind the pews in the area she usually chose to sit in, but despite going over the church with a fine-tooth comb, her treasured rosary chain was nowhere to be found.

I suppose someone might have found it in the street and handed it in to the Police station, Phoebe thought, it was an outside chance worth exploring. She decided to call in to the Wellfield Road Police station and register the loss.

The duty officer behind the counter sucked through his teeth when Phoebe told him about the lost rosary.

"So, Miss Horwat, you *think* the item was made of silver then," Sergeant Giles made copious notes.

"Well, I never checked it out or anything Sergeant because it was a gift from my Godmother when I was a child, but she told me it was genuine silver, so I'm pretty sure it must have been. Whatever it was made of it certainly meant a lot to me." Phoebe felt the loss of her precious rosary keenly, it was one of the few things she'd taken with her the night her mother, in a towering rage, showed her the door and threw her out of the family home for falling pregnant and breaking her father's heart.

"Would you say it was of any great monetary value?" Sergeant Giles peered over the top of his glasses.

"I really don't know Sergeant Giles …. At least I don't think it was, the chain was light, and the beads were rather small… but on the other hand, it was very pretty and quite finely wrought, so yes I suppose it *could* have been valuable, now I come to think about it. "

Phoebe was beginning to get exasperated; she had already been told that no such item had been handed in, so all these questions seemed to be getting them nowhere, *how on earth was she supposed to know what the rosary was worth!*

"Miss Horwat, the reason I'm asking about the value, is that your rosary might have been stolen."

Phoebe's eyebrows shot up.

"If you did drop it in the street and it *looked* like it might be valuable, then someone might have pocketed it hoping to make a few bob. However devotional items like this don't get worn as jewellery so it doesn't make any real sense to be sold on in a pub or to a dodgy jeweller, this is a specialist item, not exactly easy to sell on. Still, a casual thief will turn his hand to anything if the opportunity arises," Sergeant Giles spoke from twenty years of experience.

Phoebe was beginning to think that Sergeant Giles was smarter than she took him for. "I see," she said slowly.

"Do you think anyone might have stolen it from your home Miss Horwat, you did say the item was quite often left lying around for anyone to see?"

"Certainly not! My lodgers don't come into my private rooms." Phoebe said hotly.

"You seem very certain of that and are you sure you haven't had any workmen or odd job men in the house recently, or any strange visitors who don't usually come into your private rooms in the house but might have come in for some other reason." Sergeant Giles pushed Phoebe to consider all possibilities.

"I'm absolutely certain no stranger or workman has come in the house. For heaven's sake the only visitors I've had are my best friend Betty who I'd trust with my life and the two young children from next door who sometimes come in to visit me if their Mam is busy."

"Hmm, young children pop in you say…. And what ages would these children be?"

Phoebe's jaw dropped, "what are you suggesting! Both the children next door are well behaved and … and delightful."

"I'm not suggesting anything Miss Horwat, but you would be surprised to see how many youngsters pass through our doors; girls *and* boys from good homes caught shoplifting or worse, it happens all the time. And every time some poor mother is crying her heart out saying that their little angel was a good child who never normally put a foot wrong," Sergeant Giles gave Phoebe a knowing look. Children could be deceptively criminal in his experience; a child could often fall to temptation because they didn't always consider how easily they might get caught out.

"Well in this case it's the truth! Jennifer and Frank Prosser are delightful, well brought up children, and they would never steal…. Never." Phoebe said vehemently.

"I'm pleased to hear it; in that case Miss Horwat I think I have all the information I need, and the information will stay on our files." Sergeant Giles closed his notebook. "If, however, the item turns up please let us know and if by some chance it is handed in by a member of the public, we will contact you straight away. Good morning to you Miss Horwat."

Phoebe trailed out of the police station; her mind was in a whirl. It was unthinkable to contemplate that she might have a thief in her house… *and as for implying that somehow the Prosser children, her own grandchildren, might have had something to do with the loss of the rosary…. Well, that was plainly ridiculous.*

Phoebe decided to hurry back home and search again, this time she would hunt in unlikely places such as upstairs and in drawers and even under her bed. As far as Phoebe was concerned there were only two possible outcomes to this puzzle; either the rosary was lost somewhere in the house and it still might turn up eventually or, she had dropped it in the street on her way home from church, and someone had picked it up, any other scenario was just unthinkable.

Phoebe wouldn't rest until she got to the bottom of the mystery.

Rushing back to Alma Road, Phoebe bumped into Betty doing her shopping, usually she would stop for a gossip with her friend, but not today, she had a mystery to solve.

"Hello Betty, I really can't stop for a chat now, why not pop around and see me tomorrow, I have something rather strange I'd like you to give me some advice on."

"Something strange?"

"I don't want to say any more about it Betty, not until I've had a good look in the house…. I'll see you tomorrow."

With that, Phoebe scurried up the road leaving Betty mystified. *What could Phoebe be talking about?*

*

Phoebe hunted high and she hunted low, she pulled things out and turned things upside down, her fingers probed down the crevices at the side of the armchairs and she even lifted the mats. The rosary was nowhere to be seen.

A loud knocking came on the door, the same special triple rap she'd asked the Prosser children to use. When Phoebe opened the door she saw Frank was stood there alone. Frank wouldn't normally come on his own without Jennifer. His sister came quite often without her brother, happy to help making cakes or to do the dusting, but never Frank unless it was on an errand.

"Hello Aunty Phoebe, can I come in? Mam has taken Jennifer shopping for a new pair of shoes and it's boring being in the house on my own," Frank flashed a winning smile, his unsteady voice warbling and ranging from high to low. The lad was only about eleven, but he was already turning into a young man.

"Of course, you can Frank, I'm a little bit busy at the moment but I can stop for a chat."

"What are you doing Aunty Phoebe," Frank could see the chair cushions scattered over the living room floor.

"I…. I seem to have lost something, something that is important to me… my rosary." she looked the lad straight in the eye…. Did she capture a glimpse of shiftiness there?

No, it was impossible to even think that either Frank or Jennifer could have had anything to do with the lost rosary. "I'm sure it will turn up soon… at least I hope it will; sometimes these things just seem to re-appear from nowhere like magic."

Why did she say that? Was she trying to hint to him that if he did take it, then he could always put it back? She was irritated with herself for letting such a dreadful thought creep into her mind. *Stop it!*

"Come on in Frank and shut the front door behind you. I'm sure I might have a packet of Trebor sweets for you in the kitchen pantry," she said, trying to atone for her disloyal thoughts. Malcolm Goode kept her well stocked with sweet treats to give to the children next door.

"Thanks Aunty Phoebe, but I've had rather a lot of sweets lately and Mam said I wasn't to eat anymore or else all my teeth would start falling out. I'm going to see the dentist for a filling next week and I don't want any more." Frank said ruefully, he was dreading the slow tortuous drilling out of his tooth rot and at night his Mam had given him a wad of cotton wool soaked in clove oil to soothe the dull ache which frequently nagged in his lower jaw.

"I see," Phoebe was amazed to hear Frank refusing sweets. *Where did the child suddenly get so much pocket money from that he could afford an enormous number of sweets, so many he was refusing another packet?*

Phoebe didn't like the way her thoughts kept treacherously coming back to Frank.

Stop it!

"Well, if you're certain about the sweets Frank, I'll give them to my Goddaughter June."

Later that night the treacherous devil on Phoebe's shoulder kept whispering in her ear…. *valuable items don't just disappear! How did Frank get all those sweets?*

When Phoebe had tossed and turned and made herself wretched through grief, worry and lack of sleep it suddenly came to her…. Whoever had the rosary would need to sell it to make some money, a nice lad like Frank could never do that.

Frank was a child of eleven, he couldn't just walk into a respectable jeweller or pawnbroker and sell the rosary even if he had taken it…. Which she was now certain he hadn't, so if he had extra sweets then he had got them by other means. This wasn't Tiger Bay where street children like Tomasz Nowak slid down alleyways, mixed with low life and did shady deals, this was Roath for heaven's sake!

Phoebe would discuss her thoughts with Betty tomorrow. Betty always helped her settle her mind and come to a decision. Phoebe finally drifted off to sleep in the early hours; the whereabouts of her precious rosary haunted her dreams.

Chapter 5

Eileen was bursting with happiness, at first she had wanted to stand on the rooftops and broadcast her good news to the neighbourhood, but caution made her keep her secret close.

There was no doubt about it now, she was expecting a baby.

Sean cried tears of joy when Eileen told him Dr Arnold had pronounced her pregnant… no ifs, no buts or maybes she was expecting their baby in about six months, and she was in fine fettle. It was the miracle Eileen had prayed for. Even so they agreed to wait a week or two before telling anyone else apart from Eileen's Mam Ida.

Now the deadline was passed, and Eileen was like a dog with two tails, so happy she couldn't stop grinning. She'd wanted to tell the world for weeks of her happy condition and now she could… she was going to be a mother!

The first person she told was Ivy Benson. "I must tell you our good news Ivy…. We have been blessed with a baby," Eileen said shyly. She still couldn't quite believe that underneath her taut belly a new life was starting to grow.

"That's such good news Eileen, you and Sean must be so happy." Ivy was genuinely thrilled for the sweet-natured Eileen and gave her a hug. When Eileen had moved into the top of Wilson Road with her young husband looking frail and walking unsteadily with sticks, tongues had wagged, and the rumour mill worked overtime; for the couple to be expecting a baby was the best news ever.

"This year seems to be *our* lucky year Ivy." Eileen crossed her fingers.

"Sean is starting to feel more like his old self, and he is going for an interview with the trolley bus company on Tuesday. He's hopeful they might give him a job as a driver, his legs might be a bit crook after the accident, but he reckons he can manage to drive a bus as good as any man." Eileen smiled, she was so proud of her husband and his fierce determination to live life to the full.

"I'm so pleased for you both, really I am. And if you'll take my advice Eileen, you'll have a chat to Norah Ashworth, she was an absolute Godsend when I was pregnant with June. What that woman doesn't know about being pregnant and having babies is not worth knowing I can tell you." Ivy knew kind-hearted Norah had been through the mill with Gareth and the measles virus which raged through Wilson Road over Christmas, but her friend was bouncing back and making the best of things, she knew Norah would be thrilled to hear about Eileen's pregnancy. It wasn't like practical Norah to be down in the dumps for long.

"When is Norah's baby due?" Eileen felt elated to have joined the mother's club to be discussing due dates, babies, and nappies with another mother. It was a club she'd wanted to join for such a long time; now she was its newest member eager to learn all she could about the craft of being a mother.

"I believe she's due in about four weeks' time Eileen, but since this is baby number five for Mrs Ashworth it might come along a little sooner than expected." Ivy made a mental note to pop over and pay her friend Norah a visit.

The news of Eileen's pregnancy spread like wildfire and soon all of Wilson Road was party to the happy event expected in the Riley household. Within days it seemed that just about everyone Eileen met was keen to hear about the baby and Eileen was delighted to have such a willing audience.

Men clapped Sean on the back and wished him well when he ventured to the pub with Jack Ashworth. Sean felt like after existing in a long dark tunnel he'd re-joined the land of the living with hopes and dreams just like any ordinary fellow, and it felt good. A new window was opening for them both and he thanked God for it.

*

Betty couldn't wait to share the good news with Phoebe, Alice's baby and Eileen's pregnancy was certainly something to chat about and of course there was Phoebe's mystery to discuss.

When Phoebe answered the door Betty could see the dark circles under her friend's eyes. Phoebe looked done in.

"Goodness me Phoebe! You look like you've been up half the night, what on earth's the matter? Are you ill?" Betty asked anxiously.

"You'd better come in Betty, I'm in such a tizz I can't think straight."

Over a cup of tea, Phoebe explained the mystery of the missing rosary. "I know its dreadful to jump to conclusions, but for a while, God forgive me," Phoebe crossed herself, "just for a short while, not long at all really," she said quickly, hating herself for ever doubting Frank, "I worried it might have been Frank who'd taken it." Phoebe paused to take a breath; her heart was racing as she recalled the mental torture she experienced last night.

Betty could see Phoebe was in torment, to have to contemplate that her own Grandson might be the light-fingered thief was hateful.

"But then I realised it didn't make any sense for Frank to steal it, he wouldn't have any means of selling it on, it wasn't of value to him for sweets or pocket money, so now I don't know what to think.... I'm beginning to think that I must have dropped it in the street and that someone must have picked it up and didn't think to hand it in, maybe they thought it was just a cheap thing not worth the effort." Phoebe could feel herself tearing up, she sniffed into her handkerchief and dabbed her tired eyes.

"What shall I do Betty?" Phoebe pleaded.

"Has anything else gone missing?"

"I don't think so, but then I don't have anything else to go missing." Phoebe raised her hands in bewilderment.

"No money out of your purse or loose change left on the side?"

Phoebe thought for a moment, "no. I'm sure of it."

"In that case, if you're certain nothing else is missing from the house, then I'd lay a pound to a penny you dropped it in the street. You said you took it out of the house yourself and that you used it in church, so it makes sense to think it never came back, and it was lost somehow on the way home. Have you checked your coat pockets?"

"I've checked everything…. Twice." Phoebe said miserably.

Betty put her arm around her friend's shoulder. She knew how important the rosary was to Phoebe, it had been her most treasured possession. "Try not to fret, it might still turn up, you never know, stranger things have happened. Perhaps a fellow member of the congregation picked it up thinking it was theirs and will return it when they spot the error, or maybe a church cleaner or groundsman might discover it tucked down somewhere."

Phoebe felt a glimmer of hope, Betty was such a wise friend. "I won't give up hope just yet, you're right Betty, it might still turn up."

*

Betty decided to pop to the Albany Road shops to buy some liver for Gerald's dinner before returning home to Inkerman Street. Gerald was fancying a nice plate of lamb's liver and bacon with a rich onion gravy; it was one of his favourites.

As Betty came out of the greengrocers with a bag of onions and a savoy cabbage, she prepared to cross over to the butcher's shop to buy the liver. She spotted a familiar figure, Betty felt sure that she recognized the slim dapper figure of Phoebe's lodger Malcolm Goode standing on the other side of the road.

Betty had only ever met Malcolm once at Alma Road, and even though the man opposite had his back to her, Malcolm had made a firm impression on her and she was almost certain it was him standing outside Cohen's jewellery shop. The man had the same rakish air, tipped felt hat and wide lapelled suit. The man's hat partly obscured his face, but Betty could still swear it was Malcolm Goode.

Betty tried not to stare as she noticed the man in the pinstripe suit stop in front of the small jewellery shop, he seemed to spend a long time looking in the window. The butcher's shop was next door to the jeweller's; she decided she would not cross the road just yet. She would bide her time and try to see what Malcolm Goode, Trebor sweet salesman, was doing going in a jewellery shop on Albany Road in the middle of the day.

The man quickly checked over his shoulder before nipping inside the premises of *Cohen's Jewellers and Pawn Brokers.* Betty waited a while, she could see from the clock above the hardware shop it was nearly twelve o'clock, Gerald liked his dinner at one o'clock on the dot, she couldn't afford to wait too much longer if she wasn't going to be late; she still had the liver to buy.

Just as Betty was about to cross the road, she saw the man leave the shop. It *was* Mr Goode, he was replacing his hat as he left, but this time she got a good look at his face; there could be no doubt about it, the man leaving Cohen's the jewellers was Phoebe's lodger, Malcolm Goode *and* he had a face like thunder.

Malcolm hurried down the street like a man on a mission, she watched him disappear around the corner and melt swiftly into the crowd. *How very peculiar!*

Betty decided to risk lateness and Gerald's displeasure and pop into the jeweller's shop to see if she could gain any information about the purpose of Mr Goode's visit. Perhaps her mind was running riot and perhaps she was doing Mr Goode a big disservice, but *was* he trying to pawn something? It was just a hunch and she needed to follow it through.

As she entered the shop, she could see Mr Reuben Cohen was tidying away some trays of second-hand jewellery, the old man looked flustered and all a sixes and sevens, he was sipping from a glass of water and mopping his brow.

"I'll be with you in just a minute Madam." Reuben straightened up the goods on the tray. It was obviously a tray of goods for men, cufflinks, collar studs and tie pins. Betty's heart relaxed a little, whatever the annoyance might have been about it looked like it wasn't about a rosary, if the items on the counter were to be believed.

"No rush Mr Cohen," Betty said smoothly. "I'm only browsing at the moment; my God-daughter is getting confirmed soon and I'm looking for a nice rosary."

Betty hoped this lie might prompt Mr Cohen to chat about similar items he had for sale.

"I'm sorry Madam, we don't stock rosaries or any other such devotional items, so I'm sorry I can't be of help." Mr Cohen said with a sad smile. "I'm afraid today is not a good day for business," he raised his palms upwards and shrugged his shoulders.

"I'm sorry to hear that, still you do have some delightful items and if ever I need a gift for my husband, then I know where to come," Betty said as Mr Cohen began to unlock the shop window to replace the tray.

"Harrumph," Mr Cohen snorted. "Well, I'm pleased to hear that Madam."
Mollified, Ruben was starting to calm down.

"I try to run a respectable business with both new and second-hand items; this was my father's business before I took it over, and my son will take it over after I'm gone. Sixty years our family has been trading here, and we've built up a good reputation." Reuben Cohen said proudly, his family was well regarded in the local community and even in the war years, they'd never experienced any abuse or trouble. Then this morning, bold as brass, a man storms into his shop casting aspersions! It had unsettled him. Betty could tell that Mr Cohen was still feeling irritated by whatever had passed between himself and Mr Goode.

"Cohens has traded here for nearly forty years, and we've always been known for quality goods and fair prices, and I'd call any man a liar who said differently," Mr Cohen said firmly, getting into his stride. "Do you know, I had a man in here just twenty minutes ago accusing me of selling stolen goods…. I ask you what an accusation to make to an honest businessman like myself!"

Betty looked shocked, "how dreadful, why did he say that Mr Cohen?"
Ruben Cohen pointed to an attractive tie pin nestling on the tray, a fine, gold bar pin with a fox head and ruby eyes, "this tie pin here, the gentleman swore blind it was his, said it was just like the one he bought himself after a win on the races, said it had been stolen from him only recently, demanded I hand it over! He called me a liar to my face and threatened to go to the police!" Rueben Cohen still looked agitated as he recalled the nasty episode and the heated argument with Malcolm Goode.

"Goodness, so what did you say," Betty knew that Mr Cohen, could never survive the slanderous accusation of dealing in dodgy items.

"I told him that I'd I bought it fair and square from a very respectable source, a customer I've dealt with many times over the years and that he must be mistaken." Mr Cohen remembered the fury on Malcolm Goode's face when he refused to hand over the tie pin or give him the name of the person who'd sold him the piece.

"I'm sure you're right Mr Cohen…. surely there must be more than one fox head tie pin in the world?"

"Exactly…. That's exactly what I said!" Mr Cohen said, relieved that Betty could see his side of it.

"He said he recognized some small scratches and marks on the pin, which is a load of nonsense, because there's barely a mark on the thing. I told him if he can prove it belongs to him then he was welcome to call the police and we'll take it from there…. Between you and me I'm beginning to think he might be a con man; thought I'd be a sucker for a sob story because I'm getting on a bit, and he could talk me out of my merchandise. I might be getting on a bit but I'm not that easily taken for a fool." Mr Cohen tapped his nose conspiratorially.

Betty didn't know what to think, the mystery was getting deeper and deeper, she would tell Phoebe what she'd found out about Malcolm Goode's trip to the jewellers.

"It's not unknown for con men and tricksters to target shops like mine, I don't expect he'll have the cheek to come back and try it again though…. I told him if he came in here again then I'd call the police myself, let them sort it out!"

It was now twelve thirty and dinner would certainly be late; Betty knew Gerald would be grumpy, *still when she told him about the mysterious Mr Goode he'd understand.*

Chapter 6

Malcome Goode was furious, he knew beyond a shadow of a doubt that the gold fox head tie pin in Reuben Cohen's window was his, but he couldn't go to the police and cause a fuss and the old jeweller knew it. Malcolm had bought the tie pin second-hand from a mate of his after he'd had a win on the horses over ten years ago and he'd paid good money for it. His friend, Wilfred Osborne, was a retired antique dealer and second-hand jeweller who still dabbled in a bit of buying and selling on the side, usually in the pubs and clubs of Barry Island, doing deals on the sly.

Old Wilf was not averse to turning a blind eye to bits and pieces that came his way from some rather dubious sources which is why his prices were affordable so long as no one was asking any awkward questions or pushing for receipts.

Malcolm had treasured the gold tie pin for ten years and it was his lucky pin, probably not so lucky for the other man who lost it years ago at the Chepstow racecourse, but it was Malcolm's most precious possession and he'd bought it fair and square from Wilfred; Malcolm wasn't going to rest until he'd solved the mystery of how his pin had come to be on display in the shop window of Cohen's the jewellers.

The smirking face of old Reuben Cohen had made Malcolm's blood boil, *"why not call the police then Sir, if you are so certain the piece is yours... I'm sure they can investigate?"*

Malcolm knew the tie pin was lost to him; he couldn't prove it was his and it was hopeless to think that he could persuade Reuben to return it; Cohen had called his bluff and won. Even more annoyingly the jeweller refused to name the person who had sold it to him – *that* was who Malcolm needed to find, and he wouldn't rest until he'd discovered who'd taken it from him.

*

"So have you bought that dress yet Ivy," Phoebe asked over a cup of tea, her tone laden with exasperation. Phoebe knew Billy was insisting Ivy had a new dress for the wedding but, mindful of the cost, Ivy was dragging her heels.

"You know I haven't Aunty Phoebe, and don't tell me Billy has sent you to nag me about it, he's like a stuck record," Ivy raised her eyebrows.

"Quite rightly so Ivy, you can't wear some shabby old thing on your wedding day for heaven's sake."

Ivy snorted, she was fed up with the drip, drip, drip of nagging from Mam, Billy and Phoebe; she knew she must give in eventually.

"Tell you what Ivy, there's a new stall in Cardiff indoor market and the lady there is selling some very reasonably priced dresses, so why don't I look after June for you, and then you can go shopping for a dress this afternoon." Phoebe was not going to let Ivy slip off the hook, it was only just over six weeks to the wedding and Ivy still hadn't bought something pretty to wear.

"Mam's coming over to us for dinner today, she hasn't seen June in ages; she's staying for the afternoon so….." excuses tripped off Ivy's tongue

"All the better! I'll stop for a bite to eat, and then Betty can look after June whilst we *both* go out shopping together!" Phoebe exclaimed. "It will be fun Ivy; I might even treat myself to something new."

"But I…."

"No buts Ivy, a slice of bread and dripping will suit me, I'm not going to rob you of your dinner," Phoebe said quickly before Ivy could make any more excuses.

Recognizing that she was out-manoeuvred, Ivy conceded defeat; she would buy her dress that afternoon.

*

The indoor market was buzzing with life, more than fifty stalls decorated with jaunty striped awnings selling fruit, vegetables, meats, cheeses, floristry, and haberdashery crowded the lower level, stall holders vying for trade crying their wares to passing shoppers.

On the upstairs level, the larger fixed units housed the café, pet shops, toilets, and older more established businesses such as the clock makers, jealously guarded leases handed down from father to son.

"Dorothy's" dress and ladies clothes stall nestled in one far corner of the market near to the staircase leading to the upper level. Several attractive dresses, in the latest fashions hung from rails suspended from the awning and a smart young seamstress answering to the name of Dorothy sat busy making alterations on a Singer sewing machine.

"Here we are Ivy, that's the stall I was telling you about. Don't those frocks look nice?" Phoebe pointed to several swing dresses and circular skirts which caught the eye, there were even some of the latest design "wiggle" dresses pinned to the back canvas.

Ivy looked doubtful; she couldn't see any prices.

"I make them all myself," Dorothy muttered through a mouthful of pins, she pointed to a sign: *Clothes handmade -McCall's patterns.*

Spotting a potential customer Dorothy stopped winding the sewing machine handle and put down the pins. "Are you looking for something special ladies because I can make anything to order, or I can alter one I've already made if it doesn't quite fit." Dorothy eyed up the petite figure of Ivy Benson.

Phoebe was looking through the rails, some pretty polka dot prints were very eye catching.

"Those are nice, very popular with the younger ladies. I've started making the spring and summer looks now, so I've got some pretty things hanging up. I buy all my fabrics from Josie at the other end of the market, she gives me a good deal so I can keep my prices down." Dorothy chattered away, moving her stock around with practised fingers.

"If you don't see a fabric pattern you like here, then if you go to Josie's stall she'll look after you and I can run it up in no time, she sells all the net for the petticoats as well." As Dorothy was speaking, she was carefully selecting a few items she thought would suit Ivy's delicate colouring and shape.

"I'm not sure I can afford a new dress Aunty Phoebe, certainly not one especially made for me." Ivy looked nervous, after Billy's unfortunate incident down on the docks they'd agreed he'd stick to working at the tasty Plaice Fish bar; money was tight.

"Nonsense Ivy, it is your wedding day for heaven's sake, you *must* have a new dress for the day. And since it's not going to be in church can choose any dress you like for the occasion, some of these would be perfect." Phoebe sounded exasperated.

"Oh, you're getting married, how exciting!…. Then I'm sure we can find you something." Dorothy exclaimed. "And don't worry too much about the prices as I tell all the ladies who come to my stall, I'm cheaper than Woolworth's *and* it's going to fit you properly!"

Phoebe chuckled, "in that case I think you'd better show us some day dresses."

Dorothy had managed to create a little dressing area under the slope of the stairs with a curtain and a rail. Ivy was out of excuses and like a lamb to slaughter agreed to try on the dresses chosen by Dorothy. Ivy had ruled out anything light blue on the grounds that she wore light blue the first time around on the dreadful day she tied the knot with Jimmy Benson.

"Why not try this red spotted one on first, I'm sure it's going to look very glamorous with that gorgeous auburn hair of yours," Dorothy handed Ivy the red swing dress with white polka dots and two underskirts to puff out the silhouette.

"There's a mirror in the back and remember alterations can be done in a few hours." Dorothy ushered Ivy towards the changing area.

"Gosh, you do look gorgeous," Dorothy gasped as Ivy came out in the dress, "it's only cotton but it looks fabulous on you." Dorothy's nimble fingers started using a few pins to put a dart in the bust area and narrow the waist. "See it won't take much to make it a perfect fit."

The dress, now nipped in and fitted to Ivy's figure, looked stunning. Phoebe nodded her approval.

"It does look *very* glamorous Ivy, and certainly smart enough for a wedding, and afterwards you could wear it to go out dancing, all it needs is a simple cardigan to top it off." Phoebe tried to hold back the tears prickling her eyelids, Ivy's tiny cinched in waist, lustrous auburn hair and porcelain skin made her look as elegant as any fashion model. Billy would be enormously proud of her.

"Don't you think it's a bit too jazzy for a wedding?" Ivy said dubiously, the red dress felt as if it screamed *look at me*.

"No!" the two women chorused in unison.

Ivy fingered a soft green, sprigged print dress with cream lapels, capped sleeves and a narrow cream belt, the pretty, delicate design suited the gathered skirt. "I think I'd like to try this one."

Ivy went back into the changing room and slipped into the second dress, the muted green seemed to sing next to her auburn hair and the narrow fabric belt accentuated her tiny waist. She had to admit the green dress felt more like her. The soft green fabric wasn't as zingy and bold as the attention-grabbing bright red, polka dot fabric, but it hung nicely, and she felt pretty in it. She felt sure Billy would like it and it would get a lot more use than a bold red dress.

When she emerged from the changing area the two women made some polite comments about her looking pretty in the green dress, but it was obvious to Ivy the red dress was the favourite with Phoebe and the seamstress.

"But I like this one," Ivy said firmly, she was determined not to be steamrollered into buying a dress she felt ought to be on the back of another woman, a woman more glamorous and confident than timid Ivy Benson. The chic, red dress was just the sort of dress her glamorous blonde friend Alice might wear, and this green dress was the sort of dress Ivy would wear. She felt sure if she turned up in the sassy red dress Billy would think he was marrying a different woman.

The women could see Ivy looking conflicted.

"Don't get me wrong Ivy, you do look lovely in the green dress, and it would be very suitable for the occasion," Phoebe said hastily, not wishing to hurt Ivy's feelings.

"But then, with a figure like yours you'd look nice in almost anything," Dorothy said tactfully, she didn't want to lose a sale and the girl *had* looked uncomfortable in the eye-catching bright dress. The green dress did sit very well on Ivy and only needed a few tweaks to make it a perfect fit.

"What about that navy wiggle dress Dorothy has picked out, do you want to try that one on, it's very elegant?" Phoebe suggested hopefully, although she had to admit that Ivy didn't really have the voluptuous figure needed to carry the style off. Ivy *must* buy her dress today.

"No thanks Aunty Phoebe, my mind is made up. I don't *need* any impractical, glamorous dresses hanging in the wardrobe that I won't get much use out of; so long as this dress and the alterations aren't too dear then this will be the dress for me." Ivy smiled, she was happy in the green dress and was determined to stand her ground.

Dorothy was anxious to close the sale. "It's a good choice and a bargain; the dress is only seventeen shillings and sixpence, and the net petticoats to go underneath are another shilling. Tell you what…. because it's for your wedding day, I'll throw in the alterations for free, now I can't say fairer than that can I." Dorothy smiled; she could see Ivy was relieved to have found a dress and Dorothy had her sale.

"That is good of you Dorothy, thank you," Ivy said shyly. She promised Billy she would find a new dress and she felt she'd made a good choice. Ivy even had enough money left over in her purse to buy some new shoes, a sensible cream shoe would be serviceable all spring and summer.

"Ivy, whilst you're paying and getting your final measurements done, I'm going upstairs to the toilets and then I'll treat us both to a nice cup of tea in the market cafe before we go home." Phoebe was gasping for a cup of tea, it had been like pulling teeth getting Ivy to the dress stall, but at least the mission was accomplished, Ivy had her dress for her wedding day.

Phoebe left Ivy in the capable hands of Dorothy and headed up the stairs to the ladies' toilets. The top floor of the market was never as busy as the bustling, hectic lower concourse, it was a good place to have a cup of tea and take in the theatre of the market stalls down below and to people watch through the wrought iron balcony railings.

Phoebe peered over the balcony and watched for Ivy in the crowds, she could see both the left and righthand staircases from her vantage point by the cafe. There was no rush, there was heaps of time before they needed to get back for Betty, Ivy should be along soon.

Near to the staircase on the opposite side of the market floor was a clock and watch repair stall, business looked quiet; an old man sat behind the counter mending a clock. The stall was a small unit selling a few new and second-hand items, but the advertisement proclaimed the main business- *Quality repairs, watches & clocks, bought and sold.*

Phoebe watched the man on the stall crafting the clock, then in the distance she glimpsed a familiar figure approached the corner of the marketplace. As the crowds parted Phoebe could see the familiar lady quite clearly, it was Rita Prosser going about her shopping. Phoebe smiled and her heart glowed with pride; her daughter was a handsome woman.

Phoebe observed Rita approach the watch repair stall and engage in an animated discussion with the old man behind the counter. Rita appeared to know him.

Unseen, on the upstairs balcony, Phoebe watched the small interchange between Rita and the old man whilst keeping half an eye on the staircase for Ivy.

Then Phoebe saw Rita take a small parcel out of her handbag and hand it over the counter, the old man placed his jeweller's eyeglass over his eye to get a better look at the object under discussion, Rita smiled and pointed at the long chain now dangling in the old man's hand.

Phoebe gasped; she felt as if her heart was being smashed into a million pieces, even from this distance she could see that the object the old man was holding up and turning over in his hand was no ordinary chain…. It was a rosary!

Tears rolled down Phoebe's cheeks, *it couldn't possibly be her rosary, could it?*

 "Oh, no…." Phoebe groaned softly.

"Is something the matter Aunty Phoebe?" Ivy looked concerned.

Phoebe jumped; distracted with the scene unfolding at the watch repair stall, she'd missed seeing Ivy climb the stairs.

"No, no, my lovely, nothing's the matter I'm just getting to a be silly, sentimental old lady," Phoebe hugged Ivy. "Now how about that cup of tea and you can tell me all the details about that lovely frock."

When Phoebe next glanced in the direction of the repair stall, Rita had disappeared.

Chapter 7

Ivy noticed that for all the weak smiles and nods of appreciation, Aunty Phoebe's heart just wasn't in talking about which shoes would suit the new dress or whether Ivy need a green or a cream cardigan.

When the two women parted company to go their separate ways home it was obvious to Ivy that Phoebe was relieved to be leaving the market.

"Are you sure you're alright Aunty Phoebe?" Ivy was not fooled.

"Of course, I am, now stop fussing Ivy. I've just got a bit of a headache coming on, that's all. The market was so loud and echoey upstairs it's given me a bit of a sore head, a few aspirin and a bit of peace and quiet and I'll be right as rain, so stop worrying."

"If you're sure Aunty Phoebe, then I'll be off home, Mam will be expecting me." Ivy kissed her aunt goodbye.

Phoebe headed home with a heavy heart.

*

Betty was puzzled. Ivy had come home full of information about the green and cream circle dress she'd bought for the wedding and enthusing about the skilful young seamstress Dorothy who had set up in the market making her own dresses; Ivy also told a tale of Phoebe's sudden mood switch from excitement to dull resignation, and damp squib responses.

"I really don't understand it Mam, it was as if I'd upset her somehow. I know I didn't favour the red dress she preferred, but surely that wouldn't put her in a mood would it?"

"Of course, not Ivy, Aunty Phoebe would only ever want you to be happy, something else must have caused the sudden change of mood."

"You don't think she's unwell do you Mam?"

"I do hope not Ivy. Tell you what, I'll pop around in the morning, I've got a little story I want to tell her, and I'll try to find out what's troubling her. Don't you fret Ivy I expect it was just something and nothing."

"I do hope you're right Mam, I couldn't bear it if something happened to Aunty Phoebe, give her my love and tell her I'll see her next week.... I've got a busy day tomorrow myself; I'm going with Father Malone to visit that Catholic institution I told you about," Ivy said anxiously. Tomorrow was a big day for both Ivy and June.

Ivy hadn't ever really considered what her daughter's future might be when she reached school age. Safe at home with Billy, Aunty Phoebe, Nanna Betty, Norah, and her playmate Karen, June floated through life on a cloud of cheery happiness. It never occurred to Ivy that doors would soon start closing in June's face because she was different.

Norah Ashworth had placed little Karen's name on the waiting list for the local infant's school, St Mary's on the Grand Avenue, and Ivy fondly hoped the two girls would skip off to school together, hand in hand when the time came, but it was not to be.

Last week Ivy discovered that June would not be welcome to join St Mary's school along with all the other children in the road, and Ivy would have to find somewhere else for June to go.

Ivy was horrified to have June's application turned down, but the local school insisted that children like June were not expected to be in a class with other "normal" children. It didn't matter how much Ivy pleaded with the headmaster to relent, Mr Bridger had made it quite clear that children like June should be in an institution for the feeble and the disabled and Ivy needed to look elsewhere.

"I'm sorry Mrs Benson, but the matter is completely out of my hands and besides, the school governors would never allow it. Children like June cannot take part in a normal school education and we neither have the funds or wherewithal to look after her, she should be in an institution which can cope with her needs."

Ivy tried to protest and argue, but Headmaster Bridger would not be moved.

"Mrs Benson," he said firmly. "The local authority funds this school and does *not* provide its services for children like June, consequently we are under no obligation to take June next September. Children with June's condition are not expected to undertake formal education, nor would she benefit from such an education if you were to find a school to take her. We are perfectly within our rights to refuse her a place, I suggest you approach the health services." Headmaster Bridger peered over his glasses; his tone was becoming increasingly exasperated.

In his opinion, Ivy Benson seemed to have the most unrealistic expectations of her daughter's prospects, he was of the view that these children were best left in institutions where they receive the appropriate care until they died. *It was kinder that way.*

Ivy wept bitter tears on the way home, she hated Mr Bridger and all that he stood for with his sanctimonious smile and patronising voice condemning June to a life on the margins. It was obvious Bridger thought she was a fool for keeping June in the first place and even worse, he was judging her daughter as worthless without ever meeting her.

Her darling June judged not worthy of the same care and opportunities as all the other kiddies living on Wilson Road. How dare he!

Father Malone shared Ivy's disappointment and offered to take her to see some of the more enlightened institutions in Cardiff that might be able and willing to offer June a place where she would be happy and thrive… Ivy could only hope and pray that Father Malone was right, June needed to be with other children, she couldn't spend all her life locked away in Wilson Road with just her Mam and Billy for company.

Chapter 8

Gerald was feeling his age and he was feeling grumpy. There were no biscuits in the tin again; Betty had been out this morning and she still managed to forget a few things off the shopping list, so busy gossiping she forgot his Rich Tea biscuits to go with his cup of tea, and he sincerely hoped his lunch wasn't going to be late again today.

Gerald was a patient man and he loved Betty to bits, she was the caring, cheerful, company he wanted in his old age after his wife Janet had died, leaving him lonely and rattling around the old house.

Gerald wasn't a fool, he knew when he married Betty that there was an age gap of over twenty years between them, and it was only to be expected that as time went by the gap would start to show, but lately he felt like he was being left behind; trailing in Betty's wake as she rushed here there and everywhere leaving Gerald to his own devices. To top it all, his angina had been playing up again.

Gerald didn't want to sound like an old man grumbling on about his numerous ailments but there was no getting away from the fact that he was sixty-eight and the creaks and groans as he got out of bed each morning reminded him of his mortality. Gerald didn't want to worry Betty unnecessarily about his health, but the dull ache across his chest seemed to nag at him night and day. The Doctor suggested Gerald needed to adopt a quiet stress-free life; living with Betty lately was like living with a veritable whirlwind

Betty's constant dashing in and out the house on *vital* errands and *mercy* missions, sorting out other people's problems, helping out when needed, was pushing his tolerance to the limit. *He* needed Betty at his side. Gerald rubbed his aching chest and took some pills for his grumbling angina.

Gerald understood Betty's concern for Ivy and her little granddaughter June; but in his opinion Betty was getting far too caught up in her friend Phoebe's affairs; interfering in matters which were of no real concern of hers.

What did it matter if Betty saw Phoebe's lodger Mr Goode going into a jeweller's premises… so what if he did? Surely it didn't need a long visit to Alma Road to pass on that bit of information.

Every day Betty was either visiting and helping out at Wilson Road or running around to Alma Road at the drop of a hat. Gerald knew it was irrational, but he felt himself slipping down Betty's priority list and he didn't like it. He wondered if he ought to say something about his concerns when she came back from her morning visit to see Phoebe. How to approach the topic would be a thorny issue; his wife could be fearsome when roused.

Gerald looked at the clock, it was just gone eleven thirty, Betty said she would be home by twelve to cook the pork chop, peas, and boiled potatoes about for his dinner…. Well, if she wasn't back on time to cook his dinner today then he would be having words!

Betty was late again.

*

"Goodness Phoebe, just look at the time! I must dash, Gerald will have my guts for garters if I'm late again." Betty knew she had irritated her husband recently by dashing in late for his dinner, but this *was* especially important.

The twenty-minute chat and a cup of tea with Phoebe had turned into a two-hour heart to heart and Phoebe was very upset.

To start with, Betty told the tale of Mr Goode and the dispute over the tie pin with Mr Cohen, "apparently Mr Goode insisted it had been stolen from him, said he recognized it immediately, but Mr Cohen was having none of it, said he'd bought it fair and square and refused to hand it back. Not that I blame Mr Cohen, I mean how could Malcolm Goode's tie pin end up in his shop window?"

Phoebe looked thoughtful; she didn't really care *how* the tie pin got there, perhaps Mr Cohen had bought it in good faith from someone, but it did beg the question, if it *was* Malcolm's tie pin and if it had been stolen, then who took it?

"That certainly is a strange story Betty…. I must say I don't think Mr Goode would have the nerve to try and diddle Mr Cohen out of a piece of jewellery unless he genuinely thought it was his tie pin." Phoebe said dubiously, she liked Malcolm and had no reason to think he was dishonest. "I *have* seen Malcolm wearing a fox head tie pin….and I must admit I *haven't* seen him wearing lately."

Phoebe's mind was in a whirl, *if* Malcom Goode's tie pin had been stolen from the house, and *if* her rosary was also stolen from the house, there was only one dreadful conclusion…. There was a thief in the house *or* a thief coming into her house. Who could it be?

Phoebe hated the way her thoughts treacherously kept coming back to her neighbours. She didn't want to contemplate the awful prospect of having to confront anyone from the Prosser family about her suspicions.

"I can't bear to say this Betty, but I'm worried the Prosser family next door *might* have something to do with all this," Phoebe buried her head in her hands and wept bitterly, the very thought was tearing her apart.

"Why do you think that?" Betty gasped

"I'm almost certain I saw Rita with a rosary in Cardiff market, a rosary that looked just like mine." Phoebe groaned; she had relived the awful scene in the market a thousand times in her mind but there was no getting away from it – Rita was handling a silver rosary just like the one Phoebe had lost.

"I think she might have been selling a rosary to a watch repair man, she handed it over to him and just as I was about to see if he gave her any payment for it, Ivy turned up chattering about her purchases, and the next time I turned around Rita was gone." Phoebe groaned. "I don't know what to think anymore… perhaps Frank had something to do with it after all… God help me I'm being suspicious of my own grandson!" Phoebe sobbed; she was beside herself with despair.

There she'd done it; she had voiced her worst fears that somehow the Prosser family might be involved with stealing things from her home, and she hated herself for it.

"I see, no wonder Ivy thought you were upset the day you went shopping together."

"I know Ivy thought she'd upset me, but she hadn't… it's just that I could hardly believe my eyes when I saw Rita hand over a rosary to a stall holder, and I couldn't think straight. I couldn't tell her what I'd seen either. And now there's this missing tie pin…. It's all very fishy, perhaps Malcolm is also the victim here? What am I going to do Betty?" Phoebe wailed.

Betty held her friend in her arms, she knew how much Phoebe wanted a close and loving relationship with the Prosser family next door and the daughter she thought she'd lost forever.

"If I were you Phoebe, I'd talk to Father Malone about this, he's a wise man, you can tell him about your fears in confidence. You don't need to say that Rita is your daughter, just tell him it's a concern about a neighbour and ask his advice…. You mustn't say anything until you're sure of your ground, because if you're wrong you may end up ruining what you have with your daughter Rita and the children." Betty cautioned.

"Do you think I should ask Malcolm about his tie pin going missing?"

"No, certainly not yet Phoebe… how are you supposed to know he's lost something valuable; you can't admit to spying on him, and don't forget he might have his own theory about who took his pin if it was stolen from the house…. He might even suspect that you had something to do with it."

"No, surely not!" Phoebe looked horrified.

Betty gave Phoebe a knowing look. "Just bide your time a while Phoebe until you've talked this through with Father Malone and in the meantime keep an eye open for anything going missing and…. I hate to say this but, you must keep an eye on anyone who comes into this house and that includes Frank and Jennifer."

Phoebe moaned, she hated suspecting her own grandchildren, but Betty was right, until she knew who the thief was, she couldn't trust anyone.

Chapter 9

Ivy was feeling miserable, no worse than that… she was on the brink of despair; if ever she needed to be held by Billy and told that things were going to be alright in the end, then today was the day. But Billy was run ragged and working every hour God gave at the Tasty Plaice fish bar, and he couldn't take time off to hold Ivy's hand, she would have to be strong now for June's sake. She took a deep breath before unlocking her front door.

Crying's not going to help June or solve anything for that matter, so no more bloody useless tears, Ivy, pull yourself together. She chided herself as she blew her nose. She'd returned to Wilson Road feeling down in the dumps, and she needed to see her daughter, to hold her and erase the memory of the terrible morning from her mind.

When Ivy accompanied Father Malone on his routine visit to St Mary's institution, she'd felt hopeful that she would find a solution to June's lack of a school place. The day, which had started off so filled with hope, had turned out to be disheartening and depressing, far worse than Ivy could ever have dreamed of. Her eyes had been opened to June's future world and she didn't like what she saw.

 Now after giving herself a stern ticking off and pulling herself together Ivy vowed she would shed no more tears over a stupid, heartless system which labelled her darling daughter a misfit, a child to be cast on the rubbish heap, never expected to achieve anything worthwhile; a child to be kept out of sight.

After the school refused June a place, Father Malone had been as good as his word in seeking out an alternative to June staying at home alone with

Ivy each day, and it had been eye-opening and heart-breaking in equal measure.

The kindly priest had taken Ivy to see St Mary's Home; an Institution for the "feeble-minded," as one nurse on reception happily described the facility and the place brought tears to Ivy's eyes and left her angry beyond belief. Ivy never knew such places existed, let alone seen the inside of one. It never occurred to her that these young people, youngsters just like June, were kept away from public view.

Ivy couldn't bear to think June would end up in a place for the "feeble-minded."

Father Malone reassured Ivy that St Mary's was compassionate and kind, and suitable for people with June's condition. She'd never expected to see so many souls with trusting moon faces and almond eyes like June, but these faces were older, so much older.

"But where are all the other *young* children, Father Malone," Ivy gasped when she saw groups of young adults who looked just like older versions of June, daubing paintings, winding wool, or snipping up patch books with plastic scissors. Some individuals held dollies or teddies for comfort. Ivy had expected school rooms and playgrounds filled with chattering children and laughter, not day rooms filled with subdued young adults whiling away their days with meaningless activities.

"Most of the young people you can see in this room are aged between ten and twenty, children with this condition age a lot more quickly than normal children. These patients are not as old as you think they are." Nurse Jones said.

Ivy gasped with the realisation that there was still so much she needed to learn about children with June's condition. Ivy felt she was groping in the dark, no-one told her anything about what she could expect for June's future, she had no help or useful information; the system had just left her to fend for herself the day she walked out of the hospital with her baby. With the help of Mam and Phoebe, Ivy had always treated June as her loved daughter, a little girl who wanted for nothing and June had thrived under the love and attention…. *June chattered, ran, and skipped with the other children on Wilson Road, June was not subdued and docile like these poor souls*, Ivy thought to herself.

Since the day Ivy left the hospital and the aftercare of midwife Marion Spears, she had been cast adrift and now so many doors were closing in June's face, Ivy didn't know where to turn.

And why did Nurse Jones keep referring to them all as patients? June wasn't ill.

"We don't have many very young children with us Mrs Benson, most of our patients join us when they are about ten years old and they can stay in this particular facility until they are twenty-five before moving on to the adult ward of the local hospital to ensure their health needs are being met," the young nurse explained, she could see Ivy looking upset. Nurse Jones didn't want to upset Ivy even more by pointing out that such children were not expected to live long and healthy lives, and that many died before they ever reached that twenty fifth birthday milestone.

"After the birth of a Mongol child, most parents choose to leave the babies with the health authority and those infants who make it through babyhood are then transferred to institutions attached to the Cardiff mental hospital facility where they are looked after. However, most parents who do take their baby home with them tend to keep them in a quiet family environment until the children are old enough or settled enough to be left in facilities such as these. The patients are well looked after here, aren't they Father Malone?"

"That they are Sister Jones." Father Malone patted Ivy's hand. "June would be with her own kind if she came here Ivy. She would be treated with kindness."

Ivy was trying not to cry. As far as the world was concerned children like June shouldn't be in schools or indeed anywhere else with other "normal" children. Ivy couldn't bear to think her happy golden-haired daughter would be regarded as a patient for the rest of her life, doomed to age prematurely, unable to ever learn to read or write. *Whatever Father Malone might say, June was still being shut away from the normal world,* the injustice of the system made Ivy's blood boil.

"We do have a few younger children in the nursery area who have come to stay with us, shall we go on through and see them Mrs Benson?" The nurse turned and led the way down a hospital style corridor.

Father Malone could see Ivy was getting upset. It was never his intention to distress her by bringing her to see the home, he had hoped that Ivy would see it as a refuge if things got too much to handle. In his work, he'd seen many older parents struggle as age crept on and they worried about who would look after their adult-child when they could no longer do so.

Father Malone knew only too well that to the State it did not matter *how* good June's skills or talents were as a child, it was *what* she was that mattered, nothing else. June wore a label, and it would always decide her future.

"Come on Ivy," Father Malone took her arm and guided her towards the nursery unit at end of the corridor.

Ivy simply nodded; she couldn't trust herself not to break down in tears. She'd always treated June just like any other normal child and now she was realizing that the world saw June as a failure, less worthy, and less deserving than other children, and it was breaking her heart.

In the nursery, six children aged between three and eight sat in cot beds with the railings pulled up to stop them clambering out, most had a teddy or a doll in the bed with them for comfort. Bored and listless, on hearing visitors arriving, one or two children stood up in the robust steel cots to observe proceedings.

"Now, now, Jeremy please sit down, that's a good boy, we can't have you falling out again." Nurse Jones firmly guided the little boy to place his bottom back on the mattress. Large soulful eyes watched as the nurse walked away.

Ivy thought Jeremy looked a bit like June with his golden curls; Ivy choked back a sob as she imagined her own child sat for hours, cooped up inside a pen like that.

The dim room was plain, bland, functional. There were no toys or games to be seen. The curtains were closed.

"We find that most Mongol children are happier if they get plenty of rest and sleep during the day, some have health issues, and they can't be too stressed out by robust activities. Although we do take them out for fresh air each day for a constitutional walk." Nurse Jones chattered on.

"But my June runs about and plays outside all the time!" Ivy protested. Only that morning June had been bouncing up and down on the bed and laughing, her merry cheeks glowing with exertion.

These children sitting in cots looked pale, bored subdued; the silence was overwhelming.

"We try to ensure that the children don't get overexcited, it tends to upset them especially when they have to leave their parents. As I said, they do go outside in the grounds for exercise and fresh air…"

"Leave their parents?" Ivy squawked

"St Mary's is a residential facility Mrs Benson, but unlike many other facilities we do permit visits twice a month if the children don't find it too upsetting."

"Residential… I think there has been a misunderstanding! Father Malone, I'm not leaving June here or anywhere for that matter!" Ivy said firmly and turned to go.

The nurse turned to face Ivy. "That's all right Mrs Benson, you must do what you think is best. But that is why so many of our young people come into us when they are about ten or twelve, because as they age and grow, Mongol children can become a bit of a handful for their parents to manage." The nurse said tactfully. She had seen it so often, especially with older parents, the sheer difficulty of coping with a demanding child who grew bigger but never grew up, would take its toll until the parents, cut off from friends and support couldn't cope.

"June is *not* just a Mongol!" Ivy said hotly. "She is a sweet loving little girl who can learn and do things…. You know that Father Malone!" Ivy turned to the priest for support.

Father Malone nodded.

"June *can* do things; she was even in the church nativity play with all the other children!" Tears started to roll down Ivy's face. "All I wanted was for June to have a normal life, and to go to school like every other child. Why is everybody being so difficult?" Ivy sobbed.

Nurse Jones shot Father Malone a look as if to say that poor Mrs Benson was deluding herself.

"Mrs Benson, I'm sorry to tell you this, but *most* children with this condition are not capable of those things you describe. Your child does not just *look* different to other children, she *is* different. It's not being kind to expect things of them when they do not have the ability to do them." Nurse Jones said firmly, it was obvious Mrs Benson did not understand medical thinking about Mongoloid children.

"School places are *not* provided for these children *because* they are incapable of taking advantage of formal education. In here, our patients are calm, and content and it is our duty to keep them that way. We do not frustrate and agitate them by trying to teach them things which will always be beyond their comprehension and of which they will have no need." The nurse said kindly shaking her head. Mrs Benson obviously failed to see that without the prospect of ever going out into the world, there was no need for the patients to learn to read and write even if it was possible to teach them those skills.

Ivy looked dumbfounded; shocked that the world had written off her daughter, words could not describe how she felt about the gaping chasm which had suddenly opened in June's life – separating her from her little friends like Norah.

"Now don't go upsetting yourself Mrs Benson. If you *can* look after June at home and that is what you want to keep doing, then that is up to you; there is nothing to stop you. And if, and when, you feel it is getting too much for you then we are always here to take care of June." Nurse Jones consulted her watch, she had a terribly busy day ahead and didn't have time to spare debating the unfairness of life, she shot Father Malone a glance as if to say she was wasting her time.

"There is *no* other help on offer Ivy," Father Malone held Ivy's hand.

"But my June is so normal in so many ways, she just looks a bit different to other children." Ivy wailed refusing to accept Nurse Jones' damming dismissal of June's abilities.

"It's the system Ivy, and we must work with it. In the eyes of the state, June will *always* be different and there is nothing we can do about it." Father Malone said softly.

"Oh, can't we! Well, in that case, June stays at home with me." Ivy snapped; she'd had enough. "If June can't go to an ordinary school like every other child, then I will have to try and teach her myself, she certainly isn't going to be spending her days just being kept calm and treated like a vegetable!"

When Ivy returned home to Wilson Road, Betty could see that her daughter had been crying. Betty raised a questioning eyebrow.

Ivy shook her head, there would be time to tell her Mam all about her visit to St Mary's home another time, right now what Ivy needed was to see June.

"Come to your Mam Junie," Ivy scooped up her gorgeous child on her lap and nuzzled her neck, she drew in a deep breath and inhaled the soft perfume of her child's hair. In Ivy's eyes, June was perfect.

June giggled. "You're tickling Mam," June squirmed, her eyes bright with merriment.

"No *this* is tickling!" Ivy wriggled her fingers under June's armpit, the child screeched with laughter and jumped off her mother's knee to escape the delicious torment.

"I'm going to count to three and then I'm coming to get you," Ivy teased as June hurtled up the stairs to evade capture, shrieking and laughing.

"One… Two…. Three…. Ready or not I'm coming to find you June." Ivy called, holding back the tears.

June would never go to a home where she was kept still and docile, out of sight out of mind! Ivy vowed to herself… *Never.*

Chapter 10

George was beginning to worry about Alice.

It had been nearly six weeks since their son Rhys was born and yet Alice still struggled to get out of her dressing gown and get dressed most mornings. His pretty wife had lost weight and lost all the bounce and life he knew and loved; he wanted the old Alice back. Alice dragged herself through each day with the baby in her arms before collapsing back into bed before the eight o'clock evening news came on the wireless. Alice had no time for anything or anybody, except looking after Rhys.

George was still relegated to sleeping on the sofa, and he was longing to share his wife's bed again. Having Billy living about the place didn't help the situation either. George was counting down the weeks until Billy and Ivy were to be married, and then he and Alice would have the flat back to themselves; just the two of them….and of course Rhys.

Festoons of drying nappies and damp baby clothes garlanded every spare corner of the flat; at the end of a busy day seeing to the business and serving customers fish and chips, George wanted to relax in a neat and tidy home with a tasty supper on the table, served by his pretty, smiling wife. He did not want to dodge a clothes horse covered in damp nappies blocking the fireplace and eat a cold pork pie.

George wasn't terribly used to dealing with women, with no sisters or female cousins and just his brother Billy when he was growing up, George's experiences of women were confined to his Mam Pearl and a few bristly aunties. But even he could see Alice was a twitchy, colourless shadow of her former self. Her body might be healed from the trauma of giving birth, but it seemed as if her nerves were still battered and bruised by the whole process. If he said anything to her, she snapped and bit his head off.

"She's just got a bit of a nervous condition son, lots of women get it, especially the more delicate types… she'll get over it, it's still fairly early days yet." his mother Pearl said loftily when George described the listless, tetchy Alice.

Well, whatever it was Alice was suffering from, George didn't know how to fix it. He slunk about the flat like he was treading on eggshells.

"I'm sorry George, I'm just so exhausted, please don't." Alice rebuffed George's feeble attempts to kiss or hold her; she felt almost claustrophobic to have this child hanging off her sore breasts, constantly needing her body, demanding her attention, she couldn't bear to have her husband doing the same.

Alice struggled with the enormity of motherhood; the sleepless nights; the colic, the monotonous routine of suckling and changing a baby who soiled his nappies every five minutes, the mountains of dirty washing and above all the boredom and loneliness.

Ivy had popped by a few times to see how Alice and the baby were faring and when Alice saw Ivy holding little Rhys in her arms, she knew she was a lucky woman to have such a beautiful healthy son, *if only she wasn't so bone-achingly tired all the time.* Alice felt like an old woman

"Oh, he is absolutely gorgeous Alice… I could eat them when they are like this," Ivy snuggled up to the sleeping baby in her arms, sniffing the sweet, powdery softness of him, remembering June at the same age.

"I love them when they are like this, just a little armful, all snuggly and warm, and those dimpled hands…look at those minute fingernails; like tiny pink fish scales… it's a shame you can't bottle them and keep them at this age for ever." Ivy enthused. June was shooting up so fast now and leaving her chubby toddlerhood behind. The awful visit to St Mary's with Father Malone had brought it home to Ivy, just how quickly June was growing up.

Alice smiled wanly and tried to be grateful for what she had, to enjoy the rapture of a new-born. She knew Ivy could never have any more children; would never experience the comforting weight of another sleeping baby of her own ever again. Even so, Alice couldn't help noticing the inner glow and beauty of her old friend, a young woman content and in love, looking forward to getting married and planning her future with Billy.

Alice couldn't help but feel envious as she sat opposite a polished, pretty Ivy, chattering on about wedding plans and the smart new dress she planned to wear, whilst she felt tired, and frumpy with breasts that oozed, and a back aching from hours of pacing the boards with Rhys in her arms. "I know I'm lucky Ivy, and he *is* gorgeous…. I'm just struggling a bit that's all, and George seems to think I should snap back like a piece of bloody elastic." Alice grumbled; she pushed a piece of lank hair away from her eyes. "There just don't seem to be enough hours in the day to get things done," Alice waved her arm in the general direction of the laundry pile.

"At least my Mam comes by every day to help out, just 'til I find my feet." Alice wondered if she would ever *find her feet*.

"Well, that's a blessing," Ivy remembered her own mother doing the same thing after June was born, until her husband Jimmy put a stop to it.

"I know but she can't keep coming over forever, and I'm dreading the day when she says she can't come… she's a God send right now. I'd drown without her, honest I would." Alice sniffed; she could feel herself getting tearful.

"Just look at me Ivy, I look such a bloody mess all the time. My clothes hang off me, I smell of baby sick and I don't have a moment to even wash my hair." Ivy was her best friend; Alice knew she could open her heart to her.

"Now don't go getting upset Alice… Would you like me to take Rhys out for a walk in his pram? It will give him a bit of fresh air and it will give you some time to have a quiet bath and tidy up a bit." Ivy offered; she could see her friend looked at the end of her tether.

"I've got an hour yet before I have to get back home. Come on Alice, let me help, I remember how tough it was after I had June. With Jimmy being the way he was, I used to feel so lonely and all at sea sometimes as well. But trust me, it does get easier… honestly it does."

"Thanks for being understanding Ivy, I was beginning to feel such a useless failure, you're the only one who seems to understand how I feel, everyone else just seem to pick holes and tell me how lucky I am to have Rhys and to *just* get on with it." She smiled ruefully at Ivy. "I'm sure even my Mam thinks I'm a failure because I can't cope with everything, and George doesn't understand how I feel either. I can see him looking at me and I know he wishes he had the old Alice back. Some days, I feel like I'm going mad." Alice sobbed.

"Of course, you're not a failure!... Don't be too hard on yourself Alice. If I didn't have my friend Norah over the road to talk to when I had June, I think I'd have gone mad as well, she was like a lifeline when I felt like I was drowning. And my Aunty Phoebe helped me get through the worst of it, she was always there to talk to." Ivy remembered the calming solidity of Aunty Phoebe, always there with a wise word and a loving smile.

"And you've *always* got me Alice. If ever I can help just let me know, even if it's just for a chat, or to take Rhys for a walk… people have got to help you, you can't struggle on, you'll make yourself ill … and as for George, well, he's going to have to step up a bit until you've found your feet. It's early days he can't expect too much of you." Ivy said firmly.

"Nobody tells you it's going to be like this do they?" Alice said miserably.

Alice loved Ivy like a younger sister, they'd been friends ever since the first day Ivy started infant's school and Alice took a frightened Ivy under her wing; over the years, they'd shared everything, even the deepest and most intimate of secrets, Alice knew Ivy would always be in her corner. "No, they don't! Now I'll take Rhys out for his walk, and you have an hour to yourself, don't worry about us, we'll be fine won't we Rhys?" Ivy smiled, she loved Alice so much she couldn't bear to see her friend looking so down. *Perhaps Billy ought to have a word with George, brother to brother and find out what was really going on?*

As Alice soaked her aching limbs in the bath she wondered when she would see the light at the end of the tunnel Ivy promised.

Her older sister Phyllis had sailed through birth and babies four times, she'd never mentioned the bouts of crushing loneliness, the feelings of inadequacy and mounting despair to Alice. *Perhaps I was so wrapped up in my own life, having fun and being young that I just didn't notice my poor sister struggling.* Alice thought to herself.

Alice vowed that tomorrow she would try harder to get a grip. But, despite all her good intentions, the next day and the following days were as predictably chaotic as all the previous ones.

Alice paced the boards in the middle of every night with a squalling child who refused to be settled and was greeted each morning with a pile of chores demanding her attention. She knew her husband was getting restless for her attention too, but she felt as if she was suffocating, and she pushed George away.

Motherhood sat so easily on capable Phyllis's shoulders, why couldn't she be more like her sister Phyllis. Everyone else seems to manage to have babies and look after them, what's the matter with me? Alice raged inwardly.

Her Mam Joan eventually snapped and told Alice she needed to "get a grip and pull herself together and just get on with it."

Alice felt pulled apart, not pulled together and the gorgeous baby in her arms still cried night and day.

This morning, mindful of yesterday's telling off, Alice put a grizzling Rhys down on the bed and rushed to get dressed before her Mam arrived. Alice feared her Mam would be having words again if she didn't see Alice at least making some attempt to get on top of things today.

It was nine o'clock already, Mam would arrive soon to tackle the chores, there was no time to feed Rhys again. George was down in the fish bar, interviewing a new counter assistant and preparing for the lunchtime serving, and Alice wasn't sure if there was any milk in the flat for a cup of tea for her mother.

"I won't be a minute Rhys darling; please don't cry, you can't possibly need feeding again, I only fed you half an hour ago... I must get dressed or I'll be in trouble with Nanna." Alice, not daring to stop and wash herself, pulled on yesterday's clothes; an old milk stain sat accusingly on the shoulder of her dress. She ran a brush through her hair and picked up the child.

"Come here trouble." Alice put the child on her shoulder, a small posset of fresh milk bubbled in Rhys's mouth and landed on Alice's sleeve.

The soiled nappies from last night stood steeping in a pail in the kitchen waiting to be boiled on the stove, she knew she shouldn't really leave them for her Mam to deal with; but lifting the heavy pail up to the sink made her freshly healed stitches pull and her arms were always full of Rhys.

Thankfully there was an inch of milk left, Alice sniffed the bottle, *it would do, it smelt fresh enough.* Perhaps her Mam might watch Rhys whilst she nipped out to the shops to get some milk and something for George's dinner, her husband had grumbled about the lack of his cooked dinner again last night.

The thought of carrying her baby down the steep slippery steps and then bundling Rhys up in the pram and manoeuvring the cumbersome thing around the shops filled Alice with dread, *it would be so much quicker if she went on her own without Rhys.*

Her Mam came over from Angelina Street most mornings for an hour or two, Joan whisked in and out like a flash of lightening before going home to her own duties. She'd volunteered to help her struggling daughter find her feet, and the jobs of boiling and rinsing ten stinking terry napkins and stained muslins and tackling the mountain of ironing were what Alice needed doing this morning.

If the nappies weren't dealt with Alice would soon run out. She reluctantly had to concede that her Mam couldn't do all that *and* look after a squalling Rhys at the same time.

There was nothing for it, George would have to go out to the shops later on if he wanted something cooked for his dinner and she would have to look after Rhys whilst her Mam tackled the chores, there just weren't enough hours in the day!

One thorn in Alice's side was her in-laws. George's parents Les and Pearl visited constantly. Les was besotted with his beautiful grandson and the pair couldn't seem to stay away.

No sooner had her Mam finished the chores and gone home to get her husband's dinner than the Thomas's would turn up to view their grandson. Having her in-laws cluttering up the place all afternoon, didn't help the situation, the doting pair sat about cooing over Rhys, generally getting in the way, and expecting frequent cups of tea and biscuits as if the place was a café.

Pearl was invariably acting like the queen bee fussing over Rhys and George. Alice's Mam was a godsend, but her plump mother-in-law, Pearl, never offered to lift a finger or do something useful to help about the place, she just sat about gossiping, reminiscing, and generally getting under Alice's feet. Alice's heart sank when she heard the door knocker rapping like clockwork just after two o'clock; Alice yearned for some peace and quiet.

"He's a fine lad you've got there George. Rhys is certainly a Thomas through and through." Les was chuffed that the child carried his name, *Rhys Lesley Thomas* and as far as Les and Pearl were concerned, their grandson Rhys was the most perfect baby on the planet. Pictures of George as a baby were produced for comparison.

"Now then Les, it's impossible to tell at this age who he's going to look like," Pearl cooed. Pearl didn't want to upset Alice, but she had to admit Rhys did look the spit of young George as a baby in the photographs. George always was a handsome child.

"Come to Nanna my angel, you *are* such a good boy…. But then he's always a good boy for his Nanna aren't you my little lamb?" Pearl oozed in a sing song voice.

When Pearl and Les were in the room Alice felt like a spare part, only needed for making endless pots of tea. Annoyingly Rhys always seemed to be on his best behaviour when Grampy Les and Nanna Pearl were in the house. The baby was fascinated with Pearl's fluffy white perm and crystal beads; Pearl revelled in her role of chief baby pacifier and sat proudly rocking the baby whilst sipping endless cups of tea.

Pearl Thomas wore the role of Nanna Pearl with pride, she gestured to Alice that she would like another cup of tea, Rhys was asleep in Nanna's arms so she couldn't possibly get up!

More bloody washing up and there was no milk left!

"I'm just popping out to the shops to get some more milk Pearl; we've run out again. I won't be gone long," Alice grabbed her coat. With all the

Thomas family in the sitting room, the tiny flat felt suffocating, she was desperate to escape if only for only a few minutes.

"We'll be fine without your Mammy won't we, my angel?" Pearl crooned to the dozing child and settled back into the best armchair like a queen. Alice shot George a mutinous look and scuttled off to the shops; Pearl was *his* mother; he should be looking after Pearl, not expecting Alice to be dancing around her mother-in-law like a housemaid. Alice was sick of having visitors cluttering up the flat; she hoped they wouldn't stay too long today.

George smiled a watery smile as Alice flounced out of the door.

"Is Alice all right George, she seems a little…. Er tetchy?" Les noticed the look that Alice gave George.

"Don't be silly Les, I told you Alice has got *nerves* that's all…. Some women get them after having babies. She'll be all right in a few months once Rhys settles… she'll snap out of it, you'll see." Pearl smiled indulgently at the snoozing child in her arms, *Rhys was such a good baby, Alice didn't know how lucky she was.*

"Did you suffer with your nerves Mam?" George was not used to discussing women's topics, especially not with his mother.

"Course not son!" Peral said smartly. "But then I was always a grafter, used to hard work, that's why your Da married me." Pearl grinned. "I just got on with things… I didn't have time to indulge in having *nerves*…. Once Alice pulls herself together she'll be fine you see…. Don't let it go on too long though George, she can't let her nerves get the better of her." Pearl was of the view that Alice wasn't making as much effort as she should do to snap out of it, her precious son George needed looking after as well.

"She's a good mother to Rhys, Mam." George said loyally. George had no concerns that Alice would ever harm or neglect Rhys, in fact it was quite the opposite, Alice seemed to have no time or energy for anyone *but* Rhys. Pearl looked at the plump baby resting in her arms; she had to admit he was a fine child, at least Alice was doing something right.

"Hmm, perhaps you are right son, he is a bonny boy and that's the truth. But it takes more than *just* feeding a baby to make a good mother *and* a good wife George." Pearl said pointedly.

Les shot his wife a warning glance to hold her tongue, she would be a fool to try and start driving a wedge between George and Alice with her carping.

The door clicked and Alice came up the stairs carrying the shopping. Almost immediately after Alice entered the room, Rhys started to wriggle and grizzle.

"There, there, my little lad, Mammy's come back." Alice dropped the bag of shopping and rushed to scoop up Rhys from Nanna Pearl's lap.

Pearl pulled a face; she was beginning to see a picture and she didn't like it. George was her handsome favoured son; she couldn't bear to see him neglected. Pearl always feared the pretty Alice Tranter might be more decorative than useful when George chose her as a wife, it seemed as if Pearl might be proved right.

"Would you like me to unpack the bag Alice?" George said as he scooped up the groceries from the floor.

"Yes please, and you'd better make your Mam that cup of tea George, I won't have time to do it now, Rhys needs a feed and a change… and so do I," Alice headed for the bedroom and sanctuary; the daube of milk on her shoulder from earlier was starting to smell of sick. Alice had bought some liver and cabbage to serve for George's dinner…she wasn't sure she'd have time to cook that either.

"Here, let me do that George, you've got too much on your plate son to be doing the household chores!" Pearl grabbed the groceries. "I can make us all a nice cup of tea if Alice is too busy with Rhys." Pearl's voice had an acidic edge to it.

Les shook his head; his Pearl could be a foolish woman.

"Les said you had a new girl serving behind the counter in the fish bar today George, how was she?" Pearl said as she unpacked the groceries, she struggled to find a spare surface to put things on. Pearl tutted loudly.

The kitchen was in an even worse mess than the sitting room, Alice really needed to make an effort and get a grip, it wasn't fair that George had to put up with such chaos, perhaps she should invite her son to join them for dinner!

"Oh yes we took on a new girl today, she seems fine enough Mam. We need the extra help whilst Alice is busy with Rhys."

"So, do you think she'll do son?" Pearl had offered to serve behind the counter herself if George couldn't find anyone suitable. Pearl had spent decades helping Les with the fish bar, her skill for swiftly wrapping hot cod and chips in newspaper and serving customers in a trice was legendary *and* she'd brought up two strapping lads! In Pearl's opinion too many young women today were work shy.

"I think so Mam…She's a nice young lass called Elsie Evans and from what I can see she's got a good way with the customers; we can keep an eye on her to see if she does a good job …. Funnily enough Billy says he remembers the girl from years ago, apparently, she comes from Angelina Street, and she's an old neighbour of Alice's."

Pearl made a little moue at the mention of Alice's name, as if to say she hoped this girl had a bit more go about her than Alice did.

"Billy says young Elsie was often down at the docks with the other young lasses, when we used to go fish buying with our Da on a Sunday, but that was ages ago…. But now he's mentioned it, I do vaguely remember her."

"Oh, so *you* know her then?" Les asked.

"I wouldn't say *know* her Da, and she's a few years younger than Alice so they weren't exactly friends either. But I do think I remember her from a few years back, of course she's changed a bit since then." George added, he might not have taken much notice of Elsie before, but he couldn't fail to notice her now; the girl had transformed into quite a looker.

When Billy had pointed out that they had met the pretty Elsie Evans before, George found it hard to believe that the buxom red head with the come-hither eyes and the seductive pout serving behind his counter was indeed the same scruffy little girl who used to hang around him and Billy down on the quays.

What George didn't mention to his father, was that, once the penny had dropped, he did remember Miss Elsie Evans, he also remembered that she had been rather flirtatious trying to get George's attention, hanging on his every word, fluttering her eyelashes. In those days George only ever had eyes for the magnificent Alice Tranter and scruffy little Elsie didn't stand a chance, besides she was quite a bit younger than him.

"Well, you make sure she works hard son," Les had glimpsed the new girl through the shop window, he thought the striking redhead seemed a little *too* chatty with some of the male customers.

Flighty sorts like Elsie needed watching in Les's opinion; he'd met girls like her before and they often spelled trouble.

Chapter 11

Deirdre had settled into a cosy, companionable routine in Porthcawl, and it suited her. Regular letters from Phoebe telling her about the old house and the lives of the Prosser family next door had put her mind at rest about moving to Porthcawl and leaving her old life behind. That life was gone now; there would be no turning back, she knew it was time to embrace this new life and make new memories in her new home.

With her worries about Alma Road swept away, Deirdre could start enjoying life again without the shadow of her brother Edmund hovering over her. Porthcawl was her new chance at contentment and part of that contentment came from her growing warm friendship with her neighbour James Pugh.

Every Monday, Deirdre helped James do the Sunday Prize Crossword over a cup of afternoon tea, she would read the clues aloud and together they tackled the riddles; James, with his quick mind and a nimble intellect, invariably found the answers before she did, but she didn't mind, it was nice to feel needed and useful and besides, James made her laugh. It was a pleasant way to while away the afternoon.

Deirdre attended the little church at the far end of the promenade each Sunday as regular as clockwork and then bought the newspaper on her way back home. As was her wont for sixty years, and just like her parents before her, Deirdre observed the Sabbath in peace and quiet; she didn't do chores or even listen to the wireless on a Sunday. The crossword and newspaper headlines always waited until Monday for her meeting with James when they would attempt to solve the crossword and discuss the weekly news together.

She and James Pugh were becoming such close friends; they seemed to feed off each other and were in tune in the way that only old friends or married couples were.

When she heard his deep friendly voice speaking her name it made her smile, it had been a long time since she had felt so ease with anyone.

"So, how are we doing with the beast this week Deirdre?" James relied on Deirdre to paint a picture of the puzzle.

"Only three more clues to go James before it's completed, but one of those is a tricky cryptic one with eight letters… I'm no good at those blessed cryptic clues, give me a general knowledge question any day." Deirdre chewed her pencil.

"Only three clues to go… that's our best yet isn't it Deirdre? Well then, we will have to put our thinking caps on because I think we stand a good chance of finishing it this week and then we can send it off for once." James lived in hope of completing the weekly puzzle and today might just be the day they did it.

"Ever the optimist James," Deirdre laughed. So far, they'd never finished the jumbo Sunday prize crossword puzzle so that it could be sent off and entered in the weekly newspaper competition. Each week they started the puzzle with hope and enthusiasm and each week they were defeated.

"How about I make us a nice cup of tea to help the situation and I've got a piece of cherry cake in the kitchen if you'd like some," Deirdre offered.

"Yes please Deirdre and I'll try my best to think of that tricky cryptic clue whilst you are at it."

Deirdre bustled off into the kitchen, the tray was laid in readiness with her best teacups, and the kettle was simmering away on the hob.

"Oh no!" Deirdre gasped loudly. Her voice an anguished yelp.

James heard the shriek; he could tell something bad must have happened, but he couldn't rush out to her, he didn't know the layout of her kitchen. Had she hurt herself?

"What's the matter Deirdre?" James called anxiously. He could hear a soft moaning coming from the kitchen, the torture of not being able to see what was amiss cut him to the quick.

"Deirdre are you alright?" James was stumbling to his feet, reaching for a handhold; he had to try and go to her. Dreadful images rushed through his mind.

Deirdre trailed into the sitting room. "It's alright James, don't try to get up, I've just had a bit of a shock, I'll be alright in a minute." Deirdre clutched her heaving chest, she needed to compose herself.

James could tell Deirdre was trying not to cry. "What's happened Deirdre?" He said softly.

"It's old Bobby… he's dead." Deirdre sniffed sadly.

"Oh no, I'm so sorry Deirdre, poor Bobby" James groaned. He knew how fond Deirdre had become of the grumpy old, ginger cat who came with the house, and he remembered how bereft he'd felt when his first guide dog Nell had died of old age. Losing a loyal friend was always hard.

"How did it happen?"

"He was asleep in the kitchen on that rag rug by the cooker that he likes; and I went to give him a stroke… and he was gone, just like that… he must have died in his sleep whilst we were chatting in here…. He was fine this morning, purring and fussing as usual for his breakfast… I just can't believe it." Deirdre dabbed at her tears; it *was* only a grumpy old cat after all.

It was silly to cry over an old cat she'd only owned for a few months, she'd barely cried so much over the death of her brother Edmund, she told herself. But she she'd grown to love old Bobby in the months they'd been together; she talked to him about everything, and she could swear blind he answered her back. He was the face who greeted her in the morning demanding her attention, and he kept her company in the evening arranging himself on her lap.

With his snooty behaviour and funny antics Bobby had found a place in her heart. She knew he was an old cat when she took him on, but she'd hoped for a few more years together before they parted company. Bobby being there on the window ledge every day, was part of what made her decide to take the old bungalow, the house would seem very empty without him.

"I must tell Mrs Prosser's daughter," Deirdre sniffed. "I promised I'd look after Bobby for Mrs Prosser… and now he's dead." Deirdre sobbed. James got to his feet and followed the sound of Deirdre's voice to the middle of the room. With his limited vision he could just make out her shape a couple of feet in front of him.

"Shh… don't upset yourself Deirdre. It's not your fault he's gone," he said softly. "Bobby was an old cat and you treated him like a king in his old age, nobody could have done more for him than you did." James moved a little closer.

"I know," Deirdre wailed. "But I loved him, and he was *all* I had." James wrapped his arms around Deirdre and stroked her hair. "Shh now, you've still got me…. You'll always have me Deirdre."

Chapter 12

Yesterday Phoebe had a long chat with Father Malone about the missing rosary and her suspicions that her lodger Mr Goode *might* have had his tie pin stolen from the house and his advice was simple. "You must sit, watch, wait and pray Phoebe. If the dear Lord taught us anything it is that we must not judge our fellow man lest we be judged.

"If you are patient I feel sure you will discover the truth you are looking for, but don't start accusing people without any proof. Words once they have been said are impossible to unsay." Father Malone gave her a stern stare, he knew Phoebe Horwat well. Phoebe had attended his church for many years, and he knew what her life used to be in the shadows of Tiger Bay and yet he also knew she was a good, kind-hearted woman worthy of respect. He never judged her.

In her heart Phoebe knew the priest was right, her lodger Malcolm *might* have lost his tie pin and she *might* have lost her rosary and the Prosser family *might* be as innocent as she wanted them to be. Perhaps she'd lived too long in Tiger Bay, and it had made her cynical and suspicious. Today she decided to visit Ivy and June, she hadn't seen Ivy for days. She would take Father Malone's advice and be patient. The priest was right, God did move in mysterious ways.

Phoebe vowed to stop mithering about the rosary and cheer herself up with a visit to Wilson Road. Ivy was bound to have some news for her, and she was longing to see June again.

"Honestly Aunty Phoebe, poor Alice looked done in when I saw her on Friday. Rhys suffers badly from colic and she's up pacing the boards with him night and day; she's not getting any sleep. Her Mam does come to help her for a couple of hours most days, but Alice is feeling quite lonely and overwhelmed by everything. I promised I would try to go over more often to take Rhys out of the flat for her." Ivy confided over a cup of tea. Phoebe was extremely fond of Alice; she admired the girl for sticking by Ivy when fair weather friends and neighbours had drifted away. and asking June to be her bridesmaid when she married George had meant the world to June. Alice was a kind girl and a loyal family friend; Phoebe couldn't bear to hear she was suffering.

"Poor girl. I'm not surprised she's finding it tough living in the flat above Tasty Plaice; she probably doesn't see another soul she knows, living in amongst a row of other shops and opposite the railway line." Phoebe knew the location of the fish bar and the steep steps to the upstairs flat. It was a far cry from the doorsteps and neighbourly terraces of Alice's old home in Angelina Street or the bustle of Ivy's home on Wilson Road.

"You're right Aunty Phoebe it's no wonder Alice is lonely; trapped in that flat without other neighbours and women to chat to, and her blessed, stuck-up in-laws don't help either, hanging around the place all the time like ornaments criticising and finding fault."

Ivy was irritated by Alice's description of Pearl fussing over her beloved George like a neglected spaniel, she was even more irritated by the fact that George had taken her to one side and made it clear that Ivy was not to visit in the afternoons, in case Ivy bumped into Les and Pearl.

"I'm sorry to ask it Ivy, but if you could visit Alice in the mornings, it would save any unpleasantness if…. Well, you know what I mean," George raised his hands and shrugged his shoulders. George felt stuck in the middle of the Billy and Ivy situation, and he wanted to stay out of it; he'd enough on his plate without getting involved in a family feud over Ivy Benson.

To keep the peace, Ivy agreed to make her visits to see Alice only in the mornings.

Phoebe knew Ivy hadn't met the Thomas family since they took umbrage at Billy and Ivy getting engaged. Phoebe hadn't met them either, but she already had a very dim view of the couple for snubbing her darling Ivy and refusing to meet her let alone go to the wedding. Who did Les Thomas think he was!

Billy confessed to Phoebe only last week that his father refused to mix with "low life," as he described the Benson family. And Les wouldn't relent by coming to the wedding or welcoming Ivy into the family. Billy vowed never to speak to his father or mother again unless Les apologised for his remarks.

"Well, I can visit Alice in an afternoon, Les and Pearl Thomas can't stop that." Phoebe replied. "I could do with getting out of the house, it doesn't do me any good sitting around the house mithering about nothing all day… I don't mind staying in Alice's kitchen, doing the chores, and making pots of tea, whilst Mrs high and mighty plays the queen bee in the sitting room." Phoebe chuckled, she quite fancied taking a look at the snobby Pearl and Les Thomas, she'd never met them but, from everything she'd heard, they sounded like the in-laws from hell.

"I'm sure Alice would like that Aunty Phoebe; she could do with a few more people in her corner." Ivy loved Alice to bits, it was tearing her apart to see her friend so down in the dumps.

"In that case, I'll pop over tomorrow with a nice cottage pie that she can pop in the oven, and I'll tackle some cleaning jobs whilst Alice has an afternoon nap; and if that stuck up mother-in-law of hers has a problem with that, then I'll soon put her straight."

Ivy smiled; this was the feisty, firm, motherly Aunty Phoebe she remembered from when she had June; a tigress ready to fight Alice's corner.

"I do love you Aunty Phoebe," she gave her aunt a kiss.

*

The next morning, good as her word, Phoebe went early to the shops for some things for the baby and the groceries. She set about making a cottage pie with lots of tasty gravy and a pile of fluffy mashed potato. "That should keep George happy, and I bet Alice could do with a bit of building up an' all." Phoebe muttered to herself as she forked a neat pattern on the potato topping.

The sharp rap on the door knocker startled her; she wasn't expecting visitors and the children next door should be in school at this time of the day. She wiped her hands on her housecoat and headed to the front door.

"Just coming," Phoebe called melodiously. She could see an outline of a woman through the glass; it was Rita Prosser. Phoebe's heart gave a little flip, she hadn't seen Rita for a couple of weeks, not since she glimpsed Rita involved in some strange deal in the Cardiff market.

Phoebe opened the door; it gave her a warm glow to see her daughter's beautiful face. "Hello Rita, do come in. I'm a bit busy cooking at the moment as you can see, but I can stop for a quick cup of tea."

Phoebe felt awful for doubting the Prosser family, and she hoped that her anxiety didn't show, Father Malone was right; *she mustn't judge and jump to conclusions.*

"I can't stop long myself Phoebe, but I needed to give you something and I'd rather it didn't wait." Rita followed Phoebe through to the kitchen. "I had a long chat with Frank the other day and he told me about your rosary…."

Phoebe slumped into the kitchen chair; *her worse fears were coming true.*

"Are you all right Phoebe, you look a little pale?"

"I'm fine Rita thank you, I'm just a little tired that's all; I've not been sleeping well lately."

"Well as I said, Frank told me you had lost your rosary and so I wanted to give you this." Rita handed over a small light package wrapped in tissue paper. "It was my first rosary; my Mam gave it to me when I was six, but my Godmother gave me another, much nicer one for my first Holy Communion and I use that, this other little one just sits in the drawer, which is a real shame."

Phoebe's heart was racing; tears were threatening to overwhelm her.

"I took it to the watch repair man in the market to give it a good clean and mend a few weak links, I'm afraid I wasn't very careful with it as a child, and it's quite delicate." Rita smiled fondly, stretching out the pretty chain for Phoebe to see.

"It's so beautiful," Phoebe gasped.

"Frank said you were upset about losing yours and he and Jennifer wanted to use their pocket money to buy you another one as a present for being such a wonderful new Aunty." Rita knelt by Phoebe and pressed the rosary into Phoebe's hands.

"With all the sweets you and Mr Goode give them they have been saving quite a bit of their pocket money.... Mind you I've given Frank a lecture about the perils of too many Trebor sweets!" Rita smiled; she had become very fond of her kindly neighbour.

Phoebe raised her hands to her face and wept tears of regret. Frank and Jennifer cared about her; they hadn't been stealing from her, they had been planning to give her something. Frank hadn't been buying or stealing loads of sweets, Malcolm Goode had given them to him.

"I'm sorry Phoebe, we didn't mean to upset you." Rita said anxiously.

"You haven't... truly you haven't. Thank you so much Rita, I can't believe you are being so kind and generous to me... but it's such a precious gift I don't know that I can accept it." Phoebe sobbed her eyes sparkling with joy.

"Honestly I want you to have it Phoebe. Please take it," she urged. "The children were so pleased when I found it in the drawer and I said that we could give it to you to replace the one you'd lost, they will be terribly disappointed if I tell them you won't accept it."

"But I can't accept such a generous gift Rita, it's too much."

"The rosary means a lot to me Phoebe, which is why I'd like you to have it, but it's not silver or very valuable, really it isn't."

"It's valuable to me Rita… in fact it is the most precious thing I have." Phoebe stood up and held her daughter in her arms, "Thank you from the bottom of my heart Rita, I can't tell you what this means to me."

Chapter 13

After Rita's visit, Phoebe floated through the morning feeling on cloud nine. She almost laughed to think how wrong she had been to assume that somehow she had a thief in the house. *That will teach you to jump to conclusions Phoebe Horwat.* She couldn't wait to tell Betty the good news.

Phoebe packed up the cottage pie and the newly purchased baby bottle and cans of evaporated milk in her shopping bag and caught the bus to Caroline Street; it cheered her to think she would spread some goodwill and be able help to Alice today; the way she felt, Phoebe wanted to hug the whole world!

Phoebe threaded through the cluttered yard at the back of the shops. One miserable, short piece of clothesline was strung haphazardly over the top of a pile of discarded fish crates stacked in one corner of the yard. Four pillowcases and two wet bed sheets flapped in the soft breeze; a sheet edge licked the grubby wall. Phoebe trudged up the steep wooden steps to the flat nestled above the Tasty Plaice. Just as she was about to rap on the door knocker the door opened.

"Goodness me you made me jump." Joan Tranter yelped as Phoebe stood her hand poised to knock the door.

"Hello Joan, I've come to give your Alice a hand with a few chores and to bring a cottage pie for dinner. Our Ivy said Alice could do with a few friendly faces helping out."

"Well, I do help out as much as I can, but I've got my own home to see to and my other daughter Phyllis has four little ones of her own to look after, she needs me as well sometimes. I have to be fair; I've only got one pair of hands." Joan snapped, she felt run ragged dashing between the two girls and her husband Cecil wanted her home in time to make his dinner.

"Of course, you do Joan, and I didn't mean to imply any differently," Phoebe said hastily. Joan Tranter was famous for her feisty temper. "It's just I gather that Mr and Mrs Thomas aren't exactly helpful when they come around every day to see Rhys," Phoebe said diplomatically; she didn't want to tread on any toes.

"You can say that again," Joan snorted. "That Pearl Thomas seems to have forgotten what it's like to have a young baby around the place, she sits on that fat arse of hers, puts on airs and graces and expects to be waited on hand, foot, and finger…." *I think another cup of tea would be nice Alice.*" Joan aped Pearl's sing song voice.

Phoebe laughed and rolled her eyes as if to say she wouldn't take any nonsense from the likes of Pearl Thomas.

"I know my Alice is struggling a bit, but having a carping mother-in-law like Pearl isn't helping, she couldn't make it any more obvious than she does, that she thinks my Alice is a useless wife and mother…. Anyway Phoebe, thanks for popping by to help, I must be off. I've done the nappies and yesterday's ironing, but I haven't washed the baby's woollens. I changed the bed for her yesterday, and I pegged the clean sheets out first thing, so they might be dry and ready for ironing in a few hours if this breeze keeps up."

"Well, I've come prepared to do a few jobs so that's what I'll do…. Don't worry Joan between us we'll make sure Alice gets a bit of rest." Phoebe said briskly.

"Thank you Phoebe I appreciate it, I'm not getting any younger, I don't have the stamina I used to. Alice is in the bedroom on the left feeding Rhys."

Phoebe gave Joan Tranter a hug and went in the flat. A smell of drying nappies greeted her in the hall. *Someone ought to string up a better washing line in that yard for the poor girl, no wonder she's struggling to keep on top of the washing if she can't peg it out.*

"Yoo, hoo Alice, it's only Aunty Phoebe," Phoebe called. Phoebe headed for the bedroom door and rapped gently, "it's me Alice can I come in?" Alice was lying on the rumpled bed, her breasts half exposed from feeding Rhys, her hair an untidy mess as if she had spent the morning raking her fingers through it; she smiled. "Hello Phoebe, it's so good to see you" Alice said softly, her voice barely creeping above a whisper, desperate not to disturb a sleeping Rhys. Alice tried slide Rhys onto the mattress and sit up.

"No don't get up Alice…. Poor love, you look absolutely exhausted!" Phoebe's heart went out to the pretty girl lying on the bed, Alice looked wrecked.

"I've just passed your Mam in the hall, and she's told me what needs doing so I'm here to roll my sleeves up and get stuck in, you stay in bed and rest for a few hours."

"Thanks Phoebe but I've got to get up anyway, George's parents will be here soon to see Rhys and George will expect me to look after them."

"Tsk," Phoebe snorted. "This little baby here needs *his* Mam to get a bit of rest, it's not helping anyone if you're exhausted all the time…. You might not know this Alice, but Ivy's Mam Betty lived with me when she was expecting Ivy, so I know how hard a new baby can be."

Alice's ears pricked up, she only knew Ivy after the girl came to live in Bute Street, Ivy's early life before then was a mystery.

"We all lived together in Railway Terrace until the bombing in the Blitz damaged the houses and we had to move out," Phoebe explained.

"I was there when Ivy was born; I helped see her into the world. For weeks after the birth, I can remember Betty going through exactly same thing as you're going through now and I helped her get through it….

You're not alone in feeling like this Alice." Phoebe's heart went out to the girl.

"Now I'll make you a nice cuppa and when I've done that I'll take Rhys and get him dressed and ready for his visitors… and you…" Phoebe gave Alice a beady stare, "you, my girl, are spending a couple of hours with your feet up and that's an order!"

"Thank you Phoebe, you are a life saver…. If I could just get an hour's nap I'm sure I'll feel much better. But Rhys might need another feed soon, he seems to need feeding every half an hour, so I might need to get up before then." Alice smiled ruefully.

"No, you won't Alice, it's all sorted. I bought a baby's bottle and some evaporated milk in the market yesterday; the little lad can have that for once if he needs it and *you* can have a well-deserved rest. It'll give you time to snooze and build up for the next proper feed." Phoebe pulled the curtains across to cover the chink of light creeping into the room.

Ten minutes later Phoebe left a cup of tea on the bedside table, Alice was already sound asleep.

Rhys was beginning to stir, a mewling grizzle starting to build.

"Shh… shhhh Rhys." Phoebe scooped the child into her arms before he could wake Alice. "Come to Aunty Phoebe you little monkey, and we'll leave your Mam get a few winks shall we."

Before Rhys could start to wail Phoebe slipped out of the bedroom with Rhys in her arms.

When Les and Pearl Thomas came to visit an hour later, they were surprised to hear from Phoebe that Alice was in bed asleep.

"What's the matter with the girl," Pearl said sharply.

 Phoebe could tell by Pearl's tone that there was no sympathy for poor Alice.

"Alice has just had a baby and I think she's getting a bit run down. I'm sure she'll be as right as rain soon." Phoebe stared hard at Pearl Thomas, the woman was a fluffy, ornamental concoction of silvery permed hair with a tint of blue rinse, rouged cheeks, and a large matronly bosom. Pearl glared back imperiously over her glasses and clicked her tongue. Rhys, content from slurping down an entire bottle of baby milk was dozing in Phoebe's arms. Pearl held out her arms to retrieve her precious grandchild from the interloper. *Pearl hadn't come all this way to watch someone else cuddling her precious grandson!*

Les stepped forward and passed Rhys to his wife. "Here we are dear…. That's it, Rhys my love…. go to your Nanna for a cwtch…." Les didn't know who this woman was, but even he thought it should be Pearl's role to hold their grandson.

Phoebe looked at Les, something about his voice sounded familiar. Did she know him?

"But just look at the little love Les, he's such a good baby, I really can't see what the problem is…. In my day we just had to get on with things." Pearl said smartly.

Les sat next to his wife and gazed adoringly at his grandson. It was obvious Phoebe was being dismissed.

"Well in that case, I'll leave you two with Rhys, I've got some jobs to do in the kitchen." Phoebe turned to go; she had a niggling suspicion that she'd met Les Thomas before. There was something about his stance and the slight incline of his head which pulled at her memory.

Rhys warm and dozy from his feed yawned and stretched his little fists above his head. "Just look at him Pearl, opening his pretty little mouth, just like a bird." Les chuckled.

Then the penny dropped. She'd heard him say those exact words; "*open your pretty little mouth*," many times before…. Phoebe knew where she had met the pompous Les Thomas. He might not remember her, but she certainly remembered him!

"Would you like a cup of tea Pearl?" Les asked solicitously, "I'm sure er…er..."

"It's Phoebe ….my name's Phoebe Horwat." She said her name slowly and emphatically, her Polish accent still strong; she watched Les's face turn ashen. *Phoebe could see now that he recognised her too.*

It might be several years since Les Thomas trawled the gloomy wharves of Tiger Bay, looking for women prepared to open their *pretty little mouths* for him. But Phoebe had a good memory, even if she didn't know a name, she rarely forgot a face or a voice, and Les had a distinctive nasal, North Wales accent.

She remembered Les searching in dark alleyways for poor, desperate women prepared to go down on their knees, women he could pay to perform acts his wife would never allow…. the same Les Thomas who told his son Billy that he didn't mix with lowlife like the Benson family. *Oh yes Phoebe had met Les Thomas before and when the time was right, she would remind him of it.*

"I'll put the kettle on for you Les, but I'm afraid you'll have to come into the kitchen and make your own tea, I've got rather a lot on," Phoebe said sweetly, she looked directly into his eyes and dared him to say something.

"Errr yes of course Phoebe, if you put the kettle on, then I'll come in a few minutes to make Pearl her tea." Les looked shifty.

The front door clicked open, and George walked in.

"Hello George," Phoebe could see that George looked surprised to see her.

"Hello Phoebe, Mam, Da…. where's Alice, is something wrong?"

Les looked at Phoebe, from the way they greeted each other it was obvious that this woman knew his son and that he knew her. *Phoebe was a family friend for heaven's sake,* so this was not just a one-off meeting, like it or not, he would probably have to see Phoebe Horwat many times again.

Les felt sick to his stomach.

"Alice is having a rest George; she was feeling bone tired. I'm going to tackle some chores and Les was just about to make your Mam Pearl a nice cup of tea, do you want one George?" Phoebe titled her head like a bird; she watched George's expression.

Pearl's mouth dropped open, *who was this woman Phoebe speaking in such a commanding fashion to her husband, telling her Les to make the tea indeed!*

George's eyebrows shot up; his father never did things like make the tea… that was women's work, Phoebe truly was a force to be reckoned with.

*

"What do you want from me?" Les looked shaken when he joined Phoebe in the kitchen, he made a big play of shutting the connecting door to the sitting room. George and Pearl must never suspect anything.

Les didn't think he'd ever see any of the women he'd used on the wharves ever again and now here one was… a prostitute he'd paid for services with her smirking face,as bold as brass, sitting in his son's flat.

It had been five years since Les last went looking for trade on the wharf, he thought that part of his life was all over now, an episode consigned to his past.

A successful well-regarded businessman with a nice home; he had too much to lose to be caught up in any police crackdown at the docks. Over the years Les had been lucky not to have been or caught out by the police, or heaven forbid, his wife Pearl. Never in a million years did Les think his past would come back to haunt him.

"Want?' Phoebe looked at him archly. "What do you mean by *want* Les?"

"To keep your mouth shut." Les hissed. He wasn't proud of how he'd behaved, during those hateful war years, or just after, when penniless women sold themselves to pay their rent. Plenty of other men had sought comfort there too. Back then he'd told himself that life was too short and brutal never to have pleasure ever again and he did still love his wife for all their bickering and carping.

Pearl might have banned him from her bed and her arms, but he didn't want to be unfaithful to her. Les didn't want to *love* another woman, sex with working girls on the wharves was different; a release. In his eyes it didn't count as being unfaithful; Les always went home to Pearl and his family.

"Now why would I want to keep my mouth shut?... It's funny Les, I find that sometimes my memory can play tricks on me if the conditions are right." Phoebe said coolly.

"And what conditions would those be Phoebe?"

Les knew when he was out foxed.

Chapter 15

"Coming to the wedding!" Ivy yelped. She wasn't sure if she was hearing things.

"Your Da *actually* said they would attend *our* wedding?" Ivy was speechless, her hands shook; the teacup rattled in the saucer slopping her brew.

Billy had popped by early in the morning to tell Ivy about the startling change of heart by his parents; he was grinning from ear to ear.

"You could have knocked me down with a feather an' all Ivy, when Da said *"perhaps he'd been a bit too hasty refusing to come to our wedding."* "I mean, in the past he's told me hell would freeze over before he came to our wedding and now he's coming and Mam's coming too... I was gob smacked; I nearly fell over!"

Ivy smiled; Billy looked so happy. She knew the quarrel with his parents had been upsetting him, his parents had forced him to choose, and he'd chosen her. Now maybe he wouldn't have to choose between them at all.

"I still can't believe it Billy... it's a miracle." Ivy had never met Les and Pearl Thomas and from what Billy had said in the past she wasn't likely to either, now, against all odds, and despite all the arguments and harsh words they were coming to the wedding.

"What's even more miraculous Ivy, is that my Da is coming around here this afternoon to meet you and June." Billy scratched his head he still couldn't quite believe it himself. "That's why I popped by this morning; I couldn't have Da turning up on your doorstep without warning you that he was coming."

"But you'll be here with me won't you Billy?" Ivy looked terrified at the prospect of meeting her future in-laws on her own. After what she'd heard from Alice about Pearl and Les, she was already shaking in her boots at the thought of them being in her home, judging her.

"I'm sorry love…. I can't come I'm needed at the Tasty Plaice," Billy knew Ivy would be nervous about meeting his parents, "but don't worry you won't be on your own with my Da; George said that Phoebe would be popping over to see you as well, about two o'clock."

Ivy felt all at sea, her head was spinning. "Is Pearl… er your Mam coming too?" She asked nervously.

"No Ivy, least wise not today, it's just Da this afternoon. Da said Mam was still taking a bit of time to get used to the idea, but that *she'd come around*…. Those were his very words Ivy." Billy kissed Ivy and hugged her to give her courage. Phoebe would help settle Ivy's nerves.

"Don't worry Ivy, you'll be fine. My Da is a good man really, it's just that he can be a bit bone headed about things sometimes, too proud to admit he was wrong… if you know what I mean."

Ivy grinned, "well that explains where you get it from then," she teased. Now she was getting over the shock announcement she could see it was all for the best. She never wanted to come between Billy and his parents. "Once he gets to know you, and June, he's going to love you as much as I do." Billy kissed her deeply.

"Another bit of good news is that Alice seems a lot happier since Phoebe came over as well. Apparently, George has finally strung up a new, longer length of washing line and cleared the yard to make room to get the pram through easily, Rhys is taking some feeds from a bottle so she can get a bit of rest, and Mam even made her own tea for once!"

"Miracles will never cease." Ivy chuckled. "Shew then…be off you Billy, or you'll be late to work."

"I wish I could stay with you." Billy nuzzled her neck.

"Soon you'll be staying here with me for good and I can hardly wait for the day." Ivy glowed with happiness.

*

Phoebe arrived at Wilson Road bearing gifts. She'd spent the morning baking Welsh cakes with Jennifer Prosser, and she had brought some fresh cakes to serve to Les Thomas when he made his momentous visit to see his prospective daughter-in-law. Phoebe was looking forward to the afternoon immensely.

After a lot of bluster Les Thomas knew he was beaten and backed into a corner. Phoebe Horwat wasn't asking for any money or even any favours for herself; the price for keeping Phoebe's mouth shut was simple; Les would have to mend the rift with Billy and accept Ivy into the Thomas family.

"But Pearl will wonder why I've changed my mind," Les protested.

"It's quite simple Les, you'll tell your wife that you've recently learned that poor Ivy was a victim of Jimmy Benson too, and that she had absolutely nothing to do with any of his activities… all of which is true by the way." Phoebe said firmly, she saw Les's shoulders droop as she spoke.

"You can say that you were too hasty to judge Ivy unfit to marry Billy." Phoebe fixed the wilted Les with a beady stare. Father Malone was so right about passing judgement on others. Les Thomas was learning his lesson about judging the hard way.

"From what I can see Les, your wife takes your lead from you, so you'd better eat a bit of humble pie and tell her you've made a mistake about Ivy and that you expect her to welcome Ivy *and* June into the family."

Les shook his head doubtfully, he could remember Pearl's acid comments about June when Alice chose her to be a bridesmaid.

Children like June should be locked away, Pearl hissed under breath when June scattered rose petals along the aisle. His wife had even gone so far as to have a quiet word with the wedding photographer to ensure June appeared in as few pictures as possible.

"I'll try my best Phoebe… I can't say more than that. I'll go to see Ivy tomorrow and I'll make my peace with Billy tonight." Les said dolefully.

"Good, I'm pleased to hear it… in which case I'm sure we are all going to get on beautifully Les." Phoebe purred.

It was agreed that Pearl and Les Thomas would attend the wedding and Les knew that Phoebe would always be hovering around in the wings to ensure he was as good as his word about being welcoming to Ivy.

"Honestly Aunty Phoebe, I'm still in shock after what Billy told me…. Les Thomas paying us a visit *and* coming to the wedding" Ivy had put on a clean frock and dressed June in her prettiest outfit for the special visit. Phoebe arrived just after two o'clock, she knew Les would be over about four o'clock after he'd been to see Rhys with his wife. It gave Phoebe time to see how Ivy was taking the news about the Thomas family.

"The silly man has realised his mistake that's all Ivy, no man wants to lose his son over a misunderstanding. I simply put him straight about your relationship with Jimmy and now he can see that he was judging you unfairly." Phoebe was busy filling the kettle, it felt good to be back in the old kitchen again.

"That's what Billy said too." Ivy was still puzzled about the sudden change of heart.

"Are you all ready for the wedding?" Phoebe swiftly changed the subject; Ivy mustn't suspect that Phoebe had too much to do with Les's change of heart.

"I think so. Mam has booked and paid for a small sandwich wedding breakfast, that reminds me, Billy didn't say if his parents were coming to that too, maybe we need to tell the hotel if two more are coming?"

An hour and a half later a flustered Les Thomas knocked the door. Earlier Pearl had given him such an ear bashing about being forced to attend Billy's wedding, *and as for having that Mongol child in the family, what would her friends make of it!…. Les was asking too much.*

"Shut up Pearl, I don't want to hear another word about it… I've said my piece and that is the end of the matter!" Les snapped and slammed the door behind him. He'd done a deal with Phoebe Horwat, and Pearl was just going to have to keep her mouth shut and do as she was told for once. Les straightened his tie, his palms were sweating.

"Go on then Ivy, answer the door. I'll go upstairs and see if June is ready to meet our guest." Phoebe nipped up the stairs to fetch June; luckily the landing was a good vantage point to hear whatever was being said on the doorstep

Ivy opened the door, a thick set man with a good head of greying hair stood on her doorstep. Ivy could see that George and Billy were the spitting images of their father.

"Good afternoon Ivy, I'm Les Thomas." Les said gruffly, he had to admit that Ivy was a very pretty, young woman. He could see what Billy saw in her.

"Hello Mr Thomas, I've been expecting you…. Do come in." Ivy could hear her voice sounding clipped and prim; she was nervous.

Ivy showed him into the little sitting room and offered him a chair. The room smelled sweetly of lavender and had been polished to within an inch of its life. Ivy was so keen to make a good impression on her future father-in-law for Billy's sake.

"Would you like a cup of tea Mr Thomas; the kettle is on the hob."

"Yes, thank you Ivy," he took a deep breath, "And please call me Les…after all we are going to be family soon." Les wasn't sure how the words managed to get out of his mouth; it took all his will power to paste a genial smile on his face.

Phoebe came down the stairs, she paused in the hall, *it seemed like Les was sticking to his side of the bargain.*

Ivy scuttled into the kitchen with a broad grin on her face. Phoebe could see that the ice had been broken.

"Good afternoon Les, how nice to see you again." Phoebe plonked down into the armchair by the fireplace.

"Ivy is so pleased you've told Billy you're coming to the wedding," Phoebe smiled a smile that didn't quite reach her eyes. "Ivy was wondering about numbers for the little wedding breakfast they are having to celebrate their happy day."

"Oh, we can't come to that…I'm… I'm busy, I've got a meeting." Les blustered, it was already like pulling teeth to get Pearl to attend the ceremony; going to the wedding breakfast would send her into a complete spiral.

"*Busy* you say," Phoebe fixed him with a serpent like stare, "would that be with some of your new councillor friends."

Les's jaw dropped, *so she knew about that as well!* Since retiring from the fish and chip shop business, Les harboured a secret desire to be local councillor. Pearl fancied hob-nobbing with the local great and good and was pushing Les to stand at the next local election.

How the hell had Phoebe discovered that, very few people knew of his ambitions to be a councillor, the woman was a bloody witch, he was sure of it.

Les knew it went without saying that any breath of scandal would kill his dreams of public office stone dead.

"Err no… nothing like that." Les stuttered.

"Oh good, then perhaps you could change the meeting to another time, I'm sure it would mean such a lot to Billy *and* Ivy to have you *both* there for the occasion." Phoebe said smoothly.

"Yes of course," Les looked at his ragged fingernails, he wished he'd never laid eyes on the meddlesome Phoebe Horwat.

Ivy entered the room carrying a heavy tea tray with her best cups and saucers and a Brown Betty tea pot. June, in her best frock and cardigan, was carefully carrying a tray of Aunty Phoebe's best Welsh cakes; she'd already eaten two in the kitchen as a bribe to be on her best behaviour.

"Hello, my angel are those nice cakes for *Uncle* Les?" Aunty Phoebe watched the child carefully approach the unfamiliar man with the sugary cakes as she had been instructed to do.

June shook her head and headed over to her favourite Aunty Phoebe with the plate before the man could help himself, the girl gave Phoebe the cakes and hid behind Phoebe's chair.

Even Les had to raise a smile.

"She's just being shy," Ivy blushed, she so wanted June to make a good impression. She handed Les his tea. "Normally she runs around the place chattering nineteen to the dozen, now I expect we won't get a peep out of her," Ivy said apologetically.

"Don't worry lass she's fine, I expect she'll come round in her own good time." Les sipped the hot brew appreciatively. He could see June was certainly not the dumb, drooling, creature Pearl kept describing. Bright blue eyes and a grinning face peeped out at him from behind Phoebe's chair.

"More good news Ivy, Les told me that he has managed to re-arrange his meeting and he and Pearl *will* be able to come to the wedding breakfast after all," Phoebe said firmly.

"Hooray for that," Ivy laughed, she knew Billy would be thrilled to have his Mam and Da at the reception.

"Hooray!" June parroted and clapped her hands, "hooray, hooray."

"She certainly is a poppet," Les had to admit with a chuckle.

Phoebe was right, he and Pearl had been fools to dismiss the idea of welcoming Ivy and June into the family. The girl couldn't help being born the way she was.

*

Les only stayed just over an hour, but it was long enough for Phoebe to see he was going to stick to his side of the bargain. By the time Les was leaving, the ice had thawed, and June was even playing peek a boo from behind the chair with him and to top it all, June had handed over one of her precious Welsh cakes.

"Well, that went very well," Phoebe started to clear the cups and saucers.

"It did," Ivy sighed with relief now the ordeal was over. "And June was such a girl for Uncle Les," Ivy bent to give her daughter a big hug.

June beamed in delight.

Just as Phoebe was about to leave, Jack raced across the road from number four and hammered on the door.

Ivy saw he had a huge grin beaming from ear to ear.

"It's a boy! Norah's had the baby about an hour ago, she popped it out like shelling peas." Jack joked.

Ivy rolled her eyes.

"I'd only been through the door about forty-five minutes and before I know it, she's had the baby upstairs in the bathroom in about ten minutes flat!" Jack looked a like a dog with two tails. "I didn't even have time to get the midwife before the little lad arrived in the world… It gave me quite a shock I can tell you."

"Is Norah all right Jack?" Ivy knew Norah had struggled with this pregnancy when Measles had wreaked havoc over Christmas.

"She seems fine Ivy, Marion Spears is with her now and I've been told to stay out of the way until I'm needed. I'm not sure if she's made anything for the kiddies tea or my dinner though." Jack's stomach was growling after a busy day working on the quays.

Ivy and Phoebe burst into gales of laughter, *how typical of a man to be thinking of his stomach at a time like this.*

"Tell you what Jack, shall I pop over and see if Norah would like me to see to the kids for you and if she's got some shopping in, then I'm sure I can rustle up a meal for you all." Phoebe offered; she was in no rush to get home yet.

"Thanks Phoebe, I'm sure Norah would appreciate it." Jack knew that he would appreciate it too, he was starving, still there was always the fish and chip shop.

"Have you chosen a name yet?" Ivy knew that Norah had been hoping for a girl because the boys were so crowded into the one bedroom; four boys and little Karen, Norah would certainly have her hands full in the years to come.

"I dunno, I didn't think to ask Norah about that," Jack scratched his head, "Perhaps we can call this one Jack after me, it's a good name and it's done me alright over the years?" Jack grinned.

To no one's surprise the latest arrival in the chaotic Ashworth household was named Jack.

Chapter 16

It was getting late, and the April sun had set a hours ago. By the time Phoebe got back to Alma Road there was already a sharp nip in the air, she was glad to get inside out of the evening chill and have a nice hot cup of tea after her busy day. She'd eaten her tea with the Ashworth household, a large plate of buttery scrambled eggs and toast had been well received by the children, and Phoebe even managed to find a few slices of bacon to go with Jack's portion.

Sometimes she missed the bustle and friendship of living on Wilson Road.

"You are a star Phoebe, bless you. Thanks for feeding the kids for me." Norah was sat propped up in bed on a mound of pillows holding Jack, dozing after his milky feed. Norah looked tired but happy.

"This little chap decided to put in an early appearance, he wasn't due for another ten days yet…. You certainly caught me on the hop didn't you little man?" Norah gazed lovingly at the sleeping baby at her breast.

"He's gorgeous Norah," Phoebe said softly. She had to admit the mantle of motherhood rested well on Norah's shoulders.

Karen sat at the foot of the bed fascinated by the bundle in her Mam's arms.

"Karen's going to help me look after Jack, aren't you my lovely?"

Karen nodded enthusiastically, this was better than any doll and Mam had promised her a hold soon.

"What a good girl Karen, your Mam is going to need some help with all these boys to look after," Phoebe smiled, Karen would certainly learn the art of motherhood at her Mam's apron strings.

"Well, this *is* certainly the last baby for me," Norah pronounced with a wry smile.

"I think I might have heard you say that before Norah," Phoebe raised her eyebrows.

"This time I mean it Phoebe!" Norah laughed.

"You need your rest now, so I'd best be off and catch my bus Norah, before it gets too late and I outstay my welcome." Phoebe grinned.

"Nonsense Phoebe…. you're always welcome here, you know that!" Norah said emphatically and she meant it, she had a lot of time for Phoebe Horwat.

"I'm visiting Ivy again in a few days so when I'm there I'll pop over and see if you want me to do a few chores…. And of course, to see how this little angel is faring." Phoebe smiled and felt a lump rise in her throat; the baby was gorgeous. Whenever Phoebe saw a newly born child it reminded her of the day when she saw her own baby for the briefest of moments before it was whisked away by the nuns, a moment so precious it was engraved on her heart.

*

Phoebe clip clopped down the empty street towards her house; she was tired; suddenly she shivered. *That felt like someone walking over my grave.* She said to herself.

Phoebe pulled her coat around her and pressed on, she would soon be inside in the warmth and safety of her own home, she checked behind her; the dark street was deserted.

*Perhaps it was just the cold…*it was still only March and with the clear sky overhead, a late frost seemed likely. Phoebe hurried the last few yards towards the dark house at the end of the street and told herself not to be so foolish.

Suddenly she thought she saw a faint glow… it was just for a moment a tiny flicker of light in the blackness… she felt sure that a small glimmer passed near the window in the upstairs front room…. *her bedroom.*

Phoebe stood outside on the pavement opposite her house, her heart racing and she watched the window. She stood for a full five minutes but the tiny light was gone.

It had been so faint, a mere glimmer, almost like a will 'o the whisp dancing past the window… and then it was gone, and it didn't return.

Perhaps she'd been mistaken about the light?

Phoebe was nervous about going into the house on her own, her trembling fingers struggled to put the key in the Yale lock. She opened the door wide to give herself room to escape if she had indeed disturbed a burglar. Phoebe flicked on the hall lights and called out a bold "hello" to announce her return. She thought she heard a small creak upstairs.

Malcolm Goode opened the door to the middle sitting room and peered out into the hallway; he was blinking and rubbing his eyes as if he'd been asleep. "Good evening Miss Horwat, are you alright?"

"I'm fine thank you Mr Goode, I didn't know if anyone else was in the house, it was so dark, with no lights on in the hall," she explained, removing her coat.

"I don't usually put the hall lights on Miss Horwat because I don't come through the front door. I think Carol Jones is upstairs though, I'm pretty sure I heard her moving around up there." Malcolm gave a large yawn.

Phoebe felt safer knowing that Malcolm and Carol were in the house, she was just being silly and jumpy; *it must have been some sort of reflection from the streetlights which caught her eye.*

At night Phoebe counted her precious new rosary and gave a prayer of thanks for all the good things in her life, she still wondered from time to time what had happened to the old one?

*

Phoebe's detailed letters about life on Alma Road came as regular as clockwork to Cartref. Deirdre was thrilled to hear all Phoebe's news especially the little titbits about Rita and the children.

Rita giving Phoebe her rosary when Phoebe had lost her own was just the sort of generous and thoughtful thing that Rita would do, Deirdre thought.

Deirdre only wished she could chatter about her snippets of news from Alma Road to James, but she knew her lips must remain sealed.

Bobby had been such a wonderful confidant; Deirdre could tell him anything and everything and he always seemed to listen intently to her chattering on, especially her news about Rita and the family. She missed having the baggy old cat to talk to.

It had been just over a week since Bobby died and with James's help they had buried him next to the shed by the flower bed where he loved to sun himself. It was a fitting, final resting place.

James had been touchingly helpful with the burial. "The hole doesn't need to be very big Deirdre; Bobby was quite small under all that fur... I'm sure we can do it between us."

"I don't know James, there are some gardening tools left by Mrs Prosser in the shed, but the ground is so very hard and dry, I don't think I can manage to do it." Deirdre said doubtfully. Growing up on Alma Road with its tiny yard and one narrow flower bed meant that Deirdre had never used a heavy spade or fork.

"Nonsense... I'm not asking you to dig the hole.... I'm asking you to help *me* dig the hole." James said kindly. He knew how much it meant to Deirdre to give Bobby a decent burial, he'd felt the same when his first guide dog Nell died.

Deirdre looked puzzled.

"If you position the fork in the ground for me and hold it upright then I can push the tines into the earth with my boot and pull back on the

handle…. Once we've broken the soil up a bit, it will be easier to shift."
James felt sure with Deirdre to guide him they could manage to dig a
suitable sized hole in no time.

"Come on, let's give it a go…nothing ventured nothing gained." James
said cheerfully trying to give Deirdre the confidence to tackle the job.

And so, Deirdre found herself with her arms around James Pugh's waist
guiding him to dig in the chosen area by the shed. She was close to his
shoulder, guiding him left and right, telling him where to put his feet,
warning him of unsteady ground or precious garden plants.

It felt a strangely intimate and poetic thing to be doing, two people in the
autumn of their lives sharing a special moment between them. Then on
their hands and knees they used some trowels to dig away the loose soil
and create a shallow grave for Bobby's resting place.

Deirdre laid the cat, wrapped in an old pillowcase, in the depression they
had created and then carefully covered the hole with the loose earth. She
was pleased with their work; she could never have done it without James's
help.

James carefully walked up and down on top of the loose soil and when the
earth was tamped down Deirdre moved a few empty garden pots on top of
the newly dug mound to protect it from disturbance. Later in the year she
would fill the pots with flowers and plant a fragrant rosemary bush next to
the tiny grave to remember him by.

"Do you mind if we say a small prayer for Bobby," Deirdre felt a little
self-conscious to be doing such a thing for a cat, but she knew that James
understood what Bobby had meant to her.

"Of course, not Deirdre," he took her small, soil covered hand and
squeezed it for encouragement.

She held James's hand and spoke softly:

"Dear Lord…. You taught us that there is no greater gift than love, and the companionship and friendship that comes with love. Thank you for bringing Bobby into my life, for all the happy times we had together and guiding me to this place… Amen." Deirdre had a catch in her voice, she was trying not to cry.

James said *Amen* and waited for her to gather herself together. He gave Deirdre a few moments of silence to mourn her lost friend. And as they stood together in silence holding hands at Bobby's grave, James began to realise he might be starting to fall in love with his kind. sweet and gentle neighbour.

Chapter 17

Phoebe was popping around to see Rita Prosser with a small photograph of Deirdre's new kitten to show the children when they came home from school.

Never in a million years did I think I would be popping around to visit my own daughter for a chat. Phoebe smiled to herself, some days she had to pinch herself to make sure she wasn't dreaming.

Before Deirdre could raise any objections to having another cat James had found a replacement for Bobby.

The canteen lady, Avril, at the institute for the blind centre James attended every Wednesday, reliably informed James that spring was an excellent time to obtain a new kitten.

"There's blessed kittens everywhere about now, the farmer near me drowns loads every year, says he'd be overrun with cats if he didn't." Avril Ferris chattered away as she served James a steaming mug of hot tea. "I could get my Reg to get you one if you wanted Mr Pugh. I always feel so sorry for the little things when the farmer gets rid of them; it seems such a waste of life." Avril was tender-hearted but she knew a pack of feral cats couldn't be allowed to breed.

"That's a marvellous idea Avril, when do you think we could get one."

"No time like the present. We'd have to be quick though he doesn't let them get too attached to their mothers, sometimes, if he finds them early, he takes them away as soon as they're born before the poor little things have even had a chance to open their eyes. It would be nice to know at least one was going to a good home for once." Avril smiled, she was glad Mr Pugh was getting on with his new neighbour, he seemed chattier and more energized of late.

"It would be the best home a cat could get Avril, and I'd be incredibly grateful if you could get me a nice ginger Tom. My friend just lost her ginger and white cat and I know she'd love another."

"I'll get my Reg to find you one and drop it over tomorrow Mr Pugh." Avril promised.

When Reg arrived the next day with the cardboard box, James didn't dare open it in case the kitten escaped. James knew he couldn't wait too long to give it to Deirdre, the meowing and scrabbling inside the box was growing frantic, the poor thing was obvious frightened of being sealed in the dark. James went straight around to Deirdre's leaving the box in his hall.

"Hello James," Deirdre was surprised to James on her doorstep late on a Thursday afternoon.

"Deirdre please come with me to my house, I have something you must see." James felt ridiculously excited, he only wished he could see her face when she opened the box and saw what was inside.

"Is something the matter?" Deirdre feared James had some sort of problem in the house, he didn't usually ask her to go around at this time of day, she was just starting to prepare some sandwiches for her tea.

"No Deirdre nothing's the matter, I've just got a parcel for you that's all and I couldn't carry it around here myself. You'll have to come and collect it and it don't think it can wait" James said.

"A parcel, for me, how intriguing." Deirdre laughed. "It's not like the postman to deliver things to the wrong address. I'll come and get it straight away" She wasn't expecting a parcel and she had no idea why James was being so mysterious.

She held his arm and escorted him back up the path.

As soon as Deirdre entered the hall, the plaintive mewing gave the game away. She could guess what was inside the cardboard box. Her face broke out into a broad grin.

"Oh, James, is it for me." Deirdre clasped her hands together.

"He needs a new home Deirdre, and I couldn't think of a better one than yours," James grinned when he handed over the battered box containing a mewling bundle of hopefully, ginger, and white fluff.

"He's been here about twenty minutes, but I think he's been inside that box quite a bit longer than that, there are a few holes for air, but he sounds ready to come out. Mr Ferris, Avril's husband, brought him around on the front of his bicycle for me. I didn't dare open the box in case he escaped into the house."

"Where are your scissors."

"In the top of kitchen drawer."

Deirdre returned with a large pair of scissors and started cutting away the string and brown tape securing the box. Her heart was all of a flutter; she'd never owned a kitten before.

The leaves of the box sprang open and a tiny ginger tabby kitten with four white feet and a white bib and startlingly blue eyes gazed back at her.

"You poor little darling locked in that box, you must have been terrified," Deirdre scooped up the kitten which seemed to weight no more than a few ounces. "He's so tiny!" She exclaimed.

"So, you like him then." James could hear the delight in her voice, he was glad he'd pleased her.

"How could you not like him, he's absolutely….. Oh, my goodness," Deirdre laughed. "I think we had better start calling this little one "*she*" it's a little girl not a boy."

James face fell, "oh…I hope you don't mind Deirdre; I did ask for a ginger and white *male* kitten, it looks like Mr Ferris doesn't know as much about kittens as I thought he did…. You don't have to keep it if you don't want it." James felt his heart sink a little, he had so wanted the surprise to be perfect.

"Don't be silly James, how could you not want anything as gorgeous as this little thing.... We aren't going to send you back, are we?" She crooned to the tiny kitten scrambling on her shoulder.

"Phew," James heaved a sigh of relief, he didn't want to tell Deirdre that all the other siblings in the litter were probably a soggy, drowned mass at the bottom the farm duck pond by now.

"So, what will you call it...er I mean her?"

"Why Bobby of course.... I wanted a cat called Bobby and I'm going to have a cat called Bobby, she doesn't know it's not a girl cat name." Deirdre chuckled.

*

Within a few hours the kitten was fed and warm and sleeping on Bobby's old rag rug. Deirdre raided the cinder patch where she tipped the sweepings from the coal fire and created a small tray for Bobby to do her business. Deirdre felt so happy she thought her heart would burst; the fact that James had been thinking of her and sought her out a new ginger and white companion touched her heart.

"You've got a lot to live up to, little Bobby. The old Bobby who used to live here was a class act," she smiled to herself as she caught herself talking to the sleeping kitten, *she had got her confidant back again.*

*

When Deirdre had a photograph of little Bobby she sent it to Phoebe and asked if Phoebe would show it to Jennifer and Frank. It would be the half term soon and Deirdre hoped the added lure of a kitten to play with would prove irresistible for the children.

Phoebe always happy to grab any chance to see Rita, Jennifer or Frank, accepted the mission gladly.

"Do come in and have a cup of tea Phoebe, I've just finished the ironing and I'm gasping for a cuppa myself." Rita looked pink from tackling a mountain of ironing.

"I don't want to disturb you if you're busy Rita, but Deirdre asked if you would show the children this picture of her new kitten." Phoebe said by way of a reason for her visit. Phoebe loved the easy way Rita had welcomed her as a new neighbour, she felt they were growing close, and it touched her heart.

"Whisht…. get away with you Phoebe, you aren't disturbing me at all," Rita sucked between her teeth. "I've been hoping someone would rescue me from all this blessed ironing, all morning, come in and take a seat whilst I put the kettle on…. Just excuse all the mess."

The little back parlour had piles of freshly ironed items waiting to be returned to their rightful home, paired socks and neatly folded tea towels sat on top of crisp bed linen… *Rita had been busy.*

"Just move things if you can't find the chairs," Rita trilled in from the kitchen.

Reluctant to move anything, Phoebe stood up and looked at the ornaments and pictures on the mantlepiece, one picture in particular caught Phoebe's eye. The beautiful image in a silver frame was of a younger Rita wearing a light-coloured jacket and spotted blouse, her hair was longer then, waved and swept to one side; the photograph must have been taken about ten years ago when she was in her early twenties.

Phoebe gasped and caught her breath; the image could have been of herself as a young woman. The likeness to Phoebe's younger self was uncanny, even the same half smile and seductive full lips. Rita aged about twenty-two looked exactly as she had done all those years ago before she met Father Edmund and her life fell apart.

Phoebe felt a sob rising in her throat. She was fatter now, less groomed than she was as a young woman, her hair so often scraped back in an unfashionable bun, no longer glorious. Phoebe's seductive, youthful glamour had faded years ago, and a hard life had etched lines and bitterness in her face. Rita might not see herself in this old Phoebe standing in her parlour, but Phoebe could see herself in this picture of a younger Rita.

"Ahh so you didn't find the chairs," Rita laughed as she came in balancing two brimming teacups. "Gosh Phoebe are you alright, you look like you've seen a ghost." Rita could see Phoebe looked pale and a little tearful.

"I'm fine thanks Rita. That's the thing about old age sometimes your emotions catch you out." Phoebe had a sob in her voice.

Rita looked puzzled, "has something upset you?"

"Oh, it was just something Deirdre said in her letter," Phoebe lied smoothly, desperate to compose herself. She thrust the picture of the new Bobby towards Rita. "This gorgeous little thing is Deirdre's new kitten and she told me that all the others in the same litter had been drowned by the farmer." Phoebe blew her nose loudly into her handkerchief. "It suddenly struck me looking at the picture how sad and cruel life can be," Phoebe sniffed.

She hated lying to Rita, but she couldn't tell her the real reason for her distress.

Rita put down the teacups and gave Phoebe a hug. "Don't upset yourself Phoebe, at least Deirdre managed to rescue this one from a terrible fate and if I know Deirdre, she will spoil this kitten rotten."

"You are right of course," Phoebe sniffed. "I'm just a bit overly sentimental sometimes."

"Ha…. My Mam was just like that too; she was incredibly kind-hearted, always helping others. Any sad story or any poor thing that needed rescuing would tug at Mam's heart strings; my Da used to tell her off for caring too much and taking the troubles of the world on her shoulders." Rita said remembering the bickering over her mother's need to nurture and rescue any waif or stray who came her way.

Phoebe recognised herself in that description, *it seemed Edmund had found a good, caring mother for their child.*

"I must go now Rita, thanks for the tea… by the way Deirdre said that she hoped the children would come and visit her over half term and meet the new kitten."

"I'm sure they would love to Phoebe. I'll write and tell her when we are coming."

*

Phoebe had not stayed long, she was angry with herself for losing her composure, *you've got to stop this bursting into tears, Rita will think you've got a screw loose,* she chided herself.

Phoebe opened the front door, and a draught blew through the house; upstairs she heard a door slam, and then footsteps and another quieter click quickly followed.

Phoebe wondered what was going on upstairs, at this time of the day it was usually just her in the house… Perhaps Carol was home and having a late morning bath or maybe it was Mr Goode having his weekly bath, salesmen did appear to keep very odd hours.

Phoebe went into the back parlour to lay the fire. When the sun went down the evenings were still chilly, she would need to light the fire later today; it was almost four o'clock now and the light was starting to fade.

Phoebe headed for the yard; the coal scuttle needed refilling. She saw Malcolm Goode coming through the back gate from the lane whilst she was filling the coal scuttle from the yard bunker, *so it couldn't have been Malcolm she heard upstairs.*

Malcom had a face like thunder.

"Is something the matter Mr Goode?" Phoebe asked solicitously.

"Yes, something bloody well is the matter!" Malcolm snapped.

Phoebe looked startled.

Malcolm lowered his voice and bent close to Phoebe's ear; his gaze drifted to the upstairs window which was open a few inches. "I'm sorry to swear Miss Horwat but I'm not prepared to put up with these *goings on* any longer!"

Phoebe's jaw dropped. "Goings on!"

Malcolm had unlocked the yard entrance to his middle room. "Please come in Miss Horwat and I'll tell you exactly what I mean by *goings on*, and then you can tell me what you're going to do about it."

Chapter 18

Ivy was brimming with happiness; Billy was reconciled with his parents and now both parents were coming to the wedding *and* the reception; it was better than she could ever have hoped for. She couldn't wait to tell Norah her good news and get a little cuddle with the latest addition to the Ashworth brood.

It had been four days since Norah Ashworth had given birth to her fifth, and if Norah was to be believed, her *last baby* and Ivy had only seen Norah and little Jack for a few minutes. Today being Monday meant the house would be quieter and hopefully the two women would have time for a catch up and an exchange of gossip.

"Come on June, shall we go and see Karen's new little brother, and if you're a good girl we can ask Aunty Norah if you can have a little cuddle with baby Jack." Ivy smiled, June loved her baby dollies, she would be so envious of Karen having a real baby to hold and cuddle.

June tugged fiercely at Ivy's hand as they crossed over to number four Wilson Road.

"Come on Mammee….," June was impatient to see the new arrival.

"Careful June, you'll pull your poor Mam over at this rate," Ivy laughed at June's desire to see baby Jack.

Karen was waving through the window and rushed to answer the door.

"Hello Aunty Ivy, I've got a brand-new baby brother." The little girl boasted proudly with a grin stretching from ear to ear. She bounced up and down from foot to foot with excitement.

"Aren't you the lucky one," Ivy ruffled Karen's curls, she really was an adorable little girl. "Is your Mam busy Karen?"

Karen shook her head, her Mam didn't look busy, the last time she'd looked around the bedroom door about an hour ago, her Mam was fast asleep and snoring very loudly.

"Be a good girl for me then and go tell Mam that Aunty Ivy has come for a cup of tea, and I'll go in the kitchen and put the kettle on…. Don't disturb her if she's busy mind."

Karen scampered up the stairs to give her Mam the message and Ivy headed for the kitchen to make the tea. She could always take Norah's tea up if Norah had her hands full with Jack.

The house was quiet, the three boys, Lenny, George, and Gareth were all at school and Norah's husband Jack was at work. The usually immaculate kitchen still bore the remains of the morning breakfast and piles of dirty dishes were stacked in the sink waiting to be washed. Ivy was a bit surprised to see the disarray.

Norah was usually so good at getting on top of things even when her hands were full of children and babies. If only half of Jack Ashworth's boasts about his capable wife's many accomplishments could be believed, Norah was the best housewife any man could wish for.

Ivy was in no doubt that Norah was indeed a force to be reckoned with, an exemplary wife and a stickler for order and tidiness. Norah was house-proud to a fault and woe be tide any scruffy lad who trailed in muddy footprints or brought mess into the house!

Ivy rolled her sleeves up and started to tackle the greasy plates and cups.

"Here we go June, let's help make the kitchen nice and tidy for Aunty Norah today shall we? I'm sure she will be down with little Jack soon. You can wipe this cutlery for Aunty Norah and put it away in that drawer in the dresser, just like you do at home." Ivy handed June a clean tea towel, June couldn't be trusted with crockery, but she was excellent at drying the cutlery and putting it back in the right slots.

The kettle started to boil with a high pitch whistle. It had been a good ten minutes or more and Karen still hadn't come back downstairs with a message. Maybe she had called at an awkward time and Norah was feeding Jack, or bathing him, or even having a bath herself. Perhaps she should just go home and leave them in peace; she didn't want to intrude. It was strange though that Norah didn't send Karen down with a message. Ivy decided to give it a few more minutes and then she would go upstairs to see if Norah needed her or if she would rather Ivy called back another day.

Overhead Ivy could hear the baby crying, the plaintive squawking of a new-born tugged at her heart strings.

"Oh, dear June, what noise… it sounds like Jack is exercising his lungs doesn't it?" Ivy smiled.

The noise persisted for a few moments, it was getting louder and louder. Ivy was surprised it was taking so long to quieten the baby. A small trickle of worry ran down her spine. *What was taking so long upstairs and why hadn't Karen come back down.*

"You stay here June and finish these dishes for Aunty Norah whilst I go and see if Aunty Norah needs me."

June nodded and chewed her lip as she concentrated on drying the knives and forks.

Ivy rushed up stairs, she didn't know why but a sense of foreboding was growing inside her; apart from Jack's crying, she couldn't hear voices. The bedroom door was open just a crack.

What Ivy *could* hear was snoring emanating from the main bedroom; deep, loud rasping snores which reminded her of Jimmy's snoring when he was blind drunk after too many pints down at the Red Lion with his mates.

"Hello Norah… it's only me," Ivy called softly as she entered the dark bedroom.

Little Karen, with her eyes like saucers sat on a bedside chair next to her sleeping mother trying to rock her screaming baby brother in her arms, the child looked worried, the baby lolled at an uncomfortable angle on Karen's meagre lap bawling its head off.

"Come here my darling," Ivy rushed to scoop the wriggling baby off Karen's knee before it escaped from the child's awkward grasp and landed on the floor.

"I'm trying to look after him like Mam does Aunty Ivy, because she's still sleeping," Karen said quickly, her eyes were like saucers.

"I know my angel, you've been a very good girl," Ivy said swiftly, she could see that Karen was starting to cry.

"I can't wake Mam up." Karen's bottom lip started to tremble.

"Don't worry my lovely, Aunty Ivy will sort things out," Ivy said with more confidence than she felt, it was obvious something was very wrong. Despite the screaming and bawling, Norah didn't stir. Ivy's mind was in a whirl, she might need to get help for Norah if things were as bad as they looked, "why don't you go downstairs Karen and see June and I'll see to Jack and your Mam."

Relieved to have Aunty Ivy in charge, Karen scooted out of the bedroom. Jigging Jack in her arms, Ivy drew the curtains so she could get a better look at her friend. All the while Norah continued to breath deep rasping snores.

Dear Mother of God, Ivy muttered under her breath. In the light she could see Norah's pillow was wet on one side where a trickle of saliva was drooling out of Norah's mouth. Norah's eyes were flickering half open and her face was deathly pale.

Ivy jostled Norah's shoulder in an attempt to rouse her, "can you hear me Norah….. Norah it's Ivy!" Ivy felt panic rising in her chest, Norah didn't respond.

"I'm going to get help Norah… I'll be as quick as I can…. It's going to be all right." Ivy said, she could hear the panic in her own voice.

Unsure if Norah could even hear her or where she could get help from, Ivy charged down the stairs with Jack in her arms to find someone to assist. She had no time to lose, Norah needed medical attention, *goodness knows how long she had been like that.*

She could hear Karen and June chattering happily in the kitchen, Karen was showing June where to put some tea plates. Ivy decided to take a risk it wasn't far to the telephone box at the corner on the Grand Avenue she could be there and back in ten minutes if she ran with the pram. She needed to dial 999, she was sure Norah needed to go to hospital.

Jack had stopped squalling now and was whimpering with exhaustion; he was obviously hungry but there was nothing Ivy could do for the child. She quickly looked in Norah's crockery cupboard, there were two rather old feeding bottles kept from when Karen was being weaned off the breast. She knew that she had a can of Ideal milk in her cupboard, she could make Jack up a bottle of that when she got back from ringing for an ambulance. Now she had no time to lose; Norah needed help and fast.

"Girls, I've got to make a phone call. If I cut some bread and butter for you, can you two girls stay here and eat it, whilst I run up to the corner? I'll take Jack with me, and I'll leave the front door on the latch." Karen was looking at Ivy with large, troubled eyes.

"I'll only be five minutes my lovely…. that's all and I'll be straight back. Now promise me you won't leave the house Karen?" Ivy was starting to feel frantic she bundled Jack into the pram, she was trying to stay calm, she couldn't let the girls sense the panic she felt building inside her.

"Promise me Karen you'll be a good girl and look after June?" Karen nodded.

"That's a good girl. And June you must stay with Karen, and both be very good girls together… stay in the sitting room with your bread and butter, Mam will be back very soon, so play nicely with Karen whilst I'm gone." June had no sense of time; Ivy would have to be as quick as she could.

"We'll be very good Aunty Ivy," Karen said; she was a sensible girl, and she knew she could trust her Aunty Ivy.

Ivy couldn't risk the girls going upstairs, it was important that they stayed downstairs out of the way. *They must not go up and see Norah.*

"Now please stay down here in the sitting room and do *not* answer the door…. Not to anyone, is that understood!" Both girls nodded. Ivy could do no more; she had to run for her life to the telephone kiosk with Jack in the rickety pram. At times like this she cursed her deformed leg which slowed her down and caused her to limp, she would just have to push through somehow… *Norah's very life might depend on it.*

Chapter 19

When Billy called around at seven o'clock to see Ivy, he was surprised to be greeted by Ivy holding a sleeping baby in her arms.

"Come in Billy," Ivy said softly, she rocked the child gently from side to side lulling the sleeping child. She raised a finger to her lips for Billy to keep quiet and led him through to the sitting room.

"What on earth is going on Ivy," Billy demanded, he'd never seen baby Jack before.

"Oh Billy, it's been the simply the most dreadful day…. Norah's been taken ill." Ivy tried not to cry; her voice was cracking with emotion.

"I went over to visit Norah with June and Karen let me in, but when Norah didn't come downstairs with Jack I went upstairs and found her unconscious lying on the bed making strange sounds." Ivy shuddered remembering the awful rasping snores.

"How awful…. What happened to her?" Billy looked shocked.

"We don't know but the ambulance came and took her away to hospital and I stayed with Karen in the house until the three boys came home from school. I've managed to find some baby bottles for baby Jack, and I've fed the children some tea. As you can imagine, her husband Jack is out of his mind with worry about her." Ivy had tried to keep the children calm until their father came home from work, but Gareth didn't understand why his Mam had gone away and left him and he became upset and difficult. Gareth's deafness made it hard to try and explain to him what was going on, as it was Ivy didn't really understand much about the situation herself, the child's anguished howls for his Mam tore at Ivy's heart.

Lenny, the eldest of the three lads tried to be brave for Karen's sake, but even though he was ten years old, Lenny's lip started to tremble when he heard his Mam had been rushed into hospital. "I'll look after my brothers and Karen, Aunty Ivy," the little lad sobbed. Gareth clung to Ivy's skirt, howling.

"I told Lenny I'd look after his little brother for his da until his Mam came home," Ivy looked at Billy with red teary eyes. "She's got to get better soon Billy; Jack and the children will never manage without her."

Billy put his arm around Ivy, he could see she was struggling to not breakdown.

"Try not to fret Ivy, the children are safe and well and hopefully their Mam will be back home soon…. There's no point running to meet trouble, for all we know Jack might get some good news tonight and Norah might be on the road to recovery." Billy tried to cheer Ivy, he hated seeing her so wretched.

"Please God she is Billy." Ivy said doubtfully, the last time she saw Norah, her friend looked like she was at death's door.

"Jack has gone to the hospital now, I said I would look after baby Jack whilst he's gone. It's one less thing for him to worry about; the poor man is utterly distraught." Ivy's heart bled for Jack Ashworth, the man broke down and cried bitter tears when he heard how ill his wife looked when Ivy had found her.

"So, do we know what's actually wrong with Norah?" Billy was dismayed to hear of the drama unfolding in the Ashworth household, he knew Ivy and Norah were close friends.

"We don't know yet, the ambulance men didn't tell me anything, they just took her away to the hospital. I'm hoping that Jack will find out some news tonight when he talks to the doctors. Lenny the eldest boy is going to watch the younger ones whilst Jack goes to see Norah and I said I'd take the baby in here until he's got things sorted… poor Norah, it's such a bloody mess." Ivy sobbed.

"Don't upset yourself Ivy, no-one could do any more than you're doing. Is there anything you would like me to do to help?"

"Could you please go over to Alma Road tonight and tell Aunty Phoebe what's happened?" Ivy pleaded. "I told Jack that I would ask Aunty Phoebe to help me look after the children for him; between us I'm sure we can manage, I just can't do it all on my own. Will you ask Phoebe if she could stay here for a few days with me?" Ivy felt sure Aunty Phoebe would be straight around the minute she heard about the crisis; Phoebe was enormously fond of Norah.

If Norah was seriously ill, who else was going to run the house and look after all the children for Jack to be able to go out to work each day? If Ivy and Phoebe didn't step in Jack was in dire trouble.

"With Phoebe's help, I'm sure we could manage the children and the housework until Jack knows what's going on. At the moment, he's got no idea about what's going on or when Norah will be well enough to come home. Norah needs Jack at her side whilst she's so poorly, but the children need their Mam to look after them; it stands to reason, Jack can't be in two places at once."

"Poor man, he must be in a hell of a state," Billy said sympathetically, he couldn't imagine how any man could look after four young children and a new-born baby.

"As Jack said, how can he go to work with all these children to look after and yet if he doesn't go to work, he won't get paid, and I know Norah has said that money is always tight." Ivy shook her head; Jack didn't earn very good wages, but he and Norah always scraped by each week with Norah watching the budget like a hawk and stretching the housekeeping.

"Of course, I'll go and fetch Phoebe, if she can come that is. I'll tell her it's an emergency." Billy put his coat back on. "Is there anything else you need Ivy?"

"Could you ask Phoebe to get some more evaporated milk for the baby when she goes past the shops? This little one is going to need feeding every few hours and I've got to get on top of the laundry, or the little lad will soon run out of nappies." It felt strange to be discussing baby needs with Billy, she was so lucky to have him as a strong shoulder to lean on. "Will do Ivy… now give me a kiss." Billy leant forward and kissed Ivy tenderly, the sleeping child nestled in her arms. "Don't fret Ivy, I'm sure it will be all right in the end, Norah is in the best place."

*

Jack sat next to Norah's hospital bed his eyes red rimmed with stress and tears. He held her hand and stroked it gently between his fore finger and his thumb, "come on love, try to wake up, the children are missing you… and so am I," he sobbed.

Dr Rawlings had given Jack the shocking news and there was no way to soften the blow, Norah had had as stroke as the result of a blot clot caused by her pregnancy.

"But what does it mean Dr Rawlings… I don't understand it. She had baby Jack in a about five minutes flat, I said at the time it was like *shelling peas*…. How on earth could this happen now?"

"It's a fairly *rare* occurrence Mr Ashworth, but the risk of a blood clot, is always a real and present threat to any woman giving birth, especially for older women and this *is* your wife's fifth pregnancy." Dr Rawlings shook his head. It was understandable that Mr Ashworth wanted definitive answers, absolute outcomes, but medicine and disease weren't like that, each patient was so different; it was impossible to tell Mr Ashworth all he needed to know.

The only thing for certain was Jack Ashworth's wife was in a life-threatening condition and only time would tell how much damage the rogue blood clot had done.

"She *never* wanted another baby; she said it a hundred times that four children were enough.... It's all my fault," Jack said mournfully, "If I'd just listened to her, she wouldn't be lying in a hospital bed fighting for her life." Jack felt consumed with grief and guilt, he idolized his Norah. *He'd never forgive himself or that baby if it cost Norah her life.*

"What have I done to you my love," he sobbed as he held his wife's hand; a drip fed into her arm and an oxygen mask on her face. "I'm so, so sorry, Norah."

"Please don't upset yourself in here Mr Ashworth. It's important we are calm and positive around our patients, especially those patients who are in a coma. We don't know how much a patient can hear of what's going on around them, and you might distress your wife if she can hear you getting upset at her bedside," Dr Rawlings said firmly.

"Sorry Dr Rawlings," Jack muttered; he took a deep breath to compose himself. Norah was his world; he couldn't bear to contemplate a world without her.... *She had to get better.*

"What happens now?" He gulped.

"Come with me Mr Ashworth and we can discuss all that in my office." Over a cup of strong tea, Dr Rawlings gave Jack as much information as he could, and none of it was good. "Your wife has suffered a serious post-partum pulmonary embolism," Dr Rawlings paused, he could see Jack looking totally mystified.

Jack was a simple man, he couldn't take in what the doctor was trying to tell him about Norah's future, the long words went straight over his head.

"But is my Norah going to be all right?" Jack said gruffly, he wanted the doctor to spell out what it all meant, not bamboozle him with big words he couldn't pronounce.

"We don't know yet Mr Ashworth, only time will tell." Dr Rawlings tented his fingers and peered over his glasses. He had seen cases like this before and the prognosis was never a positive one.

Jack groaned; he wanted reassurance Norah would wake up and pull through.

"You say your wife was lucid and complaining of a dull ache in her chest when you last saw her at breakfast, before you went off to work?"

"That's right, she was worried she might be getting a problem in her…. Er er, breast" Jack blushed, "you know because of feeding Jack…. She kept rubbing at it and said she might go to the doctors if the pain got any worse." Jack shook his head.

"I had no idea it might be serious Doctor, she never really complained much about anything did Norah." Jack shook his head in disbelief. "Our Karen said Norah went upstairs with Jack to give him a feed and a bit of a rest and then her Mam went to sleep…. Well, that's what Karen thought." Jack tried to piece together a timeline of when Norah might have collapsed with the clot. "I reckon it must have happened around about then."

"Well, if we work on those timings then, it seems as if your wife might have been unconscious for about three hours before your neighbour Mrs Benson discovered her and summoned an ambulance…. I'm in no doubt Mrs Benson saved your wife's life. The deep rasping snoring Mrs Benson told the ambulance men about, was your wife struggling to breath."

Jack ran his fingers through his hair and groaned. *Poor Norah.*

"How long will she be in here? I've got to go to work somehow doctor; if I don't turn up tomorrow I might lose my job." Jack knew he had to pay his bills, he'd taken a couple of days off when Norah had the baby, he couldn't afford to lose his job.

Dr Rawlings didn't like to say that in a worst-case scenario Mrs Ashworth might *never* come out of hospital. "We don't know yet Mr Ashworth. Of course, you must go to work, all we can do now is see if your wife responds well to treatment. In the meantime, are your family going to help you with looking after all the children?"

Jack looked exhausted; he shook his head. His own mother had died a few years back and although his Da still lived in Splott he was frail and elderly and needed looking after himself. Old man Ashworth couldn't help at all, and he didn't have any money to spare either.

Norah's family lived miles away up the valleys in Merthyr Tydfil; her Mam had had a hard life bringing up her own large brood, and now with all the other grandchildren to help with and her elderly husband, she couldn't just up sticks and come to Cardiff to help Jack.

It was a bloody mess, four children and a baby! Jack knew he couldn't manage to look after all the children and work; if Norah didn't pull through, he didn't know what to do. He couldn't bear to contemplate Norah *not* pulling through; Norah simply *must* get better.

"It will be a struggle, but I think we're fixed up for the moment Dr Rawlings. My neighbour Mrs Benson has agreed to look after the baby for as long as Norah is in hospital, and she said her Aunty Phoebe might come to give her a hand with seeing to all the other children until their Mam comes home." Jack had been enormously grateful when Ivy stepped in to help, but he knew it couldn't be for too long, Ivy had her own life to lead, and her disabled daughter June needed her attention. Still, it *was* only until Norah was back on her feet again and things got back to normal.

"Well, that sounds as if you are sorted for now Mr Ashworth, we can always get the Council services involved if these two ladies have a problem in the future; the childcare system is meant for cases such as these." Dr Rawlings knew that Jack would struggle to support so many children unless he could rely on friends and family to step in.

"I'm not putting any of the children in care!" Jack said hotly…. The thought of his children being taken away, especially little Gareth, filled him with dread and he knew Norah would be beside herself if she thought he'd allowed it to happen. "With the help of our neighbours we'll manage somehow Dr Rawlings, and *when* my wife comes home, things will go back to the way they were." Jack said stoutly.

Dr Rawlings nodded his head sagely…. It was better to let Mr Ashworth live in hope for the time being.

Chapter 20

Malcom Goode had come to the end of his tether, he didn't know exactly *how* it was happening, but things were going missing, there was no mistake about it, *and* he could swear his personal things were being rifled through. It was a clever job, but little mistakes gave the game away.

"Come into my room Miss Horwat I'm determined to get to the bottom of all this and I don't mean to upset you but I'm *not* ruling anything out." Malcolm said waspishly.

Phoebe looked taken aback, she didn't know what Malcolm was talking about, but she didn't like his tone. He was simmering with anger, and she wasn't sure if she felt comfortable being alone with him.

"Don't worry Miss Horwat, you're perfectly safe with me." He growled Phoebe reluctantly entered his room. "What's all this about Mr Goode?"

"Take a seat and I'll tell you." Malcolm paced about the room; his long legs restless with agitation.

"Now I have a lot of respect for you Miss Horwat, but I'm a plain-speaking man so I'm just going to say my piece." Malcolm fixed her with a piercing glare.

"As you know, I have lost my favourite fox head tie pin, I know I can't prove it, but I'll lay a pound to a penny I saw it being sold in Cohen's the jewellers on Wellfield Road."

Phoebe sighed, she thought Malcom had moved on from this old news, what was the point of him haranguing her about it now? "Mr Goode I really don't…."

"Hear me out Miss Horwat before you jump down my throat…. I know everyone thinks I am mistaken and that I must have lost the tie pin somewhere, but how does that explain all the other things that have been going on around here?"

"What other things?"

"I know for a fact that a quantity of sweets has been taken… I sometimes keep some stock in here whilst I use my van for… er other purposes."

Phoebe's heart sank a little, "sweets?" She said weakly.

"Yes sweets… not many, but that's *not* the point…. After I became suspicious about my tie pin, I set a few traps to solve the mystery and once I started looking, I spotted these things going on." Malcolm wiped his brow. He'd played a patient game and now he was certain of his ground. "A ten-bob note has been lifted from my wallet, a five-shilling postal order has gone from my bedside table drawer, a pair of silver cufflinks has disappeared, a…" Malcolm was ticking off his fingers.

"What exactly are you accusing me of Mr Goode?" Phoebe said sharply.

"That's the point Miss Horwat…. I'm not accusing *you* of anything. I'm sorry to admit it, but for several weeks I have been spying on you."

"Spying on me!" Phoebe yelped.

"Not *you* personally, but keeping an eye on your movements," Mr Goode added hastily. "At the beginning when I noticed things going missing, I had to suspect anybody who came and went in this house…. You have to see it from my point of view?" Malcom looked apologetic.

Phoebe's heart sank, she knew exactly how Malcolm felt, she nodded, her lips set in a grim line.

"Once I was absolutely certain you were not about when these things were going missing then I *knew* it wasn't you who was doing it." Malcolm could tell she was annoyed by his admission of spying, but at the beginning he didn't know if Phoebe had something to do with the mystery, or if she was a victim like himself.

"So, you see, I had to know when you were *out* of the house and when you were *in* for my plan to work" Malcolm rubbed his chin; he wasn't proud of admitting he'd been spying on his landlady's movements; he liked Phoebe.

"I now know for an absolute fact that when you are out of the house, Carol Jones goes snooping in your private rooms." Malcolm stood square in front of Phoebe and waited for his words to sink in.

Phoebe's face dropped, the strange glimmer she thought she saw from the street the other evening was not a figment of her imagination, or a reflection from a streetlight.

"As the weeks have gone by. she's been getting cocky and overconfident; thinks we'd never suspect her, but I'm on to her now."

"Are you absolutely sure Mr Goode… this is a very serious accusation." Phoebe struggled to believe that the sweet-natured, mild-mannered, music teacher was a sneak thief.

"I know it's very serious Miss Horwat, but then so is losing my property… and can you tell me, hand on heart that you haven't noticed your things going missing as well… not even small things?" Malcolm challenged.

"I…. I'm not sure," Phoebe lied.

"She's crafty, I'll give her that… it's a bit like that game we used to play as kids; you know the one, you get a tray full of things and one by one an object is removed, and then you have to say what's gone missing, and it's almost impossible to say which thing has gone. It's only when quite a few things have been removed, or something special goes that you notice the loss."

Phoebe nodded she knew the game well.

"Well, that's how Carol operates, she takes a small item, and it isn't missed, it might even take a few weeks for the loss to be discovered and then it's easy to blame the owner for losing it. I've often heard her wandering around upstairs when she has no business to, she always scarpers back to her own room if anyone comes in."

Phoebe gasped she could hardly believe her ears. Now Malcolm mentioned it, she did often hear Carol walking quickly back to her room when Phoebe came in, she'd always assumed Carol must have been using the bathroom.

"I reckon she snoops as well; reads things she shouldn't, letters, documents and the like. That's how people like her operate, they store away a bit of information until it might come in handy, if there's nothing to steal there's often something to trade."

Phoebe shivered as if someone walked over her grave, if Malcolm was right then Carol had probably read her letters from Deirdre. Phoebe wracked her brain to think if the letters contained incriminating bits of information about their relationship with the Prosser family next door. And her own letters to Deirdre, sometimes she took a couple of days to write her latest information, on more than one occasion she'd left her half-written letter tucked in the unlocked bureau. When Phoebe went out did Carol come snooping around in her rooms, looking in cupboards hunting for information to use, reading her letters?

Phoebe felt her heart hardened, *you've gone soft since you've been living here,* she thought to herself, in the past the old Phoebe of Tiger Bay would not have been duped by a smiling con artist like Carol.

"Mr Goode, thanks for letting me know this…I've obviously been a trusting fool; duped by a smartly dressed woman with a pretty face and a well-spoken voice. I never suspected Carol could do something like this. So, you say you have proof?"

"I do Miss Horwat…"

"Call me Phoebe," she interrupted, "all my friends call me Phoebe."

"I do have proof Phoebe, and you must call me Malcolm," he smiled; his eyes were softer now, he had found an ally in Phoebe.

"Carol doesn't know it yet, but today she's just taken two forged ten-shilling notes from a metal box I keep under the bed. I purposely left the box unlocked to see if she would bite….and she did, the notes are gone." Phoebe raised an eyebrow.

"Don't worry Phoebe, they aren't mine, I was given them by a friend who knows where he can get such items and I know for a fact that she will try to spend them tonight down at the Rose and Crown in Splott."

"How do you know that?" Phoebe gasped in admiration.

"I've spent a few nights following Miss Jones and she goes to the Rose and Crown at least four times a week and often meets with a bloke she knows for drinks. I reckon he's the one she passes any bits and pieces she's stolen to, her *fence* as they call them. I've watched her slip a few things to him on more than one occasion…. Whatever he is, they're in cahoots together!"

Phoebe shook her head in disbelief, she'd noticed Carol keeping late hours and she had assumed the woman had a man friend, but it seemed Carol Jones was keeping bad company, and not having a romantic affair after all.

Malcolm revealed he was good friends with the Hywel, the pubs landlord, so it was easy for him to get information about the activities of the striking Miss Jones when she visited The Rose and Crown. Many a time Malcolm watched what Carol was getting up to from a discreet distance in a booth by the bar.

"Hywel is an old mate and he's been tipped off that she's got forgeries in her purse, and he'll be on the look-out for them. The minute she tries to pass the forgeries over the counter he'll nab her and call the police."

"But how do you know she'll spend them at the pub tonight…. She might spend them elsewhere?" Phoebe had to admire Malcolm's cunning. Malcolm tapped his nose. "Whoever it is that Carol meets in The Rose, he doesn't pick up her bills for her, in fact I've noticed she often pays for him. And our sweet and smiley Carol has got quite an expensive drinking habit; rather too fond of the Gin is Carol."

"She certainly has two sides to her." Phoebe would never have guessed this was the same Carol Jones.

"Oh yes Carol can be very devious, and those smart clothes she wears cost a few bob. Never in a million years could she earn enough to pay for her fancy lifestyle from giving a few singing lessons to kids. It stands to reason, if she had a good steady income behind her she wouldn't be renting a just single room in Roath." Malcolm said.

Phoebe had to admit that Carol did always look very smartly dressed, it never occurred to her that her lodger must be living beyond her means.

"It seems Carol pours on the charm wherever she goes, I'm prepared to bet she's debts all over the place, and she has sweet talked poor Hywel in to allowing her to have a sizable tab behind the bar for her evening meals and drinks."

Now Phoebe thought about it, Carol was rarely at home in an evening, and she'd never asked Phoebe if she could use the kitchen stove. "Are you saying she eats out every night as well?"

She eats there most nights, and she doesn't stint herself either. According to Hywel she does settle the tab regularly, probably once she's sold a few things would be my guess, so he hasn't been too bothered about letting her run up a tab before; he thought she was respectable and good for the money. Now Hywel knows what she's like, he's going to ask for payment to settle the tab in full tonight…. And Hywel won't let her pass those duff notes to him." Malcolm tapped his nose and smiled wolfishly.

"Malcolm Goode, you have the makings of either a great crook or a great detective." Phoebe chuckled.

"Why thank you, Phoebe," Malcolm gave a mock bow.

"Tell me though, where *is* Carol getting all her stuff from, no disrespect to you Malcolm, but she can't get *that* much from here?"

"You're right. I don't reckon she's much of a music teacher at all. Oh, I'm sure she's got a good enough education to teach kiddies a few bits and pieces; enough to make herself look the part, but I reckon it's just an excuse to get into other homes where people have got a few bob. Once she's been invited inside the house for these lessons by the parents, she's got her opportunity. Then over the following weeks she's got the chance to lift a few things here and there…. or worse maybe even get to know when the household are away so her gentleman friend can pop in and help himself to a few things."

"Phwee," Phoebe whistled. Carol Jones was certainly a lot tougher than she looked.

"I reckon she's always shifting around and moving on when she thinks people have wangled her tricks. She won't stop here a minute longer if she knows her cover is blown."

"Is she in the house now?" Phoebe wanted to check something out.

"No."

"Right, come upstairs with me Malcolm and you keep an eye on the front door from the landing, if you see her come in alert me by knocking on the bathroom door and shouting out- *is it occupied.*"

Malcolm and Phoebe rushed up the stairs, "I'm going in my room first, if what you say is true about her snooping, then I reckon I'm missing something already." In her heart she knew Malcolm was right about Carol, it was all starting to make sense, beneath the smooth and smiling charm and girly giggles was a calculating, manipulative liar.

Malcolm stood watch on the landing whilst Phoebe headed for her dressing table, as she suspected, the little pot on the dressing table which had contained Edmund's ring from his lover Piers Loxley, was empty. *The distinctive, gold engraved signet ring was gone.*

Phoebe hurried out of her room and shut the door behind her. *The sneaky little bitch!*

"Well, I'm sorry to say Malcolm you're right about Carol going into my room, she *has* taken a man's gold signet ring which used to be in a little trinket box on my dressing table." Phoebe felt furious and sad in equal measure.

"Was it valuable?"

"Yes, in more ways than one…. And if it wasn't for you asking me to check if anything was missing, I probably wouldn't have noticed it was gone for months" Phoebe said grimly. "You keep watch Malcolm; I'm going in her room to see what I can find… two can play at this game!"

Phoebe moved quickly through Carol's things; she hunted high and low, Phoebe couldn't find anything, it appeared that Miss Jones got rid of things as quickly as she could.

But then, just as Phoebe was about to give up the hunt, she found the proof she was looking for. Tucked under Carol's underwear Phoebe found the most incriminating item of all… her precious silver rosary.

The rosary was the one item which was more difficult for Carol to offload; the gold ring, fox head tie pin and silver cufflinks were easy to sell, but a religious item, as the jeweller Mr Cohen observed, was not in demand.

You thieving little cow, Phoebe muttered under her breath.

Having seen enough, Phoebe made sure to leave everything exactly as she found it and shut the door behind her. She needed to discuss her next move with Malcolm. She couldn't risk Carol knowing they had discovered what she was up to.

Phoebe put her finger to her lips, she would tell Malcolm what she had discovered in the privacy of her back parlour.

Malcolm and Phoebe hurried back down the stairs.

"Come for a cup of tea Malcolm… I certainly owe you, without your help I would never have known I had a thief under my roof."

Phoebe related the story of the lost rosary and how she had hunted high and low for it and even reported it missing to the police. She didn't dare admit to Malcolm that for a moment she had even suspected the children next door of taking it.

"Bingo…. So, we have her!" Malcolm crowed. "She won't be able to wriggle out of that one."

Phoebe looked puzzled. "What do you mean Malcolm?"

"Well, I've been a bit concerned that the lying little minx would manage to wriggle out of trouble at The Rose and Crown. I can imagine her trying to simper in that posh voice of hers and persuade the police that she was a victim of fraud. And I thought she might bat her eyelids and tell some tall tale about a dodgy customer who must have paid her with dud notes and that she didn't know they were fake.."

Phoebe's mouth formed into a small oh, it hadn't occurred to her that Carol's plausible veneer of respectability would make it easy for her to wriggle out of trouble.

"The fact that you have reported the loss of your rosary to the police a few weeks ago means that Carol is technically guilty of theft." Malcolm laughed out loud. "The light-fingered little cow can't wriggle out of it now… even if she tries to say she found it in the street, the very fact that she made no attempt to hand it over to the police station, means in law she is guilty of theft."

"Are you sure?"

"I certainly am. If you have left the rosary exactly where she put it then when the police search her room they will find it *and* one or two more of those fake bank notes if I'm not mistaken."

Malcolm dashed down the stairs and came back with two more suspiciously fresh looking, brown ten-shilling bank notes in his hand and a small metal tie stud boasting a what looked like a diamond. "This should do the job. Don't worry Phoebe, the tie pin isn't real, it's a bit like our Carol, flashy but fake." He grinned.

Phoebe's jaw dropped; Malcolm Goode was certainly a force to be reckoned with.

Malcolm slipped into Carol's room and was out again in a trice, "job done!" Malcolm said with a self-satisfied grin on his face.

"How will we get them to search her room?"

"Don't you worry, just leave that to me Phoebe." Malcolm winked. "All I ask is that you keep a straight face and if you're asked about things going missing in the house then just make sure you back me up. Between us we'll get the better of Carol Jones and, with any luck, you'll get your rosary back tonight."

Chapter 21

Malcolm went out for the evening determined to spring the trap to catch their thief, Phoebe didn't know precisely what he was planning, but Malcolm said it was better that she left it to him and stayed well out of it. *Better not to know too much Phoebe.* Malcolm had said as he tapped his nose.

Phoebe felt jittery and on edge waiting to hear what came of his cunning plan, even though she had a cheery fire burning in the grate she still felt a chill to her bones. All she could do now was wait.

When a loud rapping came on the front door, only about an hour after Malcolm had left, Phoebe nearly jumped out of her skin. It was dark now and after her conversation with Malcolm she was nervous about answering the door, especially since she was alone in the house.

"Who is it?" she called to the figure on the other side of the glass. She switched on the porch light.

"It's only me, Billy." He shouted through the door.

Phoebe unlocked the door; *it was stupid she felt so jittery and on edge.*

"Hello Phoebe, can I come in for a few minutes? Ivy asked me to come and see you."

"Come on in Billy, don't stand on the doorstep" She could see his face looked grim. "It's not like you to call around at night, is something the matter?" Phoebe led him through to the parlour, her heart tightened a little with dread, *something must be wrong if Ivy has sent Billy.*

"Don't worry Phoebe it's not a problem for *our* family, but something is wrong over at the Ashworth's and Ivy was wondering if you would help her hold the fort until things are sorted."

Over a cup of tea Billy related the whole sorry tale of Norah's collapse and Jack's rush to hospital leaving Ivy to look after June and the five young Ashworth children.

"Oh, that poor woman!" Phoebe said sympathetically; kind, friendly Norah had a special place in Phoebe's heart. "Jack must be out of mind with worry about her, and poor Ivy finding Norah like that, it must have been one hell of a shock."

Billy nodded, he remembered Ivy's stricken face when she answered the door to him.

"Five little children and one of those a baby just a few days old needing its Mam to nurse him; it's far too much for the poor girl to cope with if she doesn't get some help. Of course, I'll come over for a few days, Ivy can't possibly manage all those children and a new-born baby on her own." Phoebe couldn't sit about mithering about the petty, mean-minded Carol Jones; this was a *real* crisis and Ivy needed her at Wilson Road.

Phoebe would just have to hope that Malcolm would deal with Carol. One thing was for certain though, Phoebe thought mutinously, *the treacherous Carol Jones will be marched out of my house as fast as her feet can carry her*.

"Thanks Phoebe, Ivy knew she could rely on you. Ivy won't let Norah down, and I know she'll move heaven and earth to look after those kiddies and do all the housework, but there are only so many hours in a day and she can't do it all on her own." Billy shook his head, he knew it was selfish of him, but he didn't want Ivy run ragged by a troop of someone else's children. Ivy already looked exhausted already.

"Everything is sorted for the children this evening Phoebe, but it's probably going to take some time before Norah comes out of hospital and Jack has to go to work in the morning.... So, Ivy really needs your help as soon as you can make it over to Wilson Road." Billy pleaded. In truth Ivy didn't have a clue how long she would need Phoebe for, but at least having Phoebe around for a while, would take the pressure off.

"Tell Ivy I'll be straight over first thing in the morning, I'll buy the milk like she's asked me to, and I'll stay as long as she needs me to… let's hope it all gets sorted in no time at all," Phoebe smiled.

Phoebe knew that time was not on their side. Ivy was getting married soon and, if the problem with Norah continued, the two bedroomed house would suddenly seem very crowded with Billy moving in after the wedding. If Phoebe was still needed to help with the children and the Ashworth baby was still there in the house with Ivy, then things could get tricky… *still they could cross that bridge when they came to it.*

"Thanks Phoebe, I'll be off now, but I will come over tomorrow to see how you and Ivy are managing, and with any luck, maybe by then Jack will have some news about Norah."

Phoebe waved Billy off and retreated to the warmth of the parlour fire. She was grateful Ivy had found such a kind man to be happy with. *Poor Norah.*

*

Phoebe must have dozed off in front of the fire, the coals had sunk low in the grate and the room was in total darkness apart from the glow from the embers and a small side lamp. The mantle clock showed it was half past ten o'clock.

"Miss Horwat…." Malcolm's voice and the light touch on her shoulder roused her from her sleep. "Miss Horwat can you wake up please the police are here." Malcolm's voice had an urgency which quickly brought Phoebe to her senses.

"Uhh… uhh." Half-awake and half-asleep Phoebe was startled awake, her eyes wide with fright.

"Don't worry Miss Horwat," Malcolm said kindly, Phoebe noticed he had reverted to a formal way of addressing her. "The police just need your permission to enter Miss Jones's room." Malcolm looked at Phoebe intently, his eyes pleading for her to go along with things and follow his lead.

Phoebe stood up, brushed the wrinkles from her dress and looked to see a constable standing in the hall.

"Mr Goode what on earth is going on?" Phoebe said sharply, she wasn't sure how she was supposed to react. "Why are the police in my house?"

"I asked the police to come back to my room Miss Horwat, but they need your permission to enter anywhere else on the premises." Malcolm explained.

"Would you mind explaining to me officer what it is that you want at this time of night in my house," Phoebe fixed the young constable with a beady stare.

Constable Hooper moved forward out of the darkness and introduced himself. "Good evening Madam, I just need to ask you a few brief questions and ask if you would be so good as to allow me to search the upstairs bedroom of your lodger Miss Carol Jones…. We have reason to believe that she may have goods in her room which might be of interest to us."

Phoebe raised an eyebrow. It still made Phoebe nervous to see a uniformed officer in her hall.

"I understand that you rent a room to a woman calling herself Miss Carol Jones?" Pc Hooper stood with his pencil poised to take notes.

"Yes, she lives here as my lodger, and she tells me that she teaches music." Phoebe said cautiously.

"Have you had cause recently to be concerned about items going missing around the house?"

Phoebe could see Malcolm fixing her with an encouraging glare.

"It's hard to say officer, I'm not a wealthy woman, but now you mention it some small items might have gone." Phoebe paused to think a moment. "I reported the loss of a silver rosary with ebony beads to the police which had great sentimental value to me …. At first, I *was* convinced it was in the house because I always keep it beside this chair and so I hunted high and low for it but was nowhere to be found. Then I thought I might have lost it coming home from church and so as I said, I did report the loss to the Wellfield Road Police Station a few weeks ago.

"I see, did you ask if either of your lodgers had seen the item in question Miss Horwat?"

"Well, you certainly asked *me* if I'd seen it Miss Horwat and I know for a fact I told Miss Jones to keep an eye out for it," Malcolm said swiftly before Phoebe could reply.

The constable sent him a warning glare.

"I remember now, I *did* ask you Mr Goode, but I can't remember about asking Miss Jones. I was so upset and flustered at the time to lose it; I believe my Godmother paid quite a lot for it; it was a special present for my first Holy Communion." Phoebe rubbed her eyes as if she was still half asleep.

"Well, I certainly mentioned it to Miss Jones, even if you didn't Miss Horwat. Malcolm said stoutly. "I told her about it because you might have dropped in the porch or the hallway and she comes into the house that way, and she told me she hadn't seen it."

"Constable Hooper what is this all leading to, as I said I reported the loss a few weeks ago?" Phoebe sounded and looked weary.

"We are just trying to build up a picture Miss Horwat, and it would help us enormously if we could search the lady's room." Pc Hooper was giving nothing away.

"You'd better follow me then," Phoebe looked at Malcolm, he gave a brief incline of the head as if to say *trust me.*

"I must say officer, it's quite upsetting to have the police in the house… I do hope I'm doing the right thing letting you in to go through her private things." Phoebe's heart was racing she knew that the officer would discover things in Carol's room, she tried to keep a composed face.

"It won't take more than a few minutes Miss Horwat. I promise I shan't make a mess and if you could stand in with me and watch the search then you can be satisfied everything is being done correctly and perhaps this matter can be sorted by the end of the evening. Miss Jones is currently being held at the police station, but she is adamant that she has nothing to hide and is anxious to return home." Officer Hooper had been very impressed by the well dressed and well-spoken Miss Jones.

When Hywel, the landlord of The Rose and Crown raised the roof over the fake ten-shilling notes Carol presented when he had demanded she settle her bar tab, Carol appeared rocked by the discovery of that the notes in her purse were forgeries.

"Oh, my goodness how terrible… I can't possibly imagine how they came to be in my purse." Carol oozed, fluttering her eyelashes at Hywel.

When Malcolm Goode sprang from a nearby booth, where he'd been sat enjoying a quiet pint, he suddenly pulled a dud brown bank note from his wallet and joined the fray.

"Hey Miss Jones…. This note you gave me earlier is dud an' all. You're passing off fake notes!" Malcolm declared loudly; he had the attention of the other drinkers in the pub now. "Look it's another bloody fake….

You've cheated me!" Malcolm waved the fake note for all to see, his face rigid with fury.

"Nonsense, I haven't given you a fake note, this is just some sort of silly mistake… I'm not standing around to be insulted by you Malcolm Goode, because I really don't know what you're talking about." Carol said sweetly, her face a picture of injured innocence and her eyebrows arched in surprise. She turned to go.

"Not so fast…. Oh, but I think you *do* know what I'm talking about." Malcolm grabbed Carol by the arm.

"Let go of me, you horrible man," Carol gasped. She tried to shake her arm free from Malcolm's vice like grasp, her smile dropped, and a hard sneer crossed her face. Her drinking companion, seeing the ruckus was turning serious, quickly stood up and left the pub whilst all eyes were on the drama unfolding at the bar.

"Not on your nelly, you aren't going anywhere Miss Jones. I'm making a citizen's arrest. Hywel, you call the Police, she's got some explaining to do about this fake money, let them decide who's telling the truth and who isn't." Malcolm said angrily.

Carol looked around wildly, her friend had scarpered and left her to face the music on her own.

Once the police arrived the game was up. All Carol Jones could hope to do now was convince the police that she too had been a victim of fraud, and not a perpetrator.

"This is all a big mistake officer, and I shall be making a complaint, "she said haughtily. Reluctantly, Carol had to allow herself to be taken to the local police station to make a statement and await her fate.

Malcolm Goode insisted the police come to the house and check her room before Carol Jones was released.

"She's a con-artist officer, I've met her sort before. Things have been going missing in the house and I reckon now that she's got something to do with it…. And I'll lay a pound to a penny she's got more of those duff notes tucked away somewhere, you can't let her come back to Alma Road and scarper. I'm sure the landlady, Miss Horwat will let you check her room and if Miss Jones has got nothing to hide, then she's got nothing to worry about. You can check my room as well if you like, I've got nothing to hide." Malcolm asserted confidently.

Anxious to resolve the matter before the night shift ended Officer Hooper agreed to check out the matter and hopefully the delightful Miss Jones could be on her way.

"You'd better see for yourself officer," Phoebe switched on the light. "I think you had better stay on the landing Mr Goode, I can't give you permission to come in here, not when it's just your word something is the matter." Phoebe sounded cautious.

"Thank you Miss Horwat, I'll just look in the obvious places, as I said I won't be long." Constable Hooper glanced under the iron bedstead, glimpsed under the pillows and gave a cursory look in and on top of the wardrobe. "Nothing amiss so far." The officer said loudly. "That just leaves the drawers in this chest then I think I can be on my way."

Officer Hooper pulled out the top drawer, a blush rose up on his cheeks as he saw it was a drawer full of ladies' underwear. His hand hovered over the delicate items, reluctant to interfere with such intimate garments.

Phoebe took her cue, "I think I should go through those personal things Constable Cooper, if you'd like to watch me do it."

"Good idea Miss Horwat."

Phoebe carefully took out stacks of underwear and placed them on the side a layer at a time, and there on the bottom of the pile were two, crisp ten-shilling notes, a tie pin and her precious rosary.

"That is my rosary!" Phoebe gasped… "she's got my rosary in her drawer; I'd know it anywhere." Phoebe held up the delicate intricate chain.

The officer looked in the drawer, he scooped out the notes and tie pin. "Is this tie pin also yours Miss Horwat?"

As if on cue Malcolm stuck his head around the door, "that's my tie pin Constable! I lost my gold one, or it was stolen more like it," Malcolm said darkly, "I bought that silver one as a cheap substitute until I could afford a better one; she must have taken it from my room…. I bet she took the first one an' all the thieving little cow!" Malcolm sounded furious.

The officer shot Malcolm Goode a warning glance. "Mr Goode I would appreciate it if you could keep a civil tongue in your head. Since Miss Horwat here has already reported this rosary as lost and yet it appears to be hidden away in Miss Jones's room, depriving Miss Horwat of her property, I think we now have enough evidence to keep Miss Jones at the station for further questioning."

Pc Hooper tucked the two bank notes and silver tie pin in his pocket, "I'll keep these Mr Goode," he then held out his hand towards Phoebe. "May I take that rosary away with me please Miss Horwat. I will need to take *all* these items with me to the police station as part of the ongoing investigation."

Phoebe reluctantly handed over her precious rosary, "but it's mine officer…. when will I get it back?"

"I will of course give you a receipt for all the items recovered from this room Miss Horwat and some other officers will come around tomorrow to do a more detailed search of Miss Jones's room to see if there are any other items of interest tucked away."

"But I'm not here tomorrow," Phoebe wailed.

"That's alright Miss Horwat, I'm here. If you give this officer permission to search this room again then I can let them in when they come. I'll stay with them to see they don't make a mess." Malcolm offered helpfully; he gave the officer a hard stare.

"Thank you Mr Goode, that would be a big help. I'm going to help a neighbour who has had a stroke, and I can't let her down." Phoebe smiled gratefully, it seemed as if Malcolm's cunning plan to bring down Carol Jones was working.

"Leave it to me Miss Horwat," Malcolm smiled.

Chapter 22

Phoebe packed a few things for her stay with Ivy and caught the bus over to Ely where she was needed. She would certainly be away from the house for a few days, she would have to let Malcolm deal with the police and any fallout from the arrest of Carol Jones.

Phoebe gave the officer Ivy's address on Wilson Road; they could find her if she was needed and she was going away secure in the knowledge that, thanks to Malcolm, she had cut out a thieving traitor from the heart of her home. Ivy and Norah needed her now, and her duty lay there until things were sorted. Let the police deal with her lying, two-faced lodger.

Now she knew him better, Phoebe felt safe leaving Malcolm Goode in charge of the house whilst she was away. She'd left strict instructions that Carol Jones was not to be allowed into the house to collect her things unless Malcolm or the police officer were there to keep an eye on her.

"I don't trust her an inch!" Phoebe said furiously. "And you can tell her to sling her hook if ever she comes back to collect her stuff and make sure she leaves her house key on the hall stand. I can't thank you enough for all you've done for me Malcolm; thanks to you I've got my peace of mind back." Phoebe smiled it felt good to have a new friend and ally.

After the police left Malcolm had told Phoebe how the strange evening in The Rose and Crown unfolded. Once Phoebe heard how the whole crafty trap played out, she developed a new respect for the cunning Malcolm Goode.

"Her face was absolutely priceless Phoebe, when I grabbed her arm and I announced I was making a citizen's arrest," he chortled.

"I didn't know you could actually make a citizen's arrest?" Phoebe gasped

"I didn't know for sure you could either, but then neither did she!" Malcolm grinned. "Lucky for me the police were just around the corner and the bloke she was with scarpered and left her to face the music on her own, so I just hung on to her arm until the police arrived and handed her over. People like her always have lots of skeletons in the closet, I'm prepared to bet that once the police start digging away they'll find even more on our Miss Jones."

Phoebe shook her head in disbelief, it was hard to imagine that the sweet, innocent looking Carol Jones was such a brazen trickster.

"Will you be alright looking after the house for me Malcolm?"

"I will be careful to keep a look out Phoebe. Don't forget there was that bloke with her in the pub, I've often seen him around with Carol and he might try to get her stuff when she's down the nick…. He won't get past me though."

Phoebe looked concerned.

"She's such a tricky cow she might have had a spare key cut for all you know; if I were you, I'd get the locks changed in case he tries to slip in whilst you're out, I can't be here all the time." Malcolm felt sure they hadn't seen or heard the last of Carol.

"I hadn't thought about the house keys." Phoebe gasped. "I don't reckon I'm going to get any more rent money out of her, so locking her and her fancy man out is an excellent idea." Malcolm was right, the locks must be changed immediately.

"Consider it done, I'll sort it today and you can pay me back when you come home. You go see your friend and don't worry about the house; I know where you are if I have to get hold of you Phoebe." Malcolm smiled.

"Thanks Malcolm, I owe you… I won't forget it." Phoebe smiled back, she thought how handsome he looked when his face was smiling and relaxed; the cocky, wise cracking, salesman persona he presented to the world was obviously just a front. She'd been wrong to dismiss him as a *bit of a spiv* when she first met him.

Malcolm Goode had gone up hugely in Phoebe's estimation.

"Yes and I won't accept any of those dud notes as payment either." He laughed.

*

Phoebe knocked Ivy's door, even from outside she could hear the plaintive wail of a fractious, tiny new-born. A frazzled looking Ivy answered the door.

"Thank goodness you've come Aunty Phoebe; I feel like I'm drowning." Ivy gasped. In the sitting room Jack was bawling at the top of his voice and June was clinging to Ivy's skirts sucking her thumb. Ivy had dark rings under her eyes, testament to a sleepless night spent marching up and down with a fretful Jack in her arms.

Phoebe took her coat off, rolled up her sleeves and gave Ivy a fierce hug, "don't worry luvvie, we'll manage between us. I've brought the tinned milk like you asked me to so if you make some up in a bottle I'm sure we'll have the little lad happy again."

Ivy, grateful for another pair of hands to share the load, left Phoebe jigging the hungry baby whilst she went into the kitchen and made up a bottle with the diluted tinned milk.

"That's the ticket Ivy…. Now, let me see if I can get this little lad settled for you, and you can make us both a nice cup of tea."

Over a cup of tea Ivy told Phoebe the whole ghastly story of Norah's dramatic collapse. "It's not looking good either Aunty Phoebe, Norah's in a coma and Jack doesn't know if she's going to come out of it, apparently they'll know more in the next few days."

Phoebe shook her head; the news was indeed worse than she thought. Baby Jack lay sleeping in her arms sated with a large bottle of milk and exhausted from crying.

"Norah can't breathe on her own now and *if* she does pull through the doctors have warned Jack that there might be lasting damage from the clot… it's all such a bloody mess and it's not going to be fixed anytime soon…. Poor Norah." Ivy sighed.

"How are the other children managing without their Mam?" Phoebe's heart went out to the four young children.

"Gareth is the worst in some ways… Norah always understood what he was trying to say, and he just keeps calling for his Mam poor lad, and nobody can explain to him why Norah has gone away." Tears started to roll down Ivy's cheeks, she was exhausted and frightened for her friend.

"Shh Ivy… now don't upset yourself, we've got to be strong for Norah's sake." Phoebe said firmly, it was no use to Norah if people went to pieces.

"I know Aunty Phoebe," Ivy sniffed.

"It sounds as if we are in it for the long haul my love. Does Jack have any family to help out?"

 "Jack said he's taking Lenny George and Gareth up to Merthyr for Norah's Mam Irene to look after until Norah is on the road to recovery and to take a bit of the weight off me… or should I say off us? And her sister -in-law will take Karen, it's not as hectic as it was." Ivy smiled weakly.

"That leaves us with this little mite to take care of," Phoebe nodded. That sounded a bit more manageable, but there was still June to be looked after as well. Phoebe smiled at the perfect little bundle in her arms flexing tiny starfish hands in his sleep.

"There's only room for the lads up in Merthyr and Irene said she can't manage a new-born at her age." Ivy grimaced; she had noticed that Jack

Ashworth wanted nothing to do with his baby son. Since the accident he hadn't held baby Jack, not even once; all his talk and concern was for the older children.

"How's Jack faring under the circumstances?" Phoebe asked.

Ivy just shook her head, she didn't want to speak ill of Jack, but it cut her to the quick the way he dismissed the tiny, precious bundle in Phoebe's arms without so much as giving him a hug or a hold.

Phoebe raised an eyebrow.

"I don't want to run the man down Aunty Phoebe, but I'm worried about him, he seems so angry, especially with baby Jack. He says that he wishes Jack had never been born… and if Norah doesn't recover, I'm not sure he will ever forgive the poor little lad for being born."

"What a load of nonsense… the man needs his head seeing to. It's not this little one's fault his Mam is in a hospital bed fighting for her life. He needs to pull himself together; this little lad needs his Mam *and* his Da." Phoebe said furiously. *Why did men forget they were at the root of a lot of these things? The poor baby couldn't be blamed for Norah's plight, he didn't ask to be born.*

"I know Aunty Phoebe; I think he's just lashing out; he can't *really* blame baby Jack for the stroke. Let's hope Norah makes a full recovery and then he can put all this behind him… Poor man. I know he loves Norah and he's been a good father to all his other children… I'm sure he'll come around eventually." Ivy said loyally.

He'd better or else this little one will have a very miserable future, Phoebe thought to herself, but she decided she'd mind her tongue today, there was no point in worrying Ivy any more than was necessary about the fate of baby Jack. For now, Phoebe and Ivy would have to give baby Jack all the love and cuddles he needed.

Chapter 23

As soon as Malcolm Goode grabbed her arm and caused a hullabaloo in the pub, Carol Jones knew she'd been rumbled; she'd been careless; and she was paying the price for that carelessness. Now all she could do was brazen it out and hope for the best, with any luck she'd get off lightly again; magistrates were always suckers for a well-spoken voice, a pretty face, and a sob story.

Carol blamed Roger for getting her into this scrape. He'd kept pushing her to get more items for him to sell and move on; and despite all his promises to her to be better, he was back to his old bad habits spending far too much money down at the bookies and pouring copious amounts of whiskey down his throat; she was sick of his lazy, whining ways. If it hadn't been for Roger nagging her to get more money, she wouldn't have gone into Malcolm's room a second time and got caught trying to pass those fake notes she found under the bed.

To cap it all, Roger, the slippery bastard, had legged it from the pub leaving her to explain everything to the police. If she ever managed to wriggle out of this scrape, she would cheerfully swing for Roger Pritchard; they'd been married ten years and in all that time the spineless, greedy, sot of a man had brought her nothing but trouble and a never-ending mountain of gambling debts to pay off.

Roger had always promised her he would stop the heavy drinking and gambling, but he always fell at the first hurdle; he was nothing but trouble, always was and always would be.

She shouldn't have listened to him; it was always her taking all the risks whilst he watched from the side-lines and kept his nose clean. *You broke the golden rule Carol, you should never piss on your own doorstep.*

Carol thought she had the old spinster Phoebe Horwat wrapped around her little finger, flattering her, smiling sweetly, charming the old girl when the rent was a few days late. But she never did like Malcolm Goode; Carol was sure he was on the fiddle with Trebor, and he always looked at her as if she was a turd on the bottom of his shoe. I'm certain he was up to something, I just never found out what it was, but I won't stop looking. Carol seethed as she sat in the police cell; she wished she'd trusted her instincts where Malcolm Goode was concerned.

All her flattery and girlish simpering had been wasted on Malcom, he'd seen right through her and now he'd trapped her in her own deceit. She could tell by the triumphant look on Malcolm's face it was a set up; he'd out foxed her…. and fool that she was, she had fallen for it.

Whatever happens, I'm not finished yet, revenge is dish best served cold, and I have an excellent memory, Carol fumed to herself.

I still have a few aces up my sleeve which might come in handy for the future and when I get out of this miserable hole, I'll make it on my own. She vowed inwardly. *I'm done with that greedy, useless husband of mine dragging me down like a ball and chain; he was the one who lost me my job as a music teacher at that posh school in the first place and now look what he's brought me to!*

Any officer glancing into the cell would see an anxious, pretty woman looking distressed and nervous, trapped in a cell over an apparent misunderstanding; but underneath the sweet smile and down cast eyes Mrs Carol-Ann Pritchard was plotting and scheming.

The letters her landlady had tucked away in her bureau had made for *very* interesting reading and maybe one day Carol could use the information she'd gleaned to her advantage. She wasn't letting Phoebe Horwat off the hook that easily.

*

It was eight o'clock when Billy called around to see how Phoebe and Ivy were managing; he was worried Ivy was taking on too much and their wedding seemed to have got entirely forgotten in all the upset at the Ashworth household; he hadn't even bought Ivy a wedding ring yet; he needed her to go shopping with him and soon.

Phoebe answered the door, "hello Billy," she kept her voice low, "come on in Ivy is just putting June to bed, she'll be down in a few minutes. Phoebe led Billy into the sitting room, pressing her finger to her lips for Billy to keep quiet. "Jack's asleep in here," Phoebe whispered.

The baby lay sleeping on the sofa wrapped in a shawl, his arms flung above his head and his eyelids flickering in a deep sleep, rosebud lips gave the hint of a smile.

"He's a little smasher," Billy said softly, and they both tip toed out to the kitchen.

"He is that… and a proper angel, it's a shame his father can't see it though." Phoebe pursed her lips, Jack Ashworth had flown in and out at teatime to tell Phoebe and Ivy the latest news about Norah and he hadn't so much as glanced at baby Jack, it was as if the child didn't exist.

Billy's eyes widened in surprise; *how could any man not feel for his infant son who was only just over a week old?*

"The man blames baby Jack for robbing Norah of her health. Yet the reality is that the poor woman had told Ivy at least a dozen times that she didn't want any more children, but Jack wouldn't listen and now Norah is paying the price of having another baby. Jack thinks it's the baby's fault she's had a stroke and he can't even bear to look at the poor little lad." Phoebe shook her head; she was angry Jack had turned his face away from his tiny, innocent son.

"How is Norah doing?" Billy was hoping that Norah would make a speedy recovery for more than the obvious reasons; the normally tidy little house he would soon be moving into was crowded and chaotic and Ivy never had a moment to herself.

"It's not looking good, she's still in a coma and the doctors have warned Jack it doesn't bode well, but Jack still lives in hope she'll bounce back… He keeps going on about the miraculous recovery made by Sean Riley who lives at the top of Wilson Road."

Billy had seen the limping Sean Riley a few times in the street when he visited Wilson Road, the man was far from a picture of health, if that was the best Norah had to look forward to, then Phoebe was right to be worried.

"Sean was at death's door after that accident he had down on the docks, and he *has* made a marvellous recovery, all things considered." Phoebe admitted, "but Sean's still not right and it took years of hospital treatments and nursing by Eileen to get the man this far, who is going to do all that for Norah *and* look after all these children whilst she's on the mend, you tell me that?" Phoebe was irritated that Jack seemed to be in such denial about Norah. Even if Norah survived, her recovery might take years. What did Jack think would happen to his young family in the meantime? Billy grimaced; the situation did look bleak for the whole Ashworth family. Phoebe had made a fair point even if Norah did survive the damage done by the clot, she was looking at an awfully long recovery if Sean's example was anything to go by. Ivy couldn't spend her life looking after Norah and all the children.

"Five young children! I mean I ask you…it's a lot for a fit young woman to tackle but, who knows what state Norah's going to be in if she comes home? I reckon Jack needs to ask the doctors what they think her future's likely to be and to start making some proper plans. He can't just bury his head in the sand and hope for the best." Phoebe said darkly.

"That's such a shame Phoebe, the man certainly has got a lot on his plate and the bills will still need paying." Billy had sympathy for Jack, the man was the family breadwinner.

"Exactly, he's got to go out to work every day, so who does he think is going to be doing all the rest about the house as well as looking after those kiddies? Norah's Mam is keeping the three boys for as long as she can but that still leaves Karen and the baby." Phoebe could hear baby Jack starting to stir in the front room.

"If Norah doesn't make a good recovery, what do you think will happen to the baby then Phoebe?"

"I reckon Jack might give him up for adoption Billy, he's a good-looking lad and he's come from a good home he'll make some childless couple very happy. If Norah isn't on the mend soon then I reckon Jack Ashworth won't want to see his little face every day anyway. Jack has already said that Norah's Mam Irene has ruled out looking after the baby because she couldn't cope with a young 'un."

Billy could see Phoebe looked upset.

"If Norah can't pull through and make a quick recovery then I reckon that little lad in there will lose both his Mam and his Da," Phoebe said sadly… Her heart bled for the blameless, unwanted child.

Chapter 24

Bobby had made herself wonderfully comfortable nestled on James's lap; his faithful black Labrador dog Nero sat by his master' side, was not impressed by the tiny, fluffy interloper, but Nero knew better than to register his disapproval.

"Here's your tea James, and I've popped a shortbread finger on the saucer…. Well, I must say you certainly look popular." Deirdre smiled to see Bobby purring contentedly on James's lap and Nero with his noble, black head resting on James's knee.

"I'm irresistible aren't I, Bobby," James groped forward and tickled the kitten under the chin; and was rewarded with a loud rumbling purr of contentment.

"Harrumph," Deirdre snorted, "I feed and clean up after the fussy little madam and she lavishes all her attention on you… ungrateful creature!" Deirdre chuckled. James looked very at home settled on her armchair next to fire with her cat on his knee. *This is how Darby and Joan must feel,* she thought to herself.

Since burying old Bobby, and James getting her the new kitten the two of them had grown closer and more comfortable around each other.

"Deirdre, you and I have become good friends since you moved here, and it's really gladdened my heart to have found a new friend… thank you." James couldn't understand why a good, kind-hearted woman like Deirdre was living such a solitary life in Porthcawl. Deirdre was well spoken and thoughtful, kind, and practical in equal measure, what quirk of life had left Deirdre Thomas to be so overlooked? *Perhaps like him, she had a past she was keeping hidden, and she had re-invented herself in Porthcawl?*

A while ago James had mentioned to Deirdre that he had a long-lost daughter Ivy who was getting married soon. Deirdre absorbed the nugget of information and didn't pry, with her own complex situation with Phoebe, Rita and Edmund, Deirdre knew better than to ask awkward questions, if James wanted to tell her all about it, he surely would in his own good time.

"Umm…. Deirdre, you know I mentioned that my daughter Ivy was getting married, well I wanted to ask your advice about something." James cleared his throat; it had been bothering him for days about whether he should ask Ivy if he could attend the wedding.

Ivy had told him all about her fiancée Billy and how happy she was to be getting wed, but she hadn't actually invited James to attend the wedding to see her get married; he knew it was being petty and irrational, but his feelings were hurt. Was Ivy ashamed of him or did she just assume it was too much for him to travel such a long way?

Ivy had told him it was going to be a very small, no fuss no frills sort of affair, but it tugged at his heart that he had so little role in his daughter's life especially on her wedding day. Perhaps she hadn't mentioned to him about going to the registry office because it would it raise too many awkward questions about his past relationship with Betty. The doubt and anxiety were eating him up, he felt sure Deirdre would know what to do for the best.

"Of course, James, if I can help you in any way then I will." Deirdre smiled; she could feel that James was starting to trust her judgement.

"Ivy is my daughter, but I never knew I had fathered her until just before Christmas last year. Her mother Lizzie never told me I'd got her pregnant all those years ago and if she had I would of course done the right thing by her." James took a deep breath; he didn't know what Deirdre must think of him for having ruined an innocent young woman.

"I went off to war with her brother John, he was my best friend… but only one of us came back from the front and I know now that she took pity on me because of my injuries." James struggled to hold back a sob.

 It was hard for James to admit that whilst he did love Lizzie, he knew they had been foolish to do what they did. But the haunting memory of their lovemaking, and the beautiful soft comfort of Lizzie's body had lived with him and sustained him in his darkest hours; he *never* regretted loving her, he only wished their lives had turned out differently; he wished she had told him she was having his baby.

Deirdre held his hand and patted it, giving him encouragement to go on. "Lizzie had a dreadful time bringing up *our* daughter, her parents threw her out and she went through hell trying to survive with a baby to look after. I never had any idea that she had suffered so much and all the while she thought I must be dead." James remembered those dark days when he wished he *was* dead, stuck in hospitals gasping for breath with rotten lungs. Days when breathing felt like drowning, and only the memory of Lizzie stopped him giving up.

"But it was all a big mistake Deirdre, I was alive and living here in Porthcawl recovering my health as best I could, with my old Mam looking after me." James shook his head mortified that he had brought such shame and hardship on Lizzie; he was frightened that now Ivy might be ashamed of him and would prefer her life to be kept in two neat, separate compartments.

"When Lizzie found me again Deirdre, she was so kind and generous…. She's married of course now, and I don't want to upset her ever, *or* her new husband for that matter, but thanks to Lizzie, I know about my daughter, and even just having a small part in Ivy's life is so precious to me."

"Shh James, don't be so hard on yourself." Deirdre soothed, she thought of Rita Prosser, the baby who Phoebe had named Angela and was forced to give away. *How differently people cope with the hand Fate dealt them.*

"Ivy hasn't asked me to go to the wedding Deirdre, and I don't know why…. Oh, I know she's dismissed it as just a two-minute affair in a registry office with no fuss or ceremony, just a legal process to be got through, but I'd give anything to be there on her wedding day." James said longingly, his voice was choking with emotion.

"Does Ivy know how you feel?"

"No…. I haven't wanted to upset her or look like I'm barging in where I'm not wanted." James said sadly.

"Why don't we write to her, tell her how you feel and let her decide for herself… for all you know she might be delighted that you are prepared to make the effort to attend the wedding." Deirdre suggested.

"Do you think so Deirdre?" James brightened a little. "But I don't know if it's possible to go even if Ivy said "yes." How would I, an almost blind man, get there for heaven's sake?" James said glumly; the obstacles seemed insurmountable.

"Let's worry about the journey once you have your answer James…. If Ivy is pleased for you to go then I will make sure you get there," Deirdre said in her usual efficient manner.

"You are good to me Deirdre, what would I do without you?" He said softly and he meant it.

"Get away with you James…. What are friends for? Now shall I get a pen and paper and then you can dictate your letter to Ivy? I've got a first-class stamp in my purse and if I hurry, we can catch the last post. In a few days you will have your answer, one way or the other."

Chapter 27

Norah's breath seemed weaker today; ragged and shallow. Jack had to put his face so close to hers to hear the soft sound of air being pumped in and out of her lungs. Norah lay on the starched hospital bed looking, for all the world, like a wax doll, her pretty hair spread across the pillow and her impassive face a dull, lifeless white. There were no roses in her cheeks now and her sparkling eyes were closed. He could feel she was slipping away from him.

Jack sat as close to his wife's bed as he could and wept, "Oh God Norah, I'm so sorry…. I wish this had never happened; I love you Norah… I love you." It was a mantra Jack said to her repeatedly, hoping his words would filter into her deep sleep and comfort her.

Forgive me Norah…. I'm so sorry. Jack was not a religious man, but he prayed that she could hear him, that she knew he loved her and that she would forgive him for desiring her body and loving her too much.

The doctors told Jack to talk to her normally as *if* she could hear him, he tried but it didn't come naturally to him. Today he had news about Karen. "Your sister-in-law Alice is going to have Karen stay with them for a while…. Just 'til you come home," he added hastily. "Alice says her young 'un Carol will be glad of the company; she says Carol gets lonely being about the house on her own all day and they've got plenty of room for Karen to have her own little room, now all their others have grown up left the nest."

Jack hadn't been too sure about Karen going to stay with Alice and John in Swansea, he'd always found Alice's daughter Carol quite a trial with her strange noises and outbursts of shouting. Carol was a Mongol, like June Benson, and still lived at home with her aging parents; she was the autumn baby John and Alice had never expected to come along so late in life. But as the years progressed, Carol had become increasingly difficult and unmanageable; prone to angry outbursts and shouting. Alice, now in her fifties, struggled to cope with her twelve-year-old daughter who was turning into a young woman.

"Anyway Norah, you're not to worry about the children you just get better and come home to us. Alice said it'll be fine to have Karen to stay for as long we like, and it will take the pressure off Ivy…. She's certainly got her hands full with *the* baby." Jack said sourly, he couldn't bear to say his son's name.

Norah lay under the sheets without so much as a flicker of movement. She reminded Jack of one of those lifelike marble statues which graced the tops of important tombs in the churchyard, the thought sent a shiver down his spine.

"And your Mam is coping…. Well just about… as you can imagine their house is crowded with the three lads staying there, but she said to tell you that Lenny, George and Gareth are being good boys for Nanna Adams. I think your Da is even helping out a bit too, which is a miracle. Fancy that? Your Da doing the washing up!" Jack managed a half laugh; he knew Norah's parents were doing as much as they could under the circumstances for the boys. Norah's parents were not exactly in the best of health themselves.

"I do give your Mam some extra house-keeping for the lads, and I try to go up every other day, but it's a fair old trek up the valleys to Merthyr and I want to be here with you as much as I can." Jack held Norah's hand and stroked it gently, willing her to wake up.

Jack sat there quietly holding Norah's hand just loving her, trying to remember the bouncy young girl he married and wishing she would find a way back to him.

A young nurse popped her head around the door and frowned, she scuttled off to get the doctor.

Norah Ellen Ashworth, aged thirty-five years, was pronounced dead at four o'clock

*

"Norah's dead! Oh, dear God no…. poor Jack….and those poor children." Ivy crumpled onto the sofa with baby Jack in her arms. Tears rolled down her cheeks, weeping for the motherless mite sleeping blissfully in her arms.

Jack Ashworth had knocked the Benson's door at seven o'clock and told Phoebe the tragic news. Phoebe was still reeling from the shock.

"I did ask him to come in Ivy love, to have a cup of tea, but the poor man was beside himself and just wanted to go home to have a bit of time to himself… said he needed to think." Phoebe looked at the tiny scrap cradled in Ivy's arms, she knew Jack Ashworth was beside himself with grief, but he didn't so much as ask after his baby son. *If ever there was a time to hold Norah's baby in his arms it was now.* Phoebe thought to herself.

"So, what happens now?" Ivy felt numb. She slipped Jack down carefully onto the sofa and threw her arms around Aunty Phoebe and wept.

The two women had worked their fingers to the bone caring for the children, seeing to the housework, catering for Jack and now Norah wasn't coming back to them, Ivy couldn't bear it.

"She was such a good friend to me Aunty Phoebe, I can't believe she's gone," Ivy sobbed.

"I know, she was the best, and she was a wonderful mother too, those poor children have lost something very precious." Not normally given to weeping, even Phoebe struggled to hold back the tears. "Come on let's have a cup of tea and pull ourselves together before Billy gets here, we can't have him seeing you looking like this can we." Phoebe brushed away a tear from Ivy's mottled face.

"Death is a very tricky business Ivy, there's always so much to do when someone dies. Jack will have his work cut out over the next few days sorting out all the arrangements for Norah. We've got to be strong because Jack is going to need us now more than ever to lean on." Phoebe sipped her tea.

Phoebe remembered helping Ivy after the death of her husband Jimmy, the number of forms to be filled in and the mountain of paperwork was overwhelming. *I shouldn't be surprised if Norah will have to have an autopsy too, to find out what killed her.*

"What do you think he will do now?" Ivy worried what the future might be for five beautiful children who'd lost a devoted mother.

"I don't know love, it's too early to say but it's obvious Jack can't stay here living on his own in Ely with all those children to see to. Norah's Mam, Irene Adams, has got the three boys and from what I've heard the poor woman is already struggling to manage, especially since Jack is in Cardiff half the time…. Three growing lads will need their Da to keep them in line, Irene can't be expected to do that; perhaps Jack might have to go and live up that way, but he's still got to work somehow, and it's too far to get to the docks every day." Phoebe's voice was flat, whichever way you looked at it, Jack Ashworth had more on his plate than any man could manage.

"But what about Karen… and the baby, who's going to take care of the baby Aunty Phoebe?" Ivy was beginning to see that Jack's family were going to be shattered by Norah's death in more ways than one.

"I reckon Alice might want to keep Karen now, at least that way Karen is staying with her family. Alice's own daughter Carol is *always* going to need help and companionship, so an extra pair of hands and eyes as Carol grows up might prove a Godsend to John and Alice." Phoebe could see that Jack would struggle to look after a little girl, Karen staying with her Aunty and Uncle and her cousin seemed the obvious solution.

"But what about the baby… he's such a tiny mite. Who's going to look after the baby?... He's never even going to remember his poor mother." Ivy struggled to stay composed.

"I know love, but I expect Jack will have to make some tough decisions, he can't possibly look after the baby himself and unless another family member steps in to take over, then I'm afraid he doesn't have much choice." Phoebe raised her hands in surrender and shrugged… Jack's choices were limited.

"What do you mean Aunty Phoebe…. Are you saying that Jack would give the lad away… put him into care? Surely not… not give away his own flesh and blood." Ivy was incensed, she could never imagine giving her own child away.

"Don't judge him too harshly Ivy, as they say *needs must when the Devil drives.* Jack Ashworth is not a wealthy man, and he doesn't come from a family where there is any money to spare to pay for hired help. The children need to be cared for and he can't do it himself. I know only too well that sometimes you must do what you think is for the best when your back is up against the wall." Phoebe knew she was sounding snappish, but Ivy needed to be realistic, Jack couldn't manage four young children *and* a baby.

A small wail came from the sitting room, the baby was stirring, "I'll get him," Ivy jumped to her feet before Aunty Phoebe could say any more. Ivy's heart bled for the poor motherless child… *well I'd love you to bits if you were mine,* Ivy muttered to herself.

Chapter 28

It was their first proper argument and Ivy was boiling with misery and rage. When Billy came around to see Ivy at eight o'clock and heard the shocking news about Norah he sided with Phoebe's assessment of the situation.

It didn't matter which points Ivy made about not allowing baby Jack to be taken into care Billy was infuriatingly practical and agreed with Phoebe that it was the only feasible option for Jack Ashworth now that he'd lost his wife, and she hated Billy for saying it.

She knew Billy and Phoebe were only being practical and logical, but her heart felt fit to burst when she saw the tiny baby in her arms… how could Jack Ashworth just hand him over like a parcel to be dealt with by the authorities, especially since it would break Norah's heart if she knew about it.

"But the man doesn't have many choices in the matter Ivy, the lad will *have* to go into care, what else is there for him to do?" Billy watched as she rocked the baby gently in her arms. June was in bed and Ivy was enjoying the soft warmth of a new-born cuddled close to her heart.

Ivy gave him a withering look, she wasn't going to argue with him anymore, *they were all wrong!*

"When *are* we going shopping for your wedding ring Ivy, we've got our own lives to think about as well you know, and it's only a week to the wedding…. we're running out of time to get a ring." Billy said swiftly, trying to change the subject.

Billy was getting a trifle fed up with playing second fiddle, he felt sad for Jack Ashworth's loss, but he wanted the old Ivy back, he felt that he and June were being neglected whilst all of Ivy's focus had been on looking after Jack Ashworth's children. His patience was being stretched to the limit… he'd been nagging on to Ivy about going wedding ring shopping for days, but each time he'd suggested it she'd declared that she *was too busy to just drop everything and go shopping.*

"I've told you Billy, that I'm quite happy wearing my engagement ring as a wedding ring, we don't need to buy another ring." Ivy knew that she was being awkward, but she didn't care.

"But I want you to wear *my* wedding ring Ivy. And we need a ring to get married with." Billy could feel himself getting irritated.

"Then take this one and buy another one the same size," Ivy wrenched Jimmy's old wedding ring off her finger, "unless you'd prefer to use that one, because it's all the same to me. I'm not leaving this little one just to go shopping for a ring I don't need!" Ivy said waspishly and promptly burst into floods of tears.

"Don't cry Ivy love." He put his arm around her shoulder…. "Let's not squabble just before our wedding. I know you're upset about Norah." He kissed the top of her hair. "You've got such a kind heart Ivy and I love you for it, but June and I need you too."

Ivy looked into his eyes and took a deep breath, "Billy, if you say that you love me *and* my kind heart then," Ivy garnered her courage…."then you will understand why I want to ask Jack Ashworth if *we* can keep the baby if he says he intends to give Jack into care," the words tumbled out of her mouth almost before she knew that she was saying them; until that moment she hadn't thought about her and Billy adopting baby Jack, but with Norah's death and all the talk of giving the child away her heart suddenly rebelled and seemed to take over. Ivy saw Billy's face drop.

"I know it's a lot to ask Billy," she pleaded, her eyes shining with tears, "but I would so love to keep him Billy, and I know Norah would prefer that I brought him up instead of some strange family she'd never met….

"She was such a good kind friend to me, and she would always help anybody when they needed it…. Jack *needs* us now Billy." Ivy's face lit up with excitement, the more she thought about the idea, the more perfect the plan sounded.

Billy looked dumbfounded, he'd gone through hell and back to be able to marry Ivy and now she was asking him to not only be a stepfather to June, but to bring up another man's child as well, a baby who would demand all Ivy's attention. On top of that, their tiny house would be very cramped indeed with another child *and* it was another mouth to feed when they had precious little money to spare as it was for just the three of them.

"I don't know Ivy love," Billy said grudgingly, he hated clashing with Ivy.

"Just think Billy, I could tell baby Jack all about his Mam when he's older, and his Da would know he's gone to a good home, he could even see the lad sometimes if he wanted to,…. Don't you see Billy, it would be perfect!" Ivy's face was shining with enthusiasm.

Billy wasn't sure it was perfect at all. Phoebe trailed into the kitchen just as Ivy finished explaining her plan to Billy. Phoebe took a deep breath and rolled her eyes; she could hardly believe what she was hearing; without so much as a bye your leave Ivy was proposing that she and Billy should adopt baby Jack.

Ivy was asking such a lot of Billy, he'd faced down the sneers about Ivy's relationship with Jimmy Benson, he'd accepted June as his own and he'd even accepted that he would never have a child of his own because of Ivy's hysterectomy…. Now this… surely it was too much to ask of any man.

"I dunno Ivy," he said hesitantly. "You've caught me on the hop, that's the truth," Billy scratched his head.

"I think you're jumping the gun Ivy; we don't know for a fact that Jack Ashworth *will* want to put the baby into care," Phoebe said swiftly, anxious to defuse the tension between Billy and Ivy.

"I see, well you can't have it both ways Aunty Phoebe, one minute you're both telling me that Jack will have no choice but to put his baby son up for adoption and the next minute you say I'm jumping the gun." Ivy glared at the pair of them.

"If the lad *is* to be given away then I want him." Ivy said stoutly. "I would love this little baby as if he were my own and I'd be honoured to bring up Norah's son…. The son she gave her life for!" The last time Ivy felt such a passionate fury for a child was the day the doctors and Jimmy tried to bully her into leaving baby June behind in the hospital to be cared for in an institution; *she fought to get her way then and she was going to fight for this baby's future now.*

"He's *not* going into a council home, not if I've got anything to do with it." Ivy hugged the child close to her and wept.

Billy looked at Phoebe unsure how to react.

"Look, we're all upset… why not go home and think about it Billy, you don't need to decide now, and I'll have a chat with Ivy." Phoebe said softly. She hated to think that all Ivy's hopes of happiness with Billy might be dashed because of a disagreement over the Ashworth baby. Phoebe tried to usher him out of the door before he said anything hasty that they might both regret.

"I don't know if I can do it Phoebe," he muttered under his breath.

"Sleep on it, Billy… the reality is that the authorities won't let Ivy just keep the child unless she has some support, if you can't *both* come to an agreement over this then Ivy might not have any say in the matter however much she wants to keep the baby."

"If you loved me Billy then you'd say yes," Ivy sobbed.

"But I do love you Ivy, you know I do!" Billy shook his head in disbelief, *it wasn't fair that she was making him choose… how had they come to this*? Billy turned to leave, he felt miserable and backed into a corner.

"Then just say yes." Ivy called after his retreating back

Phoebe shook her head and saw Billy to the door. "Go home and think about it Billy, things will seem different in the morning."

Billy shrugged his shoulders; he didn't know what to think.

"She's grieving for Norah, please don't think too badly of her. Ivy has got such a kind heart she can't bear to see someone suffering," Phoebe said softly.

"I know Phoebe…." Billy trailed home feeling wretched.

Chapter 29

Phoebe recognized the precise, neat handwriting the minute the letter landed on the door mat of Wilson Road and the Porthcawl post mark confirmed it; *it was a letter from Deirdre Thomas*. But this time, the envelope was addressed to Mrs Ivy Benson not Phoebe; Phoebe was intrigued. At least it wasn't yet another bill to be paid, there had been too many of those turning up lately.

It was gone eight o'clock when the morning post arrived, and June was noisily tucking into her breakfast in the kitchen; Ivy was up and about now but was still far too busy seeing to baby Jack to come downstairs and join them for breakfast. Yet again it had been left to Phoebe to keep June out of Ivy's way, to get June dressed and to make porridge for the child, *a taste of hectic family life to come* Phoebe thought ruefully?

Phoebe picked up the envelope from the mat and took it into the kitchen she could tell from the feel of it, that there were several sheets of writing paper inside; she was intrigued.

Ivy was still upstairs feeding and changing Jack's nappy before trying to settle him back into June's old cot for a few more hours sleep. As if sensing the family discord, baby Jack had been up half the night wailing loud enough to raise the dead and squalling as if his little heart was breaking. Even through the bedroom walls Phoebe could hear the baby's high-pitched screams in the middle of the night and the creak of the boards as Ivy paced about trying to soothe the fractious child.

Phoebe struggled to get a few hours' sleep; luckily, oblivious to all the commotion going on in the next bedroom, June had slept through it all in the bed they shared together.

Poor Billy, it will be an earth shock if this is what greets him on his honeymoon night, Ivy isn't thinking what taking on this baby would mean for her and Billy if she pushes him into agreeing to it. Phoebe thought anxiously, having your own child keeping you awake all night is difficult enough, Billy won't know what's hit him.

Worrying about Ivy's emotional outburst over the baby had niggled away at Phoebe as she lay in the darkness desperately trying to shut out the incessant screaming which was driving all hope of sleep away.

It was a blessed relief when baby Jack finally gave in to exhaustion in the early hours of the morning and silence descended over the household; it was still dark, and Phoebe must have eventually drifted off for a few hours. But there was to be no lying abed for Phoebe, within a few brief hours June was up and about chattering, laughing, and demanding her breakfast and Phoebe was back to worrying about what trials the new day might bring.

When Phoebe got out of bed with June it was just gone seven o'clock and all was still quiet in the next-door bedroom, Ivy and Jack weren't up yet. Phoebe and June crept stealthily down the stairs to the kitchen, leaving Ivy to get up when she was ready.

"Is that porridge nice June?" Phoebe spooned in a generous dollop of golden syrup and topped the hot cereal off with the cream off the top of the milk. June was shovelling her breakfast down as if her very life depended on it, a curtain of golden hair covering her face, June raised her head and nodded enthusiastically, her mouth rimmed with sticky porridge. "Goodness me what a mess!... You've got porridge all around your chops young lady.... We'd better tidy you up before your Mam comes down and sees you looking like a rag-a-muffin." Phoebe laughed and reached for the damp dishcloth to clear away the smears.

Phoebe itched to open the letter and find out what it contained; she hadn't found time to write to Deirdre for a few days she'd been so caught up helping Ivy with looking after baby Jack; writing to Deirdre had slipped her mind completely. She felt guilty.

The unsettling revelation that the smiley, charming Miss Carol Jones was really a devious, light-fingered thief still vexed Phoebe; she didn't know what was happening about her tricky lodger or what the police intended to do about the accusations. The house on Alma Road and Malcolm Goode needed her attention too; answering Billy's summons for help, she'd rushed off out the house leaving poor Malcom to pick up the pieces and it wasn't fair on the man; and for all she knew there was a mountain of post on her own door mat waiting to be opened.

Phoebe's thoughts were starting to crystalize. She nursed her cup of tea and watched June mopping up the last of her porridge. Phoebe loved visiting Wilson Road and seeing June, but she had stayed long enough, the wedding was only a week away now and the small house was already feeling too crowded; it was time she left the couple to themselves again. It was high time Phoebe went back to her own home to sort things out and with any luck, Carol's personal things would be gone, and the room would be vacant and ready for a new lodger.

Phoebe knew that she really ought to start searching for another tenant to replace Carol; without Carol's rent coming in every week, Phoebe's own bills would soon start to turn into rent demands. Phoebe had pushed all this to the back of her mind as the Ashworth drama had unfolded, now it was time to return home to her own problems.

After all, Phoebe reasoned, she was only a bus ride away if her help was needed. Jack Ashworth wasn't trekking up to the hospital now to sit with his wife every evening since she had passed away and the children were sorted and being cared for: Karen was living with Aunty Alice; the three Ashworth boys were settled with his mother-in-law Irene Adams, and Ivy was looking after the baby until the baby's future was decided…. She really *wasn't* needed at Wilson Road any longer; it was time to go home to her own problems.

Besides, Phoebe reasoned, if Ivy really was so determined to take on this baby, then maybe a few days coping on her own with the baby night and day, and looking after June and all the chores, might bring Ivy to her senses. *It was time she went home to her own life, and time Ivy got on with hers.*

With her mind made up to be on her way, Phoebe decided that she must tell Ivy of her decision to leave when she came down. Phoebe wondered what Billy had decided to do about the baby after Ivy's outburst and ultimatum last night.

In Phoebe's opinion Ivy was asking an awful lot of Billy; pushing him into a corner, *was it a push too far?* Phoebe resolved to wait and see what happened between Ivy and Billy tonight and then she would pack her bags and leave first thing in the morning with a clear conscience; she had tried her best.

Phoebe could only hope that once Jack Ashworth had had some time to gather his thoughts that he would come to a swift decision about his young family, she would hate it if Ivy was left living in limbo with false hope about keeping the baby.

It wouldn't surprise Phoebe at all, that once the dust had settled, the grieving father might even want to move away from Ely to be near Norah's family and his older boys, and that contrary to first impressions, he still might want to reclaim his small son and take Jack with him to Merthyr… Or another family member might offer to take the child off his hands and keep baby Jack as a member of the extended Ashworth family. The possibilities were a worryingly complex, just the thought of them all was giving Phoebe a headache.

Phoebe fretted about an even worse possibility, Jack might already be talking to the authorities about placing the tiny baby into care and then Ivy would have no say in the matter. Ivy's front door could be knocked at any moment by officials who'd come to take the child away and put him up for adoption. Phoebe gave a small shudder.

Phoebe could see stormy waters and rivers of tears looming ahead. Whatever Ivy, or even Ivy and Billy for that matter, might want or decide to do, it wouldn't necessarily count for a whole hill of beans if Jack Ashworth had already started to make plans for the child's future… Jack might well thank Ivy for her help but tell her to mind her own business as far as his son was concerned.

Ivy eventually trailed down into the kitchen still in her dressing gown, looking shattered from lack of sleep. Ivy pushed a lock of tousled hair out of her eyes and inspected the teapot to see if there was any tea left which wasn't too stewed.

 Ivy ruffled June's hair and planted a kiss on top of the child's head "Morning my lovely, have you had a nice breakfast with your Aunty Phoebe?"

Ivy, functioning as if on autopilot, removed some of the dirty breakfast crockery from the table and headed for the sink.

"Here, you let me do that Ivy… you look completely done in," Phoebe jumped to her feet, "and that tea in the pot will be cold and horrid by now, I made it ages ago when I made June's breakfast." Phoebe made the subtle dig which sailed straight over Ivy's head. "Take a seat Ivy and I'll make you a nice fresh pot and I'll put some toast under the grill for you as well." Phoebe bustled about the kitchen.

"By the way, there's a letter come for you," Phoebe pointed to the mysterious envelope propped on the table by the jam pot; she was itching for Ivy to open it.

Ignoring the fact that she had missed getting June's breakfast for the third morning in a row, Ivy sat down with a tired sigh and allowed herself to be fussed over by her doting aunt.

Ivy turned the envelope over and inspected the post mark.

"I'm pretty sure that's Deirdre's handwriting," Phoebe said helpfully wishing Ivy would just tear open the envelope so she could know what was going on.

"It's burning Aunty Phoebe," June yelped and pointed to the toast as smoke started to fill the kitchen.

"Oh, no, damn and blast… that grill is so fierce!" Phoebe leapt across the kitchen and snatched the grill tray from under the gas jets. The signed bread accused her of inattention, and Phoebe started to rescue the toast by scraping the blackened bread into the sink with a metallic *scrinch, scrinch, scrinch,* noise; they couldn't afford to waste good food.

"What's the letter about Ivy," Phoebe called over the rapid scraping; luckily the toast had been caught in time.

"It's a message from James… I mean my Da," Ivy corrected herself, it still didn't come easily to her to refer to the man she barely knew, as her father.

Ivy had Phoebe's full attention.

"He's asked Deirdre to write to me because of our wedding," Ivy sipped her tea and pondered the precise phrasing on the page, it was obvious her father had thought long and hard about what he wanted to say to her when he composed the letter. It broke Ivy's heart that she seemed to have hurt her father's feelings.

Phoebe's ears pricked up; this was an unexpected turn of events; she could see Ivy's troubled expression. "I see Ivy… so what does James have to say then?"

"He says that he hopes we will consider inviting him to the wedding as he wants to share our special day, but…." Ivy gulped; she could feel tears prickling her eyes, "but that he will understand if for some reason we don't want him there." Ivy dabbed her eyes with her dressing gown sleeve.

"I didn't think he would *want* to come Aunty Phoebe… not all that way from Porthcawl, after all the ceremony is only a formality so Billy and I can be together; neither of us wanted any fuss, especially when we thought Billy's parents wouldn't attend either," Ivy reasoned.

"And even with Billy's parents coming now it's still not a big event; it *never* occurred to me that he would travel here for the day," Ivy looked to Phoebe for guidance.

"Well, it's certainly going to cause a bit of a stir Ivy if James Pugh just turns up out of the blue, and if he comes to the reception then questions are bound to be asked about who he is. Do Billy's parents know that your Mam had a relationship with James, or do they still know the old story and think that your real Da is the fictional Mr Jenkins who died when you were tiny?" Phoebe said bluntly.

Ivy looked shocked, she wasn't sure what Billy had told his parents about her parentage, but she was prepared to bet they didn't know the true story. Ivy could feel her heart pounding in her chest; *this request to attend the wedding was certainly going to throw the cat amongst the pigeons.*

Ivy's former relationship with Jimmy Benson had caused Mr and Mrs Thomas to have a meltdown in the early days; and they'd only just relented about accepting Ivy into the family, who knows what Billy's parents would think if they discovered that Ivy was illegitimate, and that her Mam's former lover was going to be at the wedding.

Ivy groaned; she crumpled the letter between her fingers.

"And you have to ask yourself Ivy, if it will upset Gerald to see your Mam's first true love standing there on your wedding day? I don't think Gerald has even met James Pugh yet?"

Ivy shook her head; she knew that the two men hadn't met.

"I thought not … Well, you have to admit Ivy that for Gerald to see James Pugh at the wedding would certainly be a strange way to have his first introduction to your long-lost father, it's enough to give the poor Gerald a heart attack" Phoebe raised a questioning eyebrow, Betty had told her that Gerald's angina had been playing him up again of late.

"Oh, bloody hell Aunty Phoebe, what an awful mess…What am I going to do now? "Ivy buried her head in her hands, she felt overwhelmed, tired and exhausted; she just wanted the ground to swallow her up and for the whole dilemma to just be a bad dream she could wake up from.

Phoebe glared at Ivy for swearing in front of her daughter, she gave June a kiss, "off you go my darling, go and play in the front room, your Mammy's got a headache."

"I'm sorry for swearing Aunty Phoebe… but who knows what will happen if my Da does come to the wedding with his neighbour, and what do I tell Billy? Billy's cross enough with me now as it is, and even if Da just turns up, Billy might refuse to allow my Da to come along to the reception, and then what do I do!" Ivy wailed.

Phoebe shrugged her shoulders, she had to admit that Ivy was between a rock and a very hard place and whatever Ivy decided to do was bound to upset someone.

"All I do know Aunty Phoebe, is that by *not* inviting my Da, I've really hurt his feelings and I *never* wanted to do that…. He says he has a neighbour who is willing to escort him to the registry office so the journey to get here is not a problem…. *if* we say that he can come to the wedding, then he says he would love to be there on our special day." Ivy raised her hands in despair.

"I see," Phoebe guessed who the neighbour would be.

"But, the sad thing Aunty Phoebe, is that he says he's concerned the reason I didn't invite him in the first place was because I might be ashamed of him or that Mam might be embarrassed and we'd rather he stayed away…. And he says if that's the reason then he understands," Ivy sniffed back a tear.

"Well, he's not wrong on that score, is he?" Phoebe said archly.

Ivy looked indignant "That's not true, I didn't *not* invite him because he was an embarrassment!" Ivy protested.

"If you say so Ivy. How I see it is that, for whatever reason, you didn't invite James. In your heart you could justify not inviting James to the wedding because it was only going to be a small affair and you thought it would be too difficult for him to get to it." Phoebe waited for her words to sink in.

"But the reality is your father now knows about the wedding arrangements and he wants to come however big or small the affair *and* he has someone to help him with the journey, so the distance from Porthcawl is no barrier to him. So now the only reason your Da won't come to the wedding is *if* you tell him that he can't come. So, in a way he will be right."

Ivy looked crestfallen she knew that Phoebe had put her finger on it.

"It seems to me Ivy that your father is a very perceptive man and that he can imagine all the pitfalls if he attends the wedding even if you can't. But he also acknowledges that ultimately the decision is yours and I think that you should ask yourself *why* you don't want him there and at least be honest with the man… you can't just hope he'll forget about it."

Ivy knew Phoebe was right.

"If it's too difficult for him to be there on the day then at least have the guts to tell him your reasons why, he deserves that much." Phoebe said tersely, she headed for the sink to tackle the mountain of dishes.

"By the way Ivy, I've been giving it some thought, and I really must plan to go home myself… probably tomorrow morning. As you know, I must find a new lodger for my spare room, and I've got my own life to sort out." Phoebe gave Ivy a small smile, her heart went out to her darling girl, but Ivy wasn't a child anymore and she needed to make her own decisions.

"But I need you here with us Aunty Phoebe," Ivy yelped, she couldn't bear the thought that Phoebe would leave her in the lurch.

"I can't stay here forever Ivy, you know that; you and Billy will be married soon, and you'll need the place to yourselves. You can't have me hanging about, cluttering the place up." Phoebe clattered the dishes onto the wooden draining board.

"The way things are going Aunty Phoebe, I'm not even sure that I want to get married, *and* I'm not sure that Billy is going to want to get married to me either." Ivy said, her face a picture of misery.

"Nonsense don't be silly Ivy…. Billy loves you; you'll get through this. You have some tricky decisions to make, and they *must* be made but don't let that spoil everything you have." Phoebe gave Ivy a stern look.

Ivy would be foolish to throw away everything she had with Billy just because life was proving difficult.

"I'm sorry to have to say it Ivy, but a Happy Ever After Fairy Tale, doesn't exist in real life, it's only in children's books. Life is difficult and it isn't always fair."

Upstairs Phoebe could hear a faint wail coming from the bedroom, "I think the baby needs you Ivy," Phoebe pursed her lips and tackled the sticky porridge pot. Ivy was going to be in for a difficult time.

Ivy dragged herself upstairs, as she passed the hall mirror and she saw the dark circles smudging under her tired eyes, she looked and felt like an old woman.

You look an absolute mess. Ivy muttered to herself.

Chapter 30

Jack Ashworth felt numb; without his strong capable wife at his side, he felt bereft, like a boat drifting aimlessly out to sea beset by stormy waves. The house was so empty without her; no chattering, squabbling children charging about, no comforting smell of a meaty stew bubbling on top of the stove for his dinner when he came through the door, no warm sensuous body to lie next to him in the dark.

Every day he cried bitter tears of frustration to think he'd lost his loving wife of nearly fifteen years, and all because he'd got another baby inside her; the baby which took her life, *if* he hadn't done that then she would probably be sat opposite him now chiding him about being late for work; the *what ifs* haunted him.

They were supposed to grow old together, him and Norah, but this last baby had put an end to that; how could it have all gone so horribly wrong?

Norah was the only woman Jack Ashworth had ever wanted and loved; he'd courted Norah Adams, as she was then, when she was a young, pretty shop girl of twenty who'd caught his eye one day in a Cardiff grocery store. As soon as Jack saw her laughing and joking with the customers, his heart was lost; but it would be weeks before she'd succumbed to his charm and banter and agree to go out on a date with him.

For all Norah's gentle eyes and warm flirtatious manner, she had a will of iron, and nothing would allow Jack to get past first base until Norah had a ring on her finger. Within two years of meeting the lass with the dancing eyes, Jack had proposed, and they were married just after Norah's twenty first birthday.

Now he was planning her funeral. "Oh Norah, what am I going to do without you," he groaned.

Jack was finding out to his cost that death was an expensive business; bills had started to arrive on the door mat. Jack always let Norah manage the money, but knew that he and Norah hadn't got enough put by to pay for a decent funeral; *who plans their funeral in their thirties?* They'd assumed they would have years together before they needed to worry about things like that.

Arnold Jervis, the man from the Co-op funeral home had called around at just after eight thirty in the morning with his catalogues and costings; Jack did not offer him a cup of tea.

"I'm sorry to say Mr Ashworth, but decisions do have to be made about what to do with the late Mrs Ashworth's remains." Mr Jervis cleared his throat; these conversations about choosing funeral details were never easy, and the messy, modest council house told its own story.

Jack looked at the catalogues of caskets and linings Mr Jervis had carefully spread on the kitchen table and groaned. "But I can't afford all this palaver Mr Jervis."

Mr Jervis had tried to be kind and suggest how Jack could cut a few corners with plastic golden handles instead of brass, no rouging and laying out of the corpse, a cheap pine coffin to bury her in and the headstone could wait until a later date, but, for Jack, the expense was still going to be ruinous.

Jack buried his head in his hands; he didn't want to think of Norah rotting away in a cheap coffin lying under mounds of earth in Ely cemetery without a decent headstone to mark her place of rest.

"Just go away and do your best to keep costs down Mr Jervis," Jack snapped, he saw Mr Jervis jump as he pushed away the catalogues.

"I don't want to look at these bloody things Mr Jervis… I don't want to be choosing the cost of handles, or the colour of the fabric surrounding my dead wife." Jack could hear his voice becoming shrill. Mr Jervis looked shaken.

"And don't worry Mr Jervis, I'll settle the bill somehow… you'll get paid, don't you worry about that." Jack said through gritted teeth; he would have to use the last of their savings and scrounge from the family. "Of course, Mr Ashworth; I understand, just leave it to me. We'll make sure Mrs Ashworth has a nice tasteful send-off at *ahem…* at a modest price." Mr Jervis coughed over the word *modest* and put the offending catalogues back in his large leather bag.

Jack saw the obsequious, black-suited man to the door and heaved a sigh of relief when the ordeal was over. "It's like a load of crows picking over a corpse," he muttered bitterly as he shut the door behind him.

He knew Mr Jervis was only doing his job and Jack had been told by a kindly neighbour that the Co-op was the most affordable funeral he would find but it irked him to be thinking about the cost of coffin handles when Norah was lying in the hospital morgue bearing the ragged marks of an autopsy.

At just gone eleven o'clock, Mr Perkins, the official from the Council Housing Department had also called at number seven of Wilson Road and passed on his condolences. "The council will try to help you Mr Ashworth, if they can, and of course it is understandable that you may wish to move to be nearer to relatives under…. Under the circumstances." Mr Perkins cast an eye over the pile of dirty dishes in the sink and the shambles which appeared to be enveloping the house; it was obvious Jack Ashworth needed help. Jack Ashworth was also behind with his rent.

"These family sized houses are in high demand Mr Ashworth, so if you do wish to transfer over the tenancy, we need to know sooner rather than later. If, however, you wish to apply for a council house transfer out of area then that can be arranged as well depending on availability of a property and the number of dependants you need to house." Mr Perkins was aware from the social services that currently the Ashworth children were living elsewhere with relatives. "It's always easier to get a smaller house than it is to get the larger ones." Mr Perkins pointed out helpfully.

"So, you have two options Mr Ashworth; the council can either try to find you another house in Merthyr to be nearer to your relatives or, if you choose to stay here then the council will waive the rent on this house for two months in recognition of the additional costs you are experiencing at this difficult time." Mr Perkins cleared his throat and waited.

Jack sat in front of the official with his head in his hands.

Mr Perkins waited until it was clear to him that Jack Ashworth had no intention of replying, "I know this is difficult for you Mr Ashworth, if you need some more time to think about it, then I'll leave you in peace to mull it over." Mr Perkins got to his feet, "but please don't leave it too long Mr Ashworth… we do need a decision."

"All right… thanks," Jack muttered grudgingly.

Jack Ashworth was no fool, it was no good kidding himself by thinking he had a choice; whatever Mr Perkins had to say he didn't *really* have any choice about what to do next. Jack needed help as much as money and he'd already made up his mind to move to Merthyr to be near to Norah's parents, *he just couldn't bring himself to say it out loud yet.*

Through the kitchen window Jack could see a scatter of discarded children's toys in the garden, Gareth's red bike lay abandoned on its side on the small patch of grass that Norah had been so proud of; *it was time for him to leave.*

This home in Ely held nothing but bad memories for him now and in his heart, he couldn't wait to move away. He'd decided to apply for a transfer to a council estate near Norah's Mam; he'd ring up the council offices in the morning.

Jack's final decision was what to do about the baby, it didn't matter which way he looked at it, baby Jack was just going to be a burden too much. He could just about manage the lads in a three or even a two bed-room house in Merthyr if Karen stayed with her Aunty Alice. His mother-in-law had agreed that if Jack applied for a council house transfer to Merthyr, then she would look after the boys each day when Jack was out at work; but she'd flatly refused to take on all the extra responsibility of looking after a new-born baby.

In his heart Jack knew that it would be hard to love this last child which carried his name, even if he did want to try and keep him; he couldn't bring himself to love the baby who had been the cause of Norah's death, the baby which would be a constant reminder of all he'd lost.

I'm sorry Norah but the lad has got to go to a new home, I can't manage all of it on my own…. Forgive me.

Chapter 31

In the bedroom, Alice had just got Rhys down for the evening and now she could hear the raised voices coming from the kitchen; Billy and George were locking horns in a heated discussion and the volume was increasing. *What the hell did they think they were playing at, raising the dead at this time of night?* Alice thought irritably.

Usually, Alice would have gone straight to bed after she had settled Rhys down for the night and leave the brothers to chat over a beer in the kitchen before George joined her in bed. But this was no brotherly chat at the end of a busy day in the fish and chip bar; whatever this was about it was turning into a full-blown argument by the sound of it, and Alice was going to put her foot down. She tucked the blankets around Rhys and headed for the kitchen.

Alice stood outside the door and eavesdropped for a few minutes; she didn't want the men clamming up the minute she entered the kitchen.

"She can't just give you an ultimatum for God's sake Billy, not over something like this…. Put your foot down!" George seethed; Alice could tell from the tone of his voice her husband was working himself up into a fury.

"But I love her George and I'd do anything for her… you know that. I was prepared to choose her over my own Mam and Da… but I just don't know if I can do this." Billy sounded desperate.

Alice was intrigued, she'd overheard Billy complaining to George about Ivy's preoccupation with the Ashworth baby for several days recently; it looked like something had happened to push Billy into a corner.

"If I say no George, then I think she *might* even cancel the wedding….and…"

Alice couldn't hear what Billy said next to his brother.

George thumped the kitchen table in response, "who is going to wear the trousers in your house brother? Are you just going to give in every time Ivy says she *must* have something?... Think about it, this is not just some stray dog she wants to take home with her, it's a bloody baby... it's for life, you'll be picking up the bills and the problems for life!" George seethed.

Alice opened the door, her face creased with rage, "will you both be quiet...the pair of you are making enough noise to wake the dead! I've only just got Rhys down for the night and I'll have your guts for garters if you two wake him up again with all this shouting." Alice rounded on George who had the good grace to look sheepish.

"And don't try telling Billy what to do in his relationship... it's Billy and Ivy's choice what they do; they've got to live with whatever decision they make … it's nothing to do with us George and we should stay out of it." Alice clattered over to the stove and put a kettle on to boil for a pot of tea.

George could see his wife was in dire dudgeon; Ivy was a good friend and Alice always took her part.

"All I'm saying Alice, is that I think it's a bit much of Ivy to suddenly spring on Billy that she doesn't want to hand the baby back to Jack Ashworth if he says he's going to put the child up for adoption," George tried to adopt a mollifying tone, he needed Alice to back him up, he didn't want to be rowing over Ivy Benson again; it was bad enough the last time.

"It's not just that George, I *have* been giving it some thought.... I at least owe Ivy that much." Billy looked like a puppy dog who'd had a beating, "but just imagine *if* Jack is just prepared to let Ivy hold onto the lad, you know…. allow us a casual arrangement like, and then a few years later when things are different Jack wants to change his mind about it…. Well, where does that leave me and Ivy then?" Billy looked torn; he paced the tiny kitchen. "And I just don't think it can be a simple matter of us keeping the baby like Ivy seems to think it is. I'm not sure that you can just decide to give a baby away to a neighbour like a Christmas present."

Alice had to admit Billy had a point, Ivy's plan appeared to have lots of pit falls.

"I'm sure the authorities might have some say in the matter if they get wind of the arrangement, and then what?" It had been playing on Billy's mind about his recent brush with the law over the suspicious death of Ajo Abbas, Billy wasn't sure that the authorities, if they did get involved with the case, would even allow someone like him to adopt a baby.

Alice's heart softened, Billy wasn't the easy push over his brother painted, he was a thoughtful loving man and Ivy would be lucky to marry him.

"I thought June was enough for Ivy. When I proposed to Ivy I thought it would always be just the three of us… and I've grown to love June, I really have, I think of her as my daughter and now *this* just lands in my lap." Billy looked torn.

Alice gave him a hug, "don't get yourself in a stew Billy, if you *want* to make this work, I'm sure you will."

"I dunno, Alice," Billy said doubtfully, "a tiny baby is hard work for everyone; it changes your life; nothing will ever be the same again…. but *if* I agree to this, and it is a big *if...* then I just don't know if I can live with the constant uncertainty of Jack Ashworth possibly turning up on our doorstep, maybe even in few years' time, asking if he can have his son back." Billy raked his fingers through his hair.

"Do you still want to marry Ivy, with or without this baby?" Alice said softly.

"Of course, I do Alice… I love her and *nothing* will change that." Billy said fiercely, he might have doubts about this baby, but he never had any doubts about marrying Ivy

George grunted his disapproval.

"Does Ivy know whether or not Jack Ashworth is even considering letting Jack go to a new home?" Alice asked, she ignored George's eye rolling.

"I don't know for sure," Billy admitted, "but Phoebe said Jack's made a few comments that make her think he *is* going to move away to be near Norah's Mam and that the baby won't be part of those plans…. that's what put this flipping idea in Ivy's head in the first place… up until then there was no thought of us adopting another baby."

"My point exactly Billy … it's just a whim and she'll get over it…. After a few days she'll forget all about it once Jack takes the lad away and things will go back to the way they were." George said spitefully.

Alice glared at her husband *sometimes he could be such a pompous prick.*

Billy let the comments pass. "It's just that Ivy has always said that she was happy with it being just the three of us Alice… if we add this little lad into the mix how is June going to feel… is she going to feel pushed out, you know as well as anyone Alice, that June can't always understand what's going on and she loves being the centre of attention?"

Alice nodded sympathetically, Billy was making a few very perceptive remarks, it certainly wasn't a simple task to take on this new baby.

"The thing is Alice; I know Ivy would make a wonderful mother to Jack and you can already see she's got fond of the lad, and I'd hate to let her down if this is what she *really* wants but…" Billy's voice was starting to falter

"But Phoebe has already said she's going home to Alma Road in a day or two, so Ivy won't have any help there and I gather Gerald hasn't been too well lately, so her Mam Betty won't be able to help out much either…. If we do this thing, then it's just going to be down to me and Ivy." Billy struggled with the idea of coming home to a frazzled wife, but he did so want Ivy to be happy.

The convoluted arguments for and against the decision about keeping the baby had been going around in Billy's head all evening, it wasn't just a simple matter of putting his foot down as George implied.

"You're right Billy, it *will* be tough to start with, but you'll get through it; we *all* get through it in the end," Alice said kindly, remembering the nightmare first six weeks when Rhys cried and tugged at her breast night and day until she was so exhausted, she thought she was going mad.

George was getting aggravated; yet gain Ivy Benson was the source of discord in his family. "For heaven's sake Alice, Billy doesn't even know if Jack Ashworth is going to agree to anything... whatever Ivy wants or doesn't want is irrelevant if Jack Ashworth has other ideas," George snapped.

"I'm going to bed Alice, some of us have got work to do in the morning." He gave Billy a pointed look. "I'm sick of this talk going around in circles, if Billy is mad enough to take on this baby then it seems pretty simple to me; he should approach Jack Ashworth and state his terms, not just hope that it's all going to be alright... you mightn't like me saying this Billy, but in the end this *is* a business deal and Jack Ashworth has got to promise to stick to his side of the bargain if he chooses to agree your terms.... otherwise, you've got to walk away.... As you said yourself, Jack could just waltz back into the child's life and reclaim him and then where would Ivy be!"

Alice rushed over and gave George a kiss, "you're absolutely right George.... Billy and Ivy have got to go into this with their eyes open. The best thing Billy can do is go straight over to see Jack Ashworth first thing in the morning and discuss this man to man... then Billy can give Ivy his answer."

George was pleased to get such an enthusiastic hug from his wife, but he couldn't help feeling that somehow both he and Billy had been manoeuvred into discussing the possibility of adoption with Jack Ashworth. George was too tired to argue anymore, "all I'm saying Alice is we *know* what Ivy wants but we don't *know* what Jack Ashworth wants," George headed for the bedroom.

"Just go and talk to Jack first thing Billy… at least that way you will put an end to all this speculation. I'm sure you'll do the right thing…. Ivy does love you Billy, she might be angry with the world and frightened for the baby, but she does love you." Alice gave her brother-in-law a small kiss on the cheek and left Billy to his thoughts.

"I know she does Alice."

As she lay in bed Alice pondered Billy's dilemma; if Jack Ashworth said that Ivy and Billy *could* keep the baby, but Billy still refused because he couldn't accept Jack's terms, then Alice could see trouble and heartache ahead.

Fingers crossed it would all work out for the best in the morning.

Chapter 32

It was just after seven o'clock and barely light when Billy rapped on Jack Ashworth's front door, he'd decided to catch Jack before the man went off to work. A light was still glowing in the upstairs bedroom; Jack was still home.

Billy had barely slept all night, dreading the meeting to come and the eventual head-to-head confrontation with Ivy if things went badly. There was nothing for it, Billy needed to know Jack's intentions and then decide what to do.

Across the road a curtain was just flicking across in the bedroom window of number ten; the household was getting up. Phoebe peered out across the street; she could see the familiar figure of Billy Thomas waiting on the Ashworth doorstep.

So, you're seeing Jack Ashworth before you come over to see Ivy... I wonder what you are up to Billy.

Jack Ashworth shambled to answer the front door, "who is it?" he called as he fumbled with the lock. "It's only just gone seven o'clock in the morning for heaven's sake... I'm not even bloody dressed yet," he growled.

Billy could sense Jack's bad-tempered impatience before the door had even opened.

Jack opened the door a crack to see who was bothering him at this early hour, he recognized Billy Thomas instantly, "oh it's you," he said rather ungraciously. "What do you want calling around at this time of day... because if it's money you're looking for you've had a wasted journey cos I haven't got any."

Jack looked like a man who'd gone to pot, his greying stubble spoke of a few days without shaving and it aged him, his trousers looked like they were hanging off him and the stains on his grubby vest spoke of neglect. Catching the look on Billy's face Jack relented and held the door open. "You'd better come in since you're here." Jack growled.

Jack led Billy through to the shambolic kitchen, a pile of cigarette butts filled a saucer and overflowed onto the cluttered kitchen table; "you'll have to excuse the mess," Jack waved his hand in the general direction of the filthy kitchen, "I've let things go a bit since Norah… well you know." Jack slumped onto a chair unable to finish the sentence.

"I'd offer you a cup of tea but I'm out of the stuff." Jack lit another cigarette, he dragged on it deeply and waited for the nicotine to calm his jangled nerves; Norah never used to allow him to smoke in the house; said she couldn't stand the smell of it, said it made the furnishings reek. None of those niceties seem to matter anymore; with no wife to take care of him Jack was existing on little more than cigarettes and bottles of beer.

"Don't worry about that Jack, but thanks for the thought; I won't be stopping too long." Billy was determined to keep a civil tongue whatever happened that morning, Jack wasn't usually snappish, and he was understandably frazzled by losing Norah.

"Look I'm sorry to be rude Billy, I've just got a lot on my plate," Jack muttered picking a strand of tobacco from his stained teeth.

Billy nodded; apology accepted; he could see Jack looked like a broken man.

"And don't get me wrong, I'm grateful to Ivy for minding the baby; I know it can't have been easy for the lass taking him on, but I'm not managing too well at the moment. Everybody seems to want a piece of me, *and* most people seem to want some money from me an' all," Jack screwed up his eyes as he puffed on his dwindling cigarette.

"And to top it all I've lost my job down at the docks… so like I said I'm sorry mate, if I caused offence." Jack rubbed his bleary eyes and seemed to drift into a reverie.

"No hard feelings Jack; I'm sorry to hear about the job," Billy knew there had been a lot of layoffs down at the docks lately, it seemed that for a worker like Jack, taking time off for sickness meant he was expendable. Billy took a deep breath, "the reason I'm here Jack is about the baby… don't get me wrong, I'm not asking for money or anything like that at all," he said swiftly. "Ivy's been only too glad to help out, Norah and Ivy were good friends, and Ivy would never let her down at a time like this." Jack nodded; he knew Ivy and Norah were close.

"I just wanted to say how fond Ivy has grown of the little lad in the time she's been looking after him and…" Billy paused and waited for his words to sink in.

"And what? Spit it out Billy, what are you trying to say mate?" Jack ground down the stub in the saucer, the cigarette burned down to his nicotine-stained fingers. "'Cos if you're saying she wants to keep it then …." Jack looked Billy straight in the eye, "then it's no skin off my nose one way or the other, cos *I* can't keep him, so he's got to go somewhere." Jack paused for a moment before ripping open another packet of cigarettes and lighting up. "Don't look so shocked Billy…. What would you do if you were me? No-one in the family can take him on and as you can see," Jack waved his hand towards the clutter and mess, "I can't even look after myself let alone a bloody baby." Jack promptly burst into tears, guttural sobs of frustration tore out of his throat, and he howled like an animal in pain.

"Hey, hey I'm sorry if I've upset you Jack," Billy said hastily, anxious to fix any offence he might have caused; but he didn't know what to do or say as he watched the man crumbling in front of him. He didn't know

Jack Ashworth well enough to throw a comforting arm around his shoulders, like he would do to his brother George. Awkward and embarrassed, Billy sat and waited for the storm to blow itself out.

Jack wiped his vest across his face, "sorry," he mumbled and took a deep breath. "I *can't* keep him billy, it's as simple as that, I've got no money and," Jack took a deep breath… "and, if I'm being honest I'm not sure I'd *want* to keep him even if I could. Every day I looked at him it would just eat away at me that because he's here on this earth, my Norah isn't." Jack took a deep sniff and cleared his throat.

"Look Billy, I know it's not the kiddies *fault* his Mam died," the word seemed to stick in Jack's throat, "but she did and I'm not able to bring him up even if I wanted to, I'd already decided that someone else was going to have to do that job for me…. As I said I *can't* keep him, so he's got to find a new home one way or another; I've thought about it, and I was going to tell the council man today." Jack said firmly, daring Billy to chip in with some comment.

Billy at least now had one part of his answer; he nodded.

"See it from my point of view Billy, the lad needs a good home, and I can't give it to him, it's as simple as that." Jack examined his grubby bitten fingernails, as if somehow the solution to his dilemma lay there.

"So, what are you going to do now?" Billy left the rest unsaid.

"I'm moving away from here and I'm off to Merthyr to be near Norah's Mam and Da and the boys. I'm going to look for another job up that way and try to make a new life for myself with the three lads… there's nothing left for me here and I reckon it's the best I can do." Jack looked thoughtful.

"I see."

"Norah's Da said that they need some labourers on a building site up in the valleys near them, so I might try my hand at that, I'm still fit enough."

Jack sat a bit straighter in his chair, until that moment he was slumped like a broken old man.

Billy looked at the shrunken figure sat opposite him and wondered what the future might hold for Jack Ashworth.

"I'm sorry it's such a bloody mess Jack but like I said, Ivy *has* lost her heart to your little lad, and she feels a duty to Norah to care for him if you'll let her…or should I say let us? As you know we're getting wed next week." Billy felt awkward parading his own happiness when Jack looked so shattered.

Billy felt sorry for Jack but he had resolved to be firm so he pressed on, "the only thing is Jack, if we *do* take on your lad, then I can't have Ivy's heart being broken some time down the line. *If* we take him on it's got to be for good… not that I'm saying that you can never visit him to see how he's getting on or anything like that, because of course you can," Billy added hastily, "he's your son when all is said and done, and nothing can ever change that."

Jack grunted appreciatively.

"All I'm saying is that *if* we keep him without us going through all the formal channels then I expect us both to hold up our ends of the bargain…this will be a trust thing Jack." Billy stared at Jack Ashworth, he needed to be certain the message was getting through to him.

"So, are you saying that you and Ivy will bring up the lad like your own? And that you won't be looking to me for the lad's upkeep… he'd be yours for good, with no regrets and second thoughts in the future?" Jack eyed Billy suspiciously.

To Billy's amazement he found it surprisingly easy to agree to Jack's request. "We will treat him as our own Jack, you can count on it. Ivy will make Norah proud of this little lad, and I promise you we'll love him and make him happy." Billy could feel himself welling up; *they were going to have a son, Ivy would be thrilled.*

"Good… well that's a weight off my mind Billy. It's agreed you can keep him, and I won't ask for him back; but I have two conditions."

Billy waited for the bombshell to fall. "And what might they be Jack?" He said cautiously.

"Give him a new name…I don't want him to be called Jack, that was my name for him," he gulped, "and I don't want you to ever tell him where I am. I'll have my own life by then and this lad has got to have his own with you… if you and take him on, then *you* will be his Da not me. I'm not being a father lurking somewhere in the shadows who will suddenly come back to claim him." Jack paused; it was obviously costing him a lot to talk about breaking up his family for good.

He would still have some explaining to do to his other lads who'd watched their mother bring a new brother into the world; who'd cried as if their hearts were breaking when he said that their Mam was never coming back to them. It would take time for them to settle into a new life in Merthyr

"My three older boys need me, so if you take him on, I'm *never* seeing him again. Once I leave this God forsaken house, I won't ever be back Billy… you have my word on it." Jack said levelly.

"Agreed," Billy felt sorry for the man, *never* was a very final word, it might be harsh, but it was exactly what Billy needed to hear. He wasn't going to judge Jack Ashworth for giving his son away and now he knew that Jack would stay away for good he felt easier about agreeing to Ivy's desire to keep the baby.

"Will you come over and say goodbye to him?" Billy thought it would be only kind to let the man have some time with his son before they parted company forever.

"No thanks Billy if you don't mind, I'd rather leave things as they are. And if the authorities should ever ask me where he is then I'll say that he's stopping with his Godmother Ivy who was his Mam's best friend… there's no law against that and it's not so far from the truth is it?" Jack gave a weak smile, he knew the child was going to a good home and he felt sure, that under the circumstances Norah would approve of his decision.

"No it's not, Jack," Billy didn't like to point out that baby Jack hadn't been christened yet, but he felt sure Ivy would sort that out all in good time.

"I'll be off then to tell Ivy the news…. I wish you all the best Jack." He shook Jack's hand. "Could you just drop me a line giving me your new address just in case I have to get hold of you… who knows, maybe in a few years' time we might need to get so some formal paperwork done for the lad… once the dust has settled." Billy knew that they would apply to adopt the baby at a later stage and would meet no resistance from Jack.

"Yeah of course I will," Jack mumbled. "And thanks for everything Billy, your Ivy is a grand lass."

After Billy left, Jack cried a few more tears for all that he'd lost, but he vowed they would be his last. His three lads needed him to be strong now, especially his favourite son Gareth, the little lad who existed in a confusing world of almost total silence. *I'll do my best for the kiddies Norah, I promise, and I know Ivy will look after the baby for you.*

*

It was nearly eight thirty when Billy knocked at the door of number ten Wilson Road, in the time he'd spent with Jack, Billy had come to peace with his decision. His mind was made up and now all he had to do was tell Ivy the news.

Billy knew some people would gossip and bitch about them keeping the Ashworth baby, would whisper in corners and make snide remarks about the arrangement, but Billy didn't care; making Ivy happy was all that mattered to him and in time the chatter would die away.

At Phoebe's insistence, Ivy answered the door, she had the baby in her arms. "Hello Billy, I wasn't expecting to see you so early," Ivy looked anxious; they had parted on such a sour note the night before she wasn't sure what Billy was going to say.

Billy took Ivy in his arms and kissed her, he looked down at the sleeping infant in her arms and smiled. "Here, let me hold the little lad Ivy… don't you think that if we are going to be his parents then he'd better start getting used to me." Billy grinned, Ivy's face a picture as his words sunk in.

"Really! … Oh Billy, I do love you…. thank you so much," Ivy yelped "And you're sure we're really going to keep Jack for good?" Ivy could hardly believe her ears.

"We are… I think I'd better come in and explain it all. Jack has agreed the baby is ours now… no ifs and buts, this little lad is going to be *our* son from now on." Billy headed into the sitting room with Jack in his arms, he could feel himself grinning with happiness.

"And Ivy I'm not having any more arguing about you having a bloody wedding ring either. We *are* going out to buy you one this very afternoon after I've done the lunchtime shift with George. Your Aunty Phoebe can look after this little lad whilst we do it." Billy said firmly.

Ivy felt so happy she thought her heart would burst with joy and nodded obediently.

Phoebe overheard Billy's comments about buying a wedding ring from the kitchen; it seemed that Phoebe was destined to spend one more night at

Wilson Road before she could head back home to sort out her own troubles.

Of course, in all the excitement over keeping the baby, Ivy had entirely forgotten about her letter from James… it was something that would need to be dealt with and with the wedding only a week away it was something that couldn't wait. She must talk to Ivy later after Billy had left.

Billy cradled the small bundle in his arms. *They would call their new son William… William Jack Thomas.*

Chapter 32

"Well, that was certainly a turn up for the books," Phoebe said as she brought them both a cup of tea. She watched as Ivy smothered the baby with happy kisses. Since Billy had told her of his decision, Ivy had been floating on a cloud of happiness. Baby William, as the couple had now re-named him, drifted off to sleep, milky and content, blissfully unaware of the drama surrounding him.

"I can't believe we're going to be able to keep him Aunty Phoebe," Ivy gasped, her eyes bright with happy tears. "He's such a gorgeous little lad and I just know that Billy will learn to love him as much as I do; we'll be a *proper* family now." Ivy slipped the child down onto the sofa, her face glowing with happiness.

Phoebe held her tongue and let the comment slip by; she'd already observed June, looking as if her nose was being put out of joint when she saw her Mam fussing over the new baby; Phoebe made a mental note to make a special fuss of June whenever she visited. Once the novelty of having a new baby in the house wore off, June might start to feel a bit left out.

Phoebe put her tea down and took a deep breath, "I'm pleased you and Billy have sorted out your differences, but you do owe it to your father to come to a decision about the wedding… time is running out to get a message to him." She fixed Ivy with a beady stare.

Ivy blushed, "I know Aunty Phoebe, I haven't forgotten," Ivy sipped her tea. "I've been thinking about it such a lot since I got his letter…. I know Billy just wants me to be happy," she paused, "And I haven't spoken to him about Da's letter but…." A shadow flickered across Ivy's face, she chewed her bottom lip, something she always did as a child when asked a tricky question in school.

Phoebe waited for Ivy to collect her thoughts. "Well, then?"

"But the more I think about it Aunty Phoebe, the more I think it would be better if I asked my father *not* to come to the wedding."

Phoebe raised a quizzical eyebrow; she was surprised Ivy wasn't going to even discuss the dilemma with Billy and even more surprised that Ivy was turning down James's request.

"Don't look at me like that Aunty Phoebe," Ivy caught the glance, "I know Billy would probably say that it was up to me to decide and even if he didn't say that; I don't think it's fair to put him on the spot, it's my father after all." Ivy said hotly.

"Have it your way."

Sensing disapproval Ivy pressed on. "Aunty Phoebe, I don't want Billy and I spending the afternoon debating this, not now we are going shopping for my ring... I want us to have a happy afternoon. I've made my decision and I'll write to Da today; I promise." Ivy shook her head she knew James would be hurt if he didn't come, but then a lot of other people might be hurt if he did come. It wasn't an easy decision.

"I know Billy's family have a pretty dim view of me as it is Aunty Phoebe… and now there is baby William to tell them about… they don't even know about him yet, and *that* won't be easy for them." Ivy guessed that this newest family member might set the cat amongst the pigeons. Billy might know about Ivy's inability to have any more children, but Billy's parents didn't, and she felt sure they would be hoping for a grandchild to carry the Thomas name, baby William was not what they would have in mind.

Phoebe remembered the spite in Pearl Thomas's eyes and knew Ivy was right.

"I never thought I'd get to hold another baby and call him my own Aunty Phoebe, I never dared to hope that Billy would have the joy of a child calling him Da… and now I wish we could just run away and get married and not have to go through all this rigmarole with guests and a reception, no matter how small. I just want *us* to be together Aunty Phoebe… is that so wrong?" Ivy said miserably.

Phoebe felt sorry for the little girl with the shortened leg who'd spent her life trying to please, doing as she was told and always doing other people's bidding. She'd loved and nurtured Ivy all her life, if Ivy needed her support now, she'd get it.

"Of course not," Phoebe said softly.

Ivy had a faraway look on her face, it was obvious to Phoebe that for Ivy, the wedding was just an ordeal to be got through; one day in her life she'd rather skip over.

Ivy gave a little half-smile; Aunty Phoebe always took her side. Ivy knew she would find it hard to explain her decision to her father, but after the initial argument over Billy's parents disapproving of Ivy and Billy getting married in the first place, she'd *never* wanted the fuss and the spotlight to be on her and Billy. Ivy hadn't wanted the engagement ring, the smart new dress, or the wedding ring; all she wanted was to spend her life with the man she loved, and half of her wished *nobody* else was coming to the wedding either, not the waspish Pearl, not her stern new father-in-law, not even her Mam and Gerald.

"Penny for your thoughts," Phoebe said kindly.

"Why is life always so difficult Aunty Phoebe?" Ivy sighed and looked at the angelic sleeping child, a child she would now call her own. Her good friend Norah would never see the little lad grow up and would soon be buried in Ely cemetery; Norah's life over before she'd even had a chance to really live it. The Ashworth family would be scattered and dispersed, and she and Billy would be starting out on a new and uncertain path together with possibly just as many pitfalls ahead that they just didn't know about yet.

"I don't know love… but I'm a great believer in the old saying that "when God shuts a door he opens a window," we don't always know why things happen but when they do, they set us out on a path we never even knew was being laid out for us." Phoebe got up and gave Ivy a hug.

"Would you like me to go to Porthcawl today and see your father for you and explain it to him, rather than you writing it all in a letter?"

Ivy smiled, "you are so good to me Aunty Phoebe, but no. I think I should write this letter myself… I at least owe him that much."

Phoebe knew Ivy was right.

"I know Da will be upset not to come, but I'm sure he will understand when I explain it to him." Ivy got up. "Now I think I'd better go upstairs and spruce myself up a bit before I do it though, because if I keep looking like an old bag lady, Billy might start having second thoughts about marrying me." Ivy gave a small smile; inside she was happy.

"Off you go then, I'll listen out for the baby and sort the kitchen out. If you get a move on and write the letter, it will catch the lunchtime post and, with any luck, your Da will get it by tomorrow morning."

Chapter 33

The letter was posted, and the ring purchased; Phoebe could go home to her own house in Alma Road in the morning.

Ivy had briefly mentioned to Billy that her father had written to her about the up-coming wedding and that she had written back to him and said how small the affair was going to be and that the service was not the time for him to meet all the family for the first time.

Ivy didn't relay Billy's response, but Phoebe had to admit it was probably the right decision. Even so, Phoebe's heart reached out to James, she could only hope that Deirdre would smooth things over for the man when she read Ivy's letter to him.

Phoebe could only pray that if James had any sense he would read between the lines and accept that Ivy had little choice given the sensitive nature of things.

Ivy told Phoebe that in her letter she had said it might be better for *all* concerned if he stayed away, and as she had pointed out, not even Billy's own brother George, or her best friend Alice would be attending the service either. Ivy begged for his forgiveness and understanding and promised to visit James as soon as she could. "I do hope he understands, Aunty Phoebe; I don't want to hurt his feelings, but then I don't want to cause a family upset either," Ivy said, her eyes brimming with tears.

When Phoebe took June for an afternoon walk and lifted the little girl up to the letter box to post the envelope, she knew the deed was done. There would be no change of heart; James Pugh would not be coming to the wedding like some spectre to the feast, there wouldn't be embarrassed silences or awkward questions about Ivy's parentage, all those things could be reserved for another day.

*

The letter landed with a satisfying plop on James's mat, he didn't get many pieces of correspondence arriving at the bungalow apart from the bills. He felt the ridged nature of the envelope and guessed it wasn't the usual thin brown official kind. In his heart he prayed it was an answer from Ivy.

It was still early, James finished getting dressed and decide to take Nero for his walk before knocking Deirdre's door and asking her to read his letter for him.

Nero pottered around the bungalow following James's every move; the dog could spot the signs of an outing. "I won't be long lad, I'm just getting my coat and then we'll be out of the door soon enough… you're all right this morning for an early walk, it's not raining like yesterday…. I think we might even go as far as the light house this morning," James chatted away to his faithful friend; some days he half expected Nero to answer him back.

The weather was blustery; white horses raced across the bay, and a sparkling early morning sun danced on the waves like a million diamonds catching the light. James enjoyed feeling the kiss of the salty air on his cheeks and with the wind at his back, he felt blown along the empty sea front.

It had been three days since he posted his letter to Ivy, and as each day passed his anticipation of her reply grew. He'd talked it over with Deirdre, trying to fathom what her answer might be; he knew that the request was not an easy one to grant; *but he was her father… surely she wouldn't refuse him this one thing.*

Not wanting to disturb Deirdre too early in the morning, he walked for over an hour trying to while away the time and settle his nerves. The letter seemed to burn a hole in his pocket. The return trip along the promenade meant walking into the stiff breeze, the wind caught at his hair and pulled at his coat and by the time James reached Deirdre's door at nine thirty, he was pink cheeked with exertion.

"Good morning James do come in… this is an early visit. I'm just making some tea if you'd like some?" Deirdre opened the door to let James in. She could see from the windswept look of him he'd been out walking Deirdre was dressed but still had two curlers in the front of her hair, a pink hair net perched on her head kept her perm in place, James had caught her on the hop, he didn't usually call before eleven o'clock. She quickly removed the net and curlers and fluffed her hair into place.

James reached into his pocket and pulled out the envelope which had been eating away at him since its arrival, "I'm sorry to be so early Deirdre, but this came this morning… from the feel of it I thought it might be a letter from Ivy and I couldn't wait any longer to know what it had to say." He thrust the envelope towards Deirdre.

Deirdre examined the post mark; it was from Cardiff and from the neat, even script on the envelope, Deirdre would deduce it was in a woman's hand, "I think you might be right James. Why don't you come through the kitchen with Nero, and then I can pour us both a nice cup of tea and I'll read it out for you."

James and Nero followed Deirdre through to the kitchen, James was so familiar with Deirdre's house, the lay out posed no difficulties for him now.

"I'm afraid I haven't had time to tidy up yet; but never mind sit yourself down at the table… don't worry you won't squash Bobby she's out for her morning walk." Deirdre chattered away and set the cups and saucers on a tray. She and James were easy with each other now and comfortable in each other's company.

James tried to control his breathing as he heard Deirdre slit open the envelope, she was not the sort to just tear it open with her finger, he heard the gentle rasp of a knife through paper.

"It *is* from Ivy," Deirdre said as she unfolded the letter and scanned the address in the corner. Deirdre carefully flattened out the two pages and took a deep breath, and before long she came to the nub of the matter. Deirdre's ability to read quickly meant that she could see the answer James was looking for before she'd read it out.

...so I'm sorry Da, but I must ask you not to come to our wedding next week. I appreciate that it was going to be a big effort on your part and I'm so grateful you wanted to take such a difficult journey just to share in our day.

But if the truth be told Da I don't want to even go to the wedding next week myself... not because I don't love Billy, because I do with all my heart, but because his parents don't really approve of me and originally they refused to come to the ceremony; they are not happy at having June as part of their family and I think if they discovered my Mam had me out of wedlock it would make things even worse than they already are between us.

Please try to understand Da, it's not you that I don't want to come to the wedding, I just don't want all the criticism and heart ache that would happen if you came. I can't have Mam exposed to any more sneers from the Thomas family than she gets already. As you know, I didn't even know my own past until very recently and most of the people who know us still believe the lies my Mam had to tell to protect me, if you turn up then the whole thing will crash down around her ears, and I can't do that to her.

I hope you will think about it and try to see things my way, I never thought I would have to refuse you and it breaks my heart to do it, but I have a lot of other people I must try to please as well. I feel like I'm dammed if I do

and dammed if I don't. I hope you can forgive me Da... I'll come to see
you as soon as I can. Your loving daughter Ivy. X

Deirdre took a deep breath to compose herself; James sat in front of her stony faced; he gnawed away at his bottom lip.

"I'm sorry James, I'm sure you must be so disappointed." She stood up and walked over towards him. "That couldn't have been an easy letter for Ivy to write," Deirdre said softly, "it's obvious that she's being torn in two, poor girl," Deirdre laid a comforting hand on his shoulder.

For a moment her hand just sat there until James covered it with his own, "there's a bit of me that's not surprised by her answer Deirdre, but I'd be a liar if I said I wasn't disappointed to hear it," he said sadly.

"I know James," she said softly; it was good to feel his hand on hers. She gave him a moment to compose himself, "would you like me to write another letter for you James?"

"I don't want Ivy to feel any worse than she does now, so yes please Deirdre, I would like to wish her well and tell her there are no hard feelings. She's probably right.... it would be too difficult for the poor lass if I went, and I never wanted to cause her any upset on her wedding day." James wouldn't admit it, but he was feeling cut to the quick, all the sweet anticipation of opening the letter shattered. He gave Deirdre's hand a gentle squeeze and took his own away.

"I think if we could get another letter written in time for the midday post it would put an end to the matter," James said evenly.

Deirdre could tell he was devastated.

"I'll get my pen and paper then and we can get it over and done with," she said simply.

That was one of the things James loved about Deirdre; her calm, solid dependability was soothing when he felt down. Deirdre just got on with life and took the rough with the smooth. It was only when old Bobby died that he saw a chink in her armour before she recovered her composure and accepted her lot.

"You're good for me Deirdre; you know that don't you?" James said softly, "I'd be lost without you now," and as soon as he said it, he knew it was the truth.

Deirdre didn't know what to say; no man had ever told her that before, even her first love Richard Owen, who'd gone off to war and never returned had never said something so intimate and perfect. She felt moved and uncertain of how to reply.

She knew they'd grown close over the weeks leaning on each other like a pair of old bookends, was James hinting at something more?

"Thank you," she said simply, "I think we both help each other James," Deirdre smiled, she felt a warm glow inside; it was good to be appreciated.

At that moment Bobby started pawing furiously at the window to be let in, "ah ha.. here comes your favourite cat James; even Bobby knows a good thing when she sees one," Deirdre joked. Bobby had an unerring sense of knowing when James came around to visit and returning home to her claim favourite place on James's lap.

James laughed, "she just uses me as a perch, the cheeky madam. Oh well let's get the letter to Ivy over and done with and then maybe you'd like to accompany me on a stroll to the post box Deirdre."

Deirdre had seen the breakers crashing across the bay, and if James's tousled appearance was anything to go by when he came to the door earlier it was a brisk and breezy April morning outside; she thought of her carefully permed and set hair.

"What a good idea…I'd love to James."

Chapter 34

Phoebe had decided to pop along to Inkerman Street to see Betty. If she was being honest with herself part of her was nervous about going home and seeing what was waiting for her; the pile of post, possibly information from Malcolm about Carol…and the bills…. She was dreading the bills. She must sort out getting a fresh lodger before her finances ran out.

She knew her key would probably no longer fit the front door if Malcolm had been as good as his word and got the locks changed. He'd promised to leave a new key under the mat whenever he went out, *it was yet another thing she would need to pay for.*

Betty and Phoebe were enjoying a gossip over a cup of tea whilst Gerald was out for a stroll fetching his newspaper and getting some exercise. Betty suspected Gerald also stopped for a natter with Wilf in the bookies on the corner, where Gerald was partial to a weekend flutter on the horses. Betty didn't mind Gerald's little hobby; it was good to see him getting out and about again; she'd been worried about him.

Phoebe had told Betty about James's letter asking to attend the wedding and Betty's face had been a picture, it was only when Phoebe told her of Ivy's refusal that Betty could relax again.

"I never thought James would ask to come to the wedding… Oh my God just think about it Phoebe, if he'd just turned up out of the blue!" Betty shuddered; fond though she was of James, even she could see that his presence at the registry office would be more than awkward.

"I know, and it was a hard decision for Ivy to refuse him, but it was the right one in my opinion," Phoebe nodded, she could *easily* imagine the fuss if James had just turned up on the day.

"She *has* done the right thing, that snobby Pearl Thomas would have had kittens if James had announced he was Ivy's long-lost father; she thinks Ivy's father is dead and I wasn't going to tell her otherwise," Betty gasped with relief that the crisis had been narrowly averted.

Phoebe's tale about the fall from grace of Miss Carol Jones had proved equally disquieting as they nattered over a second cup of tea. Betty was flabbergasted to hear that the slippery, but charming, Miss Jones was a really a cold-hearted sneak thief with a double life.

"I just can't believe that woman was a thief. She seemed so nice and refined… she was supposed to be a children's music teacher for heaven's sake." Betty shook her head in disbelief, once again she had been taken in by a winning smile and a bucket load of charm.

"As you say Betty, you can never judge a book by its cover… you thought Malcolm looked like the spiv when we were interviewing them for the rooms, yet it's Malcolm who has turned out to be a trustworthy diamond and it's Carol who turned out to be the dodgy one." Phoebe smiled; she was grateful to Malcolm for exposing the viper she was shielding in her nest.

"Yes, you're right Phoebe, I did get it completely the wrong way around." Betty noticed Phoebe seemed quite taken with Malcolm Goode, singing his praises, trusting him to be left in charge of the house. *Who knows, through shared adversity, perhaps the friendship might blossom?*

"Well, I best be off Betty, I need to go home and see what the damage is," Phoebe suddenly slapped her forehead. "Oh, what a fool!... I can't believe it Betty, I nearly forgot to tell you the biggest, most important piece of news of all… I must be losing my marbles."

Betty was all ears; Phoebe had already dropped two bombshells…*and there was still more to come?*

"You know Ivy has been minding the Ashworth baby, well since Norah has passed away, Jack Ashworth has decided to move to Merthyr to be nearer Norah's Mam Irene and yesterday he said that Billy and Ivy can keep the little lad if they want him,"

For the third time that morning Betty found herself goggling with amazement. "And?"

"And they've decided to take him on."

Betty took in a sharp breath, "well who'd have thought it?... Ivy having another baby."

"I know, it's a bolt from the blue and that's a fact. As you can imagine, Ivy's like a dog with two tails and I reckon Billy is quite made up about it too," Phoebe grinned; she'd watched Billy cradling the lad in his arms and saw the look of love in his eyes.

"Poor Jack, it will be hard for the man to leave Ely and his little lad behind." Betty said sadly, she had fond memories of the Ashworth family. When Jimmy was treating Ivy so cruelly, Jack and Norah were good friends to her daughter.

"Norah's death has hit him hard; just one look at him and you can see that Jack's crumbling under the stress Betty… The man can't cope on his own and the house is quickly getting in a state, keeping a new-born baby wasn't an option for him. He's doing what he thinks is for the best and you can't blame him for that."

"Well Phoebe, I think he's between a rock and a hard place and you and I both know how difficult that is," Betty smiled at her old friend, they had been through such a lot together over the years.

"My old TaTa used to say that you needed a bit of fire and heat to forge good steel. I think Jack will be all right once he's settled and it must be some comfort to him to know his son has gone to a good home. Your daughter is a lovely little mother, she'll treasure Norah's baby like it's her own."

"James might not be coming to the wedding, but is Ivy thinking of taking the baby along on the day, because *he* certainly will cause a few raised eyebrows? I assume the next thing is to let Billy's parents know they will be having a new grandson." Betty raised a quizzical eyebrow.

"Now I hadn't thought of that. I'm not sure what story Billy and Ivy are going to tell his parents, but you're right Betty, a brand-new baby will certainly cause a few raised eyebrows if it just turns up with Ivy on the day," Phoebe giggled, it would almost be worth seeing the look on Pearl Thomas's face if Ivy turned up to the registry office with a baby in her arms.

The two women hugged goodbye, and Phoebe left Betty to break the news to Gerald about their newly acquired grandson. Finally, Phoebe trailed home to Alma Road.

It was no surprise that her door key didn't fit any, Malcolm had been as good as his word and changed the locks. There was no tell-tale bulge under the mat, so she tried knocking; hopefully Malcolm would be in the house. It felt strange to be waiting to be let in through her own front door. A welcome shadow advanced towards the glass and opened the door, "Hello Phoebe, it's good to see you back, I've got such a lot to tell you." Malcolm stood aside to let her through, in a glance Phoebe could see a stack of letters piled neatly on the wooden hallstand, *she would have to deal with those later.* The hall smelt sweetly of polish; Malcolm had taken good care of the place since she went away.

"Shall I put the kettle on for you Phoebe, you look a bit done in?" Malcolm said kindly, he could see the shadows under Phoebe's eyes.

A glance in the hall mirror showed the lined, anxious face of a woman slipping into old age, looking back at her. She shouldn't be so surprised by her rather unflattering reflection, after all she was fifty-five now and her life had been far from easy. But it was getting harder and harder not to look perpetually grumpy these days; the lines and wrinkles dragged her face down into a sceptical frown, the prettiness of youth was long gone.

At least Malcolm Goode seemed genuinely pleased to see her.

"Sit yourself down Phoebe and let me make you a nice cup of tea, I've got a few things I need to tell you and whilst I'm making the tea, you might want to read this, Carol Jones said to make sure to give you this letter when you got back…I hope the thieving little cow has apologised for all she put you through." Malcolm called over his shoulder from the kitchen. Phoebe could feel her heart sink, she hoped that she had seen the back of Carol. She tore open the envelope and read the short note inside.

Malcolm clattered about in the kitchen fixing the cups and saucers, when he returned with the tray he could see Phoebe's face looked ashen, the letter lay crumpled in her lap, "what's up Phoebe you look like you've seen a ghost?"

"The devious little cow is threatening to blackmail me," Phoebe said through gritted teeth.

"Blackmail… from what the police have told me about her previous brushes with the law, I think she's almost certainly facing a jail term this time. We've seen the back of her, not unless she can wriggle out of it again with that oh so pretty face of hers, batting her eyelids at some old codger of a judge. She's a crook and a liar, and I can't see her being able to blackmail anyone without landing herself in even more hot water than she is in already. And if she does try it on, then surely you can report her; it will be her word against yours… and it's another crime for her to be found guilty of."

"I'm not so sure Malcolm… she's clever I'll give her that, her letter doesn't actually threaten to blackmail me but it's what she means if you read between the lines." Phoebe was furious.

Malcolm looked puzzled he didn't know what Phoebe was talking about. Phoebe let out a tired sigh… "I've got a secret Malcolm, a secret that I've promised someone faithfully I will *never* reveal, and the poisonous Miss Jones appears to have discovered it whilst she has been snooping through my private things."

"The bitch," Malcolm muttered under his breath.

"She's not exactly sure of her ground, but she has discovered just enough to cause enormous hurt to someone I care deeply about if she starts stirring things up; this letter is just to let me know that she has found me out…. *And* that she will look me up when she can." Phoebe wrinkled her nose in disgust.

"We all have secrets Phoebe, things we are not proud of or things we would rather didn't get out… you can't let her control you with threats; trust me *I* should know that better than anyone," Malcolm said bitterly.

"I know you mean well Malcolm, and if it *was* just about me then she could go to hell for all I care; I've seen pieces of rubbish like her many times fromwhen I lived in Tiger Bay and they don't frighten me, it's the *other* people involved in it that I'm concerned about." Phoebe's eyes looked anxious; *how could Malcolm possibly understand how she was feeling right now.*

"I don't know your secret Phoebe and I won't ask you if you don't want to tell me, but in the end she only has power over you if you let her…. I'll let you into my secret Phoebe and I *know* I can trust you."

Phoebe looked up, she wasn't expecting this from Malcolm, "really you don't have to tell me anything Malcolm, I never want to pry into your private life," she said quickly.

"Don't worry, it doesn't mean you have to tell me something in return Phoebe, not unless you want to. It's not a case of I'll show you mine if you show me yours," Malcolm grinned.

When Malcolm finished telling his story Phoebe felt a sense of overwhelming sorrow and heartache for the man sat opposite her, he had certainly been through the mill and back again. "I'm so sorry Malcolm, I had no idea…. but that certainly does explain all the dragging noises I kept hearing at night when you first moved in."

It turned out that Malcom wasn't just an ordinary travelling salesman as Phoebe thought he was, with a loving wife and family back home in Barry who he supported. Malcolm was a good man who had been sorely used and abused and as his tale unfolded Phoebe wanted to hug him and tell him how sorry she was to hear of his suffering.

"My wife Shirley was always the pretty girl in our school, the girl all the lads fancied and mooned over. She was always dainty and petite, just like a little doll with golden curls and sparkling blue eyes, and as she grew up she developed a figure like a goddess, with all her curves in the right places and lips just begging to be kissed; all the lads mooned after Shirley, and she knew it. She made all the other girls look like proper plain Janes." Malcolm had a faraway look on his face as he recalled being in awe of the gorgeous Shirley Watson and the envy of all his mates when she had started flirting with him; he'd been *her* choice when she could have had the pick of all the other lads.

"Her Mam had brought her up on her own, so there was never any money in the Watson house to spare for anything… except for young Shirley that is; whatever Shirley wanted her Mam tried to give it to her, her Mam would go without to make sure that Shirley had the best she could afford. The poor woman used to work night and day scrubbing floors in the local pubs just to keep hearth and home together; but then none of us had any money in those days, so Shirley was just the same as the rest of us…. apart from those looks which made her look like a film star." Malcolm nodded his head sadly, as if recalling some far-off time when hope was young.

Phoebe listened intently; from Malcolm's story she could picture a spoilt little madam blessed with good looks who was always used to getting her own way; twisting the local lads around her little finger.

"Shirley was an only child, so Shirley always got everything she wanted. She'd made up some fancy story that her Da had been a war hero, but I don't reckon her Mam Doris was ever married. After I married her, I soon learnt that the Shirley Watson we all *thought* we knew, didn't really exist at all, she was a creation of Shirley's imagination. Shirley was the best liar I have ever met which is why I recognised a kindred spirit when I met your lodger, Carol Jones; I'd not only seen her type before, but fool that I was, I'd married one."

Phoebe gasped.

"To begin with I was so made up that Shirley took a shine to me over all the other lads, so I never questioned why, when she could have had the pick of the local lads, why did she pick me…. I was so puffed out with winning the heart of Shirley Watson, I never occurred to me to ask myself, *why you?*"

Phoebe could see that Malcolm was still quite a handsome man with an attractive glint in his eye, she could easily imagine how proud he must have felt to secure the prize of the local glamour puss, Shirley Watson.

"Course all my mates were dead jealous when we started courting and I was stupid enough to think that she loved me…. I know now that Shirley never loves anybody apart from herself, she just needed another poor sap to replace her mother, someone doting to be at her beck and call, someone to pay the bills… someone else who she could bully and control….and *that* was why she picked me; I was the easy push over, the weak, obedient one in the herd." Malcolm eye's glittered with rage.

Malcolm told a lurid tale of hysterical shouting, threats to commit suicide, violent outbursts, and escalating violence in his marriage.

"No one ever knew what went on behind our door but as the years passed Shirley got more violent and more devious; she used sex like a weapon dishing it out when she wanted something and withdrawing it when she wanted to punish me." Malcolm recalled the misery of living with Shirley.

"For ten years she didn't get pregnant, she barely allowed me to be near her and then, suddenly, she announces that she's expecting a baby, and do you know what? I was totally made up about it Phoebe, fool that I was; bursting with pride that I was going to be a father at long last. I thought a baby might make things right between us, but I was *so* wrong, things only got worse." Malcolm could feel himself welling up, he paused to compose himself for a moment.

Phoebe could see him struggling not to break down.

"After our son was born, she banned me from our bed… said I had to sleep on the sofa or the floor, or anywhere that didn't annoy her and the baby. She started to throw things at me and threaten to hurt the baby if I upset her, and that was when I started travelling to get away from her rages."

"I'm so sorry to hear all this Malcolm, I had no idea," Phoebe said softly, this was not the happy-go-lucky chatty smiling salesman she thought she'd met the day he answered her advert for a lodger.

Malcolm rolled up his sleeve and showed a flat, crinkled white scar covering a large patch on his arm, ragged and rippled. like molten wax, "this is where I had to *let* her pour boiling water over me."

"Let her," Phoebe yelped, horrified at the image of someone casually pouring boiling water over another human being.

"She said that she would pour it over our son Roger's face unless I volunteered to be in his place and that the choice was up to me. I couldn't take the risk that she would carry out her threat to harm him… so, in the end, it *was* my choice to let her pour a kettle of boiling water over my bare arm and then I had to go to the hospital and say I'd had an accident with a pan of hot water." Malcolm shook his head, he never could understand Shirley's furies, but he would have done anything to protect his small son from harm.

Phoebe could hardly believe her ears; *the woman must be deranged.*

"I was too ashamed to admit to anyone that my tiny, beautiful wife was really a monster who bullied and beat me up when the mood took her… that I wasn't man enough to stand up to her, that I wasn't master in my own home like they were! All my mates used to say how lucky I was to be married to Shirley… if only they knew the truth… I'd have traded places with any one of them in a heartbeat," he said bitterly.

"Did you ever try to report her?"

"She used to taunt me, dared me to tell the Police … but she said that nobody would ever believe me if I tried to tell tales on her, and she was right. Who would believe a tiny, dainty woman with the face of an angel was beating up a six-foot man who was perfectly capable of defending himself?" Malcolm hung his head; he was ashamed of his own weakness, but he would never hurt a woman and Shirley knew it.

Phoebe understood Malcolm a little better now, he was staying away from his home in Barry because he feared his violent wife.

"Last time I went home she said I had to sleep in the shed like a dog, said I wasn't allowed indoors unless she said I could come in. Turns out she had another man in the house at the time." Malcolm's face wrinkled with disgust.

Phoebe looked shocked; the woman obviously cared nothing for Malcolm's feelings.

"Oh, I wasn't surprised Phoebe… not really, I knew she'd had other men, so he wasn't the first to have her and he certainly wouldn't be the last. The whole town knew what she got up to when I was away." Malcolm recalled the sleepless night he spent huddling down under sacks in the garden shed, imagining them laughing at his humiliation; too ashamed to confront the man lying in bed with his wife.

"She told me two years back that Roger wasn't my son… said I wasn't man enough to get her pregnant and that I'd been bringing up a cuckoo all these years. She laughed in my face Phoebe." Malcolm remembered the look of triumph in Shirley's eyes when she robbed him of his son. Phoebe thought Malcolm looked close to tears, *poor man*.

"I hate her, but in the end, she is my wife, *for better or worse* and all that stuff we both promised in church. To her I'm just a meal ticket, a poor sap who keeps her, whilst all the world laughs at the man who's being taken for a fool." Malcolm shivered as he remembered his wife chanting cuckoo, cuckoo in his face and laughing.

"This woman sounds like a nightmare, and do you believe her about your son," Phoebe gasped.

"Oh, believe me Phoebe she *is* a nightmare, one of your worst kind. And yes, I'm sorry to say I do believe her about Roger. As the lad has grown up, I can see that he looks nothing like me. I've had my suspicions in the past, but I would never have dared to question her, and I love him, it doesn't matter to me if I'm not his father; I still love him." It had cut Malcolm to the quick to realise the child he'd done everything to protect from his mother's rages, was indeed another man's son, but he would not abandon his son.

"Will she hurt him?"

"Oh no she'll never hurt Roger, *I'm* her punch bag. She dotes on the lad and she's doing what her Mam did before her, she's turning him into a spoilt prince who gets all his own way. I can tell from the way he looks at me that she's been dripping poison in Roger's ear, telling him lies, turning him against me. The lad's fifteen now, almost a man himself, and in time he'll come to despise me as much as she does." Malcolm shuddered, it was gut wrenching to think Shirley was warping the lad's view of him, pouring lies into his mind.

"The last time I went back to see Roger, she ordered me to get out, in front of the lad she told me to "bugger off," said she couldn't stand the sight of me; told me to leave the housekeeping money on the table and sling my hook. That's all Shirley has ever cared about is money and having nice things, but no matter how much I gave her it was never enough." Malcolm explained how he'd be doing other delivery jobs on the side to supplement his wages, using the Trebor van to drop things off for the market traders to earn bit extra; broken biscuits from the Nabisco factory, cake misshapes from the Havana bakery; anything that would bring in a bit extra money so that he could have a life as well and a few pounds in his wallet.

"Trouble was, sometimes I had a van loaded up with sweets and display shelving that I needed to deliver as well as my other deliveries to do. So, I used to have to unload all the boxes of sweets and display stands into my room so I could fill the van up again from the factories, and then I'd reload it all back in once I'd done my drop offs,"

So that was the thumping and dragging she could hear at night.

"I'm sorry about the noise, I was worried that you might ask me to leave when you complained," Malcolm smiled.

"I used to joke that you sounded like you were dragging dead bodies about," Phoebe chuckled. "So, what now Malcolm?" Phoebe felt sorry for the kindly man who sat in front of her.

"I'm staying here full time now Phoebe, I don't need to keep up the pretence of going home to see her and Roger; she's told me to stay away from the house and I will. I reckon she's got her fancy man in most nights anyway and as far as I'm concerned, the marriage is finished. She's said she'll never divorce me, but I reckon I've got grounds a plenty if ever I want to divorce her."

"How will she manage if you've left her?" Phoebe had visions of an acid tongued wife turning up on the doorstep demanding her money and looking for revenge.

"Don't worry she won't come looking for me," he said as if reading Phoebe's thoughts. "I'll post them the money nice and regular, just like I do now, I won't see my lad go without just because of her, it's not the lad's fault his Mam's a cow."

Phoebe heaved a sigh of relief.

"I've told myself that I'll do the right thing by Roger for another few years until he turns eighteen and then…. then after that who knows what I'll do." Malcolm raised his hands and shrugged shoulders, obtaining a divorce from Shirley seemed like an impossible mountain to climb but once Roger had turned eighteen, he would certainly try to cut the ties to his poisonous wife.

"All I do know is that I'm never going back to her…. Never. I'm going to be forty-eight years old in couple of weeks it's time Phoebe, that I took control. My wife Shirley has controlled and dictated my life for long enough; she enjoys the power she's got over me and that is why it's got to stop." Malcolm took a deep breath and looked Phoebe straight in the eyes, he could see he had her undivided attention.

"And that's why my advice to you Phoebe is don't let that bloody awful Carol Jones latch on to you and try to control you. People like Carol and Shirley sniff out weakness and prey on fear; they thrive on emotional blackmail." Malcolm smiled weakly; it had cost him a lot to bare his soul to Phoebe.

"Thank you Malcolm, I appreciate your honesty and trust in me, it takes a brave man to own up to something like this." Phoebe reached across and held his hand; she could see how hard it had been to share his secret.

"I know I need to think about what to do about Carol's threat; and you have certainly given me cause to think very carefully before I jump into making any rash decision."

"Good I'm pleased to hear it Phoebe, and if ever you want to talk, then you know you can always come to me, I'm good at keeping secrets." It felt good holding Phoebe's hand, and it felt good to be able to tell someone the whole truth at last, someone who didn't laugh at the idea of a strapping man of over six feet being beaten and abused by a petite woman, someone who didn't scoff at his spineless behaviour.

"Thank you Malcolm, I appreciate that. I've also got a very good friend that I will need to write to as well, she'll help me do the right thing." Phoebe knew she would have to tell Deirdre about Carol's veiled threats.

"Would you like to join me for supper Malcolm? I'm going to light the fire and I'd be honoured if you would join me, it's only corned beef hash, but you will be most welcome to share it with me." Phoebe said kindly, she knew that she had found a friend in Malcolm.

Malcolm smiled, the thought of a warm fire and good meal cheered him enormously.

"Thank you Phoebe... I'd love to."

Chapter 35

It was a crisp bright morning, and the early frosts of April were finally over, the year was turning in to spring. Alice set out bright and early with Rhys in his pram to visit Ivy on Wilson Road, the walk would do her good and she was dying to find out what Ivy's plans were now the decision to keep the Ashworth baby was made. Alice couldn't wait to see baby William; whatever the pitfalls that lay ahead of the couple, she felt certain Billy had made the right decision to allow Ivy to keep the baby. Her husband George was not so convinced.

When Billy returned from his meeting with Jack Ashworth, Alice had overheard the two brothers debating the latest twist and turn in Ivy and Billy's relationship and she could detect the note of disapproval in George's voice.

"Are you absolutely sure you are doing the right thing Billy... it's all very sudden and it's a big step to take," George was trying to tread cautiously, half of him had hoped that Jack Ashworth would simply tell Billy that he wanted to keep his son and Ivy's fantasy of keeping the baby would evaporate as quickly as it had arrived, and the other half had hoped that Jack would prefer to keep it clean and put the lad up for adoption properly with the council, it didn't seem right somehow to just hand the child over like a spare puppy from the farm litter.

"Jack has said we can keep the lad with no strings attached and so we're going to, and I'm not asking permission or advice from anybody," Billy said firmly, he gave George a hard stare. "I expect our Mam will have her two penn'orth worth when she hears about it, but when all is said and done, if Ivy was pregnant she'd have no say in the matter, and to my mind this is the same thing. We are keeping the baby and we're calling him William; he will be our son." Billy's eyes sparkled with pride.

Alice was proud of Billy for standing up for himself, for too long he'd deferred to his older brother; soon he'd be marrying Ivy and be master of his own household.

As Alice entered Wilson Road she could see a small removals van parked outside number four, loading pieces of furniture onto the van, a pile of rubbish and broken toys mounted on the scrap of a front lawn; Jack Ashworth was moving out.

Alice could see Jack standing outside smoking a cigarette, he watched as his battered sofa was upended and slipped into the van next to the bedsteads followed by chairs and a kitchen table.

Alice felt guilty, she was here to coo over Ivy's new baby and the baby's father was watching his life fall apart. When the van left Wilson Road Jack would not only wave goodbye to the pile of junk on the front lawn he would be saying goodbye to his baby son forever.

Alice took a deep breath and approached Jack. "Hello Jack, I was so sorry to hear about Norah, please accept my condolences," she said softly.

Jack grunted his appreciation, "aye, thanks Alice…. These lot are nearly finished and then I'm out of here today and I won't be coming back, nothing's the same here without Norah. I'm off to Merthyr to be near Norah's family." he said gruffly. A man in a flat cap carrying a tatty chest of drawers marched past and loaded it onto the van.

Alice could tell from the catch in his voice that Jack was struggling to keep his emotions in check. "It must be so hard without her… best of luck in Merthyr Jack, I'm sure it's for the best to be near her family." Alice paused, "try not to worry about the baby, Ivy will do her very best for him," Alice said loyally.

"I know she will lass… trouble is I reckon that my Norah was the best Mam any kiddy could ever have and she's gone." Jack gave a weak smile. "I know people will think badly of me, but I don't have too many choices in these things Alice." Jack shook his head sadly; he was penniless and jobless; hitting rock bottom without Norah to lean on

"I know it's not the lad's fault that things turned out the way they did. I was angry with him at first; angry at the entire world if the truth be told, but in the short time she had with him Norah did love the little 'un." A tear trickled down Jack's cheek, he had no control over his tears now, they just leaked out of him unbidden, he didn't even bother wiping it away, it trickled down his chin onto his grubby shirt collar.

"I'm sure she did Jack; Norah was a wonderful mother." Alice took Jack's hand and gave it a reassuring squeeze. "No-one's judging you Jack, I know Billy and Ivy will love the little lad like their own, you couldn't have found a better home for him."

"Righty oh, that's it, we're all loaded and ready for the off. You might want to give the place a quick check over before you leave mate. We've got the tools out of the shed for you as well," the man in the flat cap and overalls called across to Jack. The van door was being locked; the workers were ready for the off.

"We'll see you at the other end then mate," the man in the cap gave Jack a thumb's up and slammed the van door.

Jack nodded his approval and watched the van filled with his meagre belongings trundle up the road.

"I'd best say goodbye then Alice," Jack's eyes were bleary with crying and lack of sleep. "I'll just take one last look around the place before I drop the keys through the letter box."

Alice reached over and gave him a hug, "good luck Jack," she whispered, she could feel herself welling up.

Alice walked across the road and as she waited on Ivy's doorstep she watched as Jack, shoulders slumped and head bowed, went inside the empty house to be with his memories.

Ivy answered the door with a sleeping baby in her arms and a smile which stretched from ear to ear, "Alice how wonderful to see you, and you've brought Rhys as well!" Ivy gushed; she was brimming over with happiness.

"Come on in Alice, I've got so much to tell you." Ivy gently pulled back the shawl partly covering the baby's face, "and this is our new son William, I just know that him and Rhys are going to be the best of friends."

Chapter 36

It was six o'clock and Betty was attempting to wash June's hair and give the child her bedtime bath, without much success.

"Come on angel please be a good girl for Nanna." Betty pleaded; June tried her best to wriggle free. "Careful my lovely or Nanna will end up getting soap in your eyes."

Betty's knees were starting ache from crouching down with a jug of rinsing water, she was trying ever so carefully to get June to put her head back and get the suds rinsed off, but June was having none of it.

No sooner had the words of caution come out of Betty's mouth than June was screaming blue murder that she had soap in her eyes.

"Got soap in my eyes… Nanna, got soap in my eyes," June howled and started rubbing at her eyes furiously with her sudsy hands; splashing and wriggling trying to get up with water sloshing on the floor.

"No, no. Don't do that June, you'll only make it worse for Nanna," Betty scolded, large wet splodges now spattered the front of her dress. June was trying her patience with her wriggling and complaining; it was making Betty's back ache to spend so long bending over the bathtub; she willed June to behave.

"Shh now June… please stay still and let Nanna wipe your face with a clean flannel… if you'd just tipped your head back and kept your eyes closed tight like Nanna asked you to, then we wouldn't have all this fuss, would we?"

Betty could hear herself sounding sharp, she didn't mean to snap at June but ever since Betty had come through the door to visit Ivy and the baby, June had been playing up to get Nanna's attention.

Betty was beginning to regret offering to oversee June's bath time and hair wash whilst Ivy fed and dressed baby William for bed. It was the second time the bathwater was being used, William had been dipped in first, much to June's annoyance, and the girl had to make do with an extra kettle of boiling water to bring the bath of tepid water up to the correct temperature; June had fussed and wriggled and refused to sit down in the *baby bath* as she kept calling it; the hair washing was the final straw. "Right, well that will have to do…out you get young lady, and if you've still got soap in your hair, it's not Nanna's fault," Betty struggled to lift the slippery child out of the bath and wrap her up in a large bath towel; June promptly wriggled out of Betty's grasp and shot into the bedroom in search of Ivy.

"Mameee," June wailed holding her arms up to Ivy to be picked up.

In the darkened bedroom which she would soon share with Billy, Ivy was walking about rocking the baby in her arms, crooning a lullaby. Ivy placed her finger to her lips, "shh June… Shh, Mam, is trying to get William off to sleep."

Betty popped her head around the door, "come to Nanna June?" she whispered, beckoning to the naked child stood in the gloom.

June thrust her thumb in her mouth, shook her head vigorously and pouted.

Betty crept in with the bath towel anxious not to disturb the baby. its eyes now fluttering on the edge of sleep. "Come on there's a good girl your Mam will be finished with the baby in a minute." Betty's voice was low and coaxing.

Unmoved by Nanna's overtures, June stamped her foot and shouted "no…no Nanna," at the top of her voice.

Startled, baby William began to wail.

Betty grabbed June by the arm and yanked her out of the bedroom before the child could shout again; but it was too late, the damage was already done.

"That was naughty June, you could see your Mam was trying to get the baby off to sleep; now look what you've done." Betty was trying her best to keep her patience, William was now yelling at the top of his voice. June jutted out her bottom lip and looked as if she was about to burst into tears.

"Sorry Nanna," June's lip wobbled.

"Come on, don't cry June, Nanna will find you a nice clean nighty and then perhaps Nanna can put your hair in rags for you so it will be all nice and curly in the morning?" Betty slipped a winceyette nightgown over the child's head and led her downstairs with the promise of a mug of creamy cocoa and a biscuit.

June sat hugging her warm mug of cocoa whilst Betty combed, braided, and twisted the child's golden hair into tight twists, "this is going to look so pretty in the morning June." Betty enthused; she knew June was immensely proud of her long blonde hair.

June sat still whilst the preening and primping of her hair was underway; happy to have Nanna's undivided attention and her mug of frothy cocoa. Ivy slipped into the sitting room after half an hour spent hushing the baby to sleep and smiled; it was good to see June happy again with Nanna.

"Thank you Nanna, that's going to look marvellous in the morning." Ivy knelt beside June and hugged her tight. "You are so lucky having such pretty hair, poor baby William hasn't got any hair yet has he. Do you think he would like Nanna to give him some curls when he gets some hair?" Ivy joked.

June looked up her eyes like saucers and grinned mischievously.

"No... silly Mammee," she giggled. "June's got pretty hair," she pointed proudly to the rows of scrappy rags marching in neat lines across her head. Ivy kissed June's forehead, "Yes, June has very pretty hair."

Later, over a cup of tea the two women discussed the tantrum.

"Her nose is out of joint that's all," Betty opined.

"What can I do about it though Mam?" Ivy had noticed June looking a bit down in the mouth since William had arrived, it wasn't like her to throw tantrums, especially for Nanna.

"The poor child has had your undivided attention for five years; you can't be surprised that she's feeling a bit put out having to share you all of a sudden." Betty said logically. "It's all been very sudden for the child; she'll get used to having a new baby brother in a while."

Betty had noticed Ivy doting on the new baby, it was not so surprising that June was going to try to attract attention anyway she could. "She'll come round Ivy; you can't expect her to start loving William just like that." Betty snapped her fingers… "give her time."

"I do hope you're right Mam," Ivy so wanted them to be one big happy family. This time next week her and Billy would be married; she could hardly wait to become Mrs Thomas. Meanwhile, she told herself, she must make an extra effort with June; she couldn't have June feeling edged out by the new baby in the house.

After a bedtime story from Mam about a princess called June with wonderful golden hair and ringlets, June snuggled under the comforting weight of her blanket, content to be at the centre of her mother's world again.

"Good night my angel," Ivy stroked June's forehead, "I know you are going to be the best big sister that baby William could ever have."

June sucked her thumb, a flicker of a smile crossed her face, her eyelids began to close.

"See you in the morning sweetheart." Ivy crept out of the bedroom; she had been foolish. Ivy was so used to treating June like a normal little girl it had not occurred to her how confused and anxious June might feel about a new baby in the house. She'd forgotten how much June disliked change in her life; June's outburst over Billy and Ivy getting married should have taught her that much.

In a matter of only a few days Aunty Norah's baby Jack, who was only supposed to be visiting until Aunty Norah was better, had now turned into Ivy's new baby son and June's new baby brother. The baby had changed his name from Jack to William and was no longer visiting but here to stay. *We will have to tread carefully it's no wonder she's upset and confused;* she said to herself and vowed that tomorrow she would try to involve June as much as possible in looking after her new brother.

Chapter 37

Gerald was enjoying his Sunday breakfast; he'd had his constitutional walk and collected his Sunday morning newspaper and on his return from the corner shop a tempting aroma greeted his nostrils; *bacon*.

As a Sunday treat Betty was allowing him to have two pieces of crispy back bacon and black pudding fried in the fat, and to complete his joy, a fried egg cooked just the way he liked with a crunchy lace of brown edging to the white and a juicy runny yolk sat perched on top of the pudding. Gerald was savouring every morsel; usually Betty insisted he watched his waistline.

"She's certainly going to have her hands full now Gerald," Betty had finished relating the tale of June's tantrum's the night before.

Gerald grunted his assent; he knew Betty didn't like him speaking with his mouth full and he didn't want to interrupt his delicious breakfast with chit chat.

"Tell you what though, June hasn't half grown lately Gerald, she was so heavy to get out of the bath last night, I know she was wriggling, but even so she's certainly got quite a bit bigger recently," Betty didn't want to say June was looking chubby, but the child was certainly looking as if she'd put on a spurt.

Gerald's head snapped up, his knife and fork mid-air, "that might be a problem then." He mopped up the last of his egg with the final crumbs of black pudding and washed it all down with a cup of tea. Betty had his full attention now.

"Oh, it's not as bad as all that Gerald," Betty smiled, "June's just got a bit of puppy fat that's all, lots of children go through that phase, it's usually just before they shoot up a bit."

"No, I meant the dress, you told me that June was going to wear her favourite, pretty bridesmaid dress next week, and Alice's wedding was an entire year ago now, you can't expect the same dress to still fit the child, especially if she's grown as much as you say she has."

Betty caught her breath; she knew Gerald could be right.

"You can't squeeze a quart into a pint pot Betty, it was a perfect fit when the child wore it the last time she was a bridesmaid, this time I'll lay a pound to a penny it will be too small… how could it be otherwise?" Gerald raised a quizzical eyebrow.

"But Ivy's promised June she can wear it on the day," Betty shuddered as she recalled the bawling and tantrums of the night before when June couldn't have her own way, "June will have a fit if she can't wear her "princess" dress on the day." Betty couldn't believe the thought hadn't occurred to her before

"Someone needs to think about what to do *and* PDQ, because if the dress doesn't fit June, then Ivy will need to have something else for the child to wear on the day. Has anyone thought to try it on the child?" Gerald folded his newspaper and frowned.

Gerald loved June with all his heart and due to his chest pains, he hadn't seen as much of the child lately as he would have liked to. For weeks now, Betty had been going over to Wilson Road on her own to help with Jack Ashworth's baby. But when all was said and done, he was June's Bampa Gag, and he wasn't having the child disappointed on Billy and Ivy's wedding day. He hadn't met this new baby yet, but it certainly wasn't going to take June's place in Gerald's heart

Betty had to admit it hadn't occurred to her to ask Ivy about the dress.

"June will feel proper let down if she has to wear some everyday skirt and cardigan on the wedding day, the little lass wants to feel like a princess, and we can't let her down." Gerald said, he shot Betty a stern glance, in the excitement of keeping the new baby he could see that June was unintentionally being elbowed to one side.

Betty sat with her elbows on the table, in her heart she knew Gerald was right about the dress. They had let June down; the child wasn't to know that she was getting bigger and that some of her clothes may no longer fit; Betty could kick herself for not thinking of it herself.

They only had five days to go before the wedding. Betty decided to pop around to see Phoebe, she might be able to go over to visit Ivy and June and see if they had a problem with the dress or if Gerald was just worrying her needlessly over nothing.

*

Phoebe was giving the upstairs bedroom a final polish and going over with the carpet sweeper, all trace of Miss Carol Jones erased in a cloud of fragrant, lavender beeswax. The rugs by the bed were beaten and shaken and she hung fresh camphor balls in the wardrobes; the room was ready for inspection. Yesterday she'd placed several cards in local newsagents advertising the room to rent; it was money she could ill afford to splash out, but with any luck she would soon have a new lodger. Malcolm had promised to help her sort the wheat from the chaff.

"I've got a nose for these things, "Malcolm tapped his rather fine Roman nose and grinned. "We salesmen can spot a chancer a mile off…. Takes one to know one if you get my drift."

Phoebe did get Malcolm's *drift*, she knew that beneath Malcolm's Jack-the-lad patter and brashness, was a kind sensitive man she could trust and rely on. Malcolm had seen through Carol Jones when Phoebe had been dazzled; sucked in by a winning smile, smart clothes, and easy charm.

"This time Malcolm I'm going to be incredibly careful. I've given it a lot of thought and I'm advertising for another female straight off; I will be more confident having another woman upstairs next to my room, but I'm not going to be taken in like the last time…nice, solid and dependable that's what I'm looking for in a lodger, none of your flashy stuff like last time." Phoebe said firmly.

Malcolm grinned, "sounds like you're describing me down to a T, Phoebe," he joked.

Since Malcolm had taken her into his confidence, they had grown comfortable with each other. Phoebe, mindful of Malcolm's stretched resources and pitiful domestic life had taken him under her wing and was mothering him with the offers of a plated, tasty dinner to be reheated when he got back from work, or a slice of homemade cake left to accompany his evening nightcap. Malcolm had looked out for her and now Phoebe was going to look out for him. His tale of the ghastly Shirley had shocked her to the core.

Through the bedroom window Phoebe could see Betty bustling up the street; a woman on a mission and heading her way. *Betty didn't normally pop by on a Sunday morning.* Phoebe gave one final tweak to the counterpane and went down to answer the door.

"Good morning, Phoebe," Betty leant in and gave her friend a kiss, "I'm hoping you can dig me out of a hole." She gasped, breathless from rushing as fast as her legs would carry her.

"In that case you'd better come inside and tell me all about it," Phoebe's heart sank a little, she was tired with stress and drama in her life, *I must be getting old,* she thought to herself.

Betty marched in and started unpinning her hat. "Gerald has pointed out that we might have a problem with June's dress next Friday and I'm pretty sure that he is right," Betty waited for Phoebe to absorb the statement, she followed Phoebe into the sitting room.

"I can't believe I've been so stupid as to think that June's bridesmaid dress will just fit her like it did the day of Alice's wedding. I gave the child a bath last night and I can see that Gerald's right to be concerned, there is no two ways about it, June's got quite a bit bigger since the last time she wore her dress." Betty plumped down in a chair with a stricken look on her face.

Whilst Phoebe made the tea Betty related the tale of June's confusion and tantrums over the arrival of the new baby, "if she can't wear that dress on the day, I dread to think what she will be like on the wedding day… If last night was anything to go by, she was screaming blue murder when she couldn't have her own way."

"Of course, the child can't understand all the confusion and upset in her life now; is it any wonder? She's getting a new Da, a new brother and she's having to share her Mam with both; suddenly she's having to wait her turn and come second, and she's never had to do that before. Sometimes we expect too much of the little lass especially with her condition." Phoebe shook her head and sipped her tea.

"So, what are we going to do then," Betty paused, holding her cup to her lips. "I was hoping Phoebe, that you might be able to pop over and check out the lie of the land tomorrow morning without getting June in a stew, that still gives us time to get another dress sorted *if* she needs one; the trouble is, Ivy and Billy won't be able to pay for it." Betty said ruefully, and ever since Gerald had agreed to pay for the small wedding breakfast as their present to Billy and Ivy she couldn't ask him for any more money. Their own funds were not made of elastic and Betty had already given Ivy a few pounds to pay for things for the baby, there wasn't any more money to spare this week.

Phoebe wasn't surprised that Betty was calling on her for a favour and normally she would offer to buy the child a new party dress herself, but her own coffers were empty as well without her second lodger bringing in money. The bills and paid adverts would suck up all her spare money and she had precious little left over for essentials this week as it was, even the bus fare over to Ely to see Ivy was an expense she didn't need.

"Please Phoebe?" Betty wheedled. "I'd go myself except I promised to go with Gerald to the hospital for his monthly check up."

"All right…I'll go over in the morning Betty, but we can't work miracles if the dress doesn't fit…. Maybe there is a seam I could let out," Phoebe said doubtfully, "I can only promise to try and do my best."

"Of course, Phoebe… thank you." Betty said gratefully, the weight lifted off her shoulders and slipped on to Phoebe's.

*

The journey to Alma Road wasn't a wasted one… it solved the debate over the bridesmaid dress; the dress did not fit. Not only was it too tight around June's plump middle it was too short by a long chalk. A triangle of June's pink floral knickers was in danger of being on display for all to see whenever the child bent over.

June stood obediently on a chair whilst Aunty Phoebe tried on the dress. June was happy to display the "princess" frock with its frothy lace and pretty fabric; she smiled from ear to ear as her Mam looked on; she felt like a queen getting ready for the parade.

June grimaced a little as Aunty Phoebe shoe-horned her into the dress, the dress tugged a bit when it was pulled it over June's head; wrists bent back, and arms and shoulders squidged into holes meant for a smaller child. "Ow.." June yelped.

"There, you're in!…. Now turn around and show your Mam the back," Phoebe instructed. June, careful to keep her balance, turned on the chair to display an inch or more of vest where the zipper refused to meet at the back of the dress. Phoebe looked at Ivy and raised an eyebrow. Ivy knew better than to say anything in front of June, she screwed her face into a grimace of annoyance. Ivy could see the problem.

"Let's take this pretty dress off now shall we my lovely… we can't have it getting all creased, can we? Put your arms up nice and straight to make it easier for Aunty to pull off." Phoebe wriggled the frock over June's head and put it back on the hanger, she would have to discuss the next move without June in the room.

The dress didn't fit and there was no way it could be made to fit; June would not be able to wear her precious dress on the day of the wedding no matter how much of a fuss she made.

Chapter 38

"You were right about the dress Gerald, it's too far tight and too short; the child can't possibly wear it." Betty said glumly, "Phoebe said she's seen looser fitting sausage skins than that blessed dress. When they took June's measurements she'd grown a full inch in every direction… "more in some places than in others," Betty said archly.

June had certainly put on a bit of padding around her middle with all the treats and spoiling…. Ivy had been too busy looking after the baby to take the child out to the swings and slides to run off her energy. Washing piles of nappies and rocking a fretful child to sleep had taken precedence over strolls in the park looking for daffodils and baby ducklings with June.

"So, is someone taking the poor child shopping for a new dress?" Gerald felt the answer should be obvious.

"Ivy said she can't afford an impractical, fancy dress. And I agree, it's pointless the child having something to keep for best that she won't get any wear out of especially when money is tight. Ivy has said she'll get June something new and practical for the day."

Gerald nodded slowly; he didn't think *practical* was the order of the day for a little girl going to a wedding who wanted to look like a princess.

"I said I'd go over and look after the baby for a few hours so that Ivy can take June into the market and find something suitable for the occasion. She should find something without spending a fortune."

Gerald huffed into his cup of tea. He didn't understand women and he'd never had a daughter but even he knew that it would be no competition between a practical new frock and a fantasy princess dress of June's dreams. The child didn't see how ill-fitting and ridiculous the dress might look; to June it was a princess dress and that was what mattered.

"I hope you both know what you're doing." Gerald muttered.

The lady on the market stall, Doreen of "Doreen's Dresses," didn't know what to make of June, to her surprise she thought the child was pretty considering her condition. As she said to the lady on the next stall after June left, the child might be a bit *simple,* but she was quite a little looker despite her condition, *such a shame for the poor mother though to have one of those*, they both agreed.

"So, what are you looking for Mrs?" The stall holder eyed June up and was surprised by what she saw, she'd never seen a Mongol up close before.

"I'd like a dress for my little girl please, it must be practical and not too expensive, something a bit like that one maybe." Ivy pointed to a neat little dress with a Peter Pan collar and an attractive candy-striped cotton fabric; the price was four shillings. Ivy and knew her finances were tight especially now they had baby William to look after, she would have to watch the pennies and choose wisely; she hadn't banked on buying a new dress this week.

Doreen, a motherly lady in her fifties with impossibly red hair, could see Ivy eyeing up her cheaper wares. "I'm afraid I don't have that particular one in her size, but I do have a few others under the counter I can show you which might be suitable." Doreen pulled out and unfolded frocks for Ivy to examine.

"I could let you have that one at a bargain price," she watched as Ivy fingered a rather plain royal blue dress with a white collar, "it's not too heavy for the time of year but it was in my Autumn stock, it would be very suitable for school," Doreen added as an afterthought. As soon as Doreen had said it, she realised that June was probably not attending school, "it's nice and serviceable, I'm she'll get a lot of wear out of it," Doreen added hastily, her cheeks flushed with embarrassment.

"Do you like this one June?"

June shook her head and sucked her thumb; a deep frown crossed her forehead; the dress was plain and boring.

Ivy picked up a blue and white flowered dress with tiny buttons on this bodice shaped like forget-me-nots, it was two shillings more than the plain navy one, the fabric was softer, and the dress had pretty drape and flow to it. Ivy calculated that she could just afford it, "this one is very pretty June, look at the lovely buttons aren't they nice." Ivy held the dress up against June, it certainly had plenty of growing room and should last the child all spring and summer.

June took her thumb out of her mouth and tilted her head on one side like a bird listening for a worm, the china blue dress was indeed pretty, "Pretty mammee," June parroted and nodded her head in approval.

"That's settled then…if June likes it, then I'll take it," Ivy said and counted out the coins, her shabby leather purse felt distinctly empty. Doreen was amazed to hear Ivy chatting to June and asking her opinion about which dress to buy, "you could see the little lass was a few ounces short of a pound, but her Mam was still asking her opinion about the dresses anyway," she said to the neighbouring stall holder after Ivy left… "In my day those kids were just locked away out of sight… still it takes all sorts."

June watched fascinated as the parcel was wrapped up, the dress was pretty, it wasn't *beautiful* like her special princess dress at home, but it *was* pretty. June liked having new clothes

"I think we'd better go home now June and show this to Nanna, aren't you a lucky girl getting a nice new frock?" Ivy was pleased to see Ivy liked the dress.

*

Betty ooh and ahhed enthusiastically over the new frock, when Ivy arrived
home with the precious parcel "isn't that beautiful June… are you going to
try it on for Nanna?"

June nodded, happy to comply with the request, she wriggled out of her
plaid skirt and red jumper and stood in her vest and pants waiting to be
dressed in her new finery.

It was almost four o'clock and Betty needed to head home soon to get
Gerald's tea, "Oh you do look pretty June, it really suits you," Betty gave
Ivy a wink of approval, "isn't this much nicer than your other silly old
dress?" Betty gave a small laugh pleased that June had been won over.

June stopped twirling and puffing out the skirt, "No Nanna Betty!"

"Of course, it is," Nanna Betty chuckled, "your other dress is far too small
for you… you're growing up to be such a big girl now, the other dress is
too small for a big girl like you."

"No Nanna," June stamped her feet and started pulling at her new frock,
tearing at the buttons, and trying to lift the fabric over her head.

"Hey, hey," Ivy cried, "don't do that or you'll break it June." Ivy crouched
down beside her daughter. "I thought you told Mam you liked this dress
when we were at that nice lady's stall." She held tightly on to June's
hands to stop her scrabbling at the fabric.

"Nanna thinks this is a pretty dress and so does Mam and I'm sure Uncle
Billy is going to think you look smashing in it too." Ivy coaxed; she could
see that stormy look in June's face which hinted at trouble to come. "Let's
show it to Uncle Billy this evening, shall we?" Ivy gently removed the
dress over the child's head and started to pull the jumper over June's head.

Betty gave a small frown, Ivy couldn't give in every time June stamped her feet and shouted, the child was beginning to learn to throw her weight around.

"Come on, let's get you dressed again, and we can see what Uncle Billy thinks about your nice new frock when he comes; he's going to be here early tonight so perhaps he can read you your bedtime story if you're a good girl, and we've got your favourites…sausages for tea."

Mollified at the thought of a story from Uncle Billy and pork sausages for tea, June momentarily lost the frown.

June's dress wasn't silly, it was Nanna who was being silly. The more June thought about it the more worried she became; *what if Uncle Billy said she couldn't wear her princess dress like Nana Betty had, she began to wish Uncle Billy wasn't coming and today she didn't like Nanna Betty either.*

"She'll come around love, it's a very pretty dress and she's a lucky girl," Betty gave Ivy a hug as she was leaving, "you know what June's like she doesn't like change, but she can't expect to wear that old bridesmaid's dress forever." Betty said firmly, she thought Ivy was being too soft on June; her daughter needed to put her foot down a bit more.

"I do hope so Mam, I know she's upset about not wearing the dress, it's not her fault it's too tight on her, she doesn't really understand." Ivy said sadly.

Betty gave her daughter a hug and headed for the bus stop and the calm of her own home. *What a performance and all over a dress!*

June had quietened down a little, but she still obstinately refused to say another word to her Nanna; all entreaties were answered by June with a shake of ahead and a glower from under her mop of golden curls.

Betty regretted that she had stirred the pot with the child and upset her, but there was no getting away from it the dress *was* ridiculously too small.

Ivy knew that June was sulking upstairs with her dolls, the girl had refused to give Nanna Betty a kiss goodbye and her face looked blotchy with tears as she stamped up the stairs her bottom lip jutting out.

She'll calm down. Ivy said to herself.

Billy arrived early. It was just before five o'clock and still light, he had planned to play a game of hopscotch in the garden with June after her tea and before she got ready bed. The children in the street no longer let June join in their games and now Karen Ashworth had moved away the child didn't have a friend to share her games with. Billy felt sorry for June.

A delicious smell of sausages greeted Billy's nostrils as he came through the front door, Ivy had got him his own key now, the little house on Wilson Road was beginning to feel like home.

"Hello Ivy, I'm home," Billy called as he removed his coat and hat in the hall. Ivy was in the kitchen wearing a housecoat, her hair tucked under a scarf to protect her perm; she stood over the sink rinsing some of William's clothes whilst the sausages bubbled away in a rich onion gravy on the top of the stove.

Billy grinned, "hello you," he said, as he slipped his arms around Ivy's slender waist and kissed the back of her neck. Soon Ivy would be his wife, he couldn't wait to take her to his bed every night.

Ivy gave a half turn and pecked him on the lips, her arms still deep in the suds. "William is asleep on the sofa; I haven't long got him off to sleep and June is upstairs sulking."

"Sulking?"

Ivy explained the drama over the bridesmaid dress which didn't fit, "I thought I'd got it all sorted and she was happy to wear this new dress… I know we can't afford new dresses Billy, but it wasn't too dear." Ivy said quickly. "She would have been bereft if I made her wear her old clothes to the wedding, so I bought her a new one today in the market, but now she still wants to wear that blessed bridesmaid dress from Alice's wedding."

"Oh, dear poor June." Billy said kindly. "Where is she now?"

"She's upstairs in her room having a sulk, I haven't seen her since Mam left about an hour and a half ago. I've been busy getting William off to sleep and doing this washing." Ivy sighed, her hands were looking red and sore.

"You know how she gets Billy; she thinks we promised her that she could wear it and now Mam has let the cat out of the bag that she will be wearing this new dress *instead* of her old bridesmaid one and June is having none of it; she almost tried to rip the thing off her back." Ivy gave a grimace.

"It never occurred to me that she would still want to wear that old thing if she had a nice new dress to wear instead; the old one is really only fit for the dressing up box now." Ivy wrung out tiny vests and nighties before rolling them in a bath towel and then hanging them over the drying rack to finish off.

"What am I going to do with her Billy?" Ivy said forlornly.

"Don't worry Ivy love, I'll pop up and see her, I bet I can win her over," Billy grinned.

But June was not sulking upstairs in her bedroom playing with her dolls. Billy hunted high and low, under beds, inside cupboards, behind the sofas and in the bathroom, there was no sign of the child.

This was no game of hide and seek with mischievous giggles and legs sticking out from behind the laundry basket. After Billy searched the outside toilet and the coal bunker there was nothing else for it and nowhere else to look; he couldn't find June. In less than two hours, it would be getting dark.

When Billy came in from checking the garden his face told it all.

"She's not there either Ivy, but how on earth could she have got out of the house?" Billy was trying to wrack his brains; *was there a cupboard he'd missed?*

Then it clicked in Ivy's mind, how June had escaped from the house; "she *must* have gone out through the back door! "Ivy's face was horrified as she realised her mistake, "the back door *was* open a few inches when I came out of the sitting room after seeing to William. But I just assumed the wind must have blown it open Billy… it does that sometimes, so I shut it tight. I thought June was still upstairs." Ivy admitted with a groan; without knowing it she had shut her daughter outside in the garden over an hour ago and she hadn't thought to check.

"Bloody hell," Billy gasped.

"I *never* thought June might have gone outside Billy. June *never* goes outside on her own; I would never have shut the door if I thought she was in the garden." Ivy wailed, her heart pounding within her chest.

It seemed an impossibility that June would have gone outside without telling her Mam.

How could she not have known her daughter had slipped out of the house?

Most of the back gardens on the Ely estate were only separated by lines of wire strung between concrete posts, a small child could easily wander quite a distance across gardens and through such insubstantial boundaries. If the child happened on the right route, then June could even make it out onto the road if she headed in that direction. Ivy started to cry.

"Don't panic Ivy…Let's check everywhere in the house once again, just to be sure, you look downstairs, and I'll look up." Billy tried to keep calm; there was no point quizzing Ivy any further, it was time to act, the time for recriminations was later.

Billy sprinted upstairs calling June's name, willing the child to crawl out from a secret hidey-hole shouting *Boo* in triumph… but the little girl was nowhere to be found.

June was gone.

Chapter 39

Ivy's face was ashen, in all the kerfuffle of searching the house and shouting for June, the baby was disturbed and she clutched the squalling infant to her breast. "What do we do now Billy?" She wailed.

"June doesn't know how to say where she lives even if someone finds her, she'll be so frightened Billy… and what if someone takes her away." The note of panic was rising in Ivy's voice as she contemplated each scenario more terrifying than the last.

"She can't have gone far," Billy said firmly, he could see Ivy crumbling before his very eyes. "I'm going to rouse the neighbours, for all we know she might just be a few gardens away playing; we'll find her." Billy tried to calm Ivy down, but in his heart he was worried too.

"What was she wearing Ivy?"

"A red jumper and a navy plaid skirt, and I think she's taken Margaret with her as well," Ivy had not been able to find June's favourite doll Margaret in June's bedroom.

"You stay here Ivy in case she comes back, or in case someone brings her home, she's easy to recognize and quite a few people know June *and* where she lives, someone might knock the door at any moment and bring her home. I'll go door to door and ask the neighbours to search in their gardens and any outbuildings." Billy grabbed his coat; there was no time to lose.

Billy grabbed Ivy by the elbows, "she's a little girl whose wandered off and we *will* find her. Now pull yourself together Ivy, June needs us. I won't come home until I know something."

When the door slammed behind him, Ivy felt herself dissolving into tears, *stop it,* she muttered to herself and wiped them away; she couldn't let Billy and June down.

Billy dashed from door to door and as each neighbour answered he outlined the problem; June had escaped from the garden and was wandering around the area somewhere; he needed people to join in the search. Men grabbed coats to join Billy in the hunt; soon, half the street was scouring the neighbourhood for little June Benson.

Carol Roberts the local busybody from number three came out to see what the ruckus in Wilson Road was about. Women, arms folded across their breasts, gossiped on the doorstep as they saw their men racing up towards the Grand Avenue in case the child was heading for the shops.

"June Benson has gone missing, you know the one, the little Mongol kiddy at number twelve," her neighbour Janet Whitman passed on the scraps of information gleaned from the others further down the street, "seems the child was locked out in the garden and wandered off, leastways that's Mrs Jones told me." Janet delighted in telling Carol the latest juicy morsel of news.

The gossip about the circumstances surrounding June's disappearance had hardened, *Ivy Benson had locked her child out in the garden.*

"Locked out in the garden! And the kiddy being soft in the head like she is...well it's disgusting if you ask me! I wouldn't treat a dog like that!" Carol Roberts snarled, she had a very dim view of Jimmy Benson's widow at the best of times, and this just went to show the woman was no better than she ought to be.

In Carol's opinion if it hadn't been for the late Norah Ashworth springing to Ivy's defence after Jimmy's death, then Ivy would have been shunned by the whole estate when the truth about what Jimmy Benson got up to came out. *Well Norah Ashworth wasn't around to defend Ivy Benson now.*

"Fancy locking a child out; that woman should be ashamed of herself!
Let's hope the poor lass is found safe and well and hasn't tumbled in a
garden pond or been picked up by a kiddy fiddler," Carol said darkly.
"God forbid Carol, it doesn't even bear thinking about, I can't bear it, a
little girl like that wandering and lost…the poor little thing." Janet
Whitman shivered and crossed herself piously. Janet had three children of
her own and dirty old men in macs lurking in parks just waiting to steal an
unattended child away was one of Janet's biggest fears.

"They say Ivy Benson's got the Ashworth baby too," Carol gossiped,
eager to drip poison in her neighbour's ear, "seems to me she can't look
after her own let alone another baby. I don't know how she's come to
have that baby now Jack's left… tisn't right if you ask me." Carol left the
assertion hang in the air, she knew that it would be repeated up and down
the street, the street *always* looked to Mrs Carol Roberts for firm opinions
in times of crisis.

The hue and cry went up and down the road; men calling instructions, the
words *she's not here,* ringing out as men went from garden to garden. The
light was starting to fade; it was six o'clock with only an hour or less of
daylight left.

Billy was calling out for the missing child at the top of his voice, "June…
June," rang out up and down the road and beyond. A group of men had
dashed off to the maze of allotments behind Hiles Road each calling her
name as they went, it was a long shot but worth a look. Other men
sprinted for the park in case June had followed some other children to the
swings and slides and couldn't find her way home again.

But the park was empty and the few lads who were nearby hadn't seen a
small blonde girl with almond eyes in a red jumper and plaid skirt.

Every shed and outbuilding on Wilson Road and the roads behind which
backed onto Wilson Road gardens were searched. Some men could be

heard muttering that the police ought to be called if she wasn't found soon, Billy was beginning to wonder if they might be right.

And all Ivy could do was wait and pace about the room with baby William in her arms. Through her sitting window she could see the women of Wilson Road gathering at the ends of their paths to gossip, but Ivy didn't dare join them for fear of what she might hear.

Suddenly a cry went up, *she's here! Call off the search… she's here.* Even through the window Ivy could hear the hullabaloo. Men were shouting up and down the road, others running to convey the latest information to the search party, the lost child had been found.

Ivy's heart constricted, they had found June, she muttered a word of thanks to a merciful God.

Ivy couldn't breathe, she felt sure that she would suffocate if someone didn't come and tell her soon what they'd found. *Please God let her be alright; let her be unharmed.*

Billy came charging across the road with June lolling in his arms, "Ivy, Ivy," he called frantically as he jogged up the front path.

Ivy opened the door dreading what Billy might be about to say.

"She's fine… don't worry June's fine we found her sleeping in Jack Ashworth's old shed." Billy grinned, relief flooding over him.

Outside in the street she could hear clapping. Men yelling the news to neighbours, calling off the search; men trailing home to their abandoned hearths. The Benson girl had been found, she was safe and well.

Ivy felt as if her legs were about to crumble from under her, relief coursed through her veins.

"Oh, thank God," she mumbled, her voice choked with emotion.

Billy carried June into the sitting room, the child looked exhausted.

"We think she must have been looking for Karen," Billy explained.

"It seems that when Jack moved out the removals men cleared the shed as well, but they must have left the door unlocked because we found June fast asleep inside with her doll. It was the last garden to be searched because the house was empty."

"But why did she go there?" Ivy was almost speechless.

"I don't know but my guess is that she was bored and fed up and feeling left out so she went in search of her friend. The shed she used to play in with Karen was left open and a few old toys had been left behind, so she played there on her own and probably, tired out from walking through all the gardens, she snuggled up on some old sacks and went fast asleep."

Ivy wanted to laugh and cry at the same time, "so you mean to say that all the time I was frantic with worry, June was just across the road playing with Karen's old toys?" Ivy could feel a giggle of relief rising in her throat.

"That's about the long and the short of it, still there's no harm done, it's just been a storm in teacup hasn't it my angel?" Billy said softly, he couldn't express how worried he'd been about June; when he saw the child lying motionless on the sacks, for a moment he thought the worst must have happened.

June looked up with muddy smudges across her face and her thumb in her mouth, her face a picture of penitence.

"I think it's time for bed young lady," Ivy said covering her daughter's tired little face with kisses. I'm not sure there is any hot water left in the tank so I think you can have nice bath in the morning you mucky little pup…. It'll have to be a lick and promise tonight."

"I'm hungry Mammee,"

Ivy laughed; in all the panic she'd forgotten June had missed her tea.

"I think a nice bit of scrambled egg on toast should do the trick don't you?"

June nodded enthusiastically; small bits of twig were caught in her hair. June looked at Billy with pleading eyes, "can I wear my princess dress?" she lisped.

Billy looked at Ivy, struggling to see what the strange request was all about.

Ivy rolled her eyes; she would have to tell Billy the whole story of the dress disaster after June had gone to bed. "We'll talk about it in the morning June, I promise. Don't worry Mam won't forget, but now I think it's time for bed." Ivy felt like she was floating on air, June was unharmed.

The lights blazed in houses up and down Wilson Road as neighbours retold the dramatic discovery of June Benson discovered fast asleep in the empty Ashworth shed. Glasses of beer were raised to toast the young girl's safe recovery; everyone agreed it was a miracle that nothing bad had happened to the poor little lass whilst she was wandering around on her own.

There were always unsavoury people around looking for an unattended child, June Benson had been incredibly lucky.

Carol Roberts was of a different opinion; *Ivy Benson* had been lucky, she escaped disaster by the skin of her teeth. In Carol's opinion that woman wasn't fit to take on another child if she couldn't keep a better eye on her own girl.

"Stands to reason people ought to question Jack Ashworth's choice of Ivy Benson to look after that poor motherless baby of his," Carol dripped poison in the ear of anyone who would listen. "The poor man was obviously crazed with grief when he left the road. I'm not blaming him of course not… not at all, he's got the rest of family to think of." Her voice syrupy with fake sympathy for a man she barely knew.

Heads nodded in approval; Mrs Roberts was known for her insight on such matters.

"After all, Ivy Benson just sort of took over when Norah was struck down didn't she?" Carol allowed her audience to digest her evaluation of the matter. Heads nodded; none thought to question if they should have stepped in when the crisis arose in the Ashworth household.

"And I'm sure that she meant well at the time; but nobody expected Ivy to just keep the child, did they?" Several faces looked puzzled, Carol Roberts *had* made a valid point, nobody had given any thought what should happen to the child of poor Norah Ashworth.

Eileen Riley stood at the back of the gaggle of women cradling her growing bump. Her heart had gone out to Ivy Benson when she heard June was missing. Eileen had caught the end of the conversation and she didn't like where it was heading, Carol Roberts was trying to stir up ill will towards Ivy.

"So, what *are* you suggesting Mrs Roberts? I can't believe that anybody around here would seriously suggest the baby ought to be sent off to some council institution instead of staying with Ivy Benson, are they?" Eileen was furious; this hard-faced woman was turning a simple case of a child wandering off into a hint of neglectful mothering.

Heads turned as Eileen's soft Irish accent drifted over the heads of the other women.

"All I'm saying Mrs Riley is that it looks to *me,* as if Ivy Benson can't look after her own let alone another baby which doesn't belong to her by rights… Jack has just left him behind and from my experience of Ivy Benson *over the years,"* Carol emphasised her seniority and vast experience in the comings and goings of Wilson Road which, in her opinion, far outweighed the views of this newcomer challenging her authority, "from my *experience,* for what it's worth, the Benson family isn't necessarily the best place for a poor, motherless baby." Carol's voice was firm and authoritative, heads in the circle around her could be seen to be nodding reluctantly; few would choose to publicly disagree with Carol Roberts.

"Are you always so hard on your neighbours Mrs Roberts?" Eileen said smoothly, "it's *obvious* to me that Ivy is a wonderful mother to that little girl of hers, there's many who would have put *her* in an institution too after she was born, but Ivy didn't and all credit it to her for that." Eileen paused, she could see that a few of the women in the gaggle were nodding, some faces blushed recognizing phrases they had expressed themselves, when Ivy came home from hospital cradling a Mongol baby.

"This scare could have happened to any one of us, children *do* get involved in playing and wander off," more heads nodding. Someone at the back said, "yes my Johnny did once," in agreement.

Carol Roberts could see that she was losing her authority in front of this new upstart with the cripple for a husband, "well I can't stand around here yakking all night, my old man will wonder what I'm up to…. But have it your own way Mrs Riley since you seem to be such an expert in these matters… but ask yourself this," Carol hissed and jabbed a finger in the direction of the nodding heads, "if something ever happens to that Ashworth baby, then well…. Well, you can't say I didn't spot it coming." Carol let the awfulness of the rest of the sentence hang in the air. She drew herself up to her full five foot three inches and turned on her heels and left to go indoors. Her front door banged sharply behind her.

The gaggle of women started to disperse.

Janet Whitman sidled over towards Eileen "it's never good to get her back up love," she advised, her head nodding in Carol's direction, "she can have a nasty mouth on her, but she's got a good heart for all that," Janet added hastily, unsure of her ground yet.

Eileen looked at the pinched faced woman at her elbow, only moments before, she'd seen the woman glued to Carol Roberts's side looking for all the world as if she was Carol's best friend.

"Has she now, then I'm very glad to hear it Mrs Whitman." Eileen said doubtfully.

Janet slid away unable to prise any more comment from Mrs Riley.

Eileen headed home to tell Sean all the latest news. She felt certain she had made an enemy of the local busy body by speaking up for Ivy; but if there was one thing Eileen wouldn't tolerate, it was injustice.

Eileen made up her mind to visit Ivy the next day, she had a sinking feeling that Ivy might need friends on Wilson Road if the poisonous Carol Ashworth started stirring up trouble over the episode.

Chapter 40

In the morning Billy told George and Alice about the drama of over losing June for a few hours and the other very real drama over the unusable bridesmaid's dress.

Alice's heart had dropped when she heard how the whole drama had unfolded the evening before. When she heard that June had been safe and well, fast asleep on a pile of old potato sacks in the shed which the local children called their den, it brought tears to her eyes.

The poor lamb must have been so confused and Ivy must have been terrified.

"Thank God she was found safe and well Billy, just think of all the awful things that could have happened… I bet Ivy was beside herself with worry," Alice cradled Rhys in her arms, he rewarded her with a beaming smile, she couldn't even imagine the torture Ivy must have gone through in the hours June was missing.

"It was a nightmare, still, as I said to Ivy, there's no harm done." Billy grinned, he still felt on a high after discovering June safe and well only a few yards from home.

"Still, she shouldn't go wandering off like that again; Ivy's going to give her a stern talking to today about never going out of the garden and I'm going to get some chain link fence to put up between us and the neighbours; after all there will be two little ones to think about now." Billy knew they had had a lucky escape with June; he owed it to June and William to secure the garden for the future.

Billy had been giving the prospect of moving onto Wilson Road a lot of thought, he had plans for the house and garden, the future was looking bright for them all.

"After Friday I'll have plenty of opportunity to tackle all the jobs that need doing around the place Alice; there's lots to keep me busy once we've tied the knot. Once my name is properly on the tenancy with Ivy, I can start making a few improvements about the place," Billy gave a smile, married life and a list of chores beckoned and in his heart he couldn't be happier, *only four days to go now.*

"But has anyone got any idea why June suddenly set off?" George was amazed the child had successfully navigated her way through the backs of the gardens until she ended up at the end of Wilson Road.

"Well, we don't know for certain, because June can't always tell you what she's thinking. Partly we think that she was bored and lonely and missing her little friend Karen Ashworth, partly we think her nose is a bit out of joint because of the new baby, but mostly we think it was because of this blessed bridesmaid dress she's got her heart set on wearing." Billy explained as he sipped his mug of tea.

Last night as they sat and cuddled on the sofa Ivy told Billy how she was convinced that the episode over the dress was the main reason for June's odd behaviour.

"What's this about a dress," Alice's ears pricked up.

"June wants to wear her bridesmaid's dress to our ceremony, and I stupidly said that she could…. It never occurred to Ivy and me that it wouldn't still fit the lass, but she's grown like a weed since your wedding last year and the blessed dress is way too small for her now."

Alice could immediately see the problem. The day she brought home the bridesmaid's dress June had been beyond herself with happiness; twirling and preening in her *princess* dress as she called it. It had been hard to get the child to take it off the day she tried it on for her Aunty Alice, and on the day of the wedding Ivy said that June had even wanted to wear it to bed.

"Ivy has bought June a nice new dress for the day, but the poor girl has her heart set on wearing a *princess* dress as she calls it, and we don't have the money to spend on fripperies she won't wear for more than a day."

Billy shook his head, *if* money wasn't so tight, he would have bought the child another princess dress in a heartbeat, but it was not even a possibility he could consider, they needed to watch every penny if they were to avoid slipping into debt.

"Well, the child will just have to do as she's told," George said firmly, he thought Billy and Ivy were too indulgent with June.

Alice flashed him a hard glance, sometimes George could be so pompous.

"Poor Ivy…. And poor June," she said. Alice looked thoughtful; she knew how much June loved that special dress.

"I know Alice, it's a real shame, and Ivy is dreading the show down about it on the day of the wedding, but we haven't got money to spare, any little cash that we have is being taken up with looking after William… babies don't come cheap as you well know Alice."

"I know!... I think I've got the answer Billy." Alice suddenly looked animated.

"I bet all the other bridesmaid's dresses don't fit any more either; I bet my young cousin Ruth doesn't fit hers; but I'm willing to lay a pound to a penny she's still got it at home. I had three pretty bridesmaids and June was the youngest if you can remember Billy." Alice could feel a plan forming in her head

Billy was too busy having eyes for Ivy on the day, but he did vaguely recall three pretty maids, with only *two* being invited by his snobby mother to be part of the wedding photographs. He thought he could see where this was conversation going, there might be a solution to the dress drama after all

"Why don't I ask Ruth's Mam if we can borrow Ruth's dress for the day… it's different from the one I bought for June, but actually it's even prettier than hers was and it's still long and flowing like a princess dress. I'm sure June will remember them from the day; she won't mind it being second-hand, and we can tell her it's the big girl's dress." Alice said triumphantly.

"It might just work," Billy said slowly, although in his heart he knew that you never could be too sure with June if she got a notion in her head about something.

"Good! that's settled then; I'll pop around to see Ruth's Mam today and ask if she'll do me the favour, but I'm certain she won't mind when I explain things. The dress might even be a bit too big as Ruth is three years older than June is, but if I can borrow it then we can put some temporary darts in it for the day, which I can easily unpick." Alice's eyes were sparkling with enthusiasm, she felt sure her plan could work.

"Who knows Billy, Ruth might even be prepared to give it back to me for June to keep instead? It's pointless the thing just ending up in the dressing up box if she's finished with it," Alice grinned, "I'm sure it's going to work Billy…. We'll get June her princess dress for the day, you mark my words."

George shook his head, but he wisely said nothing; in George's opinion his wife was always getting herself too involved in other people's business. Now Alice was going to be running around for the morning chasing down a bridesmaid's dress from a cousin in Grangetown and then doing the needle work alterations, and then dashing over to Ely, and all just so that one little girl could play at being a princess for an hour.

"Thanks Alice, if you can get the dress this morning, then I can let Ivy know your plans when I drop by this morning; it will be such a weight off her mind I can tell you." Billy heaved a sigh of relief.

"Fingers crossed Billy, I'll have a princess dress for June with me today when I come over to see Ivy," Alice laughed.

*

Within three hours Alice had travelled to Grangetown and back and secured the *princess* dress; even better it was not just on loan to June, it was a gift. Alice had guessed correctly, the dress *was* sitting neglected at the back of Ruth's wardrobe deemed too tight to be worn on any future special occasion, Ruth's mother was happy to see the back of it.

The dress had obviously been well worn and played in since the wedding; the hem was a bit grubby and there was a small tear under the armpit which Alice felt sure could easily be repaired. But, best of all, it certainly looked as if the dress would be a generous fit, and with a bit of time and effort and a few alterations June would have a new princess dress to be proud of.

Alice was certain June would love it.

*

"Hello, my lovely," Alice chirruped. Alice was met at the door of Wilson Road by an extremely excited June; Alice bent to give June a kiss and a hug, she half lifted June off the floor, "my, my you are growing to be such a big girl June… Soon poor Aunty Alice won't be able to lift you if you get much bigger." Alice joked.

June grabbed her aunt by the hand to lead her through to the sitting room. June had been watching out of the window for Aunty Alice to arrive, she had something to show her favourite Aunty; she wanted to show Aunty Alice her new brother William.

Alice parked the pram outside the front door in the afternoon sunshine, Rhys was fast asleep with his arms above his head, he would probably sleep for another hour or more in the fresh air.

"Alright June, I'm coming, I'm coming, just give me a moment," Alice laughed and reached beneath the pram to fetch out her parcel. "Let's leave Rhys here on the doorstep to finish his nap, now where is your Mam?" June yanked Aunty Alice in the direction of the sitting room.

Ivy sat on the sofa giving William his bottle, the baby slurped contentedly; Ivy had gathered from all the excited squeaks and yelps that Alice had arrived, *hopefully with the dress*. "Hello Alice, thanks so much for coming" Ivy was pleased to see her friend, especially since she did have a promising parcel nestled under her arm.

"Bruvver…. My bruvver," June said proudly as she patted William rather vigorously on the head.

"June is being such a good girl with baby William, Aunty Alice, she's helping me such a lot, now that she is getting to be a *big* girl," Ivy gave Alice a theatrical wink, "Would you like to show Aunty Alice how you feed baby William, June?"

June nodded enthusiastically and bounced up onto the sofa beside Ivy; June held out her arms to receive her brother.

Ivy slid the baby across onto June's meagre lap and propped some pillows behind June's elbow. Momentarily deprived of his bottle, William grizzled his displeasure. "Here we are then, William," Ivy quickly replaced the teat in the baby's mouth and placed the bottle in June's hand. June sat a picture of contentment as William nestled into her arms, "my bruvver," she lisped again, her forehead crinkling now with concentrating on keeping the warm milk angled towards the teat as she had been shown to do.

"That's right June, William *is* your little brother, and you *are* his big sister." Ivy said emphatically, she had decided that since they were keeping William that June must feel part of the new family relationship; not left out. The child loved playing with dollies, having a real baby to hold and feed was beyond June's wildest dreams.

Alice looked on, she was so pleased to see Ivy embracing motherhood again, and it looked as if June had taken on the role of big sister with alacrity, her very *own* baby brother to hold.

Soon, William's eyes fluttered asleep, and Ivy shifted him gently onto the sofa. "Now you sit watch William for me June, whilst I make Aunty Alice a nice cup of tea." Ivy headed for the kitchen; the baby would come to no harm with Alice in the room to oversee proceedings.

Alice could see that June had indeed shot up as Billy described, but she could also see that the new dress in the parcel would be more than big enough for the child. Alice had repaired the small tear and sponged the hem and if you didn't know what you were looking for, the stains had indeed disappeared, one small smudge of grass refused to rubbed out, but otherwise, the dress was perfect.

*

"June was so excited to see her new dress George, by the time she had tried it on she had completely forgotten about wanting to wear the old one." Alice gossiped as she forked mashed potato on top of her cottage pie and put it in the oven.

George was gazing adoringly at his son and rocking the child in his arms whilst Alice finished getting his dinner ready; five o'clock was always a busy time in the Thomas household with competing demands on Alice's time and after her visit to Wilson Road in the afternoon, Alice was running rather behind tonight.

"So, the big drama is over then," George said churlishly; he liked his dinner to be on time.

Alice chose to ignore the sarcasm. "Ivy is getting June to help her with the baby, the child loves having a new brother, instead of being jealous of the little lad, June is proud to have a brother; she was even helping to give him his bottle when I was there." Alice chattered on and put the lid on the Savoy cabbage.

"Well, I hope Ivy doesn't put too much trust in the girl, she's only young herself and… er a bit… well a bit *simple* after all." George knew that Alice would resent him referring to June as a Mongol, but when all was said and done, everybody knew that they weren't like *normal* children, however much Alice glossed over the situation.

Alice glared at George, sometimes he could be infuriating, "from what I could see, June was being a kind and loving sister just like any other five-year old might be with a new baby in the family." Alice poked the cabbage vigorously with a knife.

"I'm sure she is Alice, but all I'm saying is who knows what might happen if she's left unattended with the baby." George made a mental note to secure an assurance from Billy that June would never be left in the same room as *his* baby without an adult supervising. Whatever Alice might say about June's capabilities, he wouldn't trust a Mongol to hold his precious son, who knows what June might do if she felt provoked or was distracted; she might even drop him.

"Don't be ridiculous George, Ivy isn't stupid for heaven's sake!" Alice snapped, she gave an irritated *tut* and prodded the wilting cabbage again; George's attitude to June and Ivy was infuriating on occasions.

George wasn't too sure *what* Ivy Benson was sometimes. All he did know was that she was a source of quite a few arguments and disagreements in his household.

"And just so you know George, I've promised Ivy that I will go over to the house on the day of the wedding to look after William whilst everyone else is at the registry office… since we aren't going to the wedding it's the least I can do to help out," Alice's tone brooked no argument.

"If you can't trust *me* to be left alone with William and Rhys, then you had better come with me to make sure I don't do anything silly." Alice said sourly, she was tired, and George was getting on her nerves fretting about June, *why couldn't he be happy for Billy and Ivy?* June couldn't help being born the way she was, she was a wonderful loving little girl and whether George and his family liked it or not, June would soon be a member of the Thomas family.

George huffed explosively, it reminded her of a jet of water bursting out from the nose of a hippopotamus Alice had once seen at Bristol Zoo.

"Don't be so ridiculous Alice, why do you always have to be so dramatic? Of course, I trust you with Rhys." George glared at his wife's back, he felt sure she was checking on the cottage pie again at just that moment on purpose, so that she could put her back to him.

Alice rattled and clattered with irritation as she strained the pungent green cabbage water through the colander into the sink and set about chopping the cabbage brutally with the edge of an old saucer.

"Phoebe isn't going to the wedding breakfast afterwards, so I won't be on my own with the two babies for too long, in case that bothers you," Alice snapped. "Phoebe has said that she will come straight back to the house after the ceremony, so I think I *can* manage for a couple of hours on my own if *you* are absolutely sure." Alice said waspishly she raised a challenging eyebrow, defying George to keep making a fuss about the arrangements.

Meanwhile the cabbage was being chopped and pulverised within an inch of its life by the saucer, she pressed hard on the green pad at the bottom of the colander to extract the last of the water; Alice turned to face him, head tilted on one side, waiting for his answer.

Alice knew that Friday was one of the chip shop's busiest days with Billy busy getting married, and without any extra staff taken on for the day, George could not afford to down tools to join Alice babysitting at Wilson Road. Without George in the shop, it would leave only the flighty Elsie Evans serving behind the counter and Peter the young lad working behind the scenes; the shop would be short-handed, and she knew it. Alice had a smirk on her face daring him to answer.

George had quite been looking forward to spending the day in the Tasty Plaice without Billy in the shop; eyes and ears everywhere.

Elsie Evans was always a little more flirtatious when Billy wasn't around; laughing and joking, fluttering her eyelashes, she'd even given George a cheeky kiss, *for luck,* the other day when Billy was out; the last thing George wanted to do instead was baby sit with his wife over in Ely. Besides, he hadn't planned to leave the shop unattended on a Friday; Elsie couldn't manage on the shop her own; Alice was calling his bluff.

"Of course, I'm sure Alice," George muttered feeling pushed into a corner. George always felt that when he had a disagreement with Alice, he always came off the worst of it.

"Good well that's all settled then…. I'm pleased to hear it. Now I'd better bath our son and you'd better plate up your own dinner, it's all cooked and ready in the oven; I'll have mine later." Alice scooped up Rhys from George's arms and with her head held high, she stomped off to run a baby bath full of water and fold her pile of night nappies.

"Men!" she muttered under breath.

Chapter 41

A slender, official-looking, envelope landed on Phoebe's door mat, she turned it over to try and glean a hint as to what it might contain, the embossed envelope bore the impressive crest of Cardiff County Hall. Phoebe's face dropped; this letter looked official; it was not the letter she was waiting for. She had been hoping to get a response from Deirdre; it was three days now since she sent her letter telling Deirdre about Carol Jones veiled threat.

"Any news Phoebe?" Malcolm opened his room door when he heard the post plop on to the mat, these days Phoebe said Malcolm was welcome to use the front door as well as the back. Over the last few weeks, they had become closer, Malcolm was no longer just her lodger, he was her friend. Malcolm knew Phoebe was on edge in many ways; not only was she waiting for a letter from her friend in Porthcawl, but today was the day she would choose a new lodger and she was anxious not to be duped again. Three women, chosen from a list of six, were coming to the house this morning to view the room. Two days before, Malcolm had helped Phoebe sift through the new applicants until he was satisfied they had weeded out the obvious chancers and the hopeless cases; these three women looked promising.

"You can never be certain Phoebe, but if these letters are anything to go by then any one of these three look as if they might suit you: all of them sound like decent, hardworking people; none of your fancy fly by nights like Carol. Get them to come on Wednesday and I'll help you choose, I can run my eye over them whilst you show them the room; sometimes it's body language and attitude that gives the game away, not just words on paper." Malcolm offered; he knew Phoebe valued his opinion.

"That one looks official," he could see Phoebe examining the post mark.

"I think it's from the county court Malcolm, if it is, then that means it's about Carol," Phoebe handed him the unopened envelope.

"I reckon you're right," he could see she looked nervous, she stood wringing her hands. "Would you like me to open it for you?"

Phoebe nodded she had been dreading this, she had hoped against hope that she wouldn't have to attend court if she was called to testify against Carol. This could be the summons she was fearing.

"Well, well, who'd have thought it," Malcolm grinned when he read the first paragraph. "It seems our Miss Jones is not as green as she's cabbage looking, she's actually pleaded guilty to avoid going to trial and she has asked for twenty other similar cases to be taken into account….and I bet that was just the tip of the iceberg!" Malcolm snorted in disbelief, *the tricksy cow had obviously only confessed to just enough crimes so that the police wouldn't try and hunt for any more evidence against her.*

"It seems that the police have dropped the charges of passing on fake notes due to lack of evidence… *hmm* so she managed to wangle her way out of that one." Malcolm mused.

Malcolm handed the letter back to Phoebe to read the rest of the letter. Phoebe heaved a sigh of relief and read the decision with a shaking hand.

"It says here Malcolm that because of Miss Jones's guilty plea there will be no formal trial and that she will be sentenced by the magistrate in the next few weeks… thank goodness it's all over." Phoebe smiled; a weight lifted off her shoulders. Phoebe had been anxious about being embroiled in a trial; worried that her own private life and arrangement with Deirdre might be exposed through a probing barrister out to discredit her evidence.

In hope of a lighter sentence Carol Jones had fluttered her eyelashes and maintained that she was the victim of a coercive husband who intimidated her into committing acts of theft and fraud; she asked that those factors would be considered, when she was sentenced for her crimes.

Malcolm, who knew about such things, reckoned that if anyone was doing the coercion in the relationship, then it was Carol.

"Well, she won't get off scot-free this time Phoebe, but I reckon she'll still be treated too lightly, people like her always are. With her pretty looks and devious ways, she'll probably manage to convince authorities that she's really a good person underneath, who just happened to make a few mistakes because of her nasty husband and that she's a victim herself; people like her always sweet talk their way out of things," Malcolm said bitterly. He knew that was exactly how his wife Shirley operated.

"They'll never believe you Malcolm, if you make a complaint," Shirley's favourite taunt.

"You're probably right Malcolm and none of it will bring back the things she's stolen from us or the items from all the other homes she raided." Phoebe felt sad that Carol had pilfered and sold Edmund's gold signet ring, it was precious to her as a memento of the man she had once loved, but the main thing Carol had of hers was her secret and no sentence could make Carol forget what she had discovered about Phoebe.

"Would you like to join me for a cup of tea Malcolm? The first woman to see the room will be here in half an hour, so we've got time before she arrives." Phoebe was feeling rattled, the letter had unsettled her. Phoebe had this sinking feeling that she hadn't heard the last of Carol Jones

*

The final prospective lodger left, and Phoebe and Malcolm exchanged grins, any of the plain dumpy women who had answered the advert would have done the trick but the last one to come along, Mrs Margaret Parish, a woman in her fifties had secured the coveted room. Phoebe had found her new lodger.

The minute Phoebe opened the door, she recognized Margaret Parish, "Peg" to all who knew her, as a familiar market worker from a popular stall at Cardiff market. Phoebe had bought plenty of fruit and veg from Alf and Peg's stall over the years and never once had Peg tried to short-change her or slip a rotten, or stale piece of veg into the bottom of Phoebe's bag. Now recently widowed, and with no children to take her in, Peg was looking for somewhere affordable to lodge. When Phoebe opened the door, Peg instantly recognized her old customer as well and greeted her with her usual hearty laugh.

"Peg Parish… Well, I never!... Come on in," Phoebe welcomed the woman inside and within moments the two women were chattering away. "Alf knew the lease was due up for renewal and that they wanted a lot more money for it too, but he was taken before it could all be sorted out…. And after he died Phoebe, the market authorities said they wouldn't let me take on the lease on my own even if I could find the money for it and I don't have a son or a brother to come in with me so…" Peg raised the palms of her hands in surrender and shrugged. When Alf Parish died of a heart attack overnight, their business died with him.

Phoebe sympathised with Peg, a woman running a business in a man's world was tough.

"I had to accept that I couldn't run the stall on my own Phoebe, so I had to let it go, it's a real shame after all those years working with my Alf; still, there's no point crying over spilt milk. I've had a change of tack that's all." Peg explained.

Peg was a simple soul who could barely read and write, through years of experience she could work out complex additions in her head and reckon change owed to a customer in a flash; but other than that admirable talent for money, Peg didn't understand the world of business and dealing with the authorities. Without her Alf at her side, she was struggling to keep her head above water in their old, rented house, and she'd had to let the business go; but Peg always smiled in the face of adversity and cheerfully got on with life.

"Don't worry, I've still got enough money coming in to pay my way," Peg added hastily. "I can afford the room; a cousin of Alf's has taken the lease on; they're like gold dust those leases. He's said that I can still work on his stall for as long as I want to; he knows as well as I do that I've got the loudest shout in the market; I can call them in from one end of the market to the other." She chuckled a deep throaty laugh.

"You'll never keep Peg Parish out of the market, I reckon it's in the blood, I'll probably drop dead with an apple in one hand and pound of spuds in the other." Peg grinned a toothy smile; her lips rarely covering her buck teeth which crowded her mouth and her apple shaped faced permanently creased with laughter lines; the woman radiated a perpetual state of chirpy good humour whatever life threw at her.

"It's agreed then Peg, you can take the room and if the house rules are stuck to and you pay your rent on time then I'm sure we will all get on just fine." Phoebe had already given each applicant a thorough run down on the household rules, after her unfortunate experience with Carol Jones, and she wasn't taking any chances no matter how affable *anyone* appeared including Peg Parish.

"Ta very much Phoebe," Peg grinned, "and one of the bonuses of the job is that I get plenty of free fruit and veg. I'll make sure I pass a bit your way when I've got some spare," Peg winked.

"Course I'm never too sure *what* will come my way but if it's gone past its best or is a bit bashed around the edges I can have it 'cos it'll only get thrown out at the end of a day for the pig man, which is a crying shame. Still, I reckon by the time it's been trimmed and sorted you'd never know the difference on most things; you can't beat a nice pot of vegetable soup and it saves a bit on the old house keeping." Peg chortled and patted her well-padded girth.

"Thank you Peg, the offer is much appreciated." Phoebe smiled; Peg's good humour was infectious.

So, it was agreed that Peg Parish would move in on Saturday, the day after Ivy's wedding, Phoebe wanted to be around the day the new lodger moved in, for all Peg's good humour and cosy familiarity, Phoebe thought it prudent to keep a close eye on her until they knew each other better.

"Thank you for your help today Malcolm, I feel much better now that we have found a new lodger."

"You won't regret choosing her Phoebe, trust me I know I diamond when I spot one." Malcolm grinned, "Tell you what Phoebe, how about we go out to the pub tonight to celebrate finding your new lodger and the magistrates finding Carol Jones guilty… it will be my treat."

Phoebe had to think for just a moment, it was a shift in their relationship if she accepted his invitation to go to the pub with him, to be seen out with a man in public; Malcolm made no secret of the fact that he was a married man.

Phoebe regularly had drinks with other male friends like Cappy when she lived in Tiger Bay but here things were different, if a neighbour spotted her drinking with her lodger then there might be gossip; conclusions drawn.

"I'd love to but…"

Malcolm could hear the doubt in her tone. "It's all right Phoebe I understand," his shoulders slumped a little. She could see he looked hurt as if she had repositioned their relationship; pushed him away.

"No Malcolm I really *would* love to go out for a drink but what I was going to say is… but would you mind if we went to another part of Cardiff where I'm not likely to be seen by nosey neighbours who might put two and two together and make five," Phoebe smiled.

"Of course, we can," Malcolm grinned. He hadn't thought about the sensitivity of Phoebe's position in the neighbourhood. He still knew so little about her and he wanted to know so much more if only she would let him in. He'd bared his soul to her, but she'd kept her secrets and her past close; perhaps in time she would learn to trust him

"Shall we catch a bus at about seven o'clock then Phoebe, you just say where you would like to go, and we'll go there?" Malcolm offered.

"Agreed," Phoebe felt a warm glow, she was going out for a pleasant evening in the company of a man who treated her like a lady, she was growing very fond of Malcolm. For once in her life a man wasn't just trying to use her, and it felt good.

Chapter 42

"Only one day to go now Ivy, and the weather looks set fair for the day," Betty smiled, she watched as Ivy was doing the ironing and Betty was enjoying a cuddle with baby William; the child certainly was a handsome little lad she could see why Ivy was so desperate to keep him after Norah died.

"It does look set to be fine Mam, but I shall be happy to get married to Billy whatever the weather brings." Ivy took care to neatly fold and iron a pile of tiny vests and matinee jackets. For Ivy, life felt better than it had ever done before; she was sure she could almost burst with happiness. From tomorrow, she could share her bed with Billy without fear of twitching curtains and neighbourly gossip and spend the rest of her life with the man she loved, and to top it all, their family had been made complete by the arrival of baby William into their lives.

The one cloud on Ivy's happiness was the loss of her good friend Norah; it was a bittersweet pleasure to see Norah's beautiful little lad every day and be reminded of her dear friend who would never see her son grow up. So many happy memories of Norah with her noisy exuberant family; laughter and tears from the very first day Norah took her under her wing when she and Jimmy moved onto Wilson Road; love and kindness when Jimmy turned out to be such a brutal husband.

Ivy felt blessed to be raising Norah's son, but since Norah had gone, she didn't feel that she had a loyal friend and confidant on Wilson Road who she could trust and turn to when times get tough. Norah had been her rock and she missed her every day.

The new lady from the top of Wilson Road, Eileen Riley, who popped in to wish her well after June was found safe did seem to be sweet and friendly; Ivy had hopes that in time they could be friends. Eileen was a new inexperienced mother like she used to be, Eileen might welcome a friend herself in the coming months.

Eileen had confided in Ivy that her own baby was due in four months' time, *if it was a boy, it could be a playmate for William.* Ivy vowed to try to cultivate Eileen's friendship once the wedding was out of the way; she needed to stop being so insular.

"I'm so pleased Alice is coming to look after William for me tomorrow Mam, I think it would give Pearl Thomas an apoplexy if I turned up to get wed with a new-born baby in my arms," Ivy giggled. Billy had told Les and Pearl about the arrival of baby William into their lives and Ivy knew that Pearl was less than impressed by the news. His father Les seemed to take the announcement in his stride; at least it kept the family name going like Les always wanted, but his mother Pearl seemed more concerned about how on earth she would explain this latest convoluted twist in her son's relationship with the former wife of a child abuser to all her nosey neighbours.

Pearl thought Ivy Benson couldn't shock or surprise her any more than she had already… and then she did! Convinced that her and Ivy would never get on, Pearl still grudgingly recognized it was better to gain Ivy as a daughter in law than to lose her son by falling out over the woman her son loved. In the battle with her son over Ivy Benson, Pearl knew she had lost.

"What time are you setting out tomorrow, Ivy? It still seems strange you won't have anyone to see you off on your wedding day." Betty had suggested Ivy and the children stayed over with her and Gerald the night before the wedding and Alice do the baby sitting at Inkerman Street, but Ivy argued against it.

"It's far easier for Alice to come here and look after William Mam, all the baby things are here and with any luck if I get him settled just before I leave he might sleep in his cot most of the time. Alice can wave me off, it's not like I haven't done this before is it." Ivy giggled.

Her Mam shot a disapproving glance, she didn't need reminding of Ivy's first disastrous marriage to Jimmy.

"I can see you haven't lost your touch Mam," Ivy changed the subject; she watched her mother rocking and jigging William to sleep; the child unable to resist the seductive rhythm was lolling in Betty's arms.

"Once you are a mother you never lose the knack…. He certainly is a little smasher Ivy and it's good to see June trying to mother him." Betty was surprised to find June giving William a bottle when she had arrived earlier on. Despite Nanna Betty offering to take over the task June refused to hand over William.

"*My* brother Nanna," June had announced proudly when Nanna reached out to William.

"June *is* very good with him," Ivy admitted, "at first I think that she was a bit jealous and confused by it all. One minute the baby was Karen's little brother Jack who we were looking after for Aunty Norah until she came out of hospital, the next minute he's turned into *her* brother who has come to stay for good *and* we've changed his name from Jack to William."

"When you put it like that it's no wonder the lass had a bit of a strop, it's enough to confuse anyone." Betty admitted.

"Still as Billy said, there's no harm come from June's little escapade and now that she's come around to the idea, I reckon she will be the best big sister any baby could hope for." Ivy laughed; she could see that June had latched on to her baby brother William with a passion.

"Let's hope he's a good boy for his Aunty Alice and Aunty Phoebe tomorrow then," Betty said. She lay the sleeping child on the sofa.

"He's always a good boy," Ivy knelt down and gave the child a kiss, "we wouldn't be without him now for all the tea in China." Ivy suddenly looked worried; she shivered as if someone had walked over her grave.

"Penny for your thoughts," Betty said, she saw the troubled frown flit across Ivy's face. "Is something the matter Ivy?"

"You once said to me Mam that *nothing good or bad lasts forever…* and I know it's stupid to think this way but sometimes I almost feel as if I'm cursed and now, I'm beginning to think that all this," Ivy's arm swept the room, "all this happiness with Billy and June and the baby might crumble into dust. I'm wondering if by saying my Da couldn't come to the wedding I've somehow hexed us with bad luck yet to come." Ivy started to sob.

"There, there Ivy, don't cry." Betty hugged her daughter tight, "this is just pre wedding jitters, your father wouldn't curse you for not inviting him to the wedding, that's a silly thought; he just wants you to be happy as do we all. Let's have no more nonsense about being cursed with bad luck." Betty remembered thinking herself that the old saying *nothing good or bad lasts forever* sounded like both a blessing and a curse.

Surely Ivy was due a bit of good luck in her life, surely the wheel of fortune wouldn't turn that quickly? Her daughter was a loving, kind-hearted girl who deserved to be happy.

"I know," Betty said brightly, anxious to lift Ivy's mood, "why don't you go out for a little walk in the fresh air; get yourself out of the house for half an hour and blow the cobwebs away? I'll watch June and William for you. I think a nice walk around the block or a quick pop to the shops would do you a power of good, and then when you get back, we can have a nice cup of tea together before I head for home. You're just getting overtired that's all." Betty coaxed, she could see that Ivy was working herself into a lather, Ivy might not have given birth to William, but she was having all the same sleepless night experiences of any new mother, her daughter looked worn out and run ragged.

"Thanks Mam," Ivy blew her nose and wiped her eyes. "I know I'm being silly, but what with the baby to look after and the scare over June, I've been living on my nerves a bit lately."

"Of course, you have Ivy, now off you pop, have half an hour's peace and quiet, I'll put the ironing away for you." Betty soothed. "Here take this Ivy," Betty rummaged in her purse and handed Ivy a half a crown.

"Why not pick up a nice cake from the bakery and we can have a bit of afternoon, tea before I catch my bus home. I'm sure June would like that, and you need to feed yourself up a bit my girl." Betty knew that her own well-padded middle didn't need feeding up at all, but Ivy was looking very slender these days.

"Thanks Mam."

Ivy strolled up the road with her hands in her pockets, it was good to take a moment to herself and think, to get away from the house and the chores. Her Mam was probably right, it *was* just pre-wedding jitters. Tomorrow she would be married to a man who adored her, she offered up a small prayer of thanks to a God she wasn't always too sure was always on her side.

The April sun was on her face and the wind ruffled her curls; Ivy felt a calmness descend on her as she ambled towards the shops. Tomorrow she would be Mrs William Thomas, the dreadful title of Mrs Benson thrown away with the stroke of a pen.

On the corner of Wilson Road Ivy spotted Mrs Carol Roberts deep in conversation with the neighbourhood gossip Janet Whitman. *Plotting, scheming, and running people down as usual I bet,* Ivy thought to herself, she didn't like Carol or the two-faced Janet. Norah had warned her against getting involved with the toxic pair not long after Ivy moved onto Wilson Road. The two women turned towards her.

There was many a time Norah had challenged Carol's catty remarks, but Ivy wasn't brave like Norah used to be, and she knew better than to rub the woman up the wrong way, given half the chance Ivy would have gone home, but Mam was expecting that cake.

Carol could have a very acid tongue on her when provoked and her limpet like devotee Janet loved to scatter tit bits of gossip and rumour far and wide on the Ely Estate. Ivy usually just tried to avoid being drawn into conversation whenever she saw them, but today she had nowhere to hide; if she was to get to the shops on the Grand Avenue, Ivy would have to keep going.

Ivy could see the women watching her as she walked up the road in the direction of the Grand Avenue shops, she could hardly just turn around now and look as if she was too frightened to stroll past them.

"Good afternoon, *Mrs Benson*," Carol said with emphasis on Ivy's name as she spotted her prey, "I see you have left the children at home today," Carol had a smirk on her face.

Ivy couldn't miss the heavy inference that somehow June and William were left unattended at home whilst she gallivanted off to the shops; she didn't need to explain herself to the likes of Carol Roberts, *nosey old cow.* Ivy just tilted her head and said nothing.

"When is the happy day to be, Mrs Benson…. I heard you were *supposed* to be getting married again soon?" Carol oozed womanly interest; trying to draw Ivy into conversation.

"We're getting married at midday tomorrow," Ivy knew that Carol wasn't really interested in wishing her and Billy good luck on the day; Carol Roberts wouldn't give Ivy the skin off a cold rice pudding.

"Well, that *is* good news, I've always liked a nice wedding…. If you ask me, it's *always* good to get things on an official footing." Carol said obscurely, Carol gave Ivy a cold stare, there was no warmth and kindness in those dead-fish eyes of hers.

"I'm afraid I must rush Mrs Roberts, I'm only popping to the shops, my mother will wonder where I've got to if I stand around chatting. Have a good afternoon." Ivy slipped neatly out of Carol's net.

As Ivy walked away, she could hear an explosion of sniggering from behind her back. Ivy held her head high and kept going; she wouldn't give them the satisfaction of turning around to see what they were laughing about. *Those two women were vile, she'd lay a pound to a penny they were mocking her gammy leg and limp.*

When Ivy returned from the Grand Avenue shops twenty minutes later with a hunk of fresh sticky lardy cake for afternoon tea, the two bitchy women were gone.

Ivy heaved a sigh of relief; she would not need to run the gauntlet a second time. When she got home Ivy could see her mother had tidied around and washed the crockery in the sink, a set of nappies was boiling vigorously on the top of the stove.

"Hello love," Betty muttered with a peg between her teeth, she pinned a damp tea towel on the airing rack to dry. "These nappies are nearly done, they just need a rinse through, they've had a good old boil for at least fifteen minutes."

Flexing her arms to lift the two handled pan Betty staggered over to the sink with the pan of grey bubbling water and tipped the steaming mass into the Belfast. "I thought they could dry overnight if we got them done now." Betty mashed away at the sodden mass; turning the nappies with wooden tongs under the running cold kitchen tap. Clouds of steam chased into the air and gathered on the ceiling.

"Thanks Mam," Ivy smiled. The tiny kitchen was a bath of steam, it was like the old times when they lived in Bute Street and something was always bubbling on the top of the stove, except in those days it was most likely to be a half pig's head being rendered down for *Betty's best brawn.* Times had been tough then, and Ivy appreciated now just how much her Mam, a woman on her own trying to make ends meet, had put herself through to bring up Ivy in the turbulent, unforgiving world of Tiger Bay. Ivy walked over to her Mam, now stood at the sink with a soaking apron wrapped around her, her hair threaded with silver; Ivy slipped her arms around her mother's matronly waist and kissed her mother's cheek.

"I love you Mam and thank you for everything." Ivy could feel herself getting emotional.

"Whist… get away with you Ivy, it's only a few nappies." Betty flushed with exertion and emotion.

"No, I mean it Mam, thank you for *everything*, it's not easy being a mother, I know that now." Ivy pushed a strand of hair away from her eyes, the steam was turning her carefully tamed locks into a tumble of unruly curls.

Betty laughed "You can say that again Ivy! Now how about you make us both a nice cup of tea whilst I put these nappies through the mangle and then I must be off to get my Gerald his tea."

Chapter 43

It was the morning of the wedding, the sun shone, and a light breeze chased away the chilly early morning mist which hung over roof tops; it was going to be a glorious day to get married, so very unlike the grey, dismal drizzle the day Ivy married Jimmy Benson at the same registry office. May and the promise of summer was just around the corner.

Ivy had barely slept a wink with thoughts of the wedding rushing through her mind keeping her awake and for the first time ever, since Ivy had looked after him, baby William had slept right through the night undisturbed; his very stillness driving Ivy's sleep away as she lay in the dark vigilant and listening to William's soft, dreamy snuffles.

Ivy held her breath each time she heard a sigh or a grunt coming from the old cot beside her bed and twice in the inky stillness, Ivy got up to check the child was still breathing. *I remember doing the same with June,* she thought fondly to herself. At three o'clock in the morning just as Ivy was abandoning all hope of getting to sleep, she finally drifted off.

June, her hair twisted in rags to encourage a mop of golden curls and bouncing with excitement at the prospect of wearing her new princess dress for the day, trotted into see her Mam at first light. June's excited squawks roused baby William and soon noisy, family mayhem crowned Ivy's wedding day.

Ivy got into her dressing gown, today was the first day of the rest of her life and, tired though she was through lack of sleep, she couldn't be happier.

Ivy's new green cotton dress hung on a hanger on the back of her bedroom door, topped off by a pretty, cream cardigan. On her dressing table a neat cream hat with a folded brim borrowed from Alice and a new pair of cream mesh gloves, a present from Mam would complete her wedding outfit; Mam had insisted that Ivy must wear the string of pearls Gerald gave Betty as her little bit of something *old*, a tiny blue forget-me-not embroidered on Ivy's handkerchief completed the *something old, something new, something borrowed, something blue* rhyme.

"Come on tuppence, let's go downstairs to get William his bottle and you can have some breakfast; it's going to be a long time until we eat our dinner today. I'll just change William's wet nappy first."

"Princess dress," June's eyes were like saucers.

"No, not yet young lady, you aren't eating porridge in your best princess dress, we are going to get you dressed when Aunty Alice arrives at ten o'clock; I expect if you ask Aunty Alice nicely, she'll do your hair for you as well." Ivy added, Alice had a way with hair, Ivy half hoped that Alice might help her with hers as well. A brief glance in the mirror confirmed that yesterday's steamy kitchen and a sleepless night had turned Ivy's hair into an unruly mess.

June beamed, she loved Aunty Alice, she tugged fiercely at the annoying rags which had been difficult and lumpy to sleep on.

Ivy swiftly untwined the rag twists before they became entangled in June's hair. "Now don't fiddle with these ringlets June, leave them for Aunty Alice to sort out."

June shook her head and corkscrews of curls sprung out. June had a mop of beautiful hair; it was her crowning glory.

Alice arrived promptly at ten o'clock, to a house full of noisy laughter; Alice had walked from Caroline Street with Rhys in his pram and was ready to help with the wedding preparations.

The wedding was to be held at twelve o'clock with a modest wedding breakfast held for the six adults and June at a venue around the corner from the registry office at the Duke of Clarence public house. But when

Alice left the flat that morning, Billy was pacing the floor anxiously twiddling his hair, he did not look a happy man.

"What on earth are you fretting about Billy," Alice laughed as she handed him a cup of tea. "I'll make sure Ivy and June catch their bus… don't worry she won't be late today."

"It's not that Alice, it's my bloody mother I'm bothered about. According to George, Mam was kicking off yesterday; bursting into floods of tears and giving my poor old Da a hard time about the wedding, telling him it wasn't too late for me to call it off."

Alice raised an eyebrow. *Pearl could be a difficult cow if she put her mind to it,* Alice could easily imagine Pearl trying to twist her husband around her little finger.

"Apparently Da wasn't having it, he told her she *would* attend the wedding whether she wanted to or not… said he'd given his word or something like that." Billy looked puzzled he had to admit that his father had made a big effort to have a good relationship with Ivy and June, he'd never worked out why his Da had changed his tune about him marrying Ivy, but he was glad that he had.

"I do hope our Mam doesn't kick off today and spoil things with being in a sour mood. I want this to be the happiest day of Ivy's life." Billy said thoughtfully, he loved Ivy so much and tonight he would go to sleep in her arms for the very first time; he tingled at the very thought of it. They didn't need a honeymoon; they had each other and that was all that mattered.

"I'm sure it will be Billy; I know Ivy can't wait to get married either. I'm sure, if there is any justice in this world, then you are both going to be very happy together; don't let your Mam spoil the day with her moods," Alice gave Billy a kiss on the cheek, "Good luck Billy; I'll take good care of William for you until you get back. You just have a wonderful day."

Alice smiled she was thrilled to be gaining Ivy as her sister-in-law.

June opened the door and let Aunty Alice in, she could see the child was fizzing with excitement.

Alice gave June a big hug. June dragged her favourite Aunty into the sitting room where Ivy sat feeding William.

"June's very pleased to see you as am I," Ivy laughed as she sat in the cluttered sitting room in her house coat.

"Good, now are you ready for Aunty Alice to do your hair June?" June nodded enthusiastically, despite Ivy's entreaties to leave the hair alone all morning, several ringlets had already unravelled.

"Firstly, we need to pop your dress on over your head so that we don't mess the hairstyle up once Aunty Alice has done it all nice for you…. Then once you have the dress on, you must sit very still like a real princess on a throne… can you manage to do that for me June."

June nodded her head vigorously. Ivy raised her eyes in disbelief, asking June to sit still was like asking the wind not to blow.

Somehow with coaxing and praise from Alice, June was transformed into a princess with flowing locks; June's hair was shaped into a soft wave, kept back with Kirby grips and Aunty Alice produced some magical hairspray from her handbag to set the creation into place.

"Perfect if I do say so myself, now go and look at yourself in the mirror June."

June trotted upstairs to preen in front of her mother's dressing table mirror.

"I must say that brings back memories of when we were girls Alice," Ivy smiled, a tear staring to gather in her eye, "do you remember years ago when you used to transform me with a bit of your Mam's hairspray before we used to nip out to meet Billy and George at that night club on

Portmanmoor Road; you trying your best to turn this ugly duckling into a swan?" Ivy giggled.

Alice snorted. "The trouble was Ivy you never *believed* yourself to be beautiful, you always looked amazing; I never transformed you, I just brought your natural beauty out; a few flicks of eyeliner and a dash of Mini-poo and a few borrowed clothes can't make someone beautiful if they're not. Billy's on to a good thing when he marries you; Billy's a lucky man and he knows it." Alice wagged her finger; she couldn't have Ivy getting all maudlin on her wedding day.

"Now are you going to get married in your house coat or are you going to smarten yourself up for this wedding of yours." Alice laughed and gave Ivy a fierce hug. "I'm so pleased you are going to be my sister-in-law Ivy; we are going to have such fun now you'll be part of the family." Alice looked deep into Ivy's eyes and smiled; she loved her friend dearly.

"I've always thought of you as my sister Alice," Ivy said simply, and it was true, from the very first day at school when the confident, pretty Alice Tranter took shy, plain little Ivy Jenkins' hand and looked after her, Ivy had loved Alice like a big sister.

"Well, as your big sister I'm ordering you to get a move on, I promised Billy faithfully that you wouldn't be late, now get dressed and I will do your hair and makeup before you leave." Alice said sternly shooing Ivy upstairs.

"Yes Alice," Ivy said obediently. "Thanks for everything… what would I do without you?" Ivy hugged Alice back and shot upstairs to get herself dressed.

An hour later Alice waved a glamorous, groomed Ivy and a delighted June, regal in her princess frock, goodbye.

Ivy, pretty in her new dress and hat, left Wilson Road holding June's hand and made her way to the bus stop, her heart fluttering with excitement.

As Ivy reached the top of Wilson Road she could see the twitch of a curtain from Carol Robert's house, Ivy held her head high and sailed past, she wasn't letting the bitchy Carol Roberts cast a shadow on her special day.

Eileen Riley stood on her doorstep, her hands folded across her bump and waved a cheery greeting to Ivy and princess June as they came past.

"All the best Ivy," Eileen called.

June waved enthusiastically back.

*

"All things considered it went ever so well Alice," Phoebe sipped a cup of strong tea and chewed on a toasted piece of yesterday's lardy cake. A few flakes of confetti were caught up in her greying hair.

It warmed Phoebe's heart to see Ivy so happy with a man who obviously adored her, the last time she'd witnessed Ivy's marriage to Jimmy at the same venue, Ivy looked like a lamb being led to the slaughter. This time it couldn't be more different, the couple couldn't stop grinning at each other, if ever a couple were head over heels in love, it was Ivy and Billy.

Alice was eager to hear every detail about the wedding; Pearl did have a bit of a frosty face on her at the registry office, but she kept her mouth shut and didn't spoil Ivy and Billy's day.

Les had been wary of Phoebe but he ensured that his wife did not upset Ivy; he'd stuck to his end of the bargain, he gave Ivy and Billy his blessing and a gift of twenty pounds to start their married life together. Once Ivy had the ring on her finger and was declared the new Mrs William Thomas, Pearl looked like a deflated balloon with all the fight gone out of her.

Billy and Ivy were wed, and no matter how much Pearl carped and sniped now, nothing Pearl said was *ever* going to change that. Having seen Ivy married, Phoebe was happy to go back to help Alice with the two babies and put her feet up for the rest of the afternoon until the happy couple returned home.

"These registry office services are all over in fifteen minutes flat, but I've never seen a happier bride than Ivy was today; she positively glowed." Phoebe smiled

Phoebe had come to relieve Alice from the duty of looking after two babies, mercifully for Alice, in the time before Phoebe arrived there hadn't been too much to tax her patience and Rhys had slept soundly for most of the first two hours, but now both babies required feeding and nappy changing.

"Here, you pass William to me Alice, I've finished my tea now. I'll change the little mite and you can see to Rhys and then they can both have a nice big bottle of milk and hopefully we'll get a bit of peace and quiet." Phoebe smiled, even with all the mayhem, she loved babies.

Both babies started squawking at the top of their voices, little lungs howling in unison as the women tackled the wet nappies; bottoms were changed, pink limbs flailed about in protest.

"Dear me, Phoebe," Alice laughed "it's hard to believe but they were as good as gold until you arrived… I'll tell you what Phoebe, I'm glad I didn't have twins; I couldn't do this every day." Both women laughed uproariously.

"They both sound hungry if you ask me." Phoebe tucked the nappy and fastened the pin in a practised fashion, William was all clean and tidy again.

"Their milk should be warm enough by now Phoebe, I'll go and get the bottles." Alice headed for the kitchen and retrieved the two bottles of tepid milk.

Just as Alice was heading back through the hall, a sharp knocking came at the front door, "blast" Alice muttered under her breath, babies were crying in unison.

"Just a minute," Alice called to the figure on the other side of the glass. "I'll be with you in just a minute."

Alice trotted into the sitting room, gave Phoebe a bottle for William, she scooped a howling Rhys up in her arms and plugged the teat in his mouth. Silence descended.

"There's somebody at the door Phoebe, I'll just see to it." Alice sounded exasperated; whoever the person was they could not have called at a more inconvenient time.

Alice marched towards the door with Rhys tucked in her arm, the suckling child now feeding greedily on the bottle; she would not put him down. Alice fumbled with the unfamiliar door lock, she struggled to release the latch with one hand. "Just two seconds," Alice called again, her voice pleading for patience from the visitor on the other side of the door.

Alice finally opened the door.

The short man on the doorstep wearing a dark pin stripe suit and carrying a brief case removed his hat. He smiled a smile which did not quite reach his eyes.

"Good afternoon …are *you* Mrs Ivy Benson?"

Chapter 44

Alice regarded the man with cool interest, she didn't grow up around Tiger Bay without learning that you don't need to answer a question just because someone has asked it.

The man gave a small cough to clear his throat, "Ha, hmm…my name is Mr Bevan and I'm a representative from Cardiff Council and I need to talk to Mrs Ivy Benson."

"I see," Alice said evenly. "Well, I'm afraid she's not in."

"So, you are *not* Mrs Benson."

"Have I not made myself clear Mr Bevan," Alice said coolly, "Mrs Benson is *not* in today, you'll have to try another time… Now I'm afraid, as you can see, I'm rather busy." Alice went to shut the door.

Before she could stop him, Mr Bevan wedged a large black shoe in the door.

"Hey… what are you playing at?... Get your foot out of the door!" Alice yelped.

In the sitting room Phoebe could hear the raised voices, *something was wrong.*

"Just a moment Mrs….?" Mr Bevan kept his foot firmly wedged in the door. "Would you mind telling me if that baby is yours?"

Phoebe headed for the door with a sleeping William in her arms. "What's going on Alice." Phoebe scanned the scene; she'd met pompous jumped-up officials like Mr Bevan many a time.

Mr Bevan assessed the scene; he now had a second baby in the hallway.

"I'm sorry Mrs?..." it irritated him that Alice refused to give him her name and now this other woman was staring him out, "but I *do* need to speak to Mrs Benson, and I was told that she lived at this address, I'm only doing my job." Hugh Bevan, whined.

"I've told the man that Ivy's not in and now he wants to know if this is my baby…. Not that I can see that it is anything to do with him!" Alice huffed indignantly.

Phoebe didn't like the way the questioning was going.

"I am trying to track down a Mrs Ivy Benson and a Master Jack Ashcroft and I was told that they both were to be found at this address," Hughl Bevan's gaze drifted over Alice's shoulder to the second baby asleep in Phoebe's arms. He'd been told that the grandmother often visited Mrs Benson, perhaps this was her.

"Is *that* baby named Master Jack Ashcroft?" Hugh Bevan asked pointedly.

"Not that it's your business, but this baby is called William," Phoebe said smartly. "Now you had better leave Mr Bevan, you can't come around here making all sorts of demands, and I'm not inviting you in." Phoebe could feel her blood turning to ice in her veins, she might get rid of the odious Hugh Bevan today but people like him always came back.

"In that case I shall be off; but I do have an important letter here for Mrs Benson, please see that she gets it." Hugh Bevan tossed the letter into the hall and removed his foot from the door, there could be no argument that this letter had got lost in the post.

Alice slammed the door behind him. Phoebe scooped the letter up from the mat.

"What an odious little man," Alice said angrily, "who did he think he was jamming his foot in the doorway like that?"

"I don't like the look of this Alice," Phoebe settled herself on the sofa and turned the mystery letter over several times in her hand.

"Why… what do you think it's all about Phoebe?" Alice was mystified by the man's firm determination to get her name and get the name of her baby.

"I'll lay a pound to a penny it's about this little one here." Phoebe said sadly, she looked at the sleeping baby in her arms; perfect rose bud lips, softly curled eyelashes and eyelids flickering with dreams.

"This will *all* be about him." Phoebe had a bad feeling about the letter. Over a cup of tea, Phoebe told Alice about the informal arrangement Billy and Ivy had agreed to with Jack Ashworth about keeping his baby son.

"But surely no-one would have a problem with that… what is going to happen to the child if Jack can't afford to keep him, he'll only end up going into a home and then be put up for adoption and who knows what sort of family he might end up with!" Alice said hotly.

"That was Ivy's exact thought when she persuaded Billy to talk to Jack about taking the baby on," Phoebe sipped her tea. "Ivy was Norah's best friend and Ivy will do her darndest to give this little scrap the best life any child could as for."

"So, all they have to do is fill in a few forms to make it official then…. I bet that's what this letter is about, it's probably to tell them they must fill in some forms and do it properly." Alice said hopefully.

Phoebe pursed her lips; she didn't share Alice's optimism about the contents of the envelope; Mr Bevan's attitude did not give Phoebe cause to hope.

"Why are you looking at me like that Phoebe, surely there can't be a problem with Billy and Ivy adopting the baby, especially not if they've got Jack Ashworth's blessing to do it." Alice reasoned.

"I sincerely hope you are right Alice because it would break Ivy's heart if the council took the baby away whilst all this is being sorted out." Phoebe shook her head sadly, what would be even worse was if the council took the baby away and placed it with another family; it didn't bear thinking about.

"It does beg the question though Alice…. Who did alert the Council to the arrangement because it won't have been Jack Ashworth will it?" Phoebe said.

Phoebe knew that some of the neighbours on Wilson Road had never warmed to Ivy after Jimmy's arrest, and people had long memories; this didn't need to be a new grudge or gripe against Ivy, just an old one well simmered and matured and now ripe for the hatching.

Outside the window laughter and familiar voices could be heard; June was trotting up the path and through the window Phoebe could see Billy with his arm around his new wife; Ivy leaning with her head on Billy's shoulder; a picture of happiness.

"It seems that we won't have long to wait before we find out what is in this letter then." Alice said, she was beginning to feel rattled; perhaps Phoebe was right to be worried, maybe the letter did contain bad news for Ivy and Billy.

"No, we won't Alice, and I don't want to be the one to upset their perfect day, but it seems that this letter is too important to wait."

Phoebe walked to the door to let the happy couple in.

Ivy was beaming, Billy was grinning from ear to ear and June was fizzing with happiness. Phoebe wished she could capture the love and the warmth oozing from the happy trio on the doorstep, instead of which she was probably going to be the bearer of news which might end up breaking their hearts.

Phoebe reached forward and hugged Ivy as if her life depended on it.

"I love you my darling girl, never forget that." Phoebe whispered.

When the couple came through the door Phoebe handed Ivy the letter.

"What's this about Aunty Phoebe?" Ivy laughed.

"I think you had better open it and find out."

Printed in Great Britain
by Amazon